Remember, Mr Sharma

Remember, Mr Sharma

A. P. Firdaus

sceptre

First published in Great Britain in 2023 by Sceptre
An imprint of Hodder & Stoughton
An Hachette UK company

2

A CIP catalogue record for this title is available from the British Library

Hardback ISBN 9781399714433
Trade Paperback ISBN 9781399714440
eBook ISBN 9781399714457

Typeset in Sabon MT by Hewer Text UK Ltd, Edinburgh
Printed and bound in Great Britain by Clays Ltd, Elcograf S.p.A.

Hodder & Stoughton policy is to use papers that are natural, renewable
and recyclable products and made from wood grown in sustainable
forests. The logging and manufacturing processes are expected to
conform to the environmental regulations of the country of origin.

Hodder & Stoughton Ltd
Carmelite House
50 Victoria Embankment
London EC4Y 0DZ

www.sceptrebooks.co.uk

For Indrani

'Very well, I shall be silent,' he replied. 'I shall be a silent hallucination.'

— Mikhail Bulgakov, *The Master and Margarita*

Delhi, 1997

It was a bird, a big one – a vulture?

He knew, the instant he opened his eyes, that Ma was gone. Rina Auntie was in the kitchen and he could tell by the way the dishes clattered in the sink. Ma would have immediately scolded her for being so careless, so loud. He could not hear his father mumbling his prayers for the morning puja, nor could he smell the agarbatti sticks that welcomed each morning with their sickly-sweet fumes. Amma, too, was quiet in her room, the way she went quiet when she was perched on the edge of her bed, trying to catch Ma's voice so she could start calling out to her.

But Adi knew before he could register any of these things. He knew from the shift in the magnetic field of the house, from the way his body seemed tense and restless, sensing that something was wrong, aching like a part of it was gone.

He fished his Casio from under the pillows and clicked a button, and it glowed blue-green, bright as a daydream, making him squint. He thought of the plankton he had seen on Discovery Channel, those ants of the sea that glowed in that same shade of blue. Fluorescent plankton, they were called. Or was it luminous?

Sitting up in bed, he shook his head and forced himself to focus. It was 09:24 – way too late for the house to be this quiet, even on a Sunday. He looked around the drawing room trying to find a clue but nothing seemed to be out of place. The coffee table was wiped spotless, its four wooden coasters arranged in a perfect square, and all his books were stacked neatly on the shelf underneath, just as Ma left them every night, often after he had fallen asleep.

Ever since Amma had shown up one evening, months ago, and taken over his room, he had been sleeping on the divan outside. He had grown to like his half-bed in the drawing room – he could watch TV without the glare of the tube light and sleep right in front of the big cooler. Ma insisted, however, that it was a temporary arrangement. She refused to let him think that he had lost his room forever. Every night, she battled the mess he created, hiding away the comics and homework notebooks abandoned mid-sentence, clearing out the forgotten glasses of orange squash left on the table, collecting all the remains of his day to restore the drawing room to its pre-Amma status. She had done it last night too, he could see, so maybe he was mistaken. Maybe Ma had, for the first time in his life, slept through the morning?

The monsoon-thirsty sky was on fire. Already, the sun was burning white through the thin curtains and, as the morning fog cleared from his mind, he began to remember things from the night before. He had been hoping to speak to Ma after dinner, but something had ignited between his parents and their bedroom door had slammed shut.

With all his years of practice, he had developed a special skill – a superpower, you could call it – to tune into whispers behind

4

walls. In the drawing room, however, with the roar of the big cooler, it proved harder to hear them. Turning the cooler off would have made them suspicious, so he had decided to give up. Their fights were the same anyway, like action replays of all the ones he had grown up hearing, with his father ranting on about Indian family values and 'foreign agents', accusing Ma of everything from taking advantage of his 'good nature' to corrupting his caste and religion. Through it all, Ma never shouted back. At times, when she reached the end of her patience, she calmly reminded him, through clenched teeth, that she could leave any time. His father often laughed at this, but however empty the threat may have been, it usually ended the fight.

With Amma's arrival, something had cracked open Ma's quiet, controlled face, and Adi had glimpsed a fury underneath, like a bubbling, popping river of magma. He had tried to ignore it, hoping that things would calm down on their own, but last night, there had been a new edge to Ma's voice, a boldness that he had not heard before. It was not a wail, a howl, a call for help. It was a battle cry. This time, when she had screamed her usual threat, it had made him turn to the wall and shut his eyes tight, and he had lain in bed determined to stay awake, until he had fallen asleep.

He went to his parents' room. The door was shut. He did not knock.

'Where is Ma?'

His father was still in bed, lying flat on his back with an arm crossed over his eyes in a way that made him look dramatically distraught. He had not shaved or bathed or changed into his saffron kurta – things he did before 06:00, without exception, so he could do his morning puja. He cracked his toes and sighed, his hole-riddled vest stretching thin over his ballooning belly, but he did not answer. The hair on his chest and in his armpits was mostly grey, unlike the thickly dyed semicircle that cradled the shining dome of his head. Once again Adi was reminded of just how much older his parents were, compared to most others he saw at the parent–teacher meetings at school.

'Where is Ma?' he repeated, flinching at the sound of his own voice, shrill as a little boy's whine. He was still waiting for his voice to break and he had been trying his best to help it along, hawking his throat in the bathroom until it was sore, or talking to Ma in low, growling whispers that made her frown and check his forehead. Now, his voice betrayed him, failing to hide the cracks that were spreading beneath the surface, fanning out across his body faster than he could stop them. Ma's reading glasses by her bedside, her maroon handbag hanging on the door, the soft tinkling of her bangles – they were all missing.

Looking at the bed, seeing the shallow, crumpled crater that Ma had left behind, the memory came rushing back to him. It had happened before, years ago, when he was in third standard. He had woken up one day, late for school, his uniform missing from its usual spot on his desk. He had wandered into his parents' room to find his father doing his morning puja, and the bed looking just as it did right now, like a whole world abandoned in a rush. He remembered now the suffocating weight of Ma's absence, the days that stretched like weeks, months, and the nights that screamed with unanswered questions. He remembered the tiniest of details – the cold, stale dinners; his lunchbox with a five-rupee note instead of food; the sniggers that his unironed uniform drew at school. And, most of all, he remembered his father's silence.

Ma had returned, eventually, and he had packed up the memory and tossed it away, never to be touched again. That was not how memories worked, he now realised. You could hide them away in the deepest, darkest corners of your mind – you could drop them at the bottom of the Mariana Trench, 11,034 metres deep – but all it took was the sight of an upturned pillow, the smell of talcum powder on a bedsheet and they could spring back up in an instant. You could try your hardest to forget, but your bones remembered.

He dropped down on the bed, next to his father, and buried his face in Ma's lingering smell. He pressed his lips tight to muffle the cry that seemed to be coming from deep within his chest, but he could not pin his shoulders down. He waited for a hand to reach out and pat his head; for a word, a whisper, a sigh. He waited until there were no more tears left.

*

When he woke up, he was back on the divan in the drawing room and Rina Auntie was once again banging pots and pans in the kitchen. For a moment, he wondered if he had dreamt it all, but the house was still empty, he could feel it in the thick, muggy air. Ma was still missing, and now it was nearly dark.

He tried to remember if he had eaten. He must have, he figured, as he wasn't hungry at all. Seeing the pristine state of the drawing room, he assumed that his father had not stepped out all day. He wondered if Amma had been fed – it was Ma's job because Amma refused to let Rina Auntie serve her meals – but he could not bring himself to care, not today.

'Chhoté Sahib?' said Rina Auntie standing at the edge of the drawing room, her back bent slightly in her perpetual bow.

'Yes, what is it?' He hated it when she called him 'little master'. Could she not see that he had grown taller than her?

'All done, Chhoté Sahib,' she said, drawing the edge of her sari over her head, smiling her shy, stained-toothed smile. 'I have made rice and dal and aloo—'

'Yes-yes, it's fine,' he said, and instantly regretted his tone; he sounded just like his father.

At least Rina Auntie had been nice enough to not mention Ma's absence. She must have been the first to notice, when she arrived for her morning shift, that Ma was gone, but she had simply carried on. She must have heard him weeping too, he realised, and he felt his ears grow hot. He was twelve now – in his thirteenth year, as Ma always put it, like she was more impatient for him to grow up than he was himself. How could he have let himself behave so shamefully? This was it, he decided, biting his tongue and swearing an oath on Hanuman-ji, his all-time number one favourite god: never again was he going to cry like that, like a child.

Out on the balcony, he moved the clothes horse aside to make room and stepped up to the railing crusted with pigeon poop. How he used to love standing behind that railing when he was little, looking out across the trees that stretched all the way to the railway tracks in the distance. He remembered how Ma used to stand out there with him, telling him about how all of East Delhi used to be a jungle full of snakes and leopards, and how people used to go swimming in the Yamuna River before it was turned into a black stream of sewage. More than the stories themselves, it was the way she told them that he missed – her chin pointed up, her voice slow and musical, the edges of her eyes crinkled with a smile.

The trees had all been replaced by apartment blocks just like theirs – an ever-expanding colony of grey five-storey buildings that stopped his gaze from straying too far. All he could really see from the balcony was the street below: a dusty, potholed road lined with broken pavements, littered with pink polythene bags and ice-cream wrappers that blocked the drains and made the sewers overflow every monsoon. The only saving grace was the lone gulmohar tree that still stood tall by the road. For a few weeks every summer, it lit up the dreary street with its fire-red canopy, showering the pavements with scarlet petals. When the gulmohar bloomed, it made people forget the heat and the filth below, just for a moment, and look up in wonder, like wide-eyed children longing to climb up the high branches and reach for the flaming flowers. Gulmohars were called mayflower trees in English, Ma had told him, because they bloomed in May. Ten months to go, he counted on his fingers, and sighed.

Bio-lumi-nes-cent – the word popped into his head, and he smiled. That was the one thing no one could beat him at: spelling. He didn't have to memorise the words, didn't even have to know them sometimes – the letters simply arranged themselves in his head, snap-snap, just like that. It was hard not to call it a superpower, if he were to be honest. His all-time number one favourite book, obviously, was *Roget's Pocket Thesaurus*. His father had once called it a waste of time, but what did he know about words? Ma understood. She had studied English Literature in college, so she knew almost as many words as him. Way more than his father, hundred per cent, who had once asked her how many l's there were in 'application'. He was supposed to be some super-smart scientist working for the government, but to Adi, it made no sense that Ma wasn't the one going to an office and his father the one supervising Rina Auntie.

He saw it from the corner of his eye, just as he turned to go back inside, and he froze. It was a shadow, a shape darker than the sky, perched on a roof across the street. It looked like an antique pot, a vase of darkness with a snake twisting out of it; a snake with a silver beak that shone in the dying light. No: it was a bird, a big one – a vulture? – and on its bald head, he could see a single eye gleaming like a marble, staring right at him. He had seen vultures before, usually on the highway by the river, but there was something different about this one, the way it stood perfectly still, its head cocked at an angle like a jeweller looking for cracks in a diamond. It felt like there was an invisible wire joining them, crackling with a dark energy, and it sent sparks right down to his toes.

Stepping back into the house, he slid the balcony door shut, turned on all the lights, the cooler and the TV, then sat down on the sofa and closed his eyes.

2.

Mind your language, Mr Sharma

'*Celebrating 50 Years of* INDEPENDENCE', the banner read, hanging limp over the school gates. '*INDE*' was saffron, '*PEND*' white and '*ENCE*' green: the colours of India's flag, just to remind everyone whose independence was being celebrated. It was not just the banner that was new; the entire school had received a makeover in the summer. The walkways had been scrubbed clean, the grass in the playground glowed green and a new coat of paint had turned the rust-brown, exposed-brick walls a luminous red, like an old scab scraped open.

Coming back to school after the holidays was always an odd feeling, a khichdi of excitement and dread. This year, however, Adi could taste no joy. The two friends he had were no longer in his class. After the last exams, Monty and J.P. had both been demoted to Section C, where everyone was slightly cooler – their hair longer, their voices louder, the air around them a little freer. Meanwhile, he was still stuck in the grave-yard of Section A with all the bespectacled *yes-ma'am*-ers. Monty and J.P. had promised to stay friends with him, but he knew that was not how it worked.

As he made his way through the crowded corridors, dodg-ing the primary school kids on the lower floors and following the swaggering seniors up the staircase, he had a sinking feeling, a sense that something had gone horribly wrong. Only on entering his classroom did the gravity of the problem hit him: All the boys were wearing trousers. All except him.

They were supposed to switch from shorts to trousers in eighth standard, he knew that. But he had assumed that the date would be announced in school, told to Ma at a parent–teacher meeting, or blasted out on the croaky PA system. It turned out to be more obvious: the switch happened on the first day of school after the summer break. How did he not know this? How come everyone else did? It didn't matter now, it was far too late. Here he was – Adi Shankar Sharma, the great smart-A.S.S., conqueror of Bournvita Quiz Contests and speller of esoteric words – caught without his pants.

He didn't even *have* trousers! And now with Ma gone, he would need to dip into his secret stash of fifty-rupee notes gifted by relatives at weddings and festivals to buy a pair himself. Even so, he was stuck for today. They were going to ridicule him all day long, whispering and giggling and calling him names. How did it matter what he wore the next day? And what was the point of trousers anyway? To hide their legs that were starting to sprout thick black hairs? His legs looked the same as last year, the same as when he was a baby – smooth and spindly and stick-figure straight.

It was all Ma's fault. She was the one who took care of his uniform, she should have known. She should have bought the trousers and had them altered to his height and put them on his desk the night before. She should never have left.

He turned away from the sneering backbenchers and looked around for safer seats. There was a spot available on the second bench in the first row, next to a big kid called Mikki. His real name was Omprakash Valmiki, and he was the size of a senior, dark and muscly with thick, hairy arms and a shadow on his cheeks. Rumour had it that he had come from a government school in Bombay where he had failed for two years straight, so he actually was a senior. Everyone was convinced that he had only managed to get into Section A by bribing the school. They had shortened his last name to Mikki, after the mouse, to cut him down to size, but it didn't seem to work.

The only other vacant spot was right in front of Mikki, on the first bench, where the weird girl who talked to herself sat alone. Sitting with a girl was not an option, unless he wanted winks and catcalls and initials scratched in hearts on his desk. He had to take a chance with the big guy.

He slipped his bag under the desk and mumbled a 'Hi'. Mikki flipped a page on his *Chip* magazine without as much as a nod. It was a relief not to have to talk, but it also brought a strange kind of emptiness.

'Quiet!' Ma'am Roy's chilling voice flooded the classroom, extinguishing all the criss-crossing conversations in an instant. She was the secondary school supervisor whose job was to patrol the corridors and find excuses to punish kids.

'Sit down, all of you. Nitin?' she called out to a boy who slowly stood up. 'Were you talking in Hindi?'

'Me? No, Ma'am!' he said, nailing the perplexed yet indignant look of the innocent.

'Don't lie! For how many years do you people have to be told the same thing? This is an English-medium, South Delhi school. You will not talk in Hindi in the classroom, except in Hindi or Sanskrit classes. Do you understand?'

'Yes, Ma'am,' they all murmured.

'Don't think I don't know what you people are up to. I know everything. All these gaalis you have learnt, they are spoiling your minds.'

'Gaali is also a Hindi word, behenchod,' Mikki mumbled, and before he could stop himself, Adi burst into giggles.

'Adi Sharma!' Ma'am Roy thundered. 'Stand up, please.'

He rose slowly, doing his best to hide his naked knees behind the desk.

'Would you care to share your joke? We all enjoy a good laugh in the morning.'

'Um, I—'

'What happened now, the cat got your tongue? Go on, speak up.'

'Uh, it's nothing, Ma'am . . . it's, um, it's not that funny.'

It was true – Mikki calling Ma'am Roy a 'sister-fucker' wasn't funny. It was so shocking, so inappropriate and yet somehow so apt, that he had to bite his tongue hard to keep himself from laughing again.

'You can tell me now . . .' Ma'am Roy looked down at him, her bulbous, kajal-lined eyes twinkling with malice. 'Or you can tell it to Father Rebello.'

He had seen this happen many times before; he knew there was no way out. It was best not to play chicken with Ma'am Roy. But he also knew that he could not snitch on his new desk partner. Many of the teachers seemed to especially dislike Mikki, and he had already been taken to Father Rebello's office twice, where the school principal was rumoured to keep a wooden ruler wide as a splayed-out palm.

'Ma'am, I . . . I was just thinking that, um, you said "gaali", so you also used a Hindi word. Technically, you should say swear word, or cuss word, or expletive or . . .'

Snorts and sniggers erupted on the backbenches but Ma'am Roy crushed them with a glare. 'I did not expect this from *you*, Adi,' she said, shaking her head.

There was not much else she could say, though, could she? He was simply following the law that nobody did, except when talking to the teachers. If anything, he was following it to the letter, better than she herself was. She couldn't punish him for that, though he knew enough not to be certain about it. There were plenty of excuses she could find, if she wanted to, and many different kinds of punishments too. There was no one more imaginative than a teacher who wanted revenge.

'Why are you wearing *half-pants*, Adi?' said Ma'am Roy, and he bit his lip. She had found his kryptonite. Giggles spread out through the class again, crashing into the backbenches where they erupted into open laughter. This time, Ma'am Roy did not shut them down. She stood and smiled at Adi, waiting for his answer.

The classroom door opened and Ma'am George, the English teacher, stepped in, and he finally let go of his breath. She liked him, Ma'am George; she would speak up for him, he was sure of it.

'Sorry, I'm late,' Ma'am George said, then paused to glance at Adi standing awkwardly behind his desk. She walked up to the teacher's desk and put her bag down. 'I'll take it from here, Mrs Roy, thank you.'

Ma'am Roy nodded, then gave Adi a tight smile and walked out in a huff.

'Take a seat, everyone.' Ma'am George turned to wipe the blackboard clean and Adi sat down. She did not look at him again, and he could not have been more grateful for it.

*

The morning slowly evaporated in the July heat and hung, heavy and humid, over their drowsy heads. The rest of the day passed by quietly, and Adi ate lunch at his desk and spent the recess flattening the aluminium foil with a fingernail. The problem arose in the Physical Education class, the last and longest hour of the day. He could not go out to the field today, no way, but he could not stay in the classroom either because some teacher would show up and create a fuss. There was only one place he could think of. Usually, he avoided it for fear of being mocked as a kitaabi keeda. Today, being called a bookworm was the least embarrassing option he had.

He rushed through the corridors, walking purposefully past the teachers' room, until he reached the open passageway on the fourth floor that connected the main school building to the library. There was a gang of seniors playing that game where they pretended that the marble slabs on the floor were lava and the lines between them were bridges. A boy was trying to hop across the lines while a girl tried to catch him, and he couldn't imagine why they would play such a childish game – and with girls, too. When the boy stumbled and nearly fell over the girl, causing her to laugh like it was the funniest thing in the world, he took a deep breath and decided to cross. He had worried for nothing – none of them paid any attention to him. Was he developing a new superpower, he wondered: the ability to walk through the world unnoticed, invisible as a ghost, silent as a spy?

The library was dim and deserted, and it smelled of yellowed books. The librarian was installed at a desk by the door like a guardian statue, a grim Ganesha warding off wayward spirits. She looked at him over the rim of her square glasses, her head bent over a *Filmfare* magazine. He gave her a respectful little bow, but she did not blink. *What trouble could he bring, this mousey little boy in his too-loose shorts?* she seemed to be thinking. Without a word, she dropped her eyes back to the shirtless Shahrukh Khan and Adi crept past her, careful not to make a squeak.

There were windows along the wall tinted a dark blue-grey and they made the place feel cool and calm, protected from the blazing afternoon. Browsing the Nature shelves, he decided that from now on, he was going to spend every PE class in there.

'What did you find?' whispered a voice over his shoulder,

and he nearly yelped. He turned to find the weird girl who sat in front of him.

'Uh, nothing.'

'Nothing?' She eyed the book he was holding.

'Just a book about . . .' He showed her the cover. 'Birds.'

'Oh, you like birds?'

'Uh, no. I hate them.'

She flicked her shining black curls and laughed. It was a funny sort of laugh, free and brash – a boy's laugh.

'Si-*lence*,' boomed the librarian's bored voice.

'Why are you reading it, then?' she whispered.

'Just.'

She blinked her round, bird-like eyes and nodded, like she understood.

'This is mine.' She handed him a slim, red-bound volume. It was a book of poetry. *Such a girl*, he mumbled in his head, and thumbed through it, just to be nice. The poems were in English script but he struggled to decipher the words.

'What, um, language is this?'

'Urdu.' She squinted at him like he was stupid. 'Don't worry, there are translations at the back.'

As she flitted across the birds, frowning at the colourful sketches of mynahs and peacocks, he found himself growing annoyed. Most kids at school could speak another language besides Hindi and English. Ma, he knew, could speak Punjabi and even some Urdu. Why had he never been taught any of it?

His father – that was the answer to most whys. Hindi is our national language, he insisted. The Chinese, the French, the

Italians, he said, were all proud to speak their national languages. The problem with India was all the 'unity in diversity' nonsense that gave us twenty-two official languages and no national one, and the 'colonial mindset' that made us prefer English over all of them. Only by accepting Hindi as the common tongue, he said, could India be united into a great superpower.

'A little childish, no?' She smiled, handing back his illustrated book about birds.

You're a little childish.

'So,' she went on, 'which bird do you hate the most?'

'Vultures.'

'Vultures?' Her big brown eyes narrowed with fascination. 'Why?'

'Because . . .' he said, and stopped. What could he say? That he had seen a vulture and it had scared him a little? He was already a weirdo lurking in the library, a half-pant loser. He had no desire to be labelled as one with a loose screw.

'Oh, the library is about to close,' she said, checking her watch. It had pink flowers on the strap and was not even digital. 'I'm going back to class.'

He checked his Casio. The library closed half an hour before the final bell, but they still had four minutes and fourteen seconds left. He tried to think of ways to get out of walking back with her, but before he could say anything, she was gone.

Going up to the librarian to get his book of birds stamped, he realised he still had her little red book in his hands. It was stamped already, on loan for three weeks, with her name on it: Noor Farooqi. *That's what her name was. Not* Kooky, as

19

everyone called her. He stood looking at the book, strangely unable to let it go, and decided to walk out with it.

Out in the open corridor, he peeked over the chest-high wall and looked around. He checked the tops of the school buildings, the eucalyptus trees towering over the road, the pale yellow apartment blocks beyond. There was no sign of the vulture, and he felt a little silly to have thought of it. Looking down towards his classroom windows, he saw the backbenchers tossing paper balls at the girls, and he could not bring himself to go back.

He missed Monty and J.P. They would have protected him from the sneers. They would probably have forgotten to buy trousers themselves, but they would have made it look cool to be in shorts. He missed his neighbourhood friends Sunny and Bunny too. Sunny-Bunny, as they were called, the Sardaar twins who loved to confuse everyone by regularly swapping their T-shirts and the polka-dotted patkas covering their heads. At least if they had been around, he would have had someone to go back to and talk about his worst-ever day at school. They would have laughed in the way they always did, with their heads thrown back at the same angle, their squeals synchronised and it would have made him laugh, just like them, like none of it mattered.

They were all gone now. Sunny-Bunny had moved to South Delhi after their father's promotion. To make things worse, he had ended up fighting with them just before they had left – over a contested no-ball in a stupid cricket match, of all things. And now he was left with zero friends, and no place to hide.

He looked up to the scorched sky again and the answer came to him.

*

The double doors to the chapel were tall and heavy, as if to keep out the weak-willed and the cowardly. He pushed them open with his shoulders. It was not like the churches in books and movies; there were no high ceilings or colourful glass windows or carved pillars. It was just about as big as two classrooms combined, and it smelled of stale incense. The windows were hidden by red curtains but the daylight was too bright for them, turning them into glowing pink portals, like eyelids shut against the sun.

It was dead quiet inside – a muffled kind of silence, the kind that made you aware of how much noise you made just by being alive. He tiptoed to one of the long benches in the front and sat down with his arms folded. There was a different kind of coolness in there, too, like a winter breeze – like air-conditioning! How had he not known this? It was the only place in the school, besides the computer labs, that had air-conditioning. Powerful things, gods and computers, they needed to be kept cool. Maybe that was why Jesus looked so calm, even though he was nailed to the cross, bleeding from holes all over his body. There was Mother Mary holding Baby Jesus (was she wearing a sari?), and Saint Francis, the only saint he could recognise, the one whose face was printed on his shirt pocket. He had a blank but alert expression, the statue, like an ID card photo. He looked like someone who might listen to a prayer. Jesus was too elevated, smiling too contentedly, to bother with little problems. Plus, all the Christian people were always praying to Jesus and practically nobody ever prayed to Saint Francis, so there was a higher chance that he might be free to help.

He joined his hands and began, 'Dear Saint Francis,' then stopped.

What were you supposed to say? He knew all the hymns and songs they had to mime along to every morning, but he had never actually prayed to a saint. (Except to Santa Claus, if that counted.) Was he supposed to ask for things, like a Sega console or the complete collection of Tintin? Or was it more appropriate to ask for vague blessings – to make his father less angry, Ma less sad? Perhaps it was best to keep it simple, he thought, and ask for Ma to come back soon. But then, did he really need to pray for such childish things? No, he decided. All he would ask for was to be made taller, stronger, louder, like Mikki, so he would not have to hide from anyone.

'Dear Saint Francis,' he started again, and the shriek of the final bell shook the school out of its slumber. He had to rush back to the classroom, he remembered, to get his bag. At the door, he stopped and turned around for one last look at the statue. The stony saint returned his gaze, unmoved.

*

There were three locks on their two front doors – a Harrison 9-lever padlock with a golden key, the lock on the iron-grille door with its long silver key that turned thrice and, finally, the one-click hole on the wooden door. What were they guarding so desperately? The sofa with its sunken cushions? The Kelvinator fridge that needed to be defrosted every two weeks? That weird golden, glass-domed clock? What was there worth stealing in their house?

He latched the door behind him, tossed his bag on the floor, and threw himself on the sofa. Flinging his shoes, one by one, across the drawing room carpet, he reached for the TV remote.

'Babu?' A low, rasping voice called out, like someone clearing their throat, and he closed his eyes. He had forgotten about Amma.

'Babu? Babu? Babu?' Amma bleated, on and on and on, until he got up and walked across the drawing room, past the dining hall and the kitchen and up to her door (his door). She was wearing her teeth and the thick glasses that made her eyes look goldfishy. Her white sari covered her head like a hood, and he thought of Skeletor, He-Man's greatest foe, but he couldn't bring himself to smile.

'Khaék,' she said, eating air with her bony fingers.

He took the leftovers from the fridge and heated them, staring at the tray spinning slowly inside the microwave oven. His father had gifted it to Ma on their anniversary, and even though Ma had been happy, Adi counted it as cheating that his father had got it as a gift himself, from a junior colleague who wanted a promotion.

When the oven pinged, he transferred the food onto Amma's special steel plate and took it to her bed (his bed!), along with her steel glass of water. He figured it would keep her busy for a while, so he went into the toilet to read the newspaper.

It took about three minutes before the plate clattered on the floor and Amma started calling out again. Her voice was loud and crackly, and it sawed through the toilet door. Behind his pinched eyelids he mumbled a little prayer to Shiva, the Lord of Death, before quickly pinching his ears to take it back.

When he stepped out, Amma's tone was different, softer. She wasn't talking to him, he realised, but to Kusésar. He didn't know anyone called Kusésar. There was no phone in the bedroom, and for a moment, he was scared. He couldn't make out much of what she was saying; she was talking in her village language that sounded like Hindi but not quite, using 'we' for 'I' like his father sometimes did on the phone.

Trying to recall if he had locked the front door, he peeked into the room. She was talking to the poster of Pete Sampras on his cupboard. He thought of taking her plate away but she had washed her hands in it with the drinking water, and now it was a yellow pool with mushy bits swimming in it. It looked like puke.

'Babu?' She spotted him. 'Rasgulla?'

Ma had forbidden Amma from having rasgullas, which had only made her more determined to ask for them every single day. They were not good for her, Ma had said, because she had 'health problems', she had to be careful. And they were not good for Adi because he had to take care of his teeth, he had to be careful too. Why were they always in the fridge, then? Who, exactly, were the spongy, syrupy cheese balls good for?

'Nahi hai.' He shook his head. 'There are no rasgullas.'

Amma gawked at him, her eyes blank as a baby's.

'Babu? Babu? Babu?' she started off again, and he shut the door and walked away. Her voice followed him like a beggar at the temple tugging at his clothes, but he was not going to get dragged into an argument with someone who refused to grasp a simple 'No'. The best way to deal with babies, he reckoned, was to ignore them. Eventually they would shut up, or go to sleep, or whatever.

*

All alone for the day with the house to himself, he could not think of a single thing to do. Everything that used to seem so enticing in maths class daydreams – playing with his G.I. Joes again, building a Hot Wheels track across the living room, beating his old high score in Super Tanks – they all seemed so last-summer, so childish.

Leaning back in his father's spot on the sofa, he clicked through the channels in the hope of finding something other than *Happy Days*. He checked his Casio: still only 14:42. Afternoons were the worst. Cheesy game shows and teleshopping ads took over most channels, and the only movies playing were crass Bollywood comedies or the strange 'Westerns' where old men in big hats stood and squinted at each other, chewing and spitting like bored rickshaw-valas. Things only got better at 16:00, with *Home Improvement*. Although the show's obsession with tools was a little confusing, he liked watching the three boys with their long hair and denim jackets and Nike shoes. They reminded him of how he and Sunny used to gang up and tease little Bunny, even though Bunny was only eight minutes younger than his brother.

The laughter track was interrupted by a crash from Amma's room, followed by a deep moan. He ran over to find Amma lying on the floor beside her wheelchair, looking like a pile of crumpled clothes. Fighting the rotten smell that radiated from her like a mix of Tiger Balm and stale bananas, he grabbed her arms. They felt rough and soft at the same time, the texture of papier-mâché, and he loosened his grip for fear of accidentally tearing them apart. He then positioned himself behind Amma and tried to pull her up, but she protested.

'Jaa-il, Babu, tu jaa-il,' she kept saying, and it took him a moment to understand that she was telling him to go away.

Her sari had got caught in the wheel of the chair, he realised, and had pulled up to reveal most of her left leg and even part of her butt. He had not noticed it earlier because it looked less like a person's leg than a crushed brown paper bag, wrinkled and shapeless. He reached over to free the end of her sari and it fell back over her leg. Only then did he realise that Amma was crying.

He left her alone and pulled the door shut, leaving a crack just wide enough to look through. She turned herself around and, very slowly, lifted herself up to the wheelchair. As she twirled the chair and rolled into the toilet, he almost felt like cheering. When she had come out of the toilet and carefully shifted herself back onto the bed, he ended his watch and returned to the sofa.

Thinking about how old Amma was, he couldn't believe how fragile she seemed, like she could snap in half at the slightest blow. He had always associated age with strength, with sturdiness, like the old peepul tree that towered over the two-storey neighbourhood temple or that giant two-hundred-year-old tortoise he had read about in the paper. He had never imagined that people, unlike trees and tortoises, could get smaller and weaker with age, until they turned back into frail little children, wailing for no reason, barely able to stand on their feet.

The drawing room had grown dark, he realised, and it made him smile. He slid the glass door open and stepped out onto the balcony. The skies had gone grey, finally, overflowing with clouds that swelled in a slow, mesmerising dance. Against it, a handful of diamonds twirled and glittered in different colours. The monsoon had arrived, and with it, the kite-flying season. Soon, the sky would be full of the little paper birds straining to break free.

In the days leading up to Independence Day, for a reason no one quite understood or questioned, all the boys lay down their cricket bats, leaving the parks and parking lots deserted, and headed to the rooftops, their sights set on the rain-softened skies. Everyone saved up to buy the best kites – the plastic ones were good, thin and strong and sparkly, but nothing could beat a proper paper kite, the kind made in Old Delhi, along with the hair-thin manja thread coated with crushed glass that was light enough to take your kite into the clouds, sharp enough to cut through the first fold of your index finger. A Band-Aid on that finger, preferably with a faint spot of blood showing through, was the ultimate badge of honour. He himself had never managed to earn it. He could not even fake it; everybody knew that he could barely get a kite off the ground. No matter how hard he yanked at the thread, the temperamental beast would only rise for a few seconds before turning with a deliberate fury, a missile-like menace, only to come crashing down on the concrete.

He saw it on the roof of the apartment building across the street, and it took him a second to register it, to accept it. It was the same vulture, staring at him in exactly the same way. It had scared him when he had first seen it, looming over him in the darkness. Now, exposed by daylight, the vulture looked far less intimidating. He examined the bird of death – its bald, pink head turned at an angle; its long, curved neck with a puffy collar of white feathers; its folded wings that made it look like the neighbourhood uncles on evening strolls, their arms locked behind their backs, their shoulders stuck in a shrug; and its large, furry torso with a little paunch that seemed to be heaving gently, like someone taking a long, deep breath before saying something. Far from being frightened by it, he now found the bird faintly ridiculous.

'Chootiya,' he mumbled under his breath, and the vulture seemed to flinch, its hooked silver beak turning up as though it was shocked.

'Kya?' he said, louder this time. 'What is it? What are you looking at?'

The vulture turned away, and he looked around to find something to throw at it. He wondered if he still had that old catapult that he and Sunny-Bunny used to take turns with, shooting pebbles at empty Fanta cans. No, he remembered: Ma had taken it away, saying it was too dangerous for little kids like them.

He looked at the bird and found it staring at him again. As he stared back, he felt his body growing stiff, his fingers clenching into fists. It was as though all the anger that had been building up through the day – the rage slowly simmering ever since Ma had left – was now beginning to rise, making him tremble like the lid on a forgotten pot of rice.

'What happened?' he screamed. 'The cat got your tongue? Speak, behenchod!'

'Ey! Mind your language, Mr Sharma. I will not accept this rowdy behaviour.'

The vulture was shaking its head. What had just happened?

'Kya . . . kya bola tu?'

'Please, I am not going to tolerate this crude tu-tu language.'

It was impossible, he knew that. The bird was too far away, all the way across the street, for its voice to be so loud and clear, as though it was being whispered in his ear. More importantly, it was a *bird*.

'So,' the vulture continued, 'if you have a question for me, firstly, you take back your foul word. Secondly, talk in proper English, with good manners. Then and only then I will entertain your request. Otherwise, I am not saying one word.'

'Fuck-shit-fuck-tuttee.'

He stumbled back into the drawing room and slid the door shut. Lying face-down on the divan with his eyes scrunched tight, he could still feel the vulture peering through the thin curtains, that hot gaze crawling on his neck. He decided to do what he hadn't done for a long time. He untucked the sheets over the sides of the divan, got down on the floor and slid sideways into his cave.

'Di?' he called out, his tongue barely moving to form the soft 'd', the hesitant 'ee?' no more than a hoarse plea gushing out from his chest.

There was no reply.

'Di? Are you there?'

Had she ever been there, even all those years ago? Had he ever really heard her warm whisper, her secret laughter or had it all been a little boy's fantasy? He was far too old to ask such questions now. And yet, he waited. In that empty house burning under the bird's wicked glare, she was all he had.

'I'm sorry,' he said. 'I thought about talking to you, many times, but . . .'

What could he say? That he had outgrown the first friend he ever had, the one who had kept him company through the loudest, loneliest nights of his childhood? Or that he only summoned her now because he could feel the old darkness rising again from the cracked, speckled floor of their house and, once again, there was no one he could turn to?

He told Di about his summer, about his parting fight with Sunny-Bunny and about Amma, and how she had peed in his bed – their bed – so there was now a rubber sheet covering the mattress and the room always smelled of death and Dettol. He told her that, on the bright side, the parents were not fighting anymore. It was a lie, but he thought it might make Di feel better to know that things could change.

There was only one thing he couldn't bring himself to tell her. He didn't know how to say it. He was supposed to be brave and strong; he had sworn it to her, so many times, on those long-ago nights. How could he let her see him like this? Like a little boy hiding in his make-believe fort, scared of a big, dumb bird.

He shook his head, and he did what he had learnt to do once he had grown too old to talk to ghosts. He closed his eyes, slowed his breathing and pretended to be asleep. He let the pulsing darkness slowly shush the voices in his head.

3.

Oh, what was left to lose?

The empty afternoons were washed away by the monsoon downpours, and despite Sunday's earthquake whose aftershocks he could still feel in his bones, the week went on – not quickly, not nearly as smoothly as before, but on it went nonetheless.

Just a few days after Ma had left, everyone in the world seemed to know about it. The chowkidaar and his plain-clothes friend who was always in the guard house for some reason (maybe he was a spy?), the Sardaar-ji from the first floor who was always stretching himself in painful ways, the aunties in flowing nighties and their little children with water bottles around their necks, the man who cleaned all the cars while managing to keep a cigarette dangling from his lips throughout, the family of four who camped outside the park and worked as one unit, morning to night, ironing the clothes of everyone in the colony – they had all stopped mid-sentence, mid-stretch, mid-thrust of the great black coal-fired iron and stared at him. There was curiosity and confusion in the looks they gave him, but more than anything else, there was the sting of pity. Look at the bechara bach-cha, the poor little boy whose mother left him, so sad, tsk-tsk-tsk, how will he survive now, how is he even alive?

By the end of the week, he had developed a routine to evade enemy eyes. The first phase was all about speed. At 06:00, his Casio detonated its two-tone bomb under his pillow. There was not a second to laze about in bed, so he jumped right up and started getting dressed. In twenty-five minutes, just before his father's puja ended, he was ready, bag slung on his shoulders, bread-butter sandwich packed in foil.

'Bye,' he said at the door, barely loud enough to let his father hear, and slammed it.

Outside, he had to switch into stealth mode. Instead of walking out to the bus stop he slipped into the narrow lane between the apartment buildings, dodging soggy cigarette stubs and empty Limca bottles and mossy puddles from the drip-drip-drip of air-conditioners, and he waited until he saw the bus appear at the head of the street. Cutting back across the lane, he emerged, ninja-like, just as the bus arrived at the stop and leapt inside before anybody could spot him. Mission accomplished.

Of course, all of this helped avoid the vulture too. He had seen it a few times now, lurking on the trees or rooftops around his house, but he had decided not to let it bother him. He was sure that he had imagined the words – he must have been tired or hungry or something. He knew vultures could not talk, *obviously*, so it must have been in his head. Nonetheless, he had no desire to try it again. He had enough problems already; he could do without losing his mind. This was the secret to trudging on through the unending days, he was starting to learn: ignoring things, not seeing them, not letting yourself stop and think about everything all at once.

*

At school, he found himself feeling calmer than ever. He was growing used to sitting at the front of the class, and he realised that it was a not a bad spot. Mikki, his new bench partner, never said a word to him – although, after Adi had saved him from another trip to the principal's office, he had begun to offer a little nod every morning. The teachers were mostly worried about what people at the back were up to, and they rarely called out the ones in front to answer questions or read passages. It was good, in a way, to have no one to talk to. What was there to say anyway? The timetable imposed its order on the day, and you could turn a part of your mind off – the annoying, childish part that started asking unanswerable questions as soon as it was idle.

It worked well most of the time, even at recess when he got odd looks for staying at his desk and reading the history text-book. The only trouble was Noor, who kept turning around to give him curious looks, as though she wanted to say something. Finally, on Friday, during a break between classes, he realised what it could be.

'Um, listen.' He cleared his throat, and she swung her head around like she had been waiting to hear his voice. Underneath her shining curls, he caught a glimpse of an earring – a tiny disco ball that sparkled in a thousand colours – but it disappeared in a flash, like a shooting star in the night.

'I have your book. That, um—'

'I know,' she said, frowning or smiling, he couldn't be sure.

'I mean . . .' He scratched his ear. 'I don't have it now, I'll bring it tomorrow.'

'Okay.' She kept staring at him, waiting for something more.

She really was weird, he thought, squirming before her laser gaze. It had a peculiar effect on him, making him want to avert his eyes, hide under the desk, melt into the raindrops pattering on the windows. At the same time, her sparkling brown eyes also made him want to tell her that he had read every poem three times over, that each time he had felt like he was reading them for the first time, discovering new meanings he had missed before. His voice, however, remained stuck somewhere down in his belly, and all he could do was rummage through his bag like a dog digging through a flowerbed for no reason at all.

'No rush,' she said, turning away as the maths teacher came in and they all stood up. For the first time, he felt grateful to the sour-faced Sir Prince for rescuing him from the awkward exchange. Then again, at the same time, a part of him wished that the conversation never had to end.

*

While school became a little easier, the journey home turned all the more tiring. As the bus lurched across Delhi, swerving through traffic on the ring road, honking its way through the chaos of flyover construction, rumbling across the new bridge over the Yamuna towards the distant east, he sank deeper into his seat, wondering if the front door would still be locked when he got home. It had been for nearly a week.

He stopped at the door and listened. There was no sound from the kitchen, no one arguing with Amma, no one talking on the phone – only the silence that rang in his ears. He considered going up to the terrace but it was too hot. After the morning showers, the sun was back with naked fury, making up for the hours it had lost.

He stepped inside and latched the door gently behind him. In just a few days without Ma, the house had begun to fall apart. There were things everywhere – rags and crumpled newspapers, lost socks and upturned shoes, open biscuit packs and ketchup bottle caps, tea-stained cups and crusty spoons. He was to blame for some of it, but most of it had been littered by his father. They had both grown used to bumbling around the house like babies in wheeled walkers, leaving behind a trail of debris. They had not realised, or cared, that someone was always there to clean up after them.

His father's solution, on the very first day, had been to find a replacement. He had offered to double Rina Auntie's salary if she stayed home all day to take care of Amma and keep the house clean. But it was too much for her to handle alone. Amma was too much for any one person, even Ma. With Rina Auntie, there was the additional problem of her being too low caste, too 'unclean' to serve Amma's food. Adi had no choice but to do it himself.

'Babu?' she called out. He had come in without a sound

and was lying dead still on the divan, barely breathing, but she could still tell that he was home. Weren't old people supposed to be hard of hearing? Amma's ears were even sharper than his own, and he knew there was no point in hiding. Once she began wailing, it would turn into a battle of wills that he simply could not win. He went to the kitchen, prepared her plate, and took it to her room.

'Babu? Tohar Mai? Kab aavéla?'

She said it twice more before he understood it. When was Ma coming back, she wanted to know. He felt like flinging the plate at her face. It was all her fault, wasn't it? If she hadn't turned up after all these years and taken over his room, their house, their whole life, none of it would have happened. Why couldn't she just go back to her village? Why didn't she just *die*?

He closed his eyes and opened them, and the anger passed. It was her fault, maybe, but not entirely. The demons she had woken had always been there, stirring under the sheets, stretching their toes. Right now, she was in the same place as him, he realised, alone in a house she didn't want to be in, told even less than he was.

'Kuch din baad,' he said slowly, setting the plate down on her bed. 'In a few days' – that was all his father had told him on Sunday, once Adi had stopped sobbing.

Amma looked up at him, her eyes floating blankly like she didn't believe him. He couldn't blame her; he wasn't sure he believed it either.

*

His father came home late, after Rina Auntie had cooked and left, and Amma had eaten her dinner and gone to sleep. He heard the shuffling footsteps before his father pressed the bell in his usual way, like he was angry at the door for not opening by itself. Adi turned the TV off and leapt to the door. He had prepared the coffee table in the drawing room, laying out the food and setting two plates next to each other, and he had waited, trying his best to ignore his grumbling stomach.

The smell entered the house before his father did, a sharp and warm and sour sting that made him hold his breath. It was the smell of those nights, years ago, when his father's curses would collide with Ma's silence, the fights often ending in a crash, a slap, a muffled sob. The battle had gone on for years, and in the end, the silence had survived, slowly seeping into the walls of their house.

With one look at his father – the loose tie and the crumpled, untucked shirt, like a schoolboy after a scuffle – he knew what to do. He fell back onto the divan and opened his little red book, careful to keep the cover hidden. The subtitle in Urdu script could have been the trigger for his father. It could have been anything, really, from the dishevelled state of his hair to the imagined disrespect in the most innocent of glances. It was like *Jurassic Park*, he thought. When the T-Rex was standing right in front of you, you had to stay still, not breathing, not blinking, just waiting for it to look around and move on. The slightest sign of life, and you'd be dead.

Once he realised that his father was not coming out of the bedroom, he cleared the table, no longer hungry himself. He lay in bed for some time, until his father's snores had reached full volume, sending vibrations through the floor, up the bed, and into his tailbone. He rose and went, slippers in hand, to unlatch the front door.

Out on the terrace, it was quiet, besides the hum of coolers and air-conditioners perched on the windows below, and there was a light breeze carrying the sweet, heady smell of wet earth.

It used to be his favourite thing in the world, rain. Monsoon rains, especially, were the most exciting event of the year, better than the yellow fogs of winter, even. When they arrived, the fat bullets slashing the sky and slamming the top of your head with a surprising force, like pebbles thrown by playful gods, you could feel the weight of the long summer lifting. Even when the sky came down in sheets, in walls of water that turned roads into rivers, cars into islands, and made the power go out, he loved the rain and the calmness it brought, slowing the world to a standstill for a few hours, drowning out all the noise that never stopped. Now, for the first time, he wished for the rain to stay away. It only reminded him of last Sunday.

Climbing the low wall that separated their terrace from the neighbours', he heaved himself onto the ledge above the door. Swinging his legs over the edge, he scanned the apartment blocks around. He did not have to search for long – the vulture was right where he had last seen it, sitting on a black water tank on the roof of a building across the street.

Oh, what was left to lose?

'Can you really talk?' he said, not much louder than a whisper, or a wish.

Silence.

'Fine, I take it back. You're not a chootiya. Buss?'

The bird turned its little head away, like a little child crossing its arms and pretending to be angry.

What was he doing, trying to talk to a bird? He shook his head and chuckled. Still, he did feel bad about yelling a gaali at it the other day. He remembered how Ma had once caught him saying 'chootiya' to Sunny. He thought it was just another word for stupid, but it had made Ma angrier than he had ever seen her. She had even used his father's threat of sending him off to boarding school and had only calmed down after making him apologise and vow on her life to never utter another gaali again. It was not a vow he should have broken, not now.

'Okay,' he sighed. 'Sir, please accept my sincere apologies for my rude language. I promise to henceforth mind my manners and speak with the utmost respect—'

'What is all this, eh? You are writing a letter to the Queen of England, is it?'

'What?' He flinched, shocked once more to hear the voice that sounded more real, more robust than his own.

'What "What?" You are making a mockery of me, Mr Sharma? I am familiar with all these tricks. You can speak normally, only no foul language please.'

'Oh–kay.'

'Now, to answer your question, let me tell you—'

40

'What question?'

'The question you were asking me, Mr Sharma. Surely, you are not having such a weak memory?'

'Oh, yeah.'

'What is this *yeah*? Say yes or no. And don't interrupt when your elder is talking, please. It is a rude habit.'

'Elder?' He couldn't stop himself from scoffing.

'What else? Am I not your elder?'

'Um, I don't know.'

'You don't know, yes. Nothing you know, is it? I am not only your elder, I am your elders' elder also. I am as old as—'

'Wait, I've read all about vultures, their lifespan is less than twenty years. You can't be that old, you're lying!'

'Lifespan is a big word, Mr Sharma. It can mean many things. We are not like you, we don't grow so slowly-slowly, wasting twenty years sitting in school. Time works differently for us. We can live seven lifespans before you learn to say your own name.'

'So, you're some kind of magical creature, then? Like, with superpowers?'

'Wah!' The creature shook his head and tsk-tsk'd in disappointment, and Adi wondered if vultures had tongues. 'Everything is magic to you people, is it? Anything you are not knowing: magic. Such simple minds you all have. No, Mr Sharma, I am not magic.'

'What are you, then?'

'I am Additional Joint Secretary and Deputy Director-General, Department of Historical Adjustment, in charge of pending case clearance.'

After a moment's silence, Adi couldn't help but laugh. 'What does that even *mean*?'

The vulture groaned like a teacher tired of answering stupid questions. 'You humans are one big headache for everyone. You are making one mess after one mess, nonstop throughout history. Then you forget about it, leaving it to rot. Naturally, it is us vultures only who must do the sweeping-mopping, yes?'

'But . . . if it's the humans' mess, why do you care?'

'Ah, yes, that is the problem. You people walk through this world like it was created for you, but not up to your satisfaction. Like everything else here is just an inconvenience to you. No. You share this world with everyone else, and when you are leaving a mess, it is our problem too. Now, our great elders, the bacteria, they have to eat plastic and fight your antibiotics, so they can keep us all alive. And look at that old gulmohar tree down there, it has to make its flowers bigger and brighter, so you won't cut it down and make the air even worse. And think of the poor dogs, the descendants of the great wolves, they have to humiliate themselves just to keep you calm, because we all suffer when you lose your senses. You see, on this Earth, everything cares about everything else. Except you people. You don't even care about yourselves. So, what choice do we have? We have to do it for you, no? And since us vultures have been here for a long time, watching you, we are helping with your biggest problem: remembering your past mistakes, so you don't repeat them. That is why the Department of Historical Adjustment was established, under the H-A-H-A.'

'Uh . . . ha-ha?'

'H. A. (H.) A. The Historical Adjustment in-brackets-Hind-sight Act. It is no laughing matter, Mr Sharma. Under this law, we are bound to keep proper records of everything in our Historical Archive. So that we can help *you* remember. To clear up the fog of the past that blurs the present, one case at a time.'

'Um, okay,' Adi nodded, as if he understood, and the vulture took a deep breath.

'And *my* job, as AJS-cum-DDG of DHA, is handling the VCRs – Very Convoluted Records – such as your family's case here. So, to put one hundred things in one, Mr Sharma, it means that I am here to resolve your family matters.'

'Oh. Okay.'

'I know what you are thinking. How come such a big officer is coming down here to do such donkey work, yes? No offence to our donkey friends, hrr-hrr.' The vulture made a sound halfway between a croak and a chuckle.

'Uh, not rea—'

'What can I say, Mr Sharma? This is the state of the Department these days. There is talent shortage, budget-cutting, the climate is getting worse day-by-day . . . but let us focus on our work.' The vulture jerked its head, as though dismissing its own worries. 'Back to your original question: what do I want? That is what you asked me, yes? Let me tell you, I want what you are wanting only.'

'And . . . you know what I want?'

'Yes, Mr Sharma. You are wanting to stop living scared-scared, like a little boy, no? You are wanting to grow up, be a *man*, yes?'

43

'Um, yeah. I mean, yes.'

'Of course. It is natural, after all. By your age, most animals are already full adults, and some are already in their old age. Even you people used to grow up faster. Your Akbar the Great was only one year older to you when he became Emperor of India. Nowadays, your parents don't teach you anything. They treat you like a child even after you have your own children.'

'That's true,' Adi mumbled. 'Sometimes they disappear and don't even tell you where they're going.'

'Ah, your mother you are talking about, yes?'

'What, you know where she's gone? You know when she'll be coming back?'

'I am not having that information, no. But if you want to find out where she has gone, you must know where she has come from.'

'Er, *what*?'

'Oh, Mr Sharma,' the vulture sighed. 'From the beginning we will have to start.'

'What are you talking about?'

'Do you know how one grows up?'

'By not talking to birds?'

'By opening one's *eyes*, Mr Sharma. By *seeing*. And you will be happy to know that this happens to be one area of expertise of yours truly. No doubt you are knowing that already, as you have read *all* about vultures, yes?'

'Yes, I know, vultures have good eyesight.' It was true, they could see a dead rat or something from miles high in the sky.

44

'Yes. And as a senior official, I have additional authority. While most of my colleagues can only see across space, I can also see across time.'

'Time travel, you mean?' He couldn't hide the scepticism in his voice. He knew all about time travel; *Back to the Future* was in his all-time top five favourite movies.

'We are not travelling in time, technically speaking. We are only seeing the original memories, just as they were recorded by our officials, without the crackle of time. You can think of it like remembering something you have not seen before.'

'That makes no sense. How can you remember something you haven't seen?'

'Memories can be shared, Mr Sharma. What one person forgets the next one remembers. And what all you people forget, we still remember. Only because we keep all the records carefully in our—'

'Wait,' said Adi. 'You said "we" will be seeing? You mean you can show me?'

'Yes, of course! What else am I talking about? But I must tell you, there are strict rules about accessing the Historical Archives. One: you may only see files related to one person, in this case your Ma, Mrs Tamanna Sharma. Two: you may access each file one time only, so please give one hundred per cent attention. And three: You *must* behave yourself.'

'What do you mean *behave myself*? And why only once? Who made these rules?'

'Please, Mr Sharma.' The vulture shook its head, and Adi could almost see it rolling its black, shining eyes. 'These are valuable historical records, the memories of the Earth, and we must treat them with respect. Memories are delicate things; they need to be preserved for everyone. Seeing them too many times can cause damage. And interfering with the originals could affect the copies that people carry – it could change what they remember about their past.'

The vulture stopped, its head jerking up like it had made a mistake, and Adi wondered what it could be.

'Anyway,' it grumbled, 'I do not make the rules, I merely follow them. If you are ready to do the same, we can proceed with your Ma's first file.'

'But . . . what do I have to *do*?'

'Oh, that is easy. You just have to close your eyes, Mr Sharma, and see.'

DHA/HA/TS/1947(1)

She is alone on the terrace and the light is bleeding out of the sky. She stands with her back to the setting sun, holding a pile of clothes in her arms, and looks towards the horizon that has already gone dark. In the distance, flickering orange fires dot the vast plains stretching as far as Adi can see, even with the vulture's super sight. He leans in closer to get a better look at the woman's face and finds his vision zooming in like a movie camera. He recognises her at once, remembering the sharp jaw, the pursed lips, the kind and radiant eyes that he has only seen in black-and-white photographs. It is Nani, Ma's ma. She is young and strong and full of colour now, her green kurta printed with pink flowers glowing despite the darkness around her.

'Toshi!' calls out a woman's voice. 'Hurry up, come and help your derani.'

'I don't understand,' Adi whispers, struggling to keep up with the Punjabi.

'Please, Mr Sharma,' the vulture shushes him. 'Just pay attention, you will understand.'

'But what's a derani?'

'Your Nani's husband's brother's wife, or sister-in-law, as they say. Now, quiet please.'

Nani crouches under a clothesline to cross the terrace and looks down into the courtyard where an old lady is sitting on a rope charpai, leaning on a cane like a wise woman, or a witch. In the middle of the courtyard lies a glowering drum made of clay, like the tandoors outside restaurants, and Nani's sister-in-law is busy sticking chapatis into it. Two little girls run in circles around the courtyard, chasing each other in turns.

Adi feels the shock, the heat of the explosion before he hears the thundering blast. At first, he wonders if the tandoor has blown up. But as he holds his breath for a long, slow moment, night turns into day, lighting up the courtyard where everyone stands frozen in place, looking up in confusion at the empty sky.

Then come the sounds – the roaring, the crackling, the scream-ing. Nani runs across the terrace and stares out to the other side with her hand over her mouth. A large building at the end of the street – a factory of some kind with a big yard full of wooden logs – is on fire. The very air around it seems to be burning in a bright halo, and orange flames grow higher with every heartbeat, leaping out of broken windows, snapping like hungry dogs.

The screams are not from people in pain, Adi realises. They are the cries of men. He sees them now, coming up the street in a tight group, chanting '*Pakistan Zindabad*'. They sound just like the fans chanting '*Ind-i-aaa–India!*' during cricket matches with Pakistan, but instead of flags and badly drawn posters, they are carrying flaming torches, waving swords that glint red and yellow in the firelight.

Nani runs down the spiral staircase, into the courtyard, and lifts one of the little girls in her arms. Her sister-in-law grabs the second girl. Just as the old woman rises from the charpai, the double doors of the house slam open and a Sardaar-ji walks into the courtyard, leaning on a crutch. The women look relieved on seeing him, but only for a moment.

'Tussi kitthé si?' says Nani, 'Where were you?' but the man does not answer. Despite his limp left leg, he stands tall and strong, broad-shouldered and bulky as a WWF wrestler. He is wearing an army uniform but instead of camouflage pants, he has wide khaki shorts over long socks that make him look slightly absurd, like a grown man in a child's clothes. Like the British-era soldiers in the history textbook, Adi realises. He has a long rifle slung over his shoulder and he is carrying a sword that shines dully in the pale night.

Behind him, a lanky man comes up with two black canisters and drops them in the middle of the courtyard. It must be the big man's brother, Adi reckons – the sister-in-law's husband.

'Bi-ji,' says the big man to the old woman, bowing to touch her feet. 'Take these.' He points to the canisters. 'You know what to do.'

He *can* understand a lot of the Punjabi, Adi suddenly realises. Perhaps all that eavesdropping on Ma's phone calls was not useless after all.

The old woman nods and pats the man on his back, and the man turns to Nani, who is standing still. He has a great black beard and his eyes look glazed over, glistening with malice, and it reminds Adi of his father's eyes from years ago, when he used to finish a bottle of Old Monk Very Old Vatted XXX Rum every night.

Nani, still holding the girl in her arms, shakes her head. She walks up to the man, yelling in such rapid-fire Punjabi that Adi struggles to pick up a single word.

The man smiles at her – a chilling smile that gleams like the sword he is carrying. He slaps Nani across her face, so hard that she nearly stumbles and falls. Nani looks at the man with fire in her eyes, and the girl in her arms begins to wail. Her sister-in-law rushes ahead and puts an arm around her, pulling her away.

Still smiling, the big man pulls his turban off and shakes his hair free, the thick curls falling down to his waist. He hands the sword to his brother, who has finished piling up broken wooden crates and newspapers and bedsheets in the middle of the courtyard, and is now standing with drooping shoulders, staring at the other little girl hiding behind Nani's sister-in-law.

'Bolé so nihaal, sutt-sri-akaal!' the big man yells, holding his rifle aloft, as if he is a general and the women are his troops going into battle. Adi has heard the words, chanted softly in a gurudwara after the end of evening prayers, but he does not quite know their meaning. They do seem to energise the younger brother, who holds up the sword and follows the big man as he limps out of the courtyard and shuts the doors behind them.

'Chhétti!' The old woman waves her cane at the canisters. 'Quick!'

Nani's sister-in-law picks up one of the metal canisters, unscrews the cap, and tilts it over the pile of wood and cloth. A clear stream the colour of pee drenches the pile. Nani covers her mouth again – in shock or because of the smell, Adi can't tell.

'Santosh?' The old woman walks up to Nani and speaks slowly, as if to a child. 'We are Sikhnis. We have the blood of Guru Tegh Bahadur Ji. We can have our heads cut off but we cannot bow before these Mussalmans.'

'But Bi-ji,' Nani protests, 'we can ask the neighbours. Doctor Ahmed will help us.'

'Look at them.' The old woman points to the house next to theirs, its doors shut, its windows boarded up. 'Where are they? Can they not see what's happening? Have they gone blind?'

'But, but Doctor Ahmed,' Nani stutters. 'He, he said—'

'They all said many things.' The old woman wipes her eyes. 'It doesn't matter now. Don't fear, my child, Wahé Guru Ji will protect us.'

The screams outside are getting louder and the smoke, billowing over the street, has taken on an eerie red glow. Nani turns to her sister-in-law, who is kneeling before her little girl, staring at her with great concentration, as if she is trying to memorise the shape of her face. Behind her, the makeshift pyre has lit up, the flames rising higher with every second.

'Come now,' the old woman says with a heavy sigh. 'It's time.'

Clasping her little girl, Nani begins to shake her head. 'No. I will not do it.'

Looking closely at the child, Adi tries to make out if it is Ma, no more than five years old here, clinging to Nani.

'Don't you know what the Mussalmans will do to you? To your daughter? Is that what you want? Come now,' the old woman takes Nani's hand. 'It has been decided. Do as your karvala said.'

'What's a karvala?' Adi whispers.

'Your Nani's husband,' the vulture says.

'But . . . that Sardaar-ji was not my Nana?'

'Quiet, please,' the vulture hisses, and he shuts up.

Another explosion, smaller than the last one, makes the ground shake. It stirs Nani's sister-in-law into action. She picks up the canister and lifts it over her head.

'No!' Nani yells, but the woman is already drenched, her long black plaits flattened into dripping ribbons, shining blue-green-purple in the shifting light. She hands the canister to the old woman, who takes it slowly and does the same. Outside, the crack of a rifle rings through the burning air, bringing a moment of stillness.

'Toshi!'

Nani hears the voice and nearly jumps. It is a hoarse scream, somehow sounding like a whisper, and it is coming from somewhere close.

'Toshi!'

Nani runs to the metal door at the back of the courtyard, padlocked and blocked by sacks of flour.

'Tariq?' she calls out at the door.

Another shot of the rifle, another moment of silence. She looks up to see a man emerging on top of the boundary wall. She stares at the silhouette glowing orange against the smoky sky. As he turns to face her, she lights up with a smile. It takes a moment for Adi to place the man. He has seen this face too, in old photographs – an older version but with the same long, crooked nose and dimpled chin. This is Nana, Ma's father. He looks like a college boy with a head of wavy hair and a sharply cut shirt that sparkles in the pale light.

'Hurry up!' says Nana. 'Lift up Kammo first.'

Kammo. That's not Ma's nickname, Adi knows; it's Munno. This must be someone else, then. Did Ma have a sister, he wonders?

Nani runs up to the wall and holds little Kammo up towards Nana's outstretched arms. By the time the old woman screams and hobbles after them, Nana has dropped Kammo outside and returned, his arm held out for Nani. She grabs on to it and, putting a foot on the old woman's charpai, heaves herself up to climb over the wall and into the smoky street.

They get on a bicycle – Nana churning the pedals with all the strength in his body, Nani straddling the rear carrier like a man with her legs dangling on either side, and Kammo sandwiched between them. As the cycle weaves through the back lanes, circling around the mobs and burning buildings, Adi tries to get a closer look at the little girl. It's hard to tell in the darkness but he can bet that she isn't Ma. Even though her eyes look somewhat familiar, there is something about her – the shape of her head, the curve of her ears, the aura of her? – that is nothing like Ma.

Unable to hold it in, he whispers to the vulture: 'This Kammo is not my Ma.'

'Correct.'

'So, who is she? And where is Ma?'

'Look at your Nani,' says the vulture. 'Like I said, pay attention.'

Nani is looking back at her house, the flames now starting to rise from the courtyard. She looks unbearably sad, but in her long, slow sigh, Adi can also sense a wave of relief. She has one arm wrapped tightly around Kammo, and the other is on her belly, softly caressing its bulge. It takes him a moment to realise what it means. He has only ever seen two types of people caress their bellies – uncles who like butter chicken and burping in public, and women who are pregnant.

Ma has not been born yet!

The cycle escapes the maze of houses and gets onto a broad road, deserted at this hour, lit only by the pale moon looming over the charred earth. Behind them, Adi can make out the lights of a city around the silhouette of a great fort, along with the glowing white domes of a grand mosque next to it. They look just like the Red Fort and the Jama Masjid, he thinks – it must be Delhi – until he spots a white milestone by the highway. He has to lean in further and strain his eyes to read it. 'Lahore, 3 mi,' it says.

Lahore, in Pakistan?

Nana and Nani stop and stare at the horizon, at the plumes of grey smoke rising from the city and climbing high into the airless night, like pillars holding up the darkness. After a brief, whispered conversation with Nani that Adi can barely hear, Nana turns the cycle around and launches off with renewed determination, Nani holding tight behind him, hugging Kammo close to her chest. On the other side too, the horizon is blurred by a cloud of flickering smoke and Adi feels a desperate urge to yell out at them, to warn them that they are going the wrong way, away from the city lights and into a sea of fire. And then he sees the milestone on the other side of the road, pointing towards their new direction. 'Amritsar, 28 mi,' it says.

Amritsar, in India.

It is such a strange, other-worldly image that it takes Adi a moment to really see it. A little further up the highway, there is a small truck by the side of the road being swallowed by orange flames. On the ground next to it are two men, sitting side by side in a pool of water, their arms tied behind their backs. They are Sardaar-jis, but their turbans lie unspooled before them, covered in locks of roughly chopped hair. Their patchy heads hang over their chests, their lips loose and drooling, and their eyes are open but they never blink. In their laps they hold pale coils of intestines spilling out of their slashed bellies. The black pool that grows around them is thicker than water, he realises. He looks at their faces again and, for an instant, he sees them morphing into boys' faces, into Sunny and Bunny, and he finds his throat choked up, unable to breathe. He opens his eyes and swallows. He leaps off the ledge to land on the terrace and away, from the shadows, he runs.

4.

Was everything alright?

One evening, just as he was starting to study for a science exam the next day, the doorbell rang, and he nearly shrieked. A whole week had passed since his encounter with the vulture and, although he thought he had pushed it all out of his mind, his body still seemed stuck on that ledge on the terrace, his legs twitching uncontrollably whenever he tried to sit still, his breath freezing in fear at the slightest sound.

As he sat wide-eyed in the quivering silence, his ears picked up a familiar sound coming from across the front door. It was faint yet unmistakable – the tinkling of glass bangles. He jumped off the divan and ran, stumbling on the edge of the carpet but not stopping, to open the door.

Years ago, on hazy winter afternoons, Ma used to take him to the little market down the road, to the magazine stall that had all the best comics – the usual *Chacha Chaudhary* and *Super Commando Dhruv*, yes, but also the latest *Archie* and *Sabrina* digests, and his old favourites, the histories and myths of the *Amar Chitra Katha*. She would tell him to pick just one, but after he had spent five minutes trying to decide between two, she would let him have both, rolling her eyes at the magazine-vala, pretending to be exasperated but turning to him with a half-bitten smile, like she was trying to keep herself from bursting with happiness. That was the smile on Ma's face, now, as she stood at the door.

She left her suitcase outside and rushed in to give him a hug. He tried to wriggle out of it, determined not to forgive her, not so easily, but she held on. She was wearing a kurta instead of a sari, pale green with faded flowers on it, like the one he remembered from her old photographs, like the Mughal Gardens in full bloom. Stuck in her grip, her arms tickling his ribs, he was worried he would break into giggles. But the real danger, he realised, was of collapsing into a puddle of tears.

When Ma finally let go of him, she looked around the house, then back at him, her smile slowly fading.

'Is everything okay? How is Amma? Have you eaten?'

There was so much to tell her, so many things to ask. He had spent the entire week wondering how to tell Ma about the vulture without sounding like he had lost all his screws. He had gone over this very moment so many times in his head, picturing Ma holding his hand and telling him how sorry she was, promising him that she will never leave him again, but after being gone for two weeks, without as much as a phone call, all she had to say was *this*? *Had he eaten?*

If she was going to pretend that it was nothing, then, he thought, so be it.

'Amma is fine. I was just going to give her dinner. You want some?'

She smiled at him again, but that glow was gone. In its place was a dark, heavy tiredness.

'Don't worry, béta, I'm here now. You go study, I'll get your food.'

Her eyes darted to their bedroom door, which was still shut. His father had not come running out to welcome her, if that was what she had been expecting. He was probably sitting before his little temple, mumbling his complaints to the gods. That was all he had been doing for more than a week, even more so after the night he had come home drunk. Every evening, he would come home and take off his shoes at the door and go straight into his bedroom, and he would sit before the gods until exactly 21:00, when he would step out briefly to get the dinner that Adi laid out on the table for him. He did not thank Adi for it, but at least he no longer seemed angry – he did not complain about the noise from the TV or bother Adi about 'wasting time' on his comics. When Rina Auntie came in the evening, it was Adi who had to instruct her on what to cook. She was well aware of their tastes, he simply said yes or no to her suggestions – always yes to dal and potatoes; always no to bhindi, those gross, gruesomely named 'ladies' fingers'. It was Adi who gave Amma her food, too, three times a day, taking away her big steel plate to wash it when she was done. He had begun to grow used to this routine – to enjoy it, even – but now, he knew, it was over. He could go back to being a child.

Ma left her suitcase in the hall and went straight into the kitchen. Adi sat on the sofa and stared at iTV, the music channel where people dialled in and you could watch them go up and down the menus to select a song. He had never called in himself but he liked to watch the others and guess what they would pick. He hoped it would be that Michael Jackson video again, the one where the *Home Alone* kid sets up huge speakers next to his sleeping father, turns the volume to 'ARE YOU NUTS!?!', yells, 'Eat this!' and sends the father flying into the sky. The caller finally picked some old Bollywood song where a chubby hero drives an open-top car alongside a train, singing to the heroine who smiles coyly at him through her carriage window. How come there was no traffic on the highway? How was he driving without even looking at the road? How could she hear him over the deafening *da-dhuk-da-dhuk* of the train? Nothing made any sense.

He switched to a rerun of *WWF WrestleMania 13*, where Bret 'The Hitman' Hart had beaten the lights out of that macho, beer-guzzling 'Stone Cold' Steve Austin, but was still booed out of the stadium. Sunny-Bunny used to be fans of Stone Cold Austin. Bunny had once tried to copy his trademark move by crushing a Fanta can over his mouth, but it had ended with him getting slapped by his mother for ruining his school uniform. Adi himself still rooted for The Hitman, even though it was obvious that the ex-champion had begun to look too old-fashioned now with his long hair and pink vest and mirrored sunglasses. Perhaps it was time to switch loyalties, he thought. God knew he could use a bit of macho-ness himself.

After he had eaten and got tired of the TV and turned the lights off, he could see the glow of Ma's bedside lamp spilling out from under their door. She had taken their dinner into the bedroom long ago, but he had still not heard a sound from the inside.

On the first day of the school year, a rumour had spread through the class at a speed that only classroom gossip could achieve. They had all huddled in small groups, boys and girls separately, and turned to page 188 in the biology textbooks. Naked men and women were what they had been expecting. Diagrams of tubes and pipes inside human outlines were all they had found. Some boy had started explaining it to the others – how the sperm from the penis swam up the vagina to meet the egg – and when someone pointed out that their parents must have done the same, everyone had screamed and howled and pretended to puke. He had wondered, even then, why he had not found it disturbing at all. Now, as he lay in bed and considered the possibility that his parents could be having s-e-x, he realised what it was. It was disgusting for the others to think of it because they *could* think of it. For him, the thought of Ma and his father doing *that* was so incredible, so far from the realm of the imaginable, that he could only snort. Perhaps he was an orphan, he thought, like in *Great Expectations*, and he had been adopted when he was too young to remember. He almost wished for that to be the case. It would certainly have explained a lot.

*

They all spent the weekend at home, together but alone, like strangers in a shared auto-rickshaw. Ma spent most of it in the storeroom unpacking her old suitcases – not frantically, like she was looking for something, but in a slow, methodical way, like she just wanted to know what was there, buried in that dark, dusty corner of their house. His father did not come out of the bedroom, and neither did Amma. The person who seemed happiest to have Ma back was Rina Auntie. She talked non-stop as she cooked and cleaned and hovered around Ma, admiring the old clothes and offering to wash and iron them. Her constant, high-pitched hum, rising and falling with questions and complaints, burrowed through the noise of the TV and the cooler, keeping Adi distracted from studying for the exams.

On any other day, Ma would have turned the TV off, made him a glass of sweet, pink Rooh Afza and told Rina Auntie to keep her voice down, but she no longer seemed to care. He thought about asking her where she had gone, what she was up to, but he could sense the wall around her – a stone wall with arrow slits and cannon turrets, surrounded by a moat filled with crocodiles. He wondered if he could find a moment to snoop in the storage room and see what she was hiding in all those suitcases. Or could he take advantage of her distracted state to root around in her room, rummage in her handbag?

He didn't care, he decided. Whatever she was doing, whichever stupid secret she was hiding, she could keep it all to herself.

What did bother him was the feeling that Ma was not fully there, at home, with them. Even as she went around doing what she usually did, serving their food, folding their clothes and rearranging the little things that always seemed to fall out of place behind her back, a part of her seemed lost in a parallel world. He knew the feeling. It was like when he used to daydream about playing *Super Contra* with Sunny when he was stuck in maths class. It was the anticipation of doing something you really wanted that drove you through the chores you had to do. Maybe she had found her Sunny-Bunny too. Were grown-ups supposed to have friends like that? Were they allowed to just leave everything and go hang out with them? He had never thought about it before. After all, Ma had no parents to tell her not to have fun, to stay at home and study and sleep on time. Why shouldn't she go off whenever she wanted?

And now that he thought about it, what was keeping her from going for good? From leaving everything behind and never coming back?

He shut his eyes and tried to tune out all the noise. He tried to foresee her departure – to dismiss, forgive, even justify it – but he could not shake away the anger that had gripped him, wrapping his fingers so tightly around the remote control that it hurt. There was only one way to prepare himself: he had to pretend she was not there. He had to get used to the idea of being alone, left to take care of Amma and his father. Perhaps it was time to switch his loyalties. If Ma was going to leave whenever she pleased, he was going to take the side of those who stayed.

5.

A list of your fears, Mr Sharma

On an especially muggy afternoon when Amma would not stop ranting at Pete Sampras, Adi stood before the cooler and waited for the tiny drops of sweat on his neck to evaporate.

After her return, Ma had begun to spend even less time at home than before. For most of the day Adi was left alone, and the afternoons became one long blur. Reheating Amma's lunch, watching *Happy Days* while eating his own, flipping through some library book while waiting for *Everybody Loves Raymond*, wondering when the sun would finally go down and Ma would return from wherever she went to. For most of the day, he tried not to wonder where she went, what she was up to, since she did not have a school or an office to go to. Maybe she was a spy and couldn't tell anyone what she did? Maybe she'd got hit by a truck and was lying on the road bleeding? Maybe she just didn't want to come home.

He was not going to ask. But didn't he deserve to know?

Walking softly across the drawing room and past the kitchen, careful not to make the slightest noise to break Amma's reveries, he stepped into his parents' room and shut the door behind him.

The first thing that struck him, as always, was the smell. The air was thick with the constant battle between the holy agarbatti fumes and Ma's floral perfume, and the gods seemed to be winning. There was a wedding procession's worth of gods in the gilded mini-temple next to the bed. Besides the usual Lakshmi-Ganesh, there were all the avatars of Vishnu – from Matsya, the mermaid who saved humanity in the great flood, to Narasimha, the lion-man who was busy disentangling some demon's intestines, and even the Buddha, whom his father counted as a Hindu god. They all sat with gloating smiles, garlanded with fake orange flowers, gathered around a gigantic picture of Ram. Unlike those family portraits where Ram was always surrounded by Sita and Lakshman and Hanuman, this one had him alone, his bow stretched taut, his eyes set on some distant enemy. He was not smiling.

The rest of the room was neat and muted, as if to compensate for the garishness of the gods. The giant box bed was covered in a white sheet embroidered with white flowers. There were two gentle pits on the mattress, far apart from each other. In the middle, where he once used to sleep, there was just a flat white desert.

Folding the bedsheet over to avoid creases, he lifted the bed's lid with a great effort. The deep, dark pit was full of old clothes, both Ma's and his father's. Most of them looked funny, like the clothes people wore in old movies – flared-out pants and shirts with huge collars and bright, flimsy saris printed with giant flowers. There were some of his old clothes too, denim dungarees and sweaters with cats on them, but they did not interest him now – he could not imagine how he had ever liked them. In a gap between two bundles, he spotted his old catapult. It was a sturdy-looking thing, heavier than he remembered – a Y-shaped weapon made of three short, stocky wooden sticks and a long, limp rubber band connected to a worn-out leather square which would hold whatever could serve as a bullet. He held it up and stretched the band as far as he could, and he was surprised to see how far it could go, how tense it could grow, trembling with a force that seemed strong enough to shatter the idols in its crosshairs. Ma had been right, he thought; it was too dangerous a toy for children.

He let go of the band and stuffed the catapult in his back pocket. He was not a child now. Plus, he had to be prepared, in case he had to defend himself against enemies unknown – ghosts or demons or blabbering birds, whatever they might be.

He dropped the bed shut and pulled the sheet over it, and went over to his father's large, polished desk that was off-limits to him. It had once ruled the room, glowing like a mahogany throne, flanked by tall shelves laden with brick-like books of physics and mathematics. Over the years, it had been pushed into a corner, next to the toilet door, and its place of pride had been usurped by the temple.

He tugged at the drawers – they were unlocked! – and took out a bundle of folders. They were the same boring beige files he had grown up seeing, all marked with a jumble of letters and numbers – DRDO/OPS/TA/0797, and so on. At the bottom of the drawer was a leather-bound diary that looked more important, embossed with the national emblem in gold, and under it:

Defence Research and Development Organisation, Ministry of Defence, Government of India.

Setting it down on the table, he carefully flipped the pages and his father's atrocious handwriting crawled out, the broken letters wiggling like insects. Pressed between the pages was a stack of forms, all titled 'Application for Central Government Housing Quarters (Type VII)'.

This was his father's greatest ambition, the thing he talked about more than anything else. Sometimes, it seemed to Adi that the sole function of his father's job as a 'Category-F Scientist' was to write applications for the government bungalow he deserved, that had been denied to him for so long. It was certainly the greatest source of his seething anger towards the government, the Congress Party, Pundit Nehru and the British and even Mahatma Gandhi. All of them had conspired, it seemed, to deprive him of his Type VII bungalow. If only his father's handwriting was better, Adi thought, his application would have gotten approved. He had half a mind to give it a shot himself – Ma'am George had once praised his handwriting in front of the whole class, waving his exam papers as an example – but he thought better of it. He dropped the diary back in the drawer and turned to the computer.

The new PC had appeared a few months ago like a blessing from some god. Since then, it had been sitting quietly on the table, its two boxes covered in flower-patterned cloth cases, like a pair of women bowing at the temple. He slid the covers off and pressed the round button, softly, to stir the tall box awake. It started with a gentle purr and grew to a roar, its little green lights blinking madly, the entire metal case vibrating like it was preparing to take off towards the faraway future.

For a long time, nothing happened. He stared at the clouds on the screen, waiting, until they seemed to start floating across the pale blue sky, along with the black dots emerging from beyond, growing bigger and bigger, turning red and blue, transforming into a bright, boxy window in the sky. *Microsoft Windows 95*: even the words looked so modern, their sharp lines so sleek and self-assured. Finally, that enchanting music echoed through the room, the sound of tinkling drops growing, then fading, as the screen came alive and made the world pale into nothingness.

His plan was to play *Minesweeper*. He had discovered it during a computers class when he was bored of practising DOS commands, but he couldn't remember where to find it now. Clicking through the folders inside My Computer, he found one called Op Shakti. He double-clicked it and the little sand clock started flipping.

'Op' meant Operation, he knew, as in Operation Blue Star that Sunny had told him about, in which Indira Gandhi had sent tanks to blow up the Golden Temple in Amritsar. When he had mentioned it to Ma, she had grown darkly quiet, but his father had gone on about how the Sikhs were terrorists who wanted another Partition, that Indira Gandhi had been the only strong leader in the country but they had killed her. It had ended, he remembered, with Ma storming into the bedroom and slamming the door. He could not tell what exactly had upset her, but he had filed the whole thing away in his own mental drawer overstuffed with topics never to be talked about.

Finally, a little box popped up asking for a password. He tried his father's name, Ma's, then his own, but none of them worked. At every family get-together, his father boasted about having 'Top Secret' meetings at the Defence Ministry, or being best friends with some General Jaggi, but Adi knew enough to not take him seriously. If you spent all day listening to eighth-standard boys, you developed a fairly reliable detector for all kinds of exaggerations, from embellished truths to barefaced lies.

Seeing this Op Shakti folder, though, he was intrigued. It seemed military-related and he imagined photos of tanks and fighter jets hidden inside. He looked in the drawers again, knowing that his father would have written down the password on a piece of paper somewhere. His father's memory was famously bad; he still called Rina Auntie 'that maid', even though she had worked at their house for as long as Adi could remember. He checked every corner of the desk but there were no clues to be found. Finally, he gave up and shut down the computer, wrapping it back in its shroud, just as he had found it.

On the way out, he stopped for one more look at the room, at the box bed with its old clothes and the grey Godrej almirah with the safe that hid Ma's gorgeous necklace made of red–blue–green diamonds. He had stopped going into the room years ago, though he could not quite remember when, exactly, or why. After all the nights spent with his ears to the wall, the room had grown in his imagination into some kind of fantastical chamber of secrets, a cross between a maiden's tower and a dragon's lair. But standing still in there for a moment was enough to see it for what it was – a plain old room with a strange smell and a dull, colourless aura. It was not just un-scary, it was boring.

He stepped out and shut the door. They could keep it all – their jewels, their files, their stupid secrets. He had more interesting ones of his own.

At the balcony door, he pulled the curtains open and looked around. After days of unending rain, the sun was having its revenge, turning the Horlicks-coloured puddles into steam, making the air seem still and soupy, almost too thick to breathe.

He did not want to do this. He had spent so much time avoiding the vulture, hiding from it, trying to forget that it existed. But, at the same time, a part of him had been itching to try it again. Terrifying as it had been, the vulture's glimpse into the past had been the most exciting thing that had ever happened to him, way better even than the only time he had ever hit a six, back in a sixth-standard cricket match.

It was only a bird, after all, he told himself. And he was now armed.

'Are you there?' he called, and the cooler's misty gale snatched his shivering voice from his lips.

'Ahem.'

He turned and followed the sound to a rooftop across the park. The vulture stood out starkly against the burning sky.

'Oh, there you are. You – you can hear me?'

'Yes, Mr Sharma, I can hear you. I am not that old.'

'No, I just meant . . . I'm not saying you're—'

'Yes, yes, it is fine. So, you are going to behave yourself now?'

'Behave? Why, what'd I do now?'

'What did you *do*?' The vulture's neck snapped down like a serpent, shooting its little head forward, and Adi nearly fell back. 'Do you know the value of our Historical Archive, Mr Sharma? Now you are having the privilege to see it and what are you doing? You are flying away like a scared little sparrow. If you are not interested, you can tell me now instead of wasting my time.'

'Wasting your time? But, you don't, um, do anything?'

'*I* don't do anything? Ha! Mr Sharma, I am DDG in charge of all the northern provinces with additional charge of the National Capital Region. I am handling hundreds of cases like yours – thousands. And now with the Department cutting our funds, I don't even have a staff. No PA, no stenographer, not even a peon to bring chai. I am hardly having two minutes to sleep. Doesn't *do* anything, he says. Watches rubbish on television all day, *he* is the one to talk. Beh!'

The vulture straightened its neck and jerked its head sideways, grunting angrily, its furry belly heaving like it was out of breath.

'Wow, you sound just like my . . . Wait, you're saying you talk to others too?'

'Why, you think you only are special, eh? Some VVIP you are?'

'You're lying. No one else talks to birds.'

'Oh? And how do you know this, may I ask? You are having a direct line into other people's heads? How do you know who anybody is talking to or not talking to?'

'Um, no, I—'

'*No.* Correct. So, please don't interfere with my work. If you are ready to be serious, then we can talk.'

'Okay, sure. I'm serious, then.'

'Good, let me find your file.' The vulture closed its eyes, lifting its head towards the sky. 'Yes, here: Mr Adi Shankar Sharma, son of Mr Mahesh Chandra Sharma and Mrs Tamanna Sharma. Interesting name you are having, like Adishankara, the great sage, but broken into two.'

'That's what it was, originally, but Ma made it shorter. Otherwise, people would have made fun of such a long name.'

His father had chosen Adishankar, after some ancient Hindu Yoda, and for a long time, he had insisted on using the full name. Ma, however, had always called him Adi. In the end, she had managed to have his name broken up on the school records, relegating the Shankar to a middle name that could easily be forgotten.

'But they are making fun of your short name also? Adi-Paadi-Shaadi, no?'

'Um, yeah. I guess.'

'You guess? What you are guessing?'

'What?'

'Never mind. Now, as you are having access to the Historical Archives, Section 42, Sub-section 3 of the H-A-H-A is in force. Meaning, you are now bound by the reciprocal protocol and obliged to disclose and address the primary factors that induce and slash or aggravate conditions of severe discomposure. So, you are having the list?'

'Uh . . . *what*? What list?'

'A list of your *fears*, Mr Sharma. How do you expect us to start if you are not even having a list?'

'I don't know. I'm afraid of many things, I guess.'

'You are guessing correctly. That is normal. Most people are afraid of many things but they do not ask why. That is the difference between the child and the mature person. One word only: why. Fear is not always bad, actually, but only if you know why. Many are fearing us vultures, for example.'

'Why?'

'Very good, Mr Sharma, hrr-hrr. It is because people think in simple equations. Vulture equals death. What they are fearing is death, you see? Day and night, they are trying not to think about death. Then they see a vulture and think, "Orey baba, Yamaraj, the Lord of Death, is here to take me." Hence, they are getting upset.'

'You do eat dead things, don't you?'

'And what do you eat, Mr Sharma? Living things, is it?'

'Um, no, I – I'm a vegetarian.'

'So you are saying plants are not living things? You should talk to that peepul tree, it has been standing here since before your father was born.'

'Great,' Adi mumbled. That's all he needed, talking trees.

'Pardon?'

'Nothing. What's your point anyway?'

'My point? *My point* is that as per the rules and regulations we require the list to proceed. As there are five files in your Ma's archive, we will need to address five of your fears in return. So, please think carefully—'

'I know!'

'Oh, good. At least something you are knowing. Proceed, please.'

'Okay, so I've always been scared of dogs. Some years ago, I was in the park and I found a puppy crying in the bushes, so I picked it up—'

'I am sorry, Mr Sharma, I have to interrupt here. I am not talking about this kind of fear. It has to be a primary fear, you understand? Something that makes you sweat in the winter, that makes your soul shiver on a summer afternoon.'

'Um, okay. I'm also afraid of going to the temple.'

'No, no, no, Mr Sharma. Dogs and gods, these are childish things. If you are not ready to mention your actual fears, I must say you are not ready to grow up. I am afraid your access to the Historical Archive will be revoked and I will have to file a report to recommend dropping your case and reassigning the Department's limited resources—'

'Talking to my father,' said Adi.

'Ah! See, now you are being serious. Good, let us start with that. Fear number one: talking to own father. That will be easy to address, yes?'

'Oh. But what, um, what will I talk about?'

'What a question! Talk about anything, Mr Sharma. The weather, the cricket, your favourite colour – it is of no concern to the Department.'

'Why should I listen to you anyway? How do you know this will work?'

'You do not know. That is the point. This is not like your politicians or your religions. You do not need blind faith, you have to try and see.'

Talking to his father – it was a task more daunting than it seemed. But he knew there was more to be discovered in the vulture's memories, and there was no other way to find out. If he wanted to know Ma's story, he had to go back.

'Alright,' he finally said. 'I'll try.'

'Good,' the vulture nodded. 'That is all you have to do.'

6.

You had to time it just right

He stood by the bathroom window, fully dressed, and stared at his Casio. 06:23. Most mornings, time raced ahead of him as he rushed to get ready and catch the school bus. Now, it was stuck. Although he had woken up early, he had decided to miss the bus. His father was not going to talk to him at home, not in front of the TV. To face Fear Number One, he would have to catch his father alone, somewhere without distractions. The only such place he could think of was the car.

Digging his thumbnail into the clay-like lining on the window pane, he wondered if he should abort the mission and make a run for the bus. No, it was already too late. Running after the bus like a loser would have been worse than asking his father to drive him to school. There was nothing to do now but wait.

The sky was blue – the sun was not yet hot enough to burn away the colour – and the little park outside was mostly empty. Except for the gang of chaddi-valas, the boys in khaki shorts who came every morning to stand at attention and chant mantras. Their teacher was a small, balding man who carried a long wooden lathi and paced up and down the line, shouting commands like some cartoon colonel. After a while, the boys stopped chanting and picked up their own lathis, and they all pretended to be Jedis, swinging their sticks around willy-nilly, startling stray dogs with hollow crashes of bamboo. It was a miracle, he thought, that they didn't knock each other dead on their little heads. They were RSS members, his father had said, being trained in the arts of discipline and self-defence. He had wondered whom they were self-defending against – were they expecting to fight Pakistan with bamboo sticks? – but he had kept it to himself. Hearing the tone of awe in his father's voice, he was worried about being sent to join their ranks and get disciplined himself. He had had enough of chaddis, he had his new trousers now. They were a darker shade of blue than the official uniform, having been urgently bought at the neighbourhood market; the difference was slight, not easily detected. It was his own little secret, a private act of rebellion against the school's countless rules, and it made him feel a little bit bolder. He even looked a tad taller in the trousers, he was sure of it.

At 06:28, he finally heard the rumble of the school bus and waited until he saw it disappear behind the park. He flushed the toilet and stepped out of the bathroom.

After Ma had come back, his father had started doing his morning puja again. He spent more time on it now than ever before and Adi couldn't tell if it was gratitude being expressed to the gods, or anger. While his father sat cross-legged before the mini temple in his bedroom, his chants getting louder as the agarbattis slowly stunk up the air, the house stood still and silent. Amma did not interrupt by calling out to Ma, and Ma tiptoed around the kitchen, carefully handling dishes to avoid

78

causing any disturbance in the divine connection. Only when his father shook the tiny bell, making the air tremble with its tinny ring, did the house let go of its breath.

Adi stood at the kitchen door until Ma turned and saw him. She almost dropped the steaming mug of chai she had made for his father.

'Adi!' she whispered, and turned to look at the clock. 'Hai Ram,' she said through her teeth. 'You missed the bus? What do I do with you?'

She put the tea back on the kitchen counter and rushed into the bedroom. Adi stayed behind, lingering in the corridor.

Amma was complaining to Pistol Pete – asking him where he had hidden her gold, from what he could understand – but she stopped when she saw him.

'Bàbu,' she whined, like he had made her wait for a long time. 'What time is it?'

'Six-thirty-two.'

'What time is it?'

'Half past six.'

She frowned, went quiet, then smiled. She had her teeth in, so it didn't look like she was crying, but he could never really be sure.

The puja bell went off and he stiffened.

He had begun to feel a little bad for Amma. The only people who talked to her were Ma and Rina Auntie, and that too was only to argue about her meal times, or to sullenly answer the question she asked over and over again, the same question she had just asked him.

'O Nawab Sahib,' his father thundered. 'Where are you now? Hurry up!'

He slowly picked up his backpack. He hated it when his father called him that. If anyone acted like a nawab in their house, lying on the sofa all day, stuffing his face and ordering people around, it was certainly not him. He could see already that this entire exercise was going to be useless. Why did he have to do these silly things? Why did he have to listen to a stupid bird?

*

In the car, his father did not say a word, and Adi tried his hardest to think of something, anything to say. He could ask about his father's work – Op Shakti – but he could not risk his father even suspecting him of snooping around on the computer. He could talk about the only thing his father some-times talked to him about – cricket – but India had just been thrashed by Sri Lanka and he decided it was best not to bring that up. He wondered what would happen if he told his father about the vulture, and the thought made him bite down a smile: it was unthinkable. There really was nothing to say.

The Maruti Suzuki 800 was a toy-like car to begin with, and with age, it had started rattling like a mango seller's cart. At the speed his father was driving at, Adi had to hold on to the seat with both hands, convinced that the whole thing was going to fall apart at any moment, sending the seat skidding across the road and under the giant twin-wheels of the truck ahead of them.

On the highway, just before the Yamuna bridge, they over-took the school bus. He would be the first one to reach school at this rate, he was thinking, when he realised what was going on. They were slowing down in front of the bus and his father was frantically waving his arm out of the window.

'Go, go quickly,' said his father, as the car jerked to a stop. Adi opened the door and stepped out.

The bus slowly came to a halt some distance behind the car, and he started walking towards it. There was something so different about the air out there – it was cool and fresh, yes, but it also had an eerie edge, like it was whistling secrets. There were farms on both sides of the highway, flat patches in different shades of green, and the sky seemed higher, wider than usual. In the distance, there was a cluster of huts under a tree, a great tree that looked like a green cloud floating over the huddled houses. On some of the farms around, he could make out men in straw hats standing with their arms stretched out, like they had started to dance but someone had called 'Statue!' They were scarecrows, he realised, just like the ones in children's books, and it made him chuckle. He passed by this stretch of land every day in the school bus, but standing out in the open, it suddenly seemed so strange. He had that unsettling feeling you get when a memory is teasing you from the corner of your eye, and he stopped to look around but he just couldn't catch it.

And then it came to him in a blinding, gut-punching flash.

It had been a cold winter morning. He was in the backseat of the same car, on the same highway. The car did not rattle as much, then, and his feet did not reach the floor. His father was slimmer, his head hairier and he was tapping the steering wheel with the rings on his fingers. Ma sat next to his father in the front, wearing one of her fancy saris with a smooth sheen that always made him want to reach out and touch it. She was looking out of the window, away from his father. Lost in his daydreams, Adi was not paying attention to what they were talking about, until his father had said something and Ma had exploded.

'Buss! Enough!' she had said, loud enough to make his father's hands flinch, making the car sway. She had accused his father and Amma of treating her like she was dirty, too polluted for their pure Brahmin blood. A 'mixed-breed bitch', she had called herself, and even though Adi did not quite understand it then, he knew that it was a foul phrase. It was the first and only time he had ever heard Ma utter a gaali.

'—Fine, I will go. You can keep the dowry, the house, your precious son. I don't need any of it.'

Adi had shut his eyes, parted his lips, and slowed his breathing down. It was not the first time he had had to pretend to be asleep. By then, he had perfected the art.

He could not remember much else after that, except that the car was silent, like their house was silent, and there was a faint song playing on the radio. It must have been 102.6 FM because it was an English song, something about a fast car, and even though he couldn't recall any of the words now, the voice still rang clear across the years, deep and doleful but somehow comforting. Sometime after, or before, or during the fight, he remembered lying on the backseat and staring up out of the window. That was when he had seen the vulture for the first time.

He could see it again now, clear as a dream. It stood on a tall lamppost, next to a nest on the broad, flat lampshade hanging over the highway. It was a fluffy little thing – cute, almost, if not for its sickly bald head. He had found it fascinating, even back then. Unlike the sparrows and mynahs that were always restless, ready to scramble at the slightest sound, the little vulture had been calm, like it was waiting for something, like it was in no rush at all.

The bus's horn nearly knocked him off his feet. The driver was saying something behind the windshield and he didn't look happy. Adi ran up to the waiting bus and, as he boarded, every eye turned to him. He slid into a seat in the second row, right behind the teachers. As the bus started moving, the two teachers watched his father's car until it reached the end of the highway and made a screeching U-turn. They whispered something to each other and turned to look at Adi, and he looked out of the window and sank in his seat and started shooting laser beams, like he used to. Blink, zap, poof, you had to time it just right. You got 10x points for every Maruti 800. If you accidentally hit a cycle, it was game over.

*

There were only two other people in the library, girls from the senior sections whispering between the biology shelves. One of them seemed to be crying and the other was holding her hand and scolding her at the same time. He found a corner away from them, between history and literature, beyond the reach of the librarian's sleepy eyes. A cloud of dust rose up as he dropped his books on the desk, a million little molecules scurrying around in panic, caught in the blaze of the afternoon sun. He picked up *Modern English Poetry Volume 2* and flipped through it for a while, waiting for his eyes to latch on to a poem's scraggly edges.

He had always struggled to read poetry, never knowing how to follow the broken lines. Now, the little red book of Urdu couplets had given him a taste for the music of words. Now, he found himself craving more. He flipped along, skipping Auden and Eliot and other names vaguely familiar from the English textbooks, but none of them matched the symmetrical symphonies of Mirza Ghalib. Why were they never taught poetry like this? Why did they have to study poems that celebrated the horrid summer when there existed such beautiful verses about the magic of monsoon rains?

The afternoon dimmed and he looked up, out of the window, and saw blue-grey clouds spilling across the sky. A cool, perfumed breeze rushed in through a gap in the window and sent the poems fluttering. He did not notice. His eyes were on the vulture sitting on a eucalyptus tree, looking around like it was bored.

'Oh, great. You're here too,' he mumbled, and the vulture turned and nodded, its bald head bobbing on its serpentine neck.

'Pleasure to see you too, Mr Sharma. Have you brought any updates on your progress?'

'Yeah, I spoke to my father.'

'Good, very good. And what did you talk about?'

'Oh, you know. The weather and stuff.'

'Uh-huh, I see. And what was your father saying about the weather?'

'Umm, he . . . he said it was hot?'

'You are lying to me, Mr Sharma. I do not appreciate this one iota. I am telling you, if you act like this—'

'You lied to me too!'

'Excuse me? Accusing a senior official of dishonesty is a serious allegation. Can you provide any evidence for this?'

'I saw you on the Yamuna bridge, many years ago, when I was a child. I remembered today when I was walking on the highway, I—'

'Ahem,' the vulture interrupted. 'You were *walking* on the highway?'

'Yes, I missed the bus to go in my father's car, but he – it doesn't matter. I saw you. I remember. You were a baby.'

'Firstly, Mr Sharma, you are not applying logic. You see one baby vulture, how do you know it is me? There were many more vultures in those days. That is where they made their nests, near the river.'

'I remember. How come there aren't any now?'

'Because . . .' the vulture sighed, and for the first time, Adi sensed sadness in its voice. 'Because that is how things work. Today you are here, tomorrow it is OK-tata-bye-bye.'

'But what happened?'

'What happened? You people created a medicine that makes the cows stronger. But when we consume the cows, we get weaker. You see, cows are very important in your culture. More important than people, actually. So then, what chance is there for poor birds like us, no? You people think eating cows is a crime fit for capital punishment, so you are not sad to see us die. In your eyes, we are criminals.'

'Do you have to eat cows? There must be other things you can eat?'

'Yes, indeed. What a great idea, Mr Sharma! We should just eat grass, or mangoes or fried potatoes like you people do. The entire food chain you have already destroyed, now you want all of nature to change as per your illogical whims.'

'Um, I – I don't even care, you can eat whatever you want. I don't like cows anyway. They're weird.'

'Yes, now you will tell me you are scared of cows too. One real fear only you have admitted, and you are not even addressing that.'

'I did try! I went in my father's car, just him and me. He was not in a good mood so he didn't talk much, I'll try again—'

'Adi?'

It took him a second to realise that the voice had come from behind him. He turned to find Ma'am George walking towards him. She couldn't have heard him, could she? He was barely whispering.

'Oh, good afternoon, Ma'am,' he said, rising to his feet.

'Were you talking to yourself?'

She had heard him. Or at least seen his lips moving. She looked more amused than concerned, however.

'No! No, Ma'am. I was just—'

'Ah! You're reading poetry? You must be the only one in class using the reference books outside of the exam syllabus.'

She bent down next to him, just a breath away from him, to read the page that was open. Her smell swept over him like the billowing monsoon clouds and threatened to lift him off the chair.

'Ah, Kipling.' She straightened, and Adi opened his eyes. ' "*If you can dream, and not make dreams your master. If you can think,*' she paused, '*and not make thoughts your aim.*" Very Victorian,' she added with a meaningful arch of her eyebrows. He had no idea what she was talking about, so he nodded and smiled.

'What are you doing here?' She checked her watch. 'Are you bunking maths class to read poetry in the library?'

'Um, no, Ma'am. I was just—'

'Very bad,' she said, but she was smiling. A secret smile, he recognised; the smile of co-conspirators. This was making no sense.

'But since you're here, here's another book you might like.'

She turned to the literature shelf and ran a finger along it, until it landed on a black, hardbound book. *The Collected Works of Lewis Carroll.*

Alice in Wonderland? Really?

'You must have seen the Disney version,' she added, reading his face. 'This is better.'

'Thank you, Ma'am.'

'But make sure you study maths too, okay? It's almost as important as poetry.'

The smile was back so he didn't know if she was being serious. Poetry was not important at all, everybody knew that. He nodded and smiled again, and she walked away.

He sat down and turned to the window. The vulture was still there.

'Um, sorry, that was my English teacher.'

'Yes, I can see. So that's who you are trying to impress with your books.'

'What?'

'Never mind, I am sure you did nothing inappropriate.'

'Of course not! Why would you say that? I was just, er, talking about my book, that poem.'

'Yes, yes, indeed. And what is the name of this poem?'

He could see it clearly, still – the strap of her bra shining silver against her dark, smooth shoulder. He had seen bras earlier, that was no big deal. Even in their neighbourhood market there were underwear stores with posters of women wearing different kinds of bras. But the one Ma'am George was wearing was not like any he had seen before. Its strap was not the usual white, thick and sturdy as a backpack strap. It was a sleek, delicate thing with a pink-purple sheen to it. Even in the dull grey shadow of the clouds, it sparkled.

'How does it matter?' he said. 'What do you want anyway? You're just wasting my time.'

'Ah! I am wasting *your* time? May I remind you that you are the one who spoke to me?'

'Whatever.'

'This is the child talking, and I have no interest in talking to children. If you complete another task, then you tell me. Otherwise, please do not disturb me now.'

Adi got up and gathered his books and flashed a middle finger to the bird, but it had already turned away.

7.

Problems of the heart

Even before he had stepped up to the front door, he knew something was wrong. He tugged at the outer metal door, lightly. It was not locked. Sticking an ear on the wooden door, he heard voices inside, and his first instinct was to turn and walk away. Ma and his father at home, together, in the middle of the afternoon? It was bound to be trouble. He could go hang out with Sunny-Bunny, he thought, before remembering once again that they were gone. He could just go down to the market and see if the magazine-vala was there, but it was a hot, humid afternoon and he was tired. He took a deep breath and opened the door.

It was not a fight. He could hear his father's voice but there was something different about it. There was an urgent energy in the house, bordering on excitement, and it was not coming from his parents' room.

Amma!

He threw his backpack on the floor and ran across the drawing room, past the kitchen and up to Amma's door. She was on the bed, propped upright with pillows, with Ma and his father standing over her. On her outstretched arm was a thick, flat band hissing and growing, making her grimace. A bald, bespectacled man was sitting next to her with one hand on her bony wrist and the other squeezing a little black balloon. It took Adi a moment to realise that it was Dr Paul. He was their regular family doctor but Adi had never seen him outside the plywood-panelled room in his clinic. He had certainly never visited their house, not even when jaundice had turned Adi's eyes yellow, convincing him that he was going to die.

Dr Paul paused for a few seconds, frowning at his watch (it was not even digital), and everyone stared at him, waiting. When he let the balloon go, Amma's armband deflated with a heavy sigh and the room let out its collective breath. Amma began to say something to his father, who tried to ignore her and listen to Dr Paul. He was trying to tell Amma that she was going to be alright, although his own furrowed forehead seemed to doubt his reassuring tone.

'Ma?'

'Adi? You're here?' she said, as if she was the one surprised, and rushed him out of the room. 'Come, change your clothes, I'll give you lunch.'

'What's happening? Is Amma sick?'

'Nothing, béta. It's just a check-up. She will be fine. Your shirt is all sweaty, what have you been doing? Go, go have a bath.'

He knew there was something Ma was not telling him. They never told him about anything that mattered, especially medical things. 'Health problems' was all they ever said, like he was too dumb to understand actual diseases, like he didn't know Dada, his grandfather, had died of a cardiac arrest, which was different from a heart attack, which his father had had when Adi was little and was the reason samosas were banned from their house. It was probably the same for Amma. Problems of the heart, they ran in the Sharmas' blood.

He went back into Amma's room and stood next to his father, determined not to be excluded anymore.

'What do you advise, Doctor Sahib? Do we need to hospitalise?'

His father was standing with a slight bow, his hands clasped before him, an earnest look in his eyes, like one of those front-benchers at school who reminded teachers about checking the class's homework. It was always funny the way his demeanour changed around doctors. As a scientist and an officer of the esteemed Indian Administrative Service, there were very many professions he deemed to be underneath him, like engineers, lawyers or businessmen. There were some – journalists, actors, musicians – whom he considered unworthy of even a greeting. Doctors were the only ones he counted as his superiors. The most noble of all people, he called them (with the exception of dentists and psychiatrists – he was convinced they were scammers). The only other people who could make him behave this deferentially were pundits.

Packing his hissy-balloon machine into his briefcase, Dr Paul talked slowly about the side-effects of some medicine while trying to ignore Amma's constant questions. The questions, Adi realised, were about Dr Paul's caste. It was not surprising – this was her first question to anyone who wasn't a family member, from the plumber who regularly came to unclog her toilet, to the boy who delivered her white saris after they were ironed. It was the reason she didn't let Rina Auntie serve her food – she called her an untouchable, and the only thing she allowed her to do was clean her toilet. Maybe she wanted to check if Dr Paul was a 'touchable', thought Adi, though he couldn't see the point: he had already touched her all over. In any case, it seemed to be making his father's face itch with annoyance. Dr Paul buckled his briefcase shut, gave Amma a respectful bow, and quickly made his way to the front door.

'Doctor Sahib?' His father hurried behind him. 'Please don't mind, she is old—'

The doctor cut him off with a polite wave. 'There's one more thing.' He bent down to tie his shoelaces. 'See if you can get a blood pressure machine. The new ones are very easy to use, and not very expensive either. It will be good for her.' He pointed his chin towards Amma's room. 'And for you too.'

'I see, I see.' His father scratched his chin. 'And, er, about the charges—'

'Don't worry, there's no rush. I will have my compounder call you. Okay, Sharma-ji,' Dr Paul rose and lightly touched his fingertips together, 'I'm running a little late.'

'Of course, of course, Doctor Sahib.' His father opened the door, nearly bowing to touch the doctor's feet. As he closed it again and turned around, he shook his head and rubbed his face.

'What's wrong with Amma?'

His father looked up to find Adi standing at the other end of the dining hall.

'Nothing, nothing. You came home early?'

'No, it's two-thirty. This is the time I come home every day.'

'Hmm,' grunted his father as he made his way towards the bedroom.

'Is Amma going to the hospital?'

His father stopped and frowned at the big clock in the corridor. It was an ancient pendulum clock mounted on a tall, wooden tower, and he often referred to it as the sum total of Adi's inheritance. He always laughed when he said it, but it was the slanted, dead-eyed laugh he used for un-funny things, like news about the Prime Minister's foreign trips, so Adi took care not to laugh along. He did not get the joke anyway.

'She is always complaining about aches and pains. How are we to know if anything is serious? It was our good luck that I was here in the morning. If she had been alone, or . . .'

His father shook his head and sighed again, then turned back towards the drawing room. Taking his place on the sofa, he reached for the remote.

'Papa?' Adi sat down on his divan. 'I can take care of Amma. I can take a few days off from school. We have tests coming up so I can stay home and revise.'

His father looked at him and smiled, and for once, there was no hint of mockery in it. 'It's okay, béta. We will adjust, you don't worry. You have already done a lot. You should be focusing on your studies now.'

It was a shock to hear the gentleness in his father's tone, the hint of gratitude in his words.

'Papa,' he ventured, emboldened by this change. 'Why is Amma unhappy? Does she not want to live with us?'

His father shook his head and gave a bitter laugh. 'Why would she want to live with us? She has royal blood in her, she is used to living in palaces. She used to be the queen of her little village, back in her day. Her chowkidaars made all the small-caste people get off their cycles and carry their shoes in their hands in front of our house. Now, she needs those same people to wipe her ass.'

He used the funny word for butt – chuttar – and Adi pursed his lips and waited until the urge to giggle had passed. 'She was a queen?'

'Arré, what queen?' His father swatted an invisible fly. 'Back then, every zamindaar owning four yards of land acted like raja-maharajas. All of India was full of them, sucking the blood of common people and donating it to the Angrez. Your Amma and Dada were no better.'

Adi was stunned to hear his father show such disrespect to his parents. He had always thought that his father too had been angry about having lost all their ancestral property after Independence. Now, he was confused.

'There was a time, I remember,' his father continued, switching channels on the TV and talking mostly to himself. 'There used to be so many people in our house – children, servants, relatives, villagers asking for favours. It was busier than a fish market. Now, there is no one left. Her husband stopped living long before he died. Her favourite son ran off to America. And now her worthless son is just a lowly civil servant with a flat smaller than her kitchen used to be.'

'But you are a scientist,' said Adi. 'That's better than being the queen of some village, no?'

His father laughed again, a little embarrassed this time, as though he had forgotten that Adi was listening. 'Yes, but who's going to make that old woman understand that? This is the problem when you don't let go of the past, you see? You become a prisoner of your own memories. Sometimes you just have to accept what happened and move on. Life goes on, it doesn't stop for anyone, there is no reverse gear in this car.' He laughed again, and Adi sensed a change in his voice. It was louder, like a kid overacting in a school play, and laced with hidden meanings. Ma walked into the drawing room and Adi realised what had changed. His father had found his audience.

'Yes,' said Ma, sitting down on the single sofa away from his father. 'What are we accepting today?'

'I'm telling your son that we should look ahead into the future, not keep digging up the past.' He always referred to Adi as 'your son'. Never 'our son'. Now Adi wondered if there was a chance that his father was not his real father. He knew there wasn't, not really – one look at their faces was enough to know that – but as Ma always said, it didn't cost eight ānnas to dream.

'I agree,' said Ma. She sat silently as his father flicked through the channels on the TV, barely pausing to see what was on. Adi thought of suggesting Star World – it was nearly time for *The Simpsons* – but he knew, just by the change in the air, that the chance for being cheeky was gone. It was time to shut up and read his book.

'But there is only one small difficulty,' said Ma. 'How can we forget the past if we pretend that it never happened? Maybe we have to remember some things first, so that we can forget them?'

The room was quiet for a while. Even the TV had stopped on a sports channel showing a snooker match, and the match was hushed as a sharply dressed man bent over the table, lining up his shot.

This was new – Ma saying such things, openly challenging his father. Adi didn't know what to make of it. What was so wrong, after all, about what his father was saying? It *was* better to look to the future, wasn't it? What had he done to deserve such curt responses? He glanced up at his father. In his haggard, unshaven face and heavy eyes, there was a tiredness that Adi had only ever seen in Ma.

Without another word, his father heaved himself off the sofa with a great sigh and walked away. Adi watched him go, hobbling lightly – his leg always fell asleep on that sofa – and a wave of pity for his father took him by surprise. Light applause broke out as the man in the bowtie knocked two balls in two separate holes, and Ma stared at the TV, her lips twitching ever so slightly, as though ready to break into a smile.

*

97

Adi had the TV turned to a whisper and was sitting with his books open and a finger on the Power button on the remote, when he heard his father's voice again. His finger pushed down and turned the TV off before he realised what was happening. His father was yelling in Amma's language, asking, over and over, if someone could hear him. He was on the phone, and at that late an hour, it could only mean one thing: he was talking to Chacha.

Chacha lived in Chicago, IL, Adi knew from the markings on the beautiful, glossy stamps on the holiday cards they received every year. Earlier, there used to be postcards from different places in America – a market glittering with Christmas lights, a lake surrounded by snow-white trees, the vast water curtains of the Niagara Falls – and they used to stand proudly on the drawing-room showcase for months.

Two years ago, Chacha had got a girlfriend – an American woman, a firangi – and the cards had changed to photographs of both of them, lighting Divali lamps or standing next to a real-life, impossibly tall Christmas tree. His father had refused to talk about this girlfriend so the cards were no longer displayed in their house, but that had not stopped Adi from examining every detail in those photographs. The fireplace with a real fire, the spotless cream-coloured sofa, the elegant paintings framed on the walls, the paper-like texture of the walls themselves – they were all things he had only seen in TV homes. Even more incredible were the two people themselves. Chacha, slim and tall, with chiselled cheekbones and clean, bright skin, was like a glossy magazine version of his father.

And his girlfriend, with red-brown hair and green-blue eyes and teeth out of a Pepsodent ad, looked stylish in a sari in a way that Ma never did. More than once he had run his fingers across those photographs, closed his eyes, and made a secret wish to be transported to that home, that family, that world that seemed to sparkle with laughter and light.

His father shouted on, as if to give his voice an extra push for the long journey to Chicago, IL, and Adi strained to understand the words. He had learnt to pick up quite a few of them, listening to Amma all day, but their similarity to Hindi somehow made them more difficult to catch. The language was always at the edge of his tongue, just out of his grasp. Ma did not speak it, and his father only used it with Amma and Chacha, so he had never had the chance to learn it. Not that he would have wanted to; it sounded like one of those dialects that were mocked at school, earning their speakers that most derogatory of labels: Bihari. He wasn't sure why all people from the state of Bihar were considered backward and uncouth. He knew that Bihar had once been home to Ashoka the Great, the ancient emperor, and Aryabhatta, the inventor of zero, even the Buddha. Still, he did not want to be one of them, such was the power of the curse 'Bihari'. In that moment, however, he wished he knew the language just enough to know what his father was saying.

Ma stepped out of the bedroom and he followed her to the kitchen to ask if Chacha was coming. His father's voice was still booming inside. 'Blood-pressure machine,' spoken in English, was the only thing he picked up.

'I don't know,' was all Ma said. 'We'll see.'

That was as close to a yes as he would ever get, Adi knew, until Chacha was actually on the flight.

'And Chacha's . . . friend?'

Ma smiled at him – her indulgent, half-bitten smile. 'Go, finish your homework, Adi. I'll tell you when I know.'

After all these years of waiting, Chacha was finally coming. It meant a trip to the airport to receive him, and it meant that he would be getting shoes and jeans and sweatshirts like the ones in *Archie* comics, carrying the warm, heady aroma of faraway foreign lands. There was no way he could do any homework now.

*

In the pale yellow darkness of the drawing room, his Casio glowed 23:15. Ma's bedside lamp was still on, he could see from the faint line under their door, but there had been no sound from the inside for at least twenty minutes. There was a small chance she might have been up, reading, but he could not wait any longer. Quietly, he got off the bed, grabbed his slippers and unlocked the front door.

There was a strong breeze on the roof, charged with the anticipation of rain. He climbed up to his usual spot and looked around at the twinkling horizon. In the distance, past the tall chimneys of the power station outlined by blinking red lights, he could see rainclouds approaching, their edges pulsing with lightning.

Leaning back against the wall and taking a deep breath, he whispered, 'Are you there?'

'Yes, Mr Sharma,' said the vulture from a lamppost across the park, sounding bored and tired.

'I did it. I talked to my father.'

'Well done. What a big liver you have, talking to your own father.'

'You try talking to him,' said Adi, laughing in much the same way his father did.

'So.' The vulture raised its head and stretched its long neck, like it had just woken up. 'What Earth-shattering discovery have you made through this difficult task? Have you learnt anything from it?'

'Just, I guess, that I'm not really scared of him?'

'Ah, I see, I see.'

'Yeah. He's just angry about some things. About Ma and Amma. But he said we should forget the past and move on. That kind of makes sense, so I guess he's not—'

'*Forget* the past and move *on*? Ha! What pearls of wisdom your father has gifted. So, if I may ask, what are you doing here, Mr Sharma? Would you like me to "move on" too? You are not interested in knowing your Ma's history anymore?'

'No! I didn't say that. I'm just saying . . . just that he's not scary, only angry.'

'I see.' The vulture nodded slowly, no longer sounding bored. 'And what about you? You are also angry?'

'Me? No? Why would I be angry?'

'Hmm,' said the vulture, and paused for a moment. In the glow of the streetlamp, its dark feathers looked softer, its round eye not so menacingly opaque and Adi realised that he was no longer scared of it either. What would he do, he wondered, if the vulture attacked him? It was big, but he was bigger; he could easily fend it off, he was sure. More importantly, he was human. He was smarter, with a way bigger brain and opposable thumbs.

And he had a catapult!

He cursed himself for forgetting to carry it with him. What good was it to have such a great weapon if he kept it stuffed under his mattress?

'Okay, Mr Sharma.' The vulture's voice sounded shaky, like it was suppressing a laugh. 'As I am also bound by the reciprocal protocol of H-A-H-A, I am obliged to share the next file from the Historical Archive. May I remind you again that you must follow the rules and regulations under section—'

'Yes, yes, I know the rules: be quiet, pay attention, things won't be repeated.'

'Yes, very good. Now if we could only follow these rules in life too, it would be so much easier, no?'

'Yes, at least you won't keep repeating yourself all the time.'

'Eyes closed, Mr Sharma.'

'They have been for the last five minutes. If you don't start soon I might fall asleep.'

DHA/HA/TS/1947(2)

Slowly, the pulsing blackness before his eyes reveals a starry sky. Under it, a yellow haze hangs over a land dotted by fiery glows, and he begins to make out the features of the land-scape. On the left are the dense, dark farms stretching into the distance. On the right, there seems to be a village. There are no lights in any of the houses but some of them are on fire, covering the village in a reddish-grey halo.

He hears a creak and swings his gaze back towards the left, where he spots the cycle with its three passengers approaching on a dirt path. Nana stops on seeing the flames and quickly dismounts, helping Nani and Kammo get off as he holds the cycle.

'Stay here,' Nana whispers to Nani and hides the cycle in the fields, beneath tall, thick canes topped with long leaves that fan out like black feathers.

Nani takes hold of Kammo's hand, who is sulkily rubbing her eyes, and crouches in the shadow of the plants. Nana begins to run towards the burning village.

The first few houses on the outer edge of the village seem untouched, though deserted and Nana keeps running past them. The only sound is that of the fires crackling all around, and the shifting shadows they cast make it difficult for Adi to follow Nana. He seems to be heading towards the centre of the village, and as Adi turns his head to scan the area, he feels his throat go dry. The path Nana is following leads to a mosque, and although Nana can't see it from where he is, the mosque is full of people. There are several jeeps and motorcycles parked in front of it and Adi can see an army of blue-turbaned Sardaar-jis in the courtyard of the mosque. They seem relaxed, even cheerful, huddled in small groups and sharing bottles of whisky, and Adi thinks that perhaps now that they have cycled across the border, things are better. Maybe in India, the Sikhs can join the Muslims in the mosque for a party.

A cheer goes up in the crowd as a few burly men step into the courtyard with a clutch of young girls. The girls are crying, trembling, and many are streaked with blood. All of them are completely naked. As everyone laughs and begins to clap and sing, the guards prod the girls with their swords. Slowly, the girls start dancing.

Outside, Nana hears the commotion and stops just as he reaches the mosque. He sees the jeeps outside and stands there for a moment with his hand covering his mouth, bent over like he is about to sneeze, or vomit. He is crying, Adi realises. Confused, he looks towards the jeeps again and sees what he has missed – the vehicles are parked in a circle surrounding a small pyramid. He did not see it at first, he realises, because of the flies. They swarm around it in a black haze, but every now and then, with a gust of the burning wind, the cloud parts and he can glimpse an arm, a leg, a face frozen in a scream. In a moment, the darkness swallows it again.

'Oye, who's there?' Adi hears a man calling out and turns to the left again.

A jeep going towards the village has stopped in front of Nani and Kammo, trapping them in its headlights. Two men step out and walk towards them. One wears the same blue turbans as the rest, and over his long, white kurta hangs a black strap carrying a kirpaan, the curved knife of the Sikhs. The other man is bald, and on the dome of his forehead is painted a red teeka in the shape of Shiva's trident.

Nani steps forward and says something, and the men nod. Kammo tries to say something too, pulling desperately at Nani's clothes, but Nani strokes her head and continues talk-ing to the men, reassured by their smiles. Adi can see what the little girl has seen – the smiles are not to be trusted.

The bald man – short and stocky with a round, friendly face – steps up to them and squats before Kammo, asking her something. When she refuses to answer, he grabs her arm and pulls her away, and Nani cries out with all her force: 'Tariq!'

'Mussalman!' yells the man to his burly companion, who rushes to grab Nani, wrapping his thick, hairy arm tightly around her neck. The little man lunges at Kammo, catching her just as she tries to run towards Nani.

The name has given it away, Adi realises. That short, sharp 'iq' is as unmistakably Muslim as a crescent moon – even he knows this. Surely, Nani should have known better? But perhaps, he wonders, names were just names back then, with-out such hard borders to divide them.

Calling out to Tariq, over and over, screaming the name that has betrayed them, Nani struggles to break free, but the big Sardaar-ji begins to drag her towards the jeep. Kammo's shrieks are loud enough to pierce through the night and echo around the village, and Adi turns to see if Nana has heard, but he is nowhere to be seen.

As Nani is brought to the back of the jeep, her captor bends over to pick up a piece of rope and his grip loosens. In a flash, Nani reaches under her kurta for her own kirpaan and stabs the man in the neck. As he staggers to the ground, dragging Nani down with him, the little man yells out and fumbles to find his own dagger in the front seat of the jeep. Seizing her chance, Kammo slips from his grip and shoots towards Nani, but the man catches up with her and lifts her up into his arms.

Nani rises and kicks the man she has stabbed, hard in the stomach, and walks around the jeep to face the little man. With her hair dripping over her face, her belly swollen under her blood-soaked kurta, and the kirpaan glinting in her hand, she is an incarnation of Kali, the goddess of doomsday herself. She lets out a scream of such ferocity that the old man steps back, flinching in fear. Adi has heard the voice before, he real-ises – it sounds exactly like Ma's voice from that night before she left.

Just as Nani starts to run towards the man carrying Kammo, another man appears from behind her and holds her back. It is Nana. He is saying something in Nani's ear but she does not stop screaming. Finally, he slaps her and points towards the man up ahead. He is holding his dagger across Kammo's quivering throat.

On the dirt path ahead, they spot two more jeeps full of men heading their way. The little man begins to run towards the approaching headlights, waving his free arm and yelling. In his suffocating grip, Kammo is no longer crying. She is still as a doll, her eyes round with terror, as she gets farther and farther away from Nani.

Dragging Nani by her arm, Nana mounts the cycle and forces her to climb on. The cycle disappears into a narrow opening in the dark fields, and Nani's screams hang in the air for a moment, before the wind picks up and blows them away.

8.

A letter from Pakistan!

'Ma?'

She was cleaning up Amma's room, carrying, with one arm, a pile of off-white saris, a plate with two half-empty teacups on it, a rag-thin towel, and a black plastic bag knotted tight, and she was still managing to wipe the desk with the other hand – his old desk that now lay crowded with medicine bottles and biscuit tins that had no biscuits and a large *Bhagavad Gita* wrapped in a faded, worn-out cloth, looking so ancient that he wondered if it was the original, written by Lord Krishna himself.

'Humko nahi maloom,' Ma said again, pushing sweat-soaked strands of hair from her forehead with the back of her hand. 'We don't know,' she kept saying, using 'we' for 'I' like Amma, who kept asking something about jevar. Jewellery.

Ma stopped at the door and looked around the room again, and shook her head. He knew what she was thinking: it was impossible to keep the room clean. She used to shake her head in exactly the same way whenever Adi made a mess of that room, but now, he thought, she would have had to admit, he was nowhere as bad as Amma.

'Ma?' he raised his voice a notch.

'Yes, béta?' she said, as she turned to walk out of the room, her arms overflowing. She reminded him of Durga – his all-time number one favourite goddess – with her ten hands holding ten random things, riding her pet tiger and slaying a blue demon with a spear, all with a bright and peaceful smile.

'I wanted to ask you something.'

'Ask.' She dumped the dirty clothes in that bottomless basket in the bathroom and turned towards the kitchen.

'What was Nana's name?'

She put the dirty dishes on the counter, tossed the plastic bag into the dustbin, washed her hands in the sink and, finally, turned to him with a glowing smile. He congratulated himself on his masterstroke – nothing worked as well to improve Ma's mood as the mention of Nana.

'Tarun Lal Sharma,' she told him. 'What happened? How come you are thinking of your Nana today?'

'I don't know.' Adi shrugged. 'I just realised I didn't know his name. Nana and Nani came from Punjab, no?'

'Yes, they came to Delhi after Partition. They used to live on the other side.'

'So, their family is still there?'

'I have told you all this, Adi,' she said, though she was not annoyed at all. Her mind had already dipped back into her childhood to dig up her favourite memories of Nana. He could have had her going for hours, he knew, just by prodding her at the right moments, but he had a mission in mind, he reminded himself. He had brought up Nana only to get Ma talking.

'I know you've told me but I keep forgetting.'

'We don't know about their families, béta. They got left behind and we lost touch with them.'

'What was Nani's name?'

'Santosh.' She turned to take out pots and pans from the cabinets.

Toshi, short for Santosh – that he knew. Tariq was still a mystery. Had Nana changed his name after getting married, like women sometimes did? Had he changed his religion too? He knew he could not ask Ma directly. Once, long ago, after hearing something his father must have said, Adi had asked Ma if she was a Muslim. She had *lost* it. She had warned him never to talk like his father, never to think of such things as religion and caste, so he had never brought it up again.

Ma was measuring rice in a steel glass now, and he could see her face growing darker. He had made a mistake mentioning Nani. He knew she had died a long time ago, when Ma was still a child, and Ma did not like being reminded of her.

'Nana liked poetry, no?'

'Oh, yes.' Her smile returned. 'He was *mad* for poetry. He could spend the whole night reading the same old poems over and over again – Mir, Ghalib, Firaq, Faiz, all the great Urdu poets.'

'Mirza Ghalib?'

'Yes,' she smiled, looking surprised. 'You know about him?'

Adi ran out into the drawing room to get Noor's book of poetry and showed it to Ma. She flipped through it, nodding slowly like she was impressed. 'Very good,' she said, handing it back to him. 'Your Nana would have been proud. He was just like you, you know, his head buried in books day and night.'

She poured water over the rice, lit the stove and moved to open the fridge.

'Ma?' He paused to clear his throat, to make his voice deeper. 'Where did you go?'

'What?' she said after a moment's pause, her smile quickly draining.

'Last month,' he said, examining his bitten fingernails. 'Where did you go?'

'I will tell you, but not today.'

'When?'

'One day, when you are older.'

There it was – the answer as familiar as a childhood friend.

'I'm old enough, I understand everything. You can tell me, whatever it is. If you and Papa are going to get a . . .'

He could not bring himself to say the word, not when he saw Ma's face. The growing darkness around her eyes, the weight on her drooping shoulders, the sadness in her sigh – it instantly made him regret opening his mouth.

'No, Adi, there's nothing like that,' she said, slowly shaking her head. 'I will tell you, béta. But right now, there are some things that even I don't know. When I find out, I will tell you.'

'Will you be going away again?'

'I don't know right now.'

It was not a no.

'Can I go with you?'

She thought about it for a moment, her lips pressing together and spreading into a faint smile and his heart leapt. Images flashed past his eyes: they would go away together, driving, no, *flying* off to some distant city. They would have a big house with a garden where she would plant flowers, and a study room which he would fill with books. Together, they would live a life filled with laughter and adventure and discussions about poetry, free from the tyranny of silence that hung over this house like a curse.

'One day—'

Adi tried not to roll his eyes.

'—I will tell you everything. Just have some patience. For now, you need to focus on your studies, revise for your exams.'

More than her frowning and lip-biting, more than her non-answers, it was this that gave it away. His exams had ended a week ago. Earlier, she would never have made this slip. She always remembered the dates of every one of his exams, even the class tests that the teachers said were just as important even though they didn't count towards the final grades. Now, she looked like she couldn't even tell today's date.

He stood and watched Ma twist a knife through a cauliflower, shredding it into little white flowers that rained all over the kitchen counter. Looking at her furrowed brows, at her lips twitching slightly, as if holding a conversation in some parallel world, he realised that he was wasting his time. It was all useless, worthless, one hundred per cent futile.

She had already left.

After Dr Paul's visit, things changed at home. In the evenings, his father started coming out to the drawing room again, wheeling Amma out as well, to eat dinner 'as a family'. Just like that, Adi's room was once again taken from him, and the quiet nights of Star World sitcoms and Channel[V] videos were hijacked by crass comedy shows or the endless drone of the news.

Most nights, there was a nervous energy in the house that made Adi rock his legs, which annoyed his father enough to make him scowl and say things like: 'A calm *body* leads to a calm *mind*.' Other than that, little was said between the four of them as they ate dinner with their eyes fixed on the TV. If there was a cricket match or an old Raj Kapoor movie on, his father became more relaxed, but it meant that he would stay in the drawing room until it ended. If, on the other hand, the news was on, he would rant at the TV, working himself up until his forehead throbbed, but it meant that he would soon toss the remote on the sofa and storm out of the room.

The news was on one evening as Adi got home, and his father was just at the muttering-at-the-TV stage.

'Where have you been?' his father asked, and it took Adi a second to realise that the question was for him. It was a question only Ma ever asked him.

'Um, just outside. With my friends.'

'The Sardaar boys?'

'No,' he mumbled, scratching his ear. 'My friends here, Suyash and all.'

Adi didn't know anyone named Suyash. In fact, he was surprised to hear the name himself, so ridiculously made-up did it sound. It seemed to satisfy his father, however, who clearly didn't even know Sunny-Bunny's names, let alone that they had moved away months ago.

'What's that?' said his father, pointing at the yellow envelope in his hand.

'Oh, this? It's a letter.'

Ever since the phone call with Chacha, Adi had started checking the letterbox obsessively, hoping to find a hint about his arrival. He had found something that day, something even more thrilling than a postcard from Chicago, IL. Now, he bit his lip and kicked himself for not hiding it under his T-shirt.

'I also have eyes, not buttons. I can see it's a letter, who is it for?'

'Ma.'

His father turned back to the TV without a word. Adi looked at him, sitting with his feet up on the table, his chin buried in the folds of his neck, his face drooping with a sadness masked by indifference. His father was just as alone as he was, Adi realised, with no one to talk to but the TV. And he knew just as little about Ma as Adi did. Didn't he have a right to know what his wife was up to, where she kept disappearing? Didn't they deserve answers too?

He walked up to his father and dropped the letter on the sofa.

The big yellow envelope, covered in stamps and markings, had sent a shock through his fingers when he had first found it. It was addressed to Ma, in beautiful calligraphic handwriting, and at the bottom, it had the sender's address:

Lajpat Road, Shahdara Town, Lahore, Punjab, Pakistan.

Most of those could have been places in India – *were* places in India. It was that word at the end that turned them into enemy territory. He had checked and checked again to make sure that it really was for Ma. A letter from Pakistan! Carrying it home in his hands, he had been tempted to tear it open and read it, but he had also felt a heavy dread, like he was holding a ticking bomb. Now, as his father turned the envelope around in his fingers, his jaws set hard and his eyes twitching, Adi braced himself for the explosion.

'What do I do with this?' said his father, tossing it back on the sofa like it was a lit match, a sizzling stick of cartoon dynamite. 'Go, give it to your mother.'

Adi walked into the kitchen, where Ma was busy preparing dinner, soaking the excess oil out of the fried aloo that his father insisted on having despite the doctor's warnings. He handed her the letter and waited to catch the look on her face. She took it and, without a glance at him, went into her room and shut the door.

*

By the time he had showered and changed and returned to the drawing room, he could sense the change in the air. His father was in his usual spot, simmering in front of the news; Ma was on the single sofa farthest from the TV. Dinner had been served and his plate was waiting for him on the divan and, as he took his place, he wondered if Ma had read the letter, where she might have hidden it and whether his father knew what it contained.

'What was so great about this Mother Teresa?' his father asked the newsreader. She had died a few days ago and the news was full of tributes to her. They had even had a special assembly at school in her honour, beginning with a two-minute silence.

'Arré, these missionaries are only interested in converting Hindus. Muslims cannot be converted, they know. Their faith is too strong. It is only our small-caste people who fall for these fraudsters. Oh, look at that, she was a foreigner too!'

She had come to India in 1929, the newsreader said. Adi did not point out that it meant she had lived in India for way longer than his father. The TV showed a picture of her with Princess Diana, who had also died recently – a rare piece of news that had brought Ma to tears. His father had mumbled about that too, wondering why anyone should care about some spoilt Angrez princess. Adi didn't know much about Diana, but he had decided that he liked her. Now, he was beginning to like Mother Teresa too.

'Useless government,' his father hissed. The newsreader was now saying something about a nuclear bomb. Prime Minister I.K. Gujral had said that India knew how to make the bombs but was not going to make them.

'Of course we know how to make them, the point is to

show the world. There,' his father pointed at the balcony door, presumably towards Pakistan, 'the Mullahs are collecting bombs like apples and here we are sitting scared of America. These people only understand one language, the language of force. If we show any sign of weakness, they will take everything. Kashmir today, Punjab tomorrow, then Rajasthan, Gujarat, what will stop them? Already they have so many agents here roaming around in broad daylight.'

The news moved on to the Samjhauta Express – the Compromise Express – the only train that ran from India to Pakistan, from Delhi to Lahore. The newsreader said that according to 'sources', it was going be shut down for security reasons.

'Lo-ji, finally,' his father laughed, then threw a glance at Ma. It was a lightning-fast flick of the eyes, but Adi caught it. Her plate seemed to have her full attention and it did not look like she was listening. She was not eating either, he realised.

'God knows whose idea it was to keep running this train. We might as well go and carry the terrorists back on our shoulders. Chalo, it's good,' his father said with a sigh, as if he was a peacekeeper breaking up an argument. 'Now maybe people will stop going here and there, and pay attention to their own homes—'

The steel plate crashed on the floor and wobbled like a top, sending bits of food flying across the room. The shrill buzz went on ringing through the walls long after Ma had walked out, gone into the bedroom and slammed the door shut.

The news turned to cricket – India had lost to Pakistan again, in Pakistan, at a place called Hyderabad, which was also a place in India. After a while, Adi stole a glance at his father – his mouth was frozen in a smile, but his eyes were burning with the glow of the TV. It was going to be a long and not so silent night.

He picked up his book and tried to read, but he could not follow the words. When his father got up to go to the bedroom, he readied himself to sneak up to the terrace and wait out the storm. Instead, his father did what Adi had never seen him do – he got the bucket and the rag that Rina Auntie used to mop the floor and started doing it himself. After a few slow blinks, Adi finally got off the bed and squatted on the floor to help sweep up the food.

He was not sure what exactly his father had said to make Ma explode like that. That was how he always talked when the news was on and, most of the time, Ma simply ignored his ramblings. Sometimes, she even rolled her eyes and snickered, or calmly corrected him when he got something wrong, like the names of Mughal emperors or pronunciations of South Indian names. This time, he knew the letter had something to do with it – the letter from Pakistan that he was now simultaneously itching to read and regretting ever having touched. If only he had hidden it better – if only he had not betrayed Ma and handed it to his father – perhaps none of this would have happened.

Watching his father panting, struggling to bend his knees and move across the floor, wobbling like an inflatable bop bag, he felt a rush of pity for him. All he probably wanted was Ma's attention, just like Adi. And just like Adi, he was starved and desperate, doing what he could to get Ma to say something.

It was all the more surprising, then, to also feel a sudden, inexplicable, almost frightening itch to kick his father in the ass.

9.

Catch the tiger by its toe

It was only mid-October but the school had begun to change colour, the dark blue of sleeveless sweaters overshadowing the white of the shirts. You could tell who the uncool kids were by noting when they started wearing sweaters. The longer you could go with your shirt sleeves rolled up, the more badass you became. Some of the boys from Sections C and D did not even *wear* sweaters, even in the foggy depths of December – they went straight to blazers over their shirts. The rule in his house was to start switching over to winter clothes right after Dussehra. It seemed as irrational as any of his father's rules – what did a festival have to do with the weather, especially one that fell on a different date each year? – but he had decided not to bother arguing. It was much easier to just take the sweater off in the bus.

Walking down the corridors buzzing with the morning rush, he rolled up his sleeves and pulled out the hem of his shirt, just short of untucking it, so that it fell over his belt in a loose, casual way. Near the classroom, he saw Ma'am George walking past on her way to another class. She gave him a brisk nod, but then stopped and turned. 'Adi?'

'Yes, Ma'am?'

'See me in the recess, in the staff room.'

She hurried off before he even had time to swallow and ask why.

*

It was the longest morning of his life. The staff room was strictly off-limits to students, unless invited, and you hoped to every god that you never got invited. The last time he had been summoned there was by Sir Prince, who had proceeded to slash almost every page on his maths assignment, before scribbling a note in blood-red ink, asking his parents to come and see him at the next parent–teacher meeting.

What could Ma'am George possibly want now? Was it about him skipping classes and hiding in the library? He couldn't believe she was going to rat him out for that – she had almost seemed happy to find him there. What else could he have done wrong?

'Shit,' he said to himself, remembering his sin. Only when Mikki sniggered next to him and Noor turned her head slightly did he realise that he had said it out loud. Fortunately, Ma'am Mishra, the Sanskrit teacher, was reciting her favourite bhoot kaal words – past tense verb forms – way too loudly for anybody to have heard him.

It had to be about that day in the library, he realised. His gaze had slipped for just a moment when Ma'am George had bent down next to him. If the vulture had noticed it, she must have too.

This was bad, he could tell – way worse than screwing up

the maths homework. If *this* got to Ma, to his father, he was one hundred per cent guaranteed dead. Worse, if it got to Father Rebello, he could not even *imagine* what might happen. He could be asked to be a murga in the middle of the ground, squatting and holding his ears to look like a rooster. Or, he could be publicly shamed in the morning assembly, like that boy who had stolen a ten-rupee note that had fallen out of a teacher's pocket.

Who was he kidding? For something like this, he was going to get expelled straightaway. He was going to turn into a school legend, whispered about for years to come, like that senior who had once peed into the petrol tank of Sir Prince's scooter.

When the recess bell finally rang out, he rushed out of the class and into the washroom. Standing in front of the mirror, he tucked his shirt back in, flattened his hair into a neat side parting and practised his confused frown. He was going to deny everything, play dumb. It was the only way out.

He knocked on the staff room door before opening it a crack and peeking in. Ma'am George was sitting behind her desk, marking exam papers with a lunchbox full of grapes in front of her. She nodded at him and pointed to an empty chair with her chin. On the chair next to it sat Noor.

'Adi,' said Ma'am George, pushing her papers aside and looking up at him. And then she gave him that secret smile of hers; the smile that always lit up the dreary afternoons; that felt, even in a crowded classroom, like it was meant only for him.

'Yes, Ma'am? Is there something wrong?'

'No, of course not,' she smiled. 'Would you like some?'

She offered him the box of grapes. He snapped one from the bunch, just to be polite, but couldn't bring himself to put it into his mouth. Eating a grape in the staffroom, in front of Ma'am George and Noor – it somehow seemed crude, vaguely obscene.

'I wanted to ask you something,' said Ma'am George, plucking another grape and popping it into her mouth.

'Yes, Ma'am?'

Why did he keep saying that? Was he an eighth-standard boy or a bloody child?

'I need someone to volunteer for a little task, and I've been wondering whom to ask. And then Noor suggested your name.' She smiled at Noor, who, Adi now saw, was grinning like a kid who has just got a gold star for reciting a multiplication table.

'Um, what task is this, Ma'am?'

'Yes,' she said, bursting another grape behind her bright pink lips, making him squirm. 'As you know, every year the English department hosts a special event—'

'The Last Word,' he interrupted, which only made her smile grow.

'Exactly. Students from every standard participate with different things – readings, debates, plays.'

She waited for a moment, but Adi did not know what to say. He'd attended the event every year. The eleventh-standard seniors were always the best. The year before, they had done William Shakespeare's *Macbeth*, and he sometimes still had dreams of the blood-soaked child's ghost that had floated across the stage in a cloud of red smoke.

'For eighth standard,' she continued, 'we have a fifteen-minute slot. Noor has volunteered to prepare something for it. Would you like to be a part of it?'

'*Me*, Ma'am?'

'Yes, why not? Are you not interested?'

'No, I mean, I – I don't know how to—'

'You will get enough time to prepare and practise. And I will be there to guide you, if you need it. The two of you can do something together or involve any of your classmates too. And don't worry, it's not for marks or anything,' she smiled again. 'Just have some fun.'

'Oh.' He glanced at Noor, who seemed to be avoiding his eyes now. Was this some kind of trick? Was she trying to get him in trouble for not returning her book?

'Okay, then.' Ma'am George checked her watch and suddenly got up and started gathering her papers. 'I will let you two decide. We will meet again in a couple of weeks and finalise it. You have time, the event will not be before February, but the faster you decide, the more time you have to practise. Okay?'

'Yes, Ma'am,' said Noor, standing up. Adi rose and nodded too. When Ma'am George had left the room, he turned to Noor.

'Why did you have to suggest my name?'

'Who else is there?' she said, with a smile that he just couldn't read. 'Anyway, don't worry, you can call your new friend.'

'What? What friend?' he asked, but she had already walked away.

*

In the library, Adi found his corner and dumped his new book on the table – *The Lord of the Rings* trilogy in one humongous hardbound tome. Everyone had been going on about it since before the summer holidays, but he had been determined to avoid it. From what he had heard, it was full of elves and dwarves and dragons and all that. He would much rather have spent his time on science fiction, or even Ma's books like *Emma* or *The Mayor of Casterbridge*, with their stiff, yellowed pages spotted with book rust, but he had finally given in and decided to give childish fantasies a try.

He sat down and opened the front page, which had a map on it. He loved maps almost as much as he loved words – the *DK World Atlas* was in his all-time top five favourite books. He had spent hours tracing the lines that ran across the world, cutting through dotted borders and dark green jungles and white-capped mountain ranges that seemed to rise out of the pages. He had imagined himself visiting star-studded capitals like Paris and Berlin and Moscow, following the railway lines to unheard-of places like Omsk and Ürümqi and Ulaanbaatar, sailing down the winding Yangtze River to Shanghai, then on to Japan, into the great wide blue of the Pacific. The map in this book, however, was so amateurishly drawn, so obviously made-up, that he sighed and gave up. What was the point of mapping lands that didn't exist, getting lost in dreams of places you could never visit?

He turned to the window, and slowly moved his eyes across the treetops. He did not have to look too hard.

'Do you follow me here every day?' he said, his words barely audible.

'Ah, Mr Sharma!' said the vulture, like it was surprised to see him. 'I could say the same to you, but I am afraid I do not have time to get stuck in the mud of metaphysics with someone yet to learn the difference between what he sees and what there is.'

Metaphysics. He had read the word in one of Ma's books – a slim, yellowed volume about wise old men from Greece – in which he had struggled to understand a single sentence.

'No offence, Mr Sharma, I am just having some difficulties in the Department. Nothing can make you question the nature of reality like our good old bureaucracy.'

'What difficulties are you having?' said Adi, curious about the vulture's life, the nature of its reality. If it really did not exist, the vulture was doing a good job of making him believe otherwise. Perhaps, if you kept thinking about something, it eventually gathered enough weight to claim an existence? If you drew a map with enough details in it, and if you spent enough time tracing its lines, perhaps you could conjure a whole new world out of thin air?

'Oh, where to begin, Mr Sharma,' the vulture sighed. 'For years and years, I work like a mule and they keep postponing my promotion.'

'That's funny, my father has the same problem.'

'I am not surprised that he is angry, then. Very few have the maturity and wisdom to rise above these things, like yours truly. But then us vultures are very good at rising high above everything, hrr-hrr.'

'Right.'

'Anyway, let us come to the business at hand. How is your progress? Have you addressed any more fears?'

'I'm not afraid of you, at least. I know you're in my head, so I control you.'

'Oh, *very* good, Mr Sharma. Knowing what is in your head is the first step to wisdom. Even your great Gautam Buddha had to sit under a tree for so many years, but you are knowing it so easily.'

Adi decided not to take the vulture's bait. He stared at it, wondering why it always kept such a great distance between them. What would happen if he decided to run out and climb that tree and grab the beast by its neck? What if he loaded his catapult with a marble and shot it through its little head? Would it fly right through? Would it make the bird disappear in a flash of fire, a puff of smoke?

'—One problem we are still having. Every time I show you one of your Ma's files you run away like a mouse. So, we are still not having a complete list of your primary fears. Do you have any suggestions for the next item?'

For the past few weeks, he had been trying his best not to think too much about the vulture's trips in time. Were they real? Could he trust them? Was it all just a bad dream that didn't seem to end? Thinking about these things felt like staring down into an endless pit of darkness, teetering on the edge of some black hole, and he held himself back for fear of tripping on a wrong question and falling in.

And yet, he was still curious to find out more about Ma, about Nana and Nani and their journey. He wanted to uncover all the things that were never remembered in his house, and never truly forgotten.

He had to know; he had no choice. He had to play along and see how far this dream could take him.

'Yes, Mr Sharma? Surely you can think of one more fear?'

'How about Father Rebello?'

'Who is this father now?'

'He's our principal. Everyone's scared of him.'

'Hmm.' The vulture paused, deliberating. 'We are not interested in what everyone is scared of. We need *your* fears. It is your father we need to address.'

'But I talked to him already!'

'Nodding and doing "hmm-hmm" like a pigeon is not enough. Only when you stand up to your father you can say that you are not afraid.'

'But, but—'

'See how you are "but-butting" like a chicken? Is this not your actual fear, Mr Sharma: standing up to your father?'

The vulture had a point, he had to concede. He may have been able to make small talk with his father but that did not mean he was no longer afraid of him. He still dreaded being trapped with him in the drawing room, without Ma. It was the reason he had got into the habit of burying his head in books – they were a shield against his father's sneers, a force field to repel his withering gaze. If he were to really face up to his father, he had to stop hiding in his comic book fort. He had to catch the tiger by its toe.

'So,' the vulture continued, 'when will you address this fear, if I may enquire? I understand you are busy these days, pursuing your lady.'

'Er, yeah, I'll try – wait, what? What lady?'

'Hah! I can see everything, Mr Sharma. Tip-top eyesight I am having. That girl who gave you the book of poems? She is looking at you all the time. Even today, was it not her plan to get you to the staff room, to have you in that little play she is planning?'

'Whatever, I don't care. I don't even want to be in some play. I don't have time to practise. I have to take care of Amma, I have to help Ma—'

'Yes, yes, it is fine.' The vulture tilted its head skywards. 'I have no interest in your romantic endeavours. I was only reminding you that you have a more serious task, so please find time for it. Sooner is better.'

'Why are you in such a hurry?' said Adi, growing more suspicious. Something about what the vulture said didn't add up. It seemed to know a lot more than it was letting on, for one, and he wondered again how exactly it knew these things. Was it really just good eyesight? Could it only know things it could see directly, or could it access what was in his mind?

'Time is precious, Mr Sharma,' said the vulture in that peculiar tone it had, bored yet jovial, laden with condescension but somehow still kind. 'You will know when you grow up, when you are running out of it. You will be missing your long afternoons then. You will be thinking, "O-ho, if only I could go back in time and sit on the sofa like a potato and watch television all day."

'Mark my words, Mr Sharma, time is like the municipal water supply. It starts out with a great roaring rush but before you know it, it is a trickle, and then you have four drops left. The only difference is that once it goes, it is gone for good.'

'Right. I'll get on with it, then.'

Adi rolled his eyes and got up. Miss those endless afternoons at home, listening to Amma go on and on? The vulture was really not as smart as it thought it was.

10.

He had to go home

He woke up with a start, as he had lately been doing, and checked his Casio. 11:03. He had missed school. Why had no one woken him up?

As he sat in bed, looking around at the house still buried under a blanket of silence, he tried to stir his brain awake. The wind had turned overnight, carrying a chill from the high Himalaya to finally sweep the long summer away. The cooler in the drawing room had fallen quiet, and the ceiling fan was churning slowly, squealing with each laboured turn. Outside too, the usual din of traffic was missing.

It was a Saturday – of course! There was no school. He let out a small sigh, but his fingers and toes remained clenched, his neck still twitching with a familiar kind of panic. There was something else. It took him a few slow blinks to realise what his body already seemed to know. Ma was gone again.

The signs had been right there to see, in hindsight, and now he felt foolish for missing them. The letter from Pakistan from two weeks ago had changed something in Ma. She had grown quiet but with concentration, not sadness – the way kids went quiet when exam papers were handed out in class. On the weekend, she had got her colourful salvaar-kameez pairs ironed, the ones she never wore at home. Even the night before, she had spent a long time in the kitchen, stocking up the fridge with food. His father had then done the unthinkable, breaking his routine and having dinner as late as 22:20, after Ma had already eaten and gone for a bath. He had switched the news on and turned up the volume, but the roar of the shower had lasted forever, washing over the house, making the silence louder still.

What more did he need to wake up? A slap in the face? How could he be so blind to things happening right before his nose?

He flung his blanket aside and walked over to Amma's room. She was in her usual place at the edge of the bed, staring out of the closed window into the deserted park outside. Once again, he was taken aback by just how *small* she was. The pallu of her sari had slipped off her head and he could see her hair, thin and silvery as a spider's web, barely enough to cover her scalp, which seemed to have spots on it, like the stains on the yellowed pages of Ma's books, like the blotches on the moon. Her lips were moving quietly, talking to one of her ghosts, or gods, and he decided to walk away, slowly, to avoid breaking her trance.

Out in the corridor, he stood and sighed. The house seemed to be at peace for once, like a dog curled up in the sun after a night of barking. Despite the clutter that had already started collecting on the dining table, despite the mess in the drawing room with his bed unmade and his books piled up on the floor, it felt nice. Only when he was all alone, he realised, could he feel his body relaxing, letting go of the muscles that were always wound tight, threatening to snap and break him into pieces.

At the end of the corridor, past the kitchen and the dining hall, he could see his parents' bedroom door lying open. He walked in and closed it behind him.

Nothing seemed to have changed in their room – not much had changed in there for years – except that the absence of Ma was even stronger, ringing in his ears like the echo of a dinner plate crashing on the floor.

He stood at the edge of the room for a while, wondering if he should start excavating, looking for clues like he remembered doing long ago, when Ma had left for the first time. The bedroom door hadn't opened fully, he realised, like there was something behind it. He turned to check and there it was, hanging from a hook on the back of the door – Ma's maroon handbag, the one she never let out of her sight. Had she really forgotten it, or had she deliberately left it behind?

He plucked the bag from the hook and emptied it on the bed. There was a lipstick, deep red and worn down to a stub; several bus tickets folded into neat, slim parcels that she always tucked under her wedding ring so as not to lose them; a pamphlet for an orphanage with branches in Delhi, Jalandhar and Amritsar; four ball pens, each missing its cap; a tiny packet of peanuts, unopened; an empty bottle of Rail Neer, the water that was sold only on trains; a whole mess of hair ties jumbled together with strands of her silky black hair; a handwritten bill from Venus Beauty Parlour for a haircut and something called threading; an old issue of *India Today*, rolled up and fraying at the edges. The letter was not there but he spotted a curious looking book – a tiny black diary full of phone numbers.

He flipped through the book, crammed full of Ma's meticulous, miniature letters, until he found a blank page at the end – blank except for one number scrawled in loose strokes and underlined twice. It had '+92' written before it in brackets. +91 was India's calling code, he knew. It was easy to guess which country the next number could belong to. He went to his father's desk, picked up the phone and started pressing the numbers. Before he could even ask himself what exactly he thought he was doing, he heard a long beep; somewhere, a phone started ringing.

'Hallo?'

It was a woman's voice, old and crackly. He tried to say hello but nothing came out.

'Hal-lo? Kaun? Koi haiga?'

It was Punjabi, but not the Delhi Punjabi that Sunny-Bunny's parents used to speak. It was the gentle, musical tongue that Ma sometimes used on the phone – the kind that Nani spoke in the memories. It was Pakistani Punjabi.

'Hello? Um, namaste ji,' he said, pausing to gather the courage to speak in Punjabi. 'I'm Adi speaking, Adi Sharma. Tamanna Sharma's son. She, um . . . is she there?'

'Who? I don't know who you are talking about.'

'Are you . . . Kammo?'

'Hain? Who?'

'Kammo? Um, Toshi's daughter?'

'Ai-hai,' said the old woman, as though she was physically pained to hear Toshi's name. And then, she began to yell. Her words, mangled and fused together by the heat of her anger, were no longer intelligible to him. He understood enough, however, to know that he had spoken to someone he shouldn't have.

He slammed the receiver down and stared at it for a while, half expecting it to ring. When it did not, he pushed the phone back in its spot, and dumped Ma's things into her bag and returned it to the door. He was itching to leave the room, regretting having set foot in it, especially when he was just starting to feel calm. As he was stepping out, a thought occurred to him. It was a flash out of nowhere, like a memory – vivid, nearly tangible – of something that you have never actually experienced; like the feeling of *knowing* a place you have never visited.

He walked to the far side of the bed, to the green-grey Godrej almirah that stood taller than anything else in the room. If there was anything of value in the house, he knew, it was inside the steel frame of the Godrej. He grabbed the handle and gave it a downward push, and the door opened with a metallic shriek, sharp enough to be heard by the neighbours. He took a deep breath and told himself it was okay – it was just a cupboard. They were only things.

It was packed from top to bottom, mostly with clothes, most of them wrapped individually in plastic bags that crackled at the slightest touch. The thing that drew his attention, however, was the safe on the middle shelf. He reached up to the topmost shelf and stuck his hand under a pile of plastic-wrapped saris. His fingers didn't have to search too far – they homed in on the small, solid brass key, as though they knew.

The key turned smoothly and the safe opened without a sound. In the small, dark space, he could make out a few jewellery boxes, folders full of laminated documents, and more keys. He stuck his hand in again, careful not to move things too much, until he found the familiar texture of the yellow envelope. He grasped it between his index and middle fingers, and slowly drew it out into the light. It was the letter from Pakistan, the envelope ripped open on one side. He blew into the gap to open it up and pulled out the letter. It was a single folded page, torn from a notebook, covered in big, quickly scribbled letters on just one side. He could not read a single word of it – it was all in Urdu. He shook his head and began to slide it back into the safe, but then he stopped. He took the letter out and stuck it into his back pocket, before returning the envelope, hiding the keys in their spot and shutting the Godrej with a final clang.

*

Just as he had settled into the sofa and turned the TV on, Amma began calling out. He turned his head up towards the fine cracks in the ceiling and let out a muted scream. In that small, stupid, silent house, there was nowhere to hide.

He got up and slowly walked to her door.

'Mohana?' Amma's entire face was crinkled, trying to see him without her spectacles. 'Is that you? How long we have waited for you. Why are you so late? You must be hungry. Tell your brother to come and eat also.'

He smiled, proud to be able to decipher most of her words now. 'It's me,' he said. 'Adi.'

She went on looking at him but it was as if she couldn't hear him, or she was seeing right through him and finding someone else. He went over to the desk to pick up her glasses and handed them to her. She held them in her shaky hands, turning them over like a baby discovering a new toy. Looking at her, a heavy sigh of sympathy weighed his shoulders down. She was not crazy, he was starting to understand. She was trapped in a hole with no one to talk to, so she did what she could – she used her memory and her imagination, and, in the blurred space between the two, she found someone to tell her stories. There was only so much silence one could take.

'We told him. You remember, don't you? We told him not to drink in a rush.' Biyah, not piyah – marry, not drink – he corrected his mental translation.

'—It is not like buying a toy you like today, throwing it away tomorrow. Marriage is an oath by fire before God.'

She was complaining about Chacha planning to marry an American woman, he assumed. She had never met the woman – no one had – but that probably didn't matter to Amma. She didn't even like people marrying someone from a different caste, let alone a whole other country.

'—not something one person can decide alone. For such a decision, you have to trust your elders, your whole family. For thousands of years our elders have done so. Now you say we are illiterate. Now you know everything. We told him, you remember? We told him Punjabi women are not right. They are too stubborn, they are like men. They don't know our ways, the duties of our women.'

She was talking about Ma. He bit his lip and squeezed his thumbs between his fists, but he could not stop listening.

'Now she has stolen my gold too. She thinks I can't see but I know she has it.'

The bloody jewellery again. She had been going on about it for so long that he had learnt to ignore it, but now it occurred to him that some of his parents' fights must have been about this. He had noticed that Ma had stopped wearing any jewellery at all these days. There were no rings on her fingers, no gold bracelet or glass bangles on her wrists and even the tiny, flower-shaped gold earrings were gone. The only thing left was the thin gold chain with black beads – the sacred mangalsutra that was meant to protect her husband. He hated the sight of those ugly beads and had often wondered why his father couldn't wear it himself if he needed protection. Now, he wished Ma were there so he could ask her to take it off and throw it at Amma's face.

'We told your Baba, you remember? We told him to say no. Punjabi girl with no mother, no family before or after, no one knows what caste, what roots. *Reph-you-gee*,' she spat out the English word, and Adi took a step back, stunned at both the disgust in her voice and the sound of English from her lips.

He felt dizzy with anger. Ma was the one person who took care of this old woman, who helped her go to the toilet and cleaned her pee-stained saris and made sure she took her medicines on time; the only person who bothered to talk to her, who told her the time fifty times a day without yelling at her. And this was what she got in return? He shook his head and shut the door. The old witch could stay hungry all day, he decided. He was not going to sit there and listen to her rambling on. He was going to walk out and let people deal with their own problems, just as Ma did.

*

He cycled aimlessly through the neighbourhood, circling the park where old ladies sat around cracking peanut shells in the winter sunshine, drifting past the market where shopkeepers sat idle before their portable TVs, crossing block after apartment block that all looked the same yet seemed to have distinct auras, from friendly to forbidding to downright haunted, until he reached the edge of Allah Colony.

The slums of Allah Colony were out of bounds for all the apartment kids. Any time his father drove through the main street cutting across the edge of the colony, he frantically rolled up the windows and locked the doors, warning Adi that the place was full of goondas, and charas-addicts and cow-butchers who kidnapped kids from 'good families' and sold them as beggars in Bombay. It was all rubbish, he knew now, like everything else his father said. He leant over the handle-bars and pedalled on.

On both sides of the road there were things he never saw in the neighbourhood market. There were tyres and tiles and half-made tables and toilet pots; there were mattress fluffers and chair-restringers, and kabaadi-valas to recycle all kinds of scrap; there were shops selling every type of bathroom fitting and every colour of wall paint, and there were shops selling nothing but window panes. It seemed like this cramped patch of unpaved streets and unpainted houses supplied everything to build and run the apartment blocks that kept growing around it, pushing it into a wedge by the side of the highway.

The slums ended abruptly, cut off by the freshly plastered walls of the temple compound, and he braked before the grand, carved gateway. Even though the vulture had refused to accept his fear of the gods, he knew it was real, though he did not know why. In fact, he could not even remember the last time he had been in a temple. Ma had stopped going long ago, and his father had his own mini temple right by his bed, so neither of them ever asked Adi to go. Most of what he knew about the gods came from the myths in the *Amar Chitra Katha* comic books. It was time to face them.

He chained his bicycle to the fence, climbed the steps leading up to the temple, hid his sneakers behind a pillar and stepped inside. It was a huge hall lit by streams of sunshine flowing down from high windows. In the middle was the mandap, a concrete pit full of smouldering ashes where they lit the fire for the ceremonial havans. All along the walls, there were mini temples housing idols of different gods, some looming like giants and others no bigger than teddy bears. Deciding to take them on clockwise, he turned left.

First up was Ganesha, the chubby, cutesy god of good beginnings. Parvati, Lord Shiva's wife, had made him out of clay one day to guard her while she was in the shower. When Shiva came home from work, he saw this boy standing outside his wife's bathroom and, taking him for some sort of creep, karate-chopped his head right off. When Parvati found out, she kicked up a fuss and Shiva agreed to resurrect the boy. But there was a problem: Shiva had tossed the boy's head into a river, or something, and since they lived alone in a jungle, there were no replacement heads around. Shiva looked around and saw an elephant minding its own business. He shrugged and said 'Why not?', and chopped the elephant's head off. He then stuck it on the boy's body and, bingo, Ganesha was born.

His father had once told him that the story had been simplified, that the real story was in fact proof of advanced plastic surgery in ancient times. All the knowledge of the world was locked in the four sacred volumes of the *Vedas*, he had said. The tragedy was that we, in India, had forgotten the password and the Angrez people had stolen the knowledge and developed modern science from it. This is why medical science only began in the West after the Portuguese, French and British came to India. Adi hadn't heard of any head transplants going on in the West, but he knew better than to express such doubts.

Next to Ganesha stood Lakshmi, the goddess of fortune, holding gold foil coins in her hand. She was a clear favourite, judging by the pile of offerings at her feet – giant fruit baskets, boxes of sweets and a gift pack of Cadbury's Dairy Milk. Next to her was Sarasvati, the goddess of wisdom and literature and art, sitting on a Lotus flower and playing her sitar. All she had received was a bunch of spotty bananas.

He walked past baby Krishna, not looking up. All this one did was play his flute and gorge himself on butter and steal girls' clothes – behaviour that would not have been encouraged in any other boy.

He stopped before Hanuman. The idol was bigger than the rest, or perhaps it was the monkey god's posture that made him look more imposing. He stood with his chest out, one muscled leg planted firmly on the ground and the other bent forward, as if ready to launch him skywards at any moment. He looked like Michael Jordan about to start his run-up towards a slam dunk, but instead of a basketball, he held in his hands a mace and a miniature mountain. Despite his warrior-like stance and WWF-grade physique, there was nothing threatening about him. Whether it was the childlike smile on his face, the long tail curving playfully behind him or his story in the *Ramayana*, where he leapt across the sea carrying a magic mountain to save Ram's brother, he was the nicest of all gods. He may not have been the sharpest one in the temple – even his weapon, the blunt, balloon-shaped gada, had a harmless look – but he was certainly the one with the biggest heart.

Bhoot-pishaach nikat nahi aavé
Mahavir jab naam sunaavé . . .

He had heard his father chant those lines a thousand times:

Ghosts and demons dare not come near
When the mighty Mahavir's name they hear . . .

For a moment, he had a strong urge to join his hands and close his eyes and pray to this generous, good-hearted god. They were all just stories, he reminded himself – kahaaniya, like Ma used to say.

He turned and walked across the hall to the other side. He could vaguely remember being here now and seeing a number of smaller idols covering that wall – intricately carved goddesses and lesser-known avatars of Vishnu and Shiva – but they were all gone now. There was only one god left: Ram. The idol seemed to have grown into a giant, surrounded by offerings and oversized donation boxes. There was a pundit washing its massive feet with milk from a silver lota, and a group of people stood with their hands joined. Before all the other idols, it was mostly women lighting diyas or mumbling prayers. Here, it was mostly men, mostly young, their heads bowed but their bodies tense.

He walked around to the side to get closer to the pundit.

'Pundit-ji?'

'Haan, béta?' The pundit turned to him with a warm, toothy grin.

'There used to be more idols here. Where did they go?'

'Ohhh, you have a good memory!' he said, and squinted, pushing his own not-so-good memory to work. 'The ones here?' He pointed to the empty wall. 'Yeesss, there used to be Mahadev. There, we had Parvati Ma, Nataraj, Garuda, Chamunda Devi. Beautiful idols carved in the old style, from the time of Emperor Akbar. We had to sell all of them.' He shook his head with a sad smile. 'This is a Ram Mandir now.

145

Ram-ji,' he joined his hands and looked up at the giant, 'gets all the donations these days. Who even knows of gods like Garuda?'

'This Garuda, Pundit-ji, was he a vulture?'

'Vulture? Noooo, that is Jataayu. You know the story of Jataayu?'

Jataayu! Of course! He had entirely forgotten that there was a vulture in the *Ramayana*. He knew the story, but seeing the kind, radiant smile on the pundit's face, he decided to hear it again.

'What happened was that when Raavan kidnapped Sita-ji from the jungle, he took her on the Pushpak Vimaan. You know about the Pushpak Vimaan?'

'The aeroplane?'

'Yeesss, the aeroplane, very good, ha-ha. But there is a story behind it. It did not actually belong to Raavan. It was stolen,' he whispered, his eyes round with scandal, and Adi giggled. 'There was only one Pushpak Vimaan in the world. It belonged to Lord Brahma and he had gifted it to Kubér. You know Kubér? He is the god of money. Very important god, no? Ha-ha. So, then, Raavan, who was actually a stepbrother of Kubér – yes, yes, Raavan started as a god and turned into a demon! Raavan stole the vimaan, and he used it to fly Sita-ji to Lanka, you see?'

'Right. But . . . Jataayu?'

'Yeesss, Jataayu, ha-ha. Jataayu was a great vulture who saw Sita-ji being kidnapped. He was so old and weak, but when he heard Sita-ji crying for help, he could not sit and do nothing, no? "I will show you," he said, and he flew high and fast and he chased the vimaan down and attacked Raavan. He tried his very best but it was not easy for the poor old bird. At first, Raavan was shocked: "Arré, where has this bird come from?" But Raavan was a powerful demon. He cut off Jataayu's wings and the poor bird fell down to Earth. Then, for many days, he lay there bleeding, crying, sad that he could not save Sita-ji. Until Ram-ji came along and found him. He told Ram-ji everything, and that was how they found out where Sita-ji was. She was in Lanka! That was when Ram-ji revealed himself as an avatar of Lord Vishnu and healed Jataayu. Not only healed him, but blessed him with immortality!'

'So, Jataayu is still alive?'

'Ha-ha, maybe, who knows?' The pundit was glowing with such childlike happiness that Adi could not help but smile.

'But that's what you just said. Being immortal means he can never die.'

'Yesss, he can never die. You see, you and I are talking about him now. His story is still alive, so Jataayu is still with us, no?'

The pundit had a point, he had to admit. Stories – kahaaniya – maybe they were the real immortals, and people were just the means of keeping them alive and passing them on, like ancestral heirlooms, or viruses.

'Jai Shri Ram,' someone said out loud, and 'Jai Shri Ram!' came the response from the men behind him, sounding less like a prayer and more like a threat.

Those few, fleeting moments from years ago emerged from the maze of his memories and flashed before his eyes. The last time they had visited the temple, it was during a celebration. A mosque had been torn down in Ayodhaya, in the spot where Lord Ram was born, and a temple was going to be built in its place. In their little temple here, the evening aarti that used to be a mellow, musical affair had turned into a roaring explosion. All the worshippers, instead of just murmuring along to the pundit's voice, had joined in to chant the Sanskrit words at the top of their voices. The only one standing quietly, refusing to be a part of it, was Ma. His father had prodded Adi to sing along too, but he had refused, snatching his hand from his father's grip and choosing to stand quietly with Ma. He remembered the fire in his father's eyes, the hush in the car on the way home and he remembered lying in bed when the silence was finally broken by the shouts in their bedroom, the accusations against Ma of 'brainwashing' Adi, of turning him into one of 'her kind'.

Rushing out of the temple, he grabbed his sneakers and stepped out into the cool evening and tried to calm his breathing. For a moment, he could not remember where he had parked his bicycle. It was hidden, he realised, behind a group of barefoot children playing hopscotch on the broken pavement, leaping, stumbling, giggling, much like the seniors in the school corridors. He walked around them, unlocked his bicycle and stood wondering whether he should go home or ride away in the other direction, onto the highway and beyond.

He still did not understand it – what made Ma different from everyone, why she refused to bow before the idols or sing the hymns like all the other women. But he had known, even back then, that the questions were somehow dangerous and so he had turned away from them.

That's how they dealt with everything – burying their secrets, locking away their memories, never speaking about their feelings, hopscotching around the past like it was lava and, at the slightest stumble, could devour you whole. This is what the vulture had been trying to tell him, he realised. If he wanted to confront the root of his fears, he had to stop hiding behind books of poetry, stop pedalling so hard to get away. He had to dive right in.

*

There was someone in the house, Adi realised, as he reached out to unlock the door. He stopped and listened to the rush of the water, the cutlery crashing in the kitchen sink and, even though his brain knew that it wasn't Ma, his body refused to believe it. He flung the door open and ran inside.

It was only Rina Auntie. She must have taken the spare set of keys from the guard. She had worked at their house long enough to be trusted even by that moustachioed hulk who guarded the colony gates with his terrifying scowl.

'Chhoté Sahib,' she said, turning around with her shy grin. 'I came early to finish the cooking.'

He nodded and checked his Casio. 14:25. Way past Amma's lunchtime.

'I asked Amma if they were hungry, they said no,' Rina Auntie smiled, using the plural as a sign of respect for some-one who refused to touch anything touched by her. It had never made sense to him why Amma created such a fuss. Surely she must know that all the food was cooked by Rina Auntie? How did it matter who served it?

'Babu?' Amma called out right on cue, and he could sense the hunger in her wavering voice.

He began to heat up her lunch in the microwave oven but remembered that she needed to have her blood pressure checked before meals. They had recently got a blood pressure machine – a sleek, white-and-blue gadget that Chacha had sent from America – and Ma took Amma's pressure twice every day and noted it down on a sheet of paper taped to a *Top Gun* poster on the cupboard. Now that Ma was not there, he had to stay calm, control his anger and do what needed to be done.

'Amma?' He peeked into her room. Her teeth and spectacles were on, and it looked like she had snapped out of her trance. 'Did someone take your BP today?'

'Ki?'

'Blood pressure.' He cupped his arm, forming the shape of the inflatable cuff. 'Did someone take it today? In the morning?'

She did not say yes. She hated having it done and blamed the strap for pain in her arm, but usually gave in after Ma scolded her for being childish. It was super simple; he had seen Ma do it several times. You kept your arm up on the table, level with your heart, strapped the strap, and pressed 'Start'. The strap puffed up until it hurt just a bit, held its breath for a few seconds, then went phuss.

Two numbers showed on the machine – 148/101 – and he wrote them down on the paper. They were higher than the last few readings, though he wasn't sure if that was a good thing.

He strapped the cuff onto his own arm and waited. When it hissed and loosened its grip, the screen flashed 124/78. He felt a little bad for scoring lower than Amma, but chalked her numbers up to her age.

'Babu, what time is it?'

Her voice was hoarse – from calling out to him, probably – and he did not have the heart to tell her how long he had been gone.

'One o'clock.'

She nodded. She was old, mostly illiterate, and not always in her senses, but she was not stupid. She must have known that it was a lie, but it was easier to accept what you couldn't do anything about. It was probably why she ate the food cooked by Rina Auntie, too. After all, she couldn't go and make it herself. There was only so much she could ask for, and if having her grandson serve her food was one, he asked himself if it was really too much.

He brought her food in and gave her twenty minutes to finish, although she rarely took more than ten. When he heard her steel plate clatter on the floor, he brought her a rasgulla in one of the glass bowls engraved with flowers that were reserved for guests. There was always a risk that she might drop the bowl and shatter it into a thousand pieces, but even if she did, he figured, what difference would it have made? It was not like they ever had any guests.

Passing by the kitchen, he stopped when he saw Rina Auntie squatting on the floor next to the dustbin, eating dry, leftover rotis.

'Auntie?' he said, trying to overcome his own embarrassment, but she looked up with her usual smile, like there was nothing odd about eating lunch like this. This was how she always ate, he knew, but he had never really understood it. She never sat on any of the furniture in the house, never came out to the drawing room for a break; whenever she was tired, she squatted on the floor in the hot, fan-less kitchen. As far as he knew, Ma had never prohibited her from sitting outside. But then, she had never encouraged it either.

'Come and sit outside, Auntie. It's hot in here.'

'No-no, Chhoté Sahib, it's okay.'

'No,' he said, as sternly as he could. 'Come and sit in the drawing room and finish your lunch.'

With a slow, sideways nod, Rina Auntie got up and carried her plate outside.

'You can sit on the sofa.'

She nodded again but went and squatted in a corner anyway, setting her plate down on the floor. Did she *like* sitting on the floor, he wondered. Was he forcing her to do something she didn't want to do? Surely, it was more comfortable to sit on the sofa and eat with the plate on the table, instead of squatting in that painful position? At least she looked relieved to be under the fan, he thought, as he switched channels on the TV.

It took her even less time than Amma to finish eating, as though she was desperate to get it over with. But as she rose with her plate and turned towards the kitchen, she stopped and looked at him.

'Chhoté Sahib?'

'Auntie, don't call me that. I don't like it.'

'Acchha, okay . . . Chhoté Bhaiya,' she nodded.

He sighed and gave up. Little Brother was slightly better than Little Master. Even though the Little was still there, at least it didn't make him sound like a mini version of the Badé Sahib, his father.

'Mémsahib is coming back on Sunday, no? Shall I cook something special?'

What?

He stared at her, unable to form a response. Did she really know when Ma was coming back?

'Auntie . . . Do you know where Ma has gone?'

'Oh, yes,' said Rina Auntie. 'She went to Punjab, no? She said she was trying to find someone, some relative.'

She had told Rina Auntie but not him? He felt his ears grow hot with anger. Did her own son really mean less to her than the maid?

Kammo.

Ma was trying to find Kammo. That's why she kept disappearing! He had wondered if there was a connection between the vulture's memories and Ma's mysterious journeys. Now, it was beginning to make sense. Now that he had seen what had happened to Kammo, maybe he could help Ma in her quest. He was still angry at her, but he knew that if he could help her find her sister, it could change everything. It could finally make him a grown-up in Ma's eyes. He needed more informa-tion, though, and since nobody at home told him anything, he had only one source for it. He had to complete the vulture's challenge to unlock the next memory. It was time to tackle the Badé Sahib.

'So, Chhoté Bhaiya,' said Rina Auntie, seeming amused at the new nickname she had given him. 'Shall I make aloo-gobhi or black dal?'

'Whatever you wish, Auntie,' he said. 'You know best.'

11.

He learns from his father

He spent all of Sunday evening cycling around the neighbourhood, just to avoid lying in bed and waiting for Ma like a baby.
When he got back home, he found the door half open and
heard voices inside and his heartbeat jumped. But it was not
Ma, he realised on seeing the shoes lying outside the door. He
stepped in to find Laddoo Uncle sitting on the sofa, peering at
his father's palm. He was a junior colleague of his father's
who visited every now and then – always with a box of oily,
orange laddoos – and Adi could never remember his name.
Today, he had brought samosas too. Neither of them looked
up as Adi shut the door and took off his shoes.

'Hmm . . .' Laddoo Uncle pushed his glasses up his nose
and turned his father's palm up to face the chandelier. Along
with being a junior scientist, Laddoo Uncle was also an
astrologer.

'Shani seems a little heavy these days,' his father muttered
in a low, grave voice. 'I was thinking of doing a Satyanarayan
puja.'

Shani – Saturn, the coolest planet in the Solar system with
its flat, multicoloured rings – was to blame for his father's
woes.

'Ah!' Laddoo Uncle lifted his own hand and turned a ring on his middle finger. 'This stone, sir, I just got it.' He rubbed his thumb over the glittering oval gemstone, the colour of morning pee. 'This will help until Shani passes.'

It took 29.5 years for Saturn to complete one orbit around the sun. (The DK *Space Encyclopedia*, obviously, was in his all-time top five favourites.)

'Arré, Nawab Sahib?' His father finally noticed Adi, just as he was about to slip past them into the dining room. 'Where have you been?'

'At Sunny-Bunny's house,' he lied, just to test his father.

'Come here, touch uncle's feet,' his father replied, failing the test.

He walked over and darted down towards Laddoo Uncle's crusty brown socks and bounced back before he could be blessed with a pat on his head.

'Which class are you in now?' Laddoo Uncle asked with a shiny grin. His cheeks were plump and glossy, pinker than the rest of his face, like they had been slapped on as an upgrade.

'Still in eighth class, Uncle.'

He threw his head back and laughed, and Adi could see the yellow bits of laddoo stuck between his teeth.

'Still in eighth, he says!' Laddoo Uncle beamed at his father. 'Looks like he's in a hurry to move up.'

'Still acts like he's in class two,' said his father with half a smile. It may have been intended as gentle, good-natured mockery but it made Adi wince, nonetheless.

'Shabaash,' Laddoo Uncle said to him. 'Very far you will go, very far.'

'I hope so,' Adi wanted to say, but did not. He retreated to his divan and turned his attention to the news on the TV, hoping that he would be left alone.

'—*one dead, over thirty injured in twin blasts at Karol Bagh market—*'

'Where is Bhabhi-ji, sir?' Laddoo Uncle turned to his father with a look of such fake concern that it nearly made Adi scoff.

'Bhabhi-ji has gone to see her relatives in Punjab,' his father answered, like it was nothing to worry about. Like it was the truth. 'Acchha, tell me this,' he switched topics with the bluntness of a kid caught lying, 'what do you think of this one, is it useful?'

It was his old ring, on his left hand, with a blood red stone on it. Laddoo Uncle did not even have to look at it to know which one it was. 'That's a Manik stone. Ruby. That's for success in work and business. For problems at home, Pukhraj is best, what they call Yellow Sapphire—'

'But I'm asking for work only, no? What's the problem at home?'

What's the problem at home? Adi could hardly believe his ears.

'—*Two more bombs, at Gurudwara Road and Ajmal Khan Road, were defused by the Delhi Police Bomb Squad—*'

'Oh,' Laddoo Uncle said after a pause. 'No, I just . . . I thought, why would you need anything for work, sir, you are already in such a high position. You are like a mentor to all of us.'

His father shook his head and laughed, like he was embarrassed, but his puffed-out chest and smirking lips said otherwise. Such fake flattery would not even have worked on the Sanskrit teacher, Adi thought, as he picked the moment to sneak out of the drawing room.

Lately, he had begun to use the dining table to study, despite the mess, as a way to avoid being too close to his father in the absence of Ma. He cleared a space, pushing away the boxes of sweets and dried fruits that had arrived as Divali gifts and the stale bananas that his father got from the office for free. Dumping his school bag on the table, he sat down and opened the maths textbook. He could still hear the TV, and the conversation, but at least they were out of sight.

'—*nine bomb blasts in the capital this month . . . the opposition questioned the government on national security*—'

'Baba Adam's bells,' his father snorted, and Adi almost burst out laughing at the quaint curse. 'This Gujral doesn't even care about the security of his own chair, let alone national security. One day he is in Scotland, next day he is in New York, then he is off to a jungle safari in Africa. Here the Pakistanis are blowing bombs like it's Divali. Look, look at that,' his father said, and Adi craned his neck to catch a glimpse of the TV. 'They put a bomb at Roshan Di Kulfi!'

He remembered being dragged to the legendary kulfi shop once, along with Ma. It was a loud, crowded place serving ice-hard kulfis with strings of faluda that tasted of nothing, blander than Maggi noodles boiled without the masala. 'Real Indian ice-cream,' his father had said, pointing to the bits of almond and pistachio. 'Not made of chemicals like those foreign brands.' All Adi could recall was how it had hurt his teeth.

'—This is amazing.' His father sounded dazed. 'This is too much.'

'You are absolutely right, sir, it is too much. We are the laughing stock of the world. It is about time this useless United Front sarkar was thrown out.'

'Arré, what United Front, this Gujral is just a Congress stooge.' Adi heard his father slap the crumbs out of his hands. 'He's not going to last long, I am telling you.'

'Oh, you have some inside information, sir?'

'All I can say is,' his father said with his mouth full of forbidden samosa, 'change is coming.'

They fell silent as the news turned to cricket, and Adi turned back to his textbook. Its pages were patterned with dots – the game he and Mikki played during class, where you started with a grid of dots and connected them, one little line at a time, to make as many boxes as you could. They always played on Adi's book because Mikki never bothered getting his own. All he carried in his backpack were dog-eared copies of *Chip* magazine, half-empty packets of crushed biscuits and a Sony Walkman. Adi had seen the sleek, silvery box glinting in his bag, but he could never bring himself to ask to try it.

They were getting along, slowly, but he wouldn't have called them friends yet. Mikki still did not say much, and he had no interest in going to the library or even to the playground. It was not only the boys who were hostile to him; the teachers disliked him outright. At first, Adi had assumed it was because of the rumours that he had been transferred from a government school where he had failed twice, but after the mid-term exams, it had become clear that he was one of the brightest students in the class. Adi was beginning to suspect that maybe he was treated the way he was simply because of how he looked. Most teachers pretended that he was invisible, and the Sanskrit teacher didn't even bother to check his homework notebook. On his part, Mikki seemed comfortable with being left alone with his magazines.

There was only one thing that made Mikki talk: computers. He seemed to know everything about them, from the difference between Intel and AMD chips to the cheat codes for *Need for Speed II*. Adi did his best to keep up with him, nodding along to his rants about the outdated PCs in the school labs, but he had no idea about any of it. The computer at home was still out of bounds for him, reserved for his father's 'Top Secret' work. He may have to start breaking that rule too, he was starting to think, if only to avoid being exposed as an outdated model himself.

He slammed his palm down on his book to flatten a fruit fly, and instantly cursed himself for doing it.

'Adi Sahib? Where are you? It's time for dinner.'

'Coming.' He closed his eyes and sighed. Rina Auntie would have prepared dinner earlier in the evening, but there was no one to serve it. On any other day his father would have served himself, but today, he wanted to show Laddoo Uncle how obedient his son was.

The son got up and went into the kitchen, gathered the plates and spoons, laid out the warm dishes on a tray and came back out into the drawing room.

'Wah!' said Laddoo Uncle, like it was a miracle to see Adi doing any work. On his father's face there was a proud smirk, as if he was the one who had arranged the tray perfectly to fit everything on it and save another trip to the kitchen.

'Arré, where is your plate?' Laddoo Uncle asked, but Adi had his answer ready.

'I will give Amma her dinner and then eat, Uncle. You start, please.'

Now, Laddoo Uncle was really impressed. He looked to his father and said, 'Very good boy, your son, sir, very good.'

'Yes,' his father nodded, heaping rice onto his plate. 'He will make a great daughter-in-law.'

As his father guffawed at his own joke and Laddoo Uncle chuckled along, Adi stood over them, his middle fingers clawing at the cuticles on his thumbs.

'Where is the salt? And the green chillies? And there are no bowls for the curd. Always does half the work.' His father rolled his eyes at Laddoo Uncle, smiling to hide his annoyance.

'At least someone does some work in this house,' said Adi.

The room went quiet as Laddoo Uncle smiled, pretending not to have heard, and his father set his plate down on the table.

'What did you say?'

Adi looked down at his father, his hands now clenched into tight, hard balls, and he smiled. 'Whatever you need you can get from the kitchen. The salt is on the counter and the bowls are in the cupboard above the sink. In case you don't know.'

'Look at that,' his father said to Laddoo Uncle. 'This is how he talks to his elders.'

'He learns from his father,' said Adi.

'You know the problem with children these days?' his father continued, talking to Laddoo Uncle, who had stopped grinning. '*Zero* discipline. They teach them nothing in school, and at home their mothers spoil them like little princes. This is why I always said boys should be sent off to boarding school while they are still young. That was how we learnt all the traditional qualities of discipline and hard work and respecting your elders.'

Adi laughed. He laughed as his father's face went red, and went on laughing as he slipped his chappals on and walked out, slamming the door behind him.

*

Out on the roof, the chill in the air made him feel lighter. He waited in the shadows, wondering if he really wanted to step out. After seeing the last memory, he had not been sure if he wanted to see any more. Those dark nights from long ago had begun to seep into his days, shocking him with flashes of bloodied bodies and crying girls, of little Kammo's face blank with terror, each time he closed his eyes. He had waited to see if they would go away, but the flashes seemed to be getting brighter, more vivid with each night, and he was scared of uncovering even darker secrets. But – he sighed – he had a mission to accomplish. He had to do it for Ma.

Settling into his spot on the ledge, he looked around. In the distance, he could see the outline of Rashtrapati Bhavan, the President's palace glimmering with the Divali lights. The new President had just moved in: K.R. Narayanan, the first Dalit President of India. He was not sure what Dalit meant, but watching it on the news, his father had snorted and mumbled something about 'reservations' again. It was one of his favourite topics to rant about: how reservations for low-caste people had ruined India, how those people took away jobs and promotions from the ones who really deserved them. He himself had been awaiting a promotion for years now, refusing to buy anything for their house because they were soon going to move into that mythical Type VII bungalow with a garden and driveway and everything.

His father had ranted about the Rashtrapati Bhavan too, once when they had driven past it. 'Angrez chalé gayé, inko chhod gayé,' he had said – the British went away but left the new rulers in their place. The Congress party, he meant. The Gandhi family – who were not Mahatma Gandhi's children, confusingly, but Nehru's – who had taken over everything and become the new maharajas. It was Nehru his father hated most of all, for partitioning India in his hunger for power, for imposing English on free India to impress his firangi girl-friend, and for taking away their family's lands and giving it to those low-caste people. Now, he said, they had given away the Rashtrapati Bhavan to the Dalits too, which he hated anyway because it was a symbol of British rule. It should be broken down, he said, and its bricks used to make schools and hospitals. It was as if there were only a finite number of bricks in the country, all locked up in its monuments, and you could only build something new if you tore down something old.

He had had enough of his father's nonsensical ramblings – all his buckvaas that never seemed to end. He was not going to take any more of it, and he had proven it tonight. He had stood up to the great roaring beast and laughed right in his face. Tonight, he was invincible.

'You there?' he said, turning to the building across the street.

'Ah, Mr Sharma,' said the vulture, its long neck curving up to lift its head, its black eye twinkling in the dim yellow light. 'At last, you have found time.'

DHA/HA/TS/1947(3)

The sky glows white hot, hazy with dust, and it takes a moment for Adi to find his bearings. It is a river of people, more people than he has ever seen, stretching far into the distance. The flat, barren land looks like a bruised battlefield, its fields and farms trampled by the tired, bedraggled army hobbling along like a horde of zombies. There are many bullock carts piled high with luggage and some carrying old people too, but most men, women and children are on foot – some on bare feet, he realises on looking more closely – weighed down by baskets on their heads or cloth bundles on their backs. Despite the number of people, the caravan is eerily quiet, the still air punctured by occasional shrieks and wails.

His gaze closes in on a makeshift tent by the side of the dirt road. It is the cloth canopy of a horse carriage, he realises, much like a rickshaw carriage without wheels, only larger. The canopy, worn out and torn in places, is barely enough to provide any privacy, but none of the passing eyes seem particularly interested in what is happening behind it. There is a lone man pacing in front of it, alert and on edge, like a child guarding a prized treasure, and Adi realises it's Nana. He looks entirely different now, clean-shaven and wearing a faded, stained white kurta in place of his slim-fit shirt and trousers, his lush hair cropped short like an army man. Without the sleek moustache balancing it, his crooked nose stands out even more starkly, rising like a lone monument in a ruined land.

Behind the canopy, Adi can see an old woman bent over and talking to someone in Hindi. Through the tears in the fabric, he can just about make out the bare legs of someone sitting on the carriage seat.

'Buss-buss, that's it, that's it,' the old woman is saying, 'no need to push too hard, let it come on its own.'

The person inside bends forward, howling in pain, and Adi catches a glimpse of that green kurta with the pink flowers, bloodstained and faded but unmistakable. It is Nani.

'Buss, it's done, nearly done,' says the old woman, massaging Nani's swollen, glistening belly.

With another surge of effort from Nani, the old woman bends down to examine something. The panicked, breathless screams of a newborn tear through the shroud of silence that hangs all around and, just for a few moments, the passing faces light up with weak, warm smiles.

'Is it done? Is she okay?' yells Nana, but he does not step behind the canopy.

The old woman whispers something to Nani, pointing to a slimy, pulsing thing that seems to be coming out of Nani's body. Nani reaches under her kurta to draw the kirpaan from its sheath. Bending forward, she slashes the cord with the curved knife, wipes the blade on her kurta, then falls back under the cover of the canopy. Leaning in to look through another gap in the canopy, Adi catches sight of the newborn. It looks just like any other baby with a wrinkled, old-person face and eyes screwed shut. It lies on a rag on the floor of the carriage and cries with all its might.

'Is it done?' Nana yells again.

'Wait, wait,' says the old woman.

She steps away from Nani and gestures to another woman waiting behind her – a woman with dark, lustrous arms wearing a brightly patterned sari, the end of which is draped over her head to hide her face – and she steps forward with a broom and a pail to clean the bloody mess. She wipes the baby, wraps it in the same rag it is lying on and puts it on the carriage seat next to Nani. The baby continues to cry but Nani does not reach out for it.

The old woman sets down two coins on the ground and steps back, and the veiled one picks them up, bows with her hands joined, and walks away.

Unable to hold himself any longer, Nana peeks in.

'Come. Congratulations,' the old woman smiles hesitantly, 'it's a girl.'

'A daughter!' yells Nana, his face beaming with joy, and the old woman looks relieved. Nana picks up the baby girl and she finally stops wailing.

'The mother and child need to be washed,' the old woman continues, 'but there's no water, so I have cleaned them with cloth for now. The mother needs milk with ghee and saffron, and the child too, for three days, until the mother's milk starts flowing. She also needs to be kept at home for forty days, but because of our circumstances . . .' She looks up at the crowds still walking past them, and sighs. 'You can ask a pundit to come and purify the mother and child later. For now, I will give you this.' She opens a tiny box and swipes it with her little finger and dabs the writhing baby's forehead with a black mark. 'This is to keep the evil eye away,' she smiles at the baby.

'How will we ever repay this debt?' says Nana.

The woman waves him off, shaking her head with a stern expression. 'This is my debt I am repaying,' she says, then joins her hands and gives him a quick nod before walking away.

On the carriage seat, Nani's eyes are still closed but she is taking deep breaths, her hands curled into fists. Nana helps her get dressed and sit up. He then brings the baby to her but she frowns at the pale white bundle like it is something suspicious, an unclaimed piece of baggage to be reported to the police.

'What should we name her?' Nana asks. She does not reply.

'How about Tamanna?' He coos at the baby, who is still refusing to open her eyes. 'Tariq and Toshi's secret wish,' he smiles. 'And her home name can be Munno. Matches your sister Kammo,' he says to the baby.

It is Ma. Adi tries to get a closer look at her, to see if he can make out any similarities with her adult self, but the baby is like any other, closer to an alien than it is to his mother.

Suddenly, Nani sits up, gathers her cloth bag and climbs off the carriage.

'Wait, Toshi!' Nana yells. 'What are you doing? Stop! You need to rest.'

Nani does not stop. She shuffles ahead slowly, the back of her kurta dark with sweat, and joins the passing crowds. Nana rushes behind her, holding the baby in one hand and pushing his cycle with the other. He continues to call out to Nani, scolding and cajoling in turns, but she keeps on walking.

Up ahead, they run into a large crowd gathered around something, or someone, and both Nana and Nani stop to have a look. It is a convoy of cars and military jeeps parked by the side of the road, with small Indian flags hanging limply from their radio antennas. Next to it, a few people dressed in crisp, white clothes stand out like diamonds in a sea of dirt. Most of the crowd seems to be attracted towards a man in a Nehru cap. He is tall and handsome, dressed in a long, grey kurta buttoned up to his neck, wearing black shoes caked with mud.

'It's Jawaharlal Nehru!' yells Adi, and the vulture shushes him. 'Sorry,' he whispers. 'But who's that next to him?'

'The Mémsahib of India,' says the vulture.

He stares at the woman, her face as white as Nehru's cap, her glossy brown hair and pearl earrings gleaming through the dusty air. Is she holding Nehru's hand? Was his father actually right about this?

'Is she . . . Nehru's girlfriend?'

'It does not matter, Mr Sharma. Please, focus on what's important.'

He catches sight of Nani as she pushes her way through the crowds and steps out into the small clearing, right before the new Prime Minister of India. Nehru nods at her, smiling politely, and says something. Nani steps forward and slaps him hard across his face. For a moment, the crowd stands absolutely still, holding its breath along with Nehru and the woman next to him.

'You've got your country, are you happy now?' Nani screams in Nehru's face. 'You're such a big man, can you bring back my daughter? Can you bring back my mother? Tell me!'

Nana manages to push through the crowd and grabs Nani's raised hand, just as several policemen come rushing in with their batons drawn.

'Here, take this.' Nani snatches the wailing baby from Nana's arms and thrusts her towards Nehru. 'This is India's bastard child. Will India take care of her?'

Nehru gestures to the policemen to step back. He takes the baby and bows before Nani. His darkened, haggard face seems to be soaked in grief, just like all the faces around him. He tries to say something, but Nani turns and storms off. Nana steps up to take the baby back, bows apologetically before Nehru and rushes after Nani. Nehru turns to a woman in a white sari and says something. The woman nods and goes running after Nana and Nani.

'What's happening?' says Adi, as his vision begins to shake and crackle, like bad TV reception during a pre-monsoon thunderstorm.

'Nothing to worry about,' says the vulture. 'There is a gap in the file, it must be skipping ahead. Please keep your eyes closed.'

The scene stabilises and he concentrates again to take in the new world. It is much darker now – pink and purple clouds hang high in the sky as the sun sets under a smoky horizon. A magnificent monument made of marble and red sandstone stands tall against the dusk sky, with a silver river flowing behind it. It looks just like the Taj Mahal, Adi thinks, though not as well kept. Its giant white dome has lost its sheen and many of the stone slabs have cracked and fallen out. All around the monument, there are rows upon rows of triangular tents like the ones he has seen near the Yamuna River, where ragpickers and charas-addicts live under the bridge.

It *is* the Yamuna flowing behind the vast field, Adi realises. The monument is Humayun's Tomb, the same one he sees from the school bus every day, the pride of Delhi's historical treasures. Here, it looks worse than a slum colony, buzzing with mosquitoes and criss-crossed with black streams of sewage.

He spots a woman in a white sari, the same one who had followed Nana and Nani before, and he follows her now as she weaves her way through the maze of tents, peeking into some of them and asking how people are doing in a gentle but robust voice. The people mostly give her slow nods, looking too tired to say anything more.

The woman stops before a tent at the far end of the field, where a man squats in front of a feeble fire, cooking a roti on a curved fragment of a broken earthen pot.

'Tarun?' says the woman.

Nana turns and smiles. He is wearing a teeka on his forehead and his wrist is wrapped in sacred red thread. It all makes sense now, Adi realises. Tariq has become Tarun, the Nana he knows. That is all it takes to erase the past and begin anew: one syllable, a good old Hindu 'un' to displace the Islamic 'iq'.

'How is she?' the woman nods at the tent, and Nana shrugs, his smile betraying a deep, tired sadness.

'Toshi?' the woman calls out as she opens the flap of the tent. Inside, Adi can see Nani lying on a charpai, looking shrunken under a thin, grey blanket. Her eyes are open and her face is blank, and his first thought is that she is dead. But she blinks when the woman holds her hand and he breathes again.

Nana opens the other flap and enters the tent, bringing some more light in with him. The baby girl, looking a little older and a lot more human, lies next to Nani on the charpai, gnawing at her own big toe. She squeals on seeing Nana and he picks her up. She smiles. It is the smile of Ma.

'Keep the faith, Toshi,' the woman tells Nani. 'It's only a matter of days now. Things are getting better, we will find you a house soon. I have some news for you too, Tarun,' she turns to Nana. 'It is not confirmed yet, but there might be a vacancy for you in the Ministry of Relief and Rehabilitation. They are looking for educated Urdu and English speakers and your college degree will help. I have spoken to some people, let's see what comes of it.'

'But, madam,' says Nana, frowning. 'We are not here to settle. We will be going back to Lahore as soon as things quiet down.'

'Yes, we'll see about that,' says the woman, 'but no harm getting some work for the time being. Oh, and I told you, call me Anis, we are friends. Now, I'm trying to get some more food arranged for everyone. These rascals,' she shakes her head, 'they are stealing food and doing black-marketing, I know. Don't worry, I will take care of it.'

Nana nods, then says something else, too softly for Adi to hear.

'Yes, things are happening in that matter too,' says the woman.

'Can't we ask the British government for help?' Nana says. 'If someone could, er, request the Viceroy? If you could—'

'The British are gone, Tarun. They drew a line on the map and left, and now we have to deal with the mess,' the woman says, waving her arm at their small, dark tent. 'But don't worry,' she nods. 'We have our own government now. They have set up a recovery committee, and both sides are going to bring in new laws to return all the lost women.'

'My Kammo was not lost,' Nani says in a hoary voice, as if she has been screaming for a long time. 'We left her behind. We sacrificed her for this one,' she points a shaking finger at Ma gurgling in Nana's arms.

'No, Toshi.' The woman takes Nani's hand again. 'Your Kammo was taken from you, like so many women were taken. Believe me, the government is working day and night on this. Gandhi-ji is talking of going on a hunger strike again. A fast undo death, he calls it. Pundit Nehru has already spoken to

Jinnah, he is going to make sure we get all our mothers and daughters back.'

'What are all these big men before Wahé Guru Ji? It is all His doing, His punishment for our deeds. I betrayed my family, my community, my panth . . . now I pay the price for this sin,' she points at Ma again, and Nana shields the baby with his hands, as if deflecting a curse.

'Don't say such things, Toshi,' the woman scolds her. 'It is not your fault, you understand? I will do everything to find your daughter and bring her back to you. For now, you have to stay strong. You still have one daughter. She needs you. Why should children have to suffer for the sins of us savages, no? Will you promise me you will be strong for her?'

'Send me back.' Nani's voice is almost too faint to hear. 'Send me back, let me jump into the fire. Let me go back to my Kammo.'

Nani turns away to lie on her side, her back turned to the woman – to Nana and Ma and everyone else.

12.

In case of an emergency

At 06:00, his Casio, buried under two pillows, burst into its cheery beeps and his eyes shot open. It was dead dark outside. The nights of November were getting longer and colder, but his father still did his puja on schedule and Ma still went to the kitchen to make tea, staying until the bell rang. He did not have much time.

It was a Sunday but he had decided to wake up early to surprise Ma. She had returned a week ago but had been unusually quiet ever since and he had an idea to cheer her up. The evening before, using some of the money he kept hidden between the pages of his old number one favourite book, a giant five-in-one collection of *The Famous Five*, he had bought a small bouquet of pink roses and a card from Archies Gallery. The card was also covered in pink roses, with something about mothers being the guiding stars on the voyage of life printed in glittery cursive letters on the inside. He had hidden both presents under his divan and had prayed to both Shiva and Saint Francis to keep the flowers from wilting.

The thick, wintery silence was stirred by the creak of his parents' bathroom door. He threw his blanket off and crouched by the bed to gather the flowers, and just as he stood up, the bedroom door opened and Ma walked out.

'Adi?' Ma stopped at the edge of the drawing room. 'You're up so early?'

It took her a few blinks to notice the flowers, and she froze.

'Happy Birthday, Ma.' He did his best to sound excited but the wish came out as a croaky whisper.

Ma took the flowers and opened the card. She stared at it for a long time, way longer than it would take to read the one cheesy line in it and he felt panic bubbling in his chest. She was smiling, but it was the wrong kind of smile.

A sudden, sharp sob from Ma made him step back, and before he could say anything, she turned and walked back into her bedroom and shut the door. He thought of going after her, trying to console her somehow, but his legs were so shaky he had to sit down. He was trembling, he realised, seized by fear, but he just could not make sense of any of it. What had he done wrong this time? What was he so afraid of? Why did his legs go on shaking, as if they were desperate to run?

*

His father left for work, Rina Auntie came and cooked and cleaned and half the day went by before Ma stepped out of her room again, and even then only to make some tea. Adi pretended he was studying, nodding when she asked if he had eaten. Why was it so hard to look at her, to ask her what was wrong? Why couldn't he stop being scared, for once, and talk to her like a grown-up? Before he could will himself into looking up, she went back into her room and shut the door.

It was funny how odd the house felt without Amma. He had come home one afternoon to find her missing and had to wait until evening to know what had happened. She had been taken to the hospital for some tests, his father had said, but the doctors had asked for her to be admitted for 'observation', like she was some kind of fascinating animal. He knew there was more to it that he was not being told, but he had not bothered to ask; he also knew the non-answers he would have received.

Amma had been gone for a week now, and only now had he begun to realise how much she had become a part of their lives. Her constant chattering with Pistol Pete, her baffling obsession with knowing the time, her wails of 'Babu, Babu,' going on and on until she saw his face – they formed the background noise of the house. Now, like the hum of fans and coolers that are never noticed until they fall silent, Amma's absence made her presence felt more acutely than ever, and he wondered what terrible disease she might be fighting, all alone in the hospital.

With the TV turned on, he decided to read another one of Ma's books that he had lifted from her shelf and stuffed under his mattress. It was a thick one, covered with plain brown paper, as if to hide it on the shelf, which was exactly why he had been intrigued enough to draw it out. It was a biography of B.R. Ambedkar, the man who wrote India's Constitution. Flipping through the pages at random, he spotted a name that made him stop – Valmiki. Mikki's surname. It was a quote by Ambedkar:

The Hindus wanted an epic, and they sent for Valmiki, an untouchable. The Hindus wanted a constitution, and they have sent for me.

Valmiki, the ancient sage who wrote the great *Ramayana*, was an untouchable? Did it mean that Mikki was an untouchable too? Was that why he was happy to be called Mikki, instead of his full name, which made him wince ever so slightly each time it was said aloud during class attendance call? Could that also be why the Sanskrit teacher refused to touch his homework notebook and barely even looked towards their desk? He thought about asking Mikki but could not imagine how to even approach the topic. What was the point anyway? All this untouchable business was from long ago, before Independence. It did not matter now; they were almost in the twenty-first century. It was all history. He shut the book and kept it away and waited for *Home Improvement*.

*

'Where is your mother?' were his father's first words, even before he had taken off his shoes.

'Inside.' Adi nodded towards their bedroom door.

'Did she come out? Has she eaten anything?'

'Just chai.'

His father's face remained stone-solid, showing no signs of anger or worry. Ma's condition must have shaken him, however, because he went into the kitchen and started making tea. He took Ma's chipped mug with flowers on it, along with a pack of her favourite Marie biscuits, and went into the bedroom.

They stayed in there for a long time, and Adi tried to listen. Despite the TV turned low, he couldn't make out a word of what his father was saying. Was he starting to lose his super-power? Was this what happened when you grew older? Or had his father finally learnt the art of whispering?

When his parents finally stepped out, together, he pretended to study again. Ma went into the kitchen and came back with the bouquet of pink roses standing tall in a glass of water and set it on the shelf behind the TV.

'Hungry?' she asked, ruffling his hair to say thank you and he shook his head. 'I'll make you a sandwich,' she said anyway, and he shrugged and kept his eyes on the history textbook, afraid to say or do anything that might have made Ma cry again.

'Listen,' his father said, and Adi looked up. 'We have some work for you.'

'Work? For me?'

'Your mother is not feeling well today, and I have spent the whole day in the hospital already. You know we need someone to stay with Amma for the night, and your mother—'

'I'll go!'

'You'll be able to manage alone?'

Was he kidding?

'I won't be alone, Amma will be there.'

'In case anything happens, or the doctors say anything—'

'I will call you. I know our number, 2219362.'

A faint smile appeared on his father's face – a smile without the slightest trace of anger – and he knew that it was real.

A whole night at the hospital, alone!

The last time he had been in one was when his father had had that heart attack years ago, but he could hardly remember any of that. This time, he thought, maybe he would get a chance to peek into an operation theatre and see an actual surgery happening or see someone getting those electric shocks that brought dead hearts back to life.

'Listen,' Ma said, 'don't worry, okay?'

'I'm not worried,' Adi replied, but his voice trembled even as he said it, and he wondered if worrying was just the adult version of being excited.

'If you can't sleep, or if you feel scared, call us and we will come get you, okay?'

'I'm not scared,' he said, dangerously close to a whine. 'Don't worry, I'll call if I need anything,' he added, using the deepest voice he could muster.

＊

As soon as Adi had stepped in, he decided that Amma's hospital room was the coolest room he had ever been in. The bed alone was more extraordinary than anything he had seen before. It had a pedal that could lift or lower it, like a barber's chair, and a remote control that made it whirr and slowly raise Amma from flat on her back to upright in seconds, without her having to move a muscle. There was a built-in table that unfolded in front of her, where she could eat while watching the TV mounted on the wall right in front of the bed. He couldn't imagine how it could get any better.

One side of the room had large windows overlooking the highway glowing with bright yellow lights and, beyond it, the dim specks of Allah Colony. Below the window was a long, hard sofa where he was meant to spend the night. On the other side, they had a private toilet fitted with long bars so Amma could go herself. The toilet bowl even had a water jet to clean your butt without having to touch it and rolls of toilet paper to dry it. And the taps on the washbasin roared with such a furious flow that there was no chance for the bacteria to cling onto your hands.

When his father had dropped him off, he had stopped and stared at Adi, and reminded him that he had to be responsible and keep an eye on Amma, that he was not to be scared and that it was only for one night. He thought of praying to some god to keep Amma there for as long as possible and wondered which one was responsible for sick people. Shiva? No, he dealt in death and destruction. It must be some avatar of Vishnu, the Maintainer of the Universe, he figured, but it was hard to keep track of them all. He thought of keeping it simple and sending his prayer to Jesus, or to Allah, but then he glanced at Amma and felt a pinprick of guilt. Despite her awesome bed and her jet-powered toilet, she still had a needle stuck into the papery skin on her hand and a bag of medicine hanging over her head, dripping slowly down a long pipe and into her veins. She looked like she was in pain.

He filled up the plastic glass of water and took it to her.

'Amma? Paani?'

She did not open her eyes. Swaddled in a pale blue blanket, it was hard to tell if her chest was moving. There was no TV screen with a beeping, zigzagging line to show that she was alive, like they had in the movies. There was a red button on the remote control for the bed, however, which he was supposed to press in case of an emergency. The nurse had not explained what an emergency might be.

He leant in close to her open mouth and listened. His nose began to twitch, filling up with the deathly smell of stale milk and unbrushed teeth, but he held his breath and stayed until he was sure he felt the faintest wisp of air on his cheeks.

Back on his sofa, he turned down the volume on the TV and switched to Star Movies. *Ace Ventura: When Nature Calls* was on. He had seen the previous one, *Ace Ventura: Pet Detective*, and although he remembered laughing through it, he could not fathom why he had found it funny. Watching Jim Carrey was like looking at those sadhu babas who walked around at traffic lights with snakes hanging from their shoulders – it was weird, but you couldn't take your eyes off it.

A nurse came to check on Amma and looked at Adi like he was doing something wrong. He muted the TV and sat up on the sofa. The nurse made Amma sit up too, then checked her blood pressure, fiddled with the hanging medicine bag and wrote something down on a notepad. Amma slept through all of it and he wondered what was in the bag, whether it was meant to make Amma better or just to keep her quiet.

After the nurse had turned the lights off and left, he could not focus on the movie anymore. Outside, the air was still hazy from all the Divali fireworks. At school, everyone had been asked to get their parents to sign a pledge for a fire-cracker-free Divali, explaining that they were bad for the atmosphere and for the poor children who made them in dirty, dangerous factories. His father had refused to sign it, calling it 'secular propaganda' and a conspiracy to make Hindus feel ashamed. He had asked why no one blamed the Muslims for butchering thousands of goats on the streets every Eid, was that not unhygienic? And what about the Christians, with their cutting of trees to decorate their houses? Where were the environmentalists then? In the end, Adi had asked Ma to sign it.

Not that the pledges had made any difference – this Divali had been louder and longer than any he could remember. Chaddha Uncle, who lived in the block opposite theirs, who had just got a promotion according to his father, had laid out an epic ladi, a string of 10,000 little red firecrackers that had circled all the way around the park, and it had gone on *forever*. Long after everyone had gotten bored and moved on, it had kept on sputtering in the background like a fire out of control, carpeting the footpath with bits of burnt paper, filling the air between the apartment blocks with foul grey smoke.

On every big festival, his father pestered both him and Ma to go downstairs and join the colony's celebrations, just so the neighbours wouldn't think that they were strange. Even the Siddiquis on the ground floor celebrated Divali and Holi with great enthusiasm, his father never failed to point out, though he never felt the need to celebrate Eid in return. Divali was one festival that Ma agreed to participate in, only because she loved phuljhadis, the silver sparklers with their hail of electric flowers. They were one of the rare things that had the power to make her giggle like a little girl. That laughter was the only thing that made it worthwhile to brave the noise and the pollution, the only firecracker that he liked. This year, however, they had decided not to celebrate Divali because of Amma being in the hospital. It was just as well: Ma seemed like she was in no mood to giggle.

Sitting up on the sofa and looking out of the window, trying to ignore Amma's shockingly loud snores, he tried to think of something, anything else that he could do. The only book he had brought along was *The Lord of the Rings* and he just couldn't bring himself to open it. He had tried for weeks to keep at it, knowing that sometimes it took time to get into books, but he couldn't even pretend to be excited about elves that talked gibberish and hairy hobbits who smoked pipes and Paragon, Son of Saridon or whatever, with his magic sword. He had had enough.

'Are you there?' he whispered into the yellow fog, and waited.

'Yes, Mr Sharma, I am here,' came the voice, that booming monotone, the drone of a dull uncle. For once, he was glad to hear it.

'Where? I can't see you?'

'Ah, yes. All thanks to your Divali festival, the great celebration of good over evil. Now, we are having so much good in the air we cannot even breathe, hrr-hrr.'

He spotted the vulture sitting on top of a half-built hospital building. It was closer to him than it had ever been, but the smoke was so thick that he still could not make out anything more than a black shape blurring into the grey-yellow smog.

'So, Mr Sharma, you are ready to face your next fear?'

'Yeah, so I was thinking, um, I'm quite afraid of Amma, actually, especially when she talks to ghosts. I thought I could spend a night with her, alone—'

'Very funny. You are trying to be smart with me? What do you think I am, a pigeon? You are not scared of your Amma, you are already staying with her and having full enjoyment. No, you will have to be serious. Please think, what is making you feel scared these days?'

'Seeing Ma looking so sad is a little scary,' he said. 'I'm terrified of making her cry again.'

'Ah, very good!' The little head bobbed up. 'And is there anything you are doing to address this problem?'

'I tried . . . I got her flowers, but she was still—'

'You gave her dead plant matter? Why are you giving dead things to someone who is already sad? That is what I give to my missus, hrr-hrr.'

'I don't know what to do, then! I don't even know why she's sad, because you don't show me all of the memories.'

'Please, Mr Sharma, do not put the blame of your laziness on my head. I am delighted to share the files with you as and when you complete your tasks. May I remind you that we are still bound by the reciprocal protocol of H-A-H-A and you are legally required to address one fear in return for each file that you are seeing.'

'Yeah, yeah, all that is fine, but can't you at least give me a hint? How am I supposed to guess what you want?'

'I, Mr Sharma? I am not wanting anything. I am merely a humble servant doing my duty, following the procedures as per section—'

'Oh, shut up,' he mumbled. 'Just . . . fly away.'

He slid down on the sofa and lay there with his eyes open, staring at the grey ceiling flickering in the glow of the muted TV. There was no point in getting angry, he told himself. It was silly to expect the answers from that useless bird; he had to figure them out himself. He would lie awake all night and think about what else he could do for Ma, he decided. He would shut his eyes just for a minute, just to clear his head.

13.

No time for dawdling

'Let us give two minutes of silence,' Father Pinto breathed into the microphone with his solemn voice and a hush descended over the playground.

Father Pinto was the School Mentor, the oldest of all Fathers, and his role consisted entirely of ambling through the corridors with his hands behind his back, his shoulders locked in a permanent shrug, his face frozen with a dazed smile. As Christmas neared, however, he came alive, leading special assemblies each week where the entire school was lined up, shivering in the morning chill, to hear his sermons. The assemblies always began with a two-minute silence. This one was for forty-six people who had died in a cyclone somewhere in Uttar Pradesh. The one last week had been for three people who had died in the bomb blasts at Chandni Chowk. Adi wondered why both got the equal two minutes – whether the silence ought to match the number of people who died. It was not practical, obviously; he had read in yesterday's paper that three hundred and fifty people had died in an LTTE attack in Sri Lanka. That would have meant an entire day of silence.

'What does Saint Francis teach us?' asked Father Pinto, making the microphone screech and scatter all the pigeons watching from the windowsills. He looked around the assembly grounds slowly, barely turning his head, as though he was trying to scan every face in all the unending columns of students, from kindergarten toddlers to moustachioed seniors. He was quiet for so long that many at the back were tempted to offer answers – maths, classical dance, sex education – but they were quickly shushed by the teachers patrolling the ranks.

'When Saint Francis went on a forty-day fast and saw an angel with six wings—'

It was Father Pinto's favourite story, and he always took so long to tell it that most kids lost track along the way and even the teachers got tired of trying to keep them from whispering among themselves.

'—he was delighted upon seeing the angel, a messenger of our Lord, and he cried tears of joy. But then he saw that the angel was on a *crucifix*—'

As the morning grogginess lifted, the strict rows ordered by ascending heights began to grow loose as places were swapped and friends clustered together. Even the teachers stopped walking around and stood at the back, chatting and occasionally shushing when someone laughed too loud.

He looked around the girls' column next to theirs and found Noor standing just three spots down from him, reading a book. Slowly, he made his way towards the front of his queue, apologising to the boys who didn't seem to care.

'Noor,' he whispered, then cleared his throat and tried again, as loudly as he dared: 'Oye, Noor!'

She turned to look at him and nearly smiled. 'Oh, hi,' she said, shutting her book.

'Listen, you can read Urdu, right?'

'Yes, obviously. Why?'

'Oh, I, um, I wanted to ask if you could translate something.' He stopped to check his pockets until he found the folded-up letter he had carried about with him for days. He looked up to find Noor frowning at him. Suddenly, she hopped across the space between their columns and joined the boys.

'Oye, move!' she hissed at the boy behind Adi, who quickly stepped back.

'What's that?' she asked. Before he could answer, the letter was already in her hands, unfolded and held down at waist level to hide it from any roving teachers.

'—Saint Francis felt the pain and suffering of our Lord in his own flesh and *blood*, in his heart and *bones*, and he fell on his knees and *wept*—'

'What *is* this?' she asked, folding the letter back up and handing it to Adi.

'What does it say?'

'It says something like, "*We don't know who you are, and we don't know anyone named Toshi or Tariq.*" Oh, and then it says, "*Don't send letters or call here to harass us again. Our uncle is the Deputy Police Commissioner and we will have you arrested.*"'

'Shit, shit, shit,' he cursed himself. Were these the people he had called? Could they really report him to the police? But then, it would be the Pakistan police, wouldn't it?

'Who's it from?' Noor asked, and he looked up to find her still frowning.

'Nobody,' he replied, and stuffed the letter back into his blazer.

Something didn't seem right. If Ma had written to these people, or even called them, they could have just ignored her. Threatening to call the police seemed like a wild overreaction, like they were trying to hide something. Maybe Ma had decided to go and find out. That's what he would've done. One hundred per cent.

'Acchha, listen. Shall we go to the drama room after this drama ends?' Noor said, rolling her eyes at Father Pinto still droning on in the background.

'Drama room?' He had no idea what she was talking about, but he was grateful that she had changed the topic herself.

'We need to decide about our play. Have you forgotten?'

'No, I know, but . . . we have classes?'

'I got a note from Ma'am George,' Noor grinned. 'We can skip any class we want.'

She was good, he had to admit. He had no idea how she managed to pull off these things, but it seemed that many of the teachers liked her just as much as the kids found her strange. Of course, it helped that she was a genius who could do geometry in her head.

'Okay,' he said, mostly because he didn't know what else to say.

'Ask your friend to come as well.'

'Mikki?'

'Yes!' she said, frowning like he was stupid. 'You've told him about it, right?'

'I, um . . .'

She pinched the bridge of her nose and shook her head. She was certainly good at drama.

'Okay, fine.' She turned towards the back of the boys' queue and began waving.

'—on his *hands*, on his *feet*, on his entire *body*, the same wounds appeared as the ones on *Christ's* body, the same iron nails going through *his* flesh, as the ones that had gone through *Christ's* flesh—'

Finally, one of the boys turned and nudged Mikki, just to make Noor stop waving and drawing attention to them. Mikki looked up with a start, as though he had been sleeping. Noor signalled him to come over towards the front, and he stared blankly at her for a moment. Then, he stepped out of the column and walked calmly towards them. Everyone around them went silent, certain that even Father Pinto would notice that hulk of a boy openly breaking ranks and trudging down the assembly grounds. Nothing happened, however. Mikki simply stepped back in line behind Adi and the column quickly adjusted to make space.

'What?' he said to Noor, who looked at Adi and giggled, clearly impressed.

'Listen,' she said to Mikki. 'Ma'am George has asked us to perform in The Last Word.'

'In what?'

'The Last *Word*,' Noor repeated, before remembering that Mikki was new to the school. She explained the annual English department event, giving examples of the kinds of performances it usually had.

Mikki listened to it all with his usual deadened expression, before asking, 'So?'

'So, you want to join us? It'll just be the three of us. We're going to the drama room after this,' she nodded towards Father Pinto, who was talking even more slowly now. 'I have a note, we can skip any classes we want.'

Mikki's eyes brightened for the first time. 'Okay.'

'—feel the suffering of others as our *own*, feel their pain in our *blood*, rise above our human *selfishness*, sacrifice our *desires*, and only *then*—'

'But we have to wait for the communion,' Mikki added.

Noor and Adi looked at each other, confused. Finally, she cleared her throat and asked: 'But you're not a Catholic, no? Are you even a Christian?'

'I like the wafers,' said Mikki.

*

The drama room was a fantastical chamber of curiosities. It was about as big as a classroom but the walls were lined with shelves carrying all sorts of strange things – animal costumes, wizard hats, plastic swords, outlandish wigs, reams of coloured chart paper and countless little bottles of paint. One half of the room was buried under all the things that could not fit on the shelves, like cardboard cutouts of trees and horses, and even a giant pumpkin carriage that he remembered from a Cinderella play last year.

Noor opened one of the cupboards and took out three folded chairs, setting them down around a long table covered in deep scratches and spots of dried paint. Mikki walked in and looked around the room for a moment, before throwing his bag on the floor and taking a seat.

'Why did you get your bag?' Noor asked.

'You said we can skip any class,' he frowned.

'So . . . you're not going to attend *any* of them?'

Mikki looked at the two of them like he was really confused now. 'What, do you like sitting in class?'

'No, of course not,' Adi said.

'I like some of them,' said Noor. 'Like English. And history.'

He looked at her, kicking himself for not saying that. Admitting it now would just look like he was copying her.

'I don't,' said Mikki, reaching into his bag for his *Chip* magazine.

Noor nodded in that way she did, like she understood what you meant without saying it. 'I hate Ghost Time, though. That Ma'am Mishra is a witch.'

Ghost Time was an inside joke in the class, their nickname for Sanskrit period – a literal mistranslation of bhoot kaal, the past tense forms that Ma'am Mishra loved to quiz them on. If they were supposed to always speak in English, it was only fair, the kids had decided, to translate Sanskrit too – and to make the translations wholly inaccurate.

Mikki's face twitched, betraying a hint of a smile, and Adi marvelled at how subtly Noor had let Mikki know that she had noticed Ma'am Mishra's behaviour towards him. Adi was the one who sat next to him. Why had he never said so himself?

'So,' Noor clapped her hands. 'Any ideas on what we can do?'

'I'm not going to speak.' Mikki was flipping through a magazine he must have read a dozen times.

'What do you mean? You want to be a mime?' said Noor.

'I can just be a tree or something.' Mikki gestured towards the cardboard tree at the back of the room without lifting his eyes.

'You can't be a *tree*! You need a role that lets you express something.'

Mikki looked up at her, then at Adi. 'I like trees,' he nodded.

'Ugh.' Noor turned away, holding her head. 'This is great. What do you want to be, Adi? A rock?'

'Actually, I have an idea,' Adi said.

'Oh?' Noor looked at him. 'What is it?'

'It's like . . . it's based on that book of poetry. You know, that red book—'

'Yes, I know. The book I lent to someone and never saw again.'

'Sorry,' said Adi, scratching his ear. 'I'll bring it back soon, I promise.'

'What's the *idea*?'

'I thought we could just, like, do a dramatic version of a poem. So Mikki can be a poet, like Mirza Ghalib or something, wearing a kurta and a tall hat. And we can be the voices in his head. So, we recite the poems – you do it in Urdu and I'll translate in English – and he can just sit at a desk and write, acting like he can't see us.'

They both turned to Mikki. He was engrossed in an article about Deep Blue, the supercomputer that had beaten Chess grandmaster Garry Kasparov. He had already nailed the part.

'Perfect,' said Noor. 'Why should we always do those foreign plays when we have such great poets and writers of our own, right?'

'Um, yeah,' he said, though he hadn't thought of it like that. It sounded vaguely like something his father would have said. But then, his father would have counted Urdu poetry as foreign too, belonging to the Muslim invaders who were even worse, in his eyes, than the British. At least the British had built the railways and the civil services, he said, unlike the Mughals who'd spent all of India's money building tombs for themselves. To Adi, it seemed like the Taj Mahal should be counted as a greater achievement than the Old Delhi Railway Station, but he knew better than to say that.

'And doing an English translation is a great idea,' said Noor. 'We can introduce people to Urdu and nobody can object because technically it's still in English. It's just *genius*, Adi!'

He nodded, hoping he wasn't blushing.

'Okay, so that's done. Should we go for the maths class now?'

'No,' said Mikki, still reading.

'No,' Adi added, deciding it was time to be a little bolder. It was nice being there with the two of them, away from all the shrill teachers and their nodding pets.

'Fine.' Noor got up. 'Have fun. We'll meet up during computers class and talk about the poems we can pick.'

'I'm not missing computers,' said Mikki.

'Why? It's useless. If you just want to play silly games, you can do it at home.'

'I don't have a computer at home.'

There was a moment of silence as Noor stood at the door, scratching the top of her nose. 'Okay. We'll catch up later, then? *By-ee*!'

'Funny girl,' said Mikki, after the door had slammed shut.

'Yeah.' Adi let out a laugh that sounded more like a snort. Mikki threw him a quick glance but he pretended not to notice it.

The morning mist had cleared and the sun was bright and sharp, flooding in through the tall windows. The room suddenly felt stuffy, so Adi went up to the windows and pushed them open, letting the cool air sweep in. He stood for a moment, looking around the streetlights and treetops, but there was no sign of the vulture. Maybe it had lost interest in him? Maybe he had finally grown up?

'Want to listen to some music?' Mikki said, and Adi swerved around to find the Walkman on the desk.

'Sure. What are you listening to?'

Mikki handed him an earbud and a cassette tape cover. Adi moved his chair closer, leaning towards Mikki and pushing the earbud in. *Savage Garden*, said the cover, next to a picture of two guys dressed in black, standing together but apart and looking in different directions.

'To the Moon and Back' was the name of the song playing, Adi realised after reading the list at the back of the cassette case. It was like no song he had ever heard before. For a few moments, it made time stand still. Usually when that happened, on long nights at home, it filled him with that familiar surge of panic that made his toes go stiff and his eyes twitch. This time, he felt his muscles relaxing, his mind slowing, his entire body sighing and letting go, like a classroom after the final bell on an exam. If this was what music could do, it was no wonder that Mikki held on to his Walkman as though it was a precious treasure masquerading as something ordinary, like that Arabian Nights story where a common parrot hides within it the soul of a king.

*

As he trudged up the stairs, dragging his backpack behind him, he found the inner wooden door open and a buzz of activity inside the house. He threw off his shoes and bag and went up to Amma's room, expecting to see her back, but found Ma and Rina Auntie instead, busy cleaning up the room. The windows were flung open, the bare mattress was propped up in the sunshine slicing through the room and Ma was clearing Amma's medicines from the desk, explaining to Rina Auntie the difference between types of silk saris.

'Ma?'

'Adi, you're back?' She wiped her forehead with the back of her hand, sweaty despite the December air rushing in through the windows. 'Wait outside, we're cleaning. I'll get your lunch soon.'

'Is Amma coming back?'

'No, béta. Not yet.'

There was something she was not telling him, as usual. Maybe Amma was never coming back? Was he going to move back into his room? He looked around at the posters on the cupboard and the walls, at the list of his favourite words he used to scrawl just beneath the windows in tiny, pencilled letters. He could still make out the 'g' words – *gargantuan*, *gregarious*, *grotesque* – the last ones he'd added before Amma had shown up. The room was exactly the same in every way. With the bedsheet changed, the clutter cleared, and the air freshened, it looked just as he had left it. Why, then, did it feel so unfamiliar, like he had never belonged there, like that cube of empty space had never belonged to him?

When Ma had put away Amma's things in a cardboard box and stuffed it under the bed, she left Rina Auntie to mop the room, then turned to Adi. She must have seen the questions flickering on his face because she offered the answer herself.

'Your Chacha is coming.'

'Chacha?' he said, half-frowning. In the few moments it took for him to take in the news of his uncle's arrival and feel the rush of excitement rise from his belly and spread out to the tips of his fingers, Ma disappeared into her bedroom. On any other day, he would not have followed her, but this was no time for dawdling.

He stood in the doorway. 'When is he coming?'

Ma had lifted the lid on the box bed and was looking through the old suitcase that kept her best saris safe, each wrapped in a clear plastic bag of its own. By the briskness of her movements and the shape of her drooping shoulders, he could tell she was not happy and he could not understand why. Chacha was the one person in his father's family whom Ma actually liked.

He remembered when Chacha had last visited, the time he had got him the red Lego briefcase; Ma had laughed more in that one week than she had in all the following years put together. Even in his parents' wedding album, he knew Ma's favourite photo was the one with Chacha standing next to the newlyweds, tall and handsome next to Ma, eclipsing the squarish figure of his father. It was the only photo in which Ma was not looking down demurely, like a good bride. She was looking straight into the camera and grinning.

'Ma?' he repeated, when she had taken out two saris and slammed the bed shut.

'Yes, Adi?'

'When is Chacha coming?'

'On Sunday.'

'Sunday?' He took a sharp breath. Just four days away. 'What time? Which airline? Can I go along to pick him up?'

'I don't know. Ask your father, he's the one in charge of everything.'

She put the saris in the cupboard and walked out. It was best to leave her when she was like this, Adi knew, but he was not going to be afraid, not today. He followed her into the kitchen.

'Will he be staying in Amma's room? What if Amma comes back? He can have the divan then. I can sleep on the floor.'

Ma filled a pot with filtered water and put it on the stove. 'Amma will have to stay in hospital for some time.'

The last he had overheard, two days ago, was that Amma was going to be discharged from the hospital on Saturday. Something must have happened.

'I can stay at the hospital, then,' he offered, as Ma began to chop onions, slicing them thin as paper.

'She has been moved to the ICU,' she said. 'We can't stay with her anymore.'

'Is she going to die?'

'Adi! Behave yourself. Don't say such things in the house. What if your father hears you talking like this?'

He scoffed and shook his head but she didn't catch it. It was not like his father cared much about Amma. He did not even know how to use the blood pressure machine.

'She had a heart attack, béta. It was not a very serious one, but they have kept her in the hospital for observation.'

'For how long?'

She put down the knife and wiped her forehead with the back of her hand. 'I don't know, we'll see.'

She looked like she was too tired to stand, and he tried to find the words to offer help. He could have made rice. He had seen her do it and it hadn't looked too hard. He could easily have heated up the leftovers in a pan, like he had often done for Amma. He could have made her a cup of tea, if nothing else.

'Go sit in the drawing room,' Ma said. 'Let me make your food.'

He went and turned on the TV, but the sound of the knife on the chopping board slashed through the hollow laughter on *Seinfeld*. He tapped his foot in time with the knife, like the ticking of a clock that paused every few seconds before going faster and faster, until he could no longer keep up.

14.

She laughed like she used to

At the airport, they waited along a glass wall from where they could see all the aeroplanes parked outside. At that late hour, it was mostly international flights with their gigantic planes emblazoned with names like JAL and KLM and Lufthansa, and he wondered where they had come from, how far they must have flown.

'Which one is Chacha's?' he asked, and his father nodded towards one slowly gliding towards the airport, little men guiding it with glowing sticks.

It was stupendously large, with two engines on each wing and a bump in the front that had two rows of windows. It was dark blue on the bottom half with a long red arrow cutting across it, and white on top with BRITISH AIRWAYS written on it. On its tail was a crown of some sort – was it Queen Elizabeth II's crown with the stolen koh-i-noor diamond on it? Why would Chacha have come on this? He was coming from America, not England. He wondered again if his father was making things up.

After a long wait, people began to trickle out of the glass doors. The first to emerge were business-like foreigners in suits and dresses, carrying sleek briefcases and tired frowns, like they were bored – bored of flying? Then, the families began to gush forth – there were many Sardaar-jis with trimmed beards and slim turbans who looked way more stylish than the ones in Delhi, and there were children wearing fancy Nikes, talking boisterously in accents straight out of Star World shows.

'There he is,' said his father, and Adi scanned the crowd. A rowdy family was blocking the gates, hugging and slapping each other's backs. When they finally dispersed, he saw Chacha walking towards them, wearing a long black overcoat and shiny boots, carrying a giant suitcase that glided gracefully on little wheels.

'Pranaam, Bhaiya,' Chacha said, as he walked up to his father and bent down to touch his feet.

His father patted Chacha's shoulder, like he was the neighbour's son, and asked him if he had eaten on the flight. Of all the things he could ask someone who had just flown halfway around the world, *this* is all his father could think of?

They argued about who would get to drag Chacha's suitcase, but it was a fake fight and Chacha finally let his father win. As they reached the car, Adi went and opened the rear door and the brothers continued talking about boring things, like they were acting in a play, reciting memorised lines.

'Good weather in Delhi for this time, isn't it, Bhaiya?'

'Oh, yes, we haven't had a proper winter yet.'

'It's good. Chicago is in a terrible state. Snow this high.' Chacha held his hand up to his flat belly. 'And the wind, baapré, it's like the North Pole.'

Looking out the window at the traffic jam outside the airport, Adi felt an aching desire to be in Chicago at that moment, walking around in a long coat in Arctic winds and snow 'this high'.

'How is Bhabhi?' Chacha asked, looking away from his father and checking for something in his briefcase.

'She must be fine. You can ask her yourself in a while. Maybe you she might tell.'

Chacha laughed, more out of politeness than amusement, and turned to Adi.

'And how is this young man? He has grown so tall since I last saw him!'

Adi smiled, unsure whether the question was meant for him or his father.

'I haven't forgotten your gifts, Hero,' Chacha grinned. That was what Chacha used to call him, he suddenly remembered: Hero. How he had longed to be called that again, in a tone that did not stink of sarcasm.

'You spoil him too much,' said his father, speeding up as they got on to the highway.

'What, Bhaiya? I have no other nephews. Or nieces. Who else will I spoil?'

It was a subtle shift in the air but Adi caught it – the tensing of Chacha's shoulders and the locking of his father's jaws. He knew something was going to be said.

'Chacha?' Adi leant into the space between the front seats. 'Did you fly over Africa?'

'No,' Chacha laughed, but not in a way that made him feel

stupid. 'Planes don't fly in a straight line across the map,' he said, and Adi smiled; Chacha had guessed why he had asked. 'My flight was actually via London, so I changed planes there and flew over Europe, then Iraq, Iran, Afghanistan, Pakistan.'

'Pakistan?'

'Yes,' Chacha laughed again. 'It's hard to tell where it ends and where India begins. You can't see any borders from the sky.'

'Hah,' his father scoffed. 'You wait for a few years, we are working on that. Fully electrified borders we will have. Visible from space too, like that wall in China.'

'Arré, Bhaiya,' said Chacha, with a childlike tone of curiosity. 'How is your work? What interesting project are you working on these days?'

'I can't tell you. It's national security.'

He had a meaningful look in his eyes, like he was working on making an atom bomb or something. As far as Adi knew, his father was still on the same project he had been for the last two years, that he sometimes discussed with Laddoo Uncle: inventing ways to make juice out of bananas. He called it an important national security project because the juice was meant for soldiers, who couldn't carry bananas around in a war because they went bad too quickly. Adi did suspect that his father was making it up – he couldn't imagine soldiers wanting bananas in battle – but his father often said that nobody knew how to waste money like the Government of India.

'You tell,' said his father, braking at a traffic light and turning to Chacha. 'How is your practice? Your patients must be more interesting than our boring lives.'

'They're normal people, Bhaiya. Like me, or you.'

'Hmm,' said his father, shifting gears and speeding up again, nodding sideways in the way he did in response to things he found incredibly dumb. Chacha was a psychiatrist, so he probably didn't think it worth his time to even argue with him.

The car was quiet for a while after that, and Adi bent low to avoid his father in the rear-view mirror and stared at Chacha. He had a shadow of a beard and dark pits around his eyes, and in the flying flashes of the yellow streetlights, Adi could make out the grey hair around his ears. Despite all that, next to his father, Chacha looked like someone out of a magazine ad. He had his father's bald spot, Adi could see, but he didn't try to hide it by combing his hair over it – his hair was cropped short and sprinkled with grey but it somehow made him look younger. His glasses were not like his father's gold-rimmed squares either, but sleek, frameless rectangles that seemed to float in thin air before his eyes. The most memorable thing about Chacha, however, was the smell. Strong and gentle at the same time, it filled the car with its heady warmth and made Adi sigh. It was probably a perfume or an aftershave, or the smell of laundry detergent, but for him, it was the smell of 'foreign', a whiff of a magical world far beyond their little lives.

*

It was past midnight when they finally arrived at home. In all the excitement, Adi had forgotten that they had not even eaten dinner yet. He was reminded of it as he entered the house and felt the fragrance of pulao stir his stomach awake.

'Pranaam, Bhabhi,' Chacha said, as Ma emerged from the kitchen in a different sari from the one she had been wearing when they had left for the airport. As Chacha bent down to touch her feet, she hugged him instead, as tightly as she had hugged Adi when she had come back from her first mystery trip.

'How long has it been, Mohan?' She gave him a frowning smile. 'Why have you not visited?'

Chacha smiled apologetically and Ma rushed him inside, towards the dining table. 'Come-come, sit, dinner is ready.'

Adi turned to shut the door, almost forgetting his father, who had just made it up the stairs. He stood aside and held the door open, as though he had been waiting.

'Dinner already? Arré, let him breathe, at least,' said his father, huffing as he slipped off his shoes.

'With a smell so delicious, how can one breathe?' said Chacha, and the smile on Ma's face reminded Adi of the smile Noor had given him in the staff room – a rare kind of smile he could not quite understand but which made him feel warm and tingly, nonetheless.

Chacha followed Ma into the kitchen and Adi could hear him talking loudly, expressing his astonishment at all the food she had prepared, including his favourite thing in the world: bhindi.

Sitting alone at the dining table, Adi felt a brief rush of happiness. Just the way Chacha and Ma talked – the bouncing, bubbling excitement of their words – made the house seem lighter, brighter, as though all the jammed windows had been flung open and a cold breeze had come in and swept away the sadness that covered their house like a thick layer of dust. How different it could have been, he thought, if Ma had married Chacha instead. Maybe they could have all gone to America, where Ma could have worn dresses and driven a car, and he could have gone to school wearing jeans and a baseball cap. Maybe he could do it himself, when he grew up – take Ma and fly away to some place where they could breathe a little easier, live a little more.

'I don't know where you get the taste for such rubbish,' said his father, shaking his head with a smile as Chacha put the steaming bowl of bhindi on the table. 'America has really broken your brain. You should become your own patient,' he laughed, but Chacha deflated his sarcastic joke by laughing right back. It was a good trick, Adi thought, and made a mental note to remember it.

Adi hated bhindi as much as his father, if not more. The limp green stalks split down the middle looked nothing like any ladies' fingers he had ever seen and the smell made him want to throw up. Now, he made it a point to eat it, chewing slowly to force his tongue to develop a taste for it.

'Start eating while the chapatis are hot,' Ma called out from the kitchen.

'No, we'll eat with you when you're done,' Chacha shouted back.

'We will go see Amma in the morning, before I go to work,'

his father said, helping himself to a mountain of rice. 'Visiting hours start at eight. It's not too early for you, is it?'

'Not at all. I'll be ready.'

Ma came out with fresh, steaming chapatis and tossed one onto Chacha's plate.

'So, tell me, Mohan.' She sat down on the chair next to Adi, facing his father but turned towards Chacha. 'How is Jean?'

His father smirked at the mention of the name. It was Chacha's girlfriend, Adi remembered. His father usually referred to her as 'Mohan's Mémsahib', but he had his mouth full so he couldn't say it now.

'Jean is very well,' Chacha nodded. 'She sends her love to everyone, and gifts for you, especially. She really wanted to come but this time it was difficult.'

'Yes, yes,' Ma nodded with a serious face. 'It would be hard to travel so far on such short notice. Anyway, this is an emergency trip. But she must come next time.'

'Arré,' said his father, 'this time hasn't started yet and you are already talking of next time? The poor guy will not come again if you get after him like that.'

Adi was stunned to find Ma laughing at this – genuinely, happily laughing at something his father had said. She laughed like she used to, like he remembered from long summers ago, when his father would sometimes drive them to India Gate in the middle of the night to get ice-cream. She would take forever to decide which one to get, and when she finally got it, his father would steal a bite and she would shriek with mock horror, and Adi and his father would burst into laughter.

He wished he could remember now, which flavour she used to pick.

*

After Ma had cleared the table, sternly refusing Chacha's offers to help, Adi lingered in the dining hall as Chacha opened his suitcase and began to take out presents.

'Bhabhi,' he called out to Ma, rummaging under piles of crisp, neatly folded shirts. 'Jean has sent a special gift for you, something she bought herself.'

Ma came out of the kitchen wiping her hands on a cloth. 'Oh-ho, what's the need for all that?' she laughed. 'But first take out what you have for him, his breath is stuck in his throat.'

She was referring to him, Adi realised, and he felt his face grow hot.

'Yes, Hero. Come, look at this.'

It was a long, grey slab of plastic with a little screen and tiny buttons. Adi had never seen one before but he knew what it was – a Nintendo Game Boy. The controls were the same as on Sunny-Bunny's video game console, though the only game on it was *Tetris*. It was a cool gadget, sure, but for someone who had grown bored of *Mortal Kombat*, making a wall out of falling bricks was hardly a thrilling adventure.

Chacha probably sensed his disappointment and fished out more gifts. There was a small RC Car (childish), a bar of

Toblerone (useful for bribing someone to share notes for skipped classes), a red-and-black Chicago Bulls cap (cool, but not allowed in school), a pale blue shirt that smelled like Chacha (oversized) and a *Star Wars* action figure set (a T-shirt would've been nicer).

When Chacha zipped his suitcase shut, Adi did his best to look thrilled with all the gifts, telling himself that they were indeed amazing presents, enough to make any kid giddy with excitement. Still, he could not help but feel a little sad.

Years ago, when Chacha had last visited, he had brought Adi the best gift he had ever received. It was a comic book, bigger than any he had seen, with a cover so beautiful he could still remember it vividly. It showed the back of a blue jeep with three people and a dog inside, racing towards a giant rocket painted with red and white squares, standing against a sky so fresh and bright it hurt his eyes. *Destination Moon*, it was called. It was the first time he had ever seen Tintin. He had known at first glance that he would never again be happy with his old comic books, knowing that *this* was out there. It had taken him two days to read the whole book, reading on the school bus, on the toilet seat, at the dinner table, devouring every glorious frame, running his eyes along the incredible details, terrified with every turn of the page that it would be the last. And when he had reached the end, he had felt his heart drop, then rise in fury. The last frame had shown the red-and-white rocket soaring into the starry sky, with questions next to it: 'What dangers await? What will happen? Will they ever return? Find out in *Explorers on the Moon*.'

All these years he had waited to find the answers that never arrived.

'Thank you, Chacha,' he said, gathering everything up in his arms.

'You're most welcome.' Chacha was looking at him with a slight frown, as though trying to look past his happy face.

'Ma,' he shouted, 'look what I got!'

He turned and ran into the kitchen, relieved to get away. There was something about Chacha's clear, sharp gaze that made him feel exposed, like all his secret thoughts were on display. He couldn't decide whether it was scary or exciting – whether he wanted to hide or lay himself bare.

*

On the first day of the school holidays, the Saturday before Christmas, Adi woke up feeling happy. It was the third Saturday of the month, which meant that his father would be gone all day for his monthly visit to the Sai Baba temple for their special prayer ceremony, followed by a trip to his astrologer to pick up another trinket meant to realign the planets or bypass the obstacles of fate.

'Good morning, Hero,' Chacha said, walking into the drawing room with a cup of coffee.

Adi smiled, rubbing his eyes and savoured the smell of coffee, light yet robust, so unlike the cloying smell of milky chai.

'First day of the holidays, huh?' Chacha sat down on his father's spot on the sofa. 'What big plans do you have?'

'I don't know,' he said. He would have been happy to stay

at home all day with Chacha and Ma, talking and laughing and drinking coffee and eating pizza like a family in some American TV show.

'Chacha?' Adi's eyes had lit up with an idea.

'Yes?'

'Let's go out somewhere. You have been at home since you came. It's been so many years since your last visit, you must be missing some places?'

'Oh,' Chacha frowned. 'This time, I just came to see Amma. I'll go sightseeing when I come later with Jean.'

'We can at least go to a market,' he said. 'You can buy something nice for Chachi.'

'Hmm.' Chacha narrowed his eyes, and Adi knew he had struck the ball through a gap.

'We can go to Lajpat Nagar,' he said. 'I'm sure you'll find something nice there.'

'Lajpat Nagar! I haven't been there in years,' said Chacha. 'I used to love going there, you know, when I was young. It was very close to my college.'

It was a lucky strike. Adi knew it used to be Ma's favourite market – she used to live right next to it – but he had no idea Chacha liked it too.

'Fine,' said Chacha. 'I do have to buy something for Jean, and for one of her nephews, who is the same age as you. Maybe you can help me pick something?'

'Okay!' Adi could not stop sounding excited as a child, and he had to force himself to breathe and deepen his voice. 'Shall we ask Ma?'

'Oh.' Chacha raised his eyebrows, like he hadn't even thought of it. 'Yes, we can ask her but I don't know—'

'What's happening?' said Ma, walking in with a bucketful of clothes to be put out to dry on the balcony.

'Ma! We're going to Lajpat Nagar to buy gifts for Chachi.'

'Oh, really?'

'You want to come?'

'Me? No-no, I have so many things—'

'Come on, Ma? It will be fun. We never go to a big market anymore.'

'Adi,' she glared at him. 'I don't need to shop, the two of you can go.'

'I just thought . . . Chacha brings us so many gifts, we should also send something back for Chachi. But it's okay if you are busy,' he shrugged.

Ma stopped in her tracks. This time, he had hit it right out of the park.

'But . . . Amma?' She glanced at Chacha.

'Bhaiya stopped by the hospital in the morning. And I will be going in the evening. We should be back in time, we'll take a taxi.'

A taxi! Adi could not even remember the last time he had been in a taxi. His father always drove his Maruti 800 everywhere and Ma always took the bus or an auto-rickshaw.

'Come, Bhabhi, it has been so long,' Chacha smiled, and Adi could see Ma melting right before his eyes.

'Acchha, fine.'

And Adi couldn't help but yell, 'Yes!' He looked sheepishly towards Chacha, but when Ma stepped out onto the balcony, Chacha raised his hand for a high-five. Adi was proud to notice that he did not even have to rise on tiptoes to clap Chacha's hand.

*

Lajpat Nagar market was a fantastical mess of shops selling nearly everything he could imagine, and many things that he could not. Nearly half of it was dedicated to women's clothes, saris and skirts and lehangas and sequinned dresses, all glimmering like Shahjahan's treasure hall in the winter sun. In the other half, there were shops selling everything from Darjeeling tea and Swiss chocolate to Christmas lights from China.

The real treasures, however, were found not in the shops but in the spaces between them, laid out upon mats on the broken pavements. There were tubs full of water with metal boats that rattled round and round, propelled by a little fire burning inside each one. There were old men who walked around blowing into loops of wire, creating streams of soap bubbles that floated over the market like a cloud of rainbows. There were puppeteers who made tiny wooden dancers leap and twirl on invisible strings, and there were Pied Pipers carrying trees of flutes, playing tunes that travelled right through the sound and fury of the market and wormed their way into your head.

And then there was the food. Every narrow street was a battlefield of clashing smells – bright red carrot halva simmering in great flat pans, golgappas dripping with water so tangy it made your eyes pop, unending coils of jalebis frying golden, and the great Ram Laddoos of Amritsar – fried dough balls topped with shredded radish and tangy green chutney, served in a cup made of dried leaves. Those alone made the trip worthwhile.

'Adi? Where are you?' came Ma's frantic call, and he scanned the crowd.

This was the only problem. In an afternoon spent in Lajpat Nagar, you could bump into more people than lived in some countries. A Saturday afternoon was better than a Sunday or a festival day, but there were still so many people that they could not take more than three steps without stopping, and Ma kept asking him to stay close, chiding him each time he paused to look at one of the shops.

'Ma!' he yelled, waving his arm, until Chacha spotted him and they came weaving through the crowd.

'Don't stop like that, béta!' Ma scowled at him. 'We'll never find you if you get lost here.'

'I'll find you.'

'Don't argue, Adi. It can be dangerous in these places, you don't know what kinds of people—'

'Then give me a hundred rupees,' he said. 'If I get lost, I'll take an auto-rickshaw and go home.'

Chacha grinned at Ma, impressed and she smiled too. His father would have probably asked him if he thought hundred rupee notes grew on trees.

'Oh, you found something interesting?' said Chacha, noticing the shop that had caught Adi's attention. It was a small music shop, its display full of audio cassettes and stereo sets and sparkling Sony Walkmans.

'For Chachi's nephew. I thought . . . a Walkman?'

'Good idea!'

'I'll be here,' said Ma, already heading to the shoe store next door as they went in.

After examining all the Walkmans, from the silver Panasonics to knock-off Aiwas, they settled on a Sony. It had a metallic blue case with a see-through flap and the prized Rewind function, so you didn't have to flip the cassette and forward it then flip it again, just to hear a song twice. It was what Mikki spent half the recess doing.

'Now, which cassettes should we get?' Chacha asked, and Adi found himself dumbstruck. It made sense – you couldn't just gift an empty Walkman to someone – but he had no idea how to even begin choosing music. The walls were stacked floor to ceiling with cassettes, divided into dozens of categories. Considering Chachi's nephew was American, he could skip over most of the wall filled with Bollywood classics and go right to Western Pop & Rock. He only knew the well-known ones – Bryan Adams, Backstreet Boys, Madonna, Michael Jackson – the same ones that played on repeat on iTV. There was no point guessing, he realised, what someone half the world away may like. He had to pick something he himself liked, something he would have been happy to rewind endlessly and there was only one such thing he could think of.

'This,' he said, reaching for the 'Latest Arrivals' shelf.

'Savage Garden,' Chacha nodded. 'I hear it's good.'

He smiled, marvelling at the fact that Chacha listened to this kind of music, that he didn't find it obscene, or 'too noisy', like his father did.

Chacha paid an eye-popping amount of money for the Walkman and the cassette – more than a thousand rupees, by Adi's count of the notes he handed over – and they walked out with a blue plastic bag. He thought of offering to carry the bag just so he could feel the weight of it, pretend that he had bought the Walkman for himself, but he couldn't bring himself to say it. It seemed a little sad, a tad childish.

Outside, Ma was haggling with the shoe seller and Chacha joined in, saying he had just seen the same pair a few shops down selling at half the price. Ma accused the shopkeeper of trying to fool women, and the shopkeeper swore on his head that he was making zero profit on the shoes. As they went on in circles, Adi turned to Rama Book Depot. It had a table set out in front of the shop, full of comic books – way more than his neighbourhood magazine-vala. There were piles of brand-new *Archie Double Digests* and proper, magazine-sized DC comics, but his attention was caught by a small stack at the back. *Tintin.*

There were only a handful of them, so he did not have much hope of finding the one he had spent years waiting for. But it was right there, second from the top: *Explorers on the Moon.* He stood holding it in his hands like it was a magical object, an apparition that could vanish in a blink.

'How much for that?' Chacha's voice came up from behind him.

'Hundred and fifty, sahib,' said the bookseller.

Chacha reached over and handed him a bundle of cash, and the man frowned at the money, perplexed.

'We'll take all five,' Chacha said.

The bookseller sprang up, stuffed all the books in a plastic bag, and handed it over to Adi with a grin. Adi took the bag and looked at Chacha, then Ma, scarcely believing what was happening.

'What, Hero? You thought we would go home without getting you a gift too?'

'You're too much, Mohan,' said Ma, shaking her head but smiling.

'Not at all, Bhabhi. There is no better use of money than buying books.'

'Say thank you to Chacha, béta,' Ma said to him, like he was a toddler. He smiled at Chacha and opened his mouth, but he was not able to say a word.

*

As they got out of the taxi, Adi rushed to pick up the shopping bags, making sure to get the Walkman, and the comics which were even heavier. Chacha carried the bronze Ganesha statue he had bought for his father and walked ahead with Ma, continuing the story he had been telling her about some distant relative's daughter who had gone to boarding school in England and fallen in love with a Pakistani boy.

'—And I just heard, they are getting married next year.'

'*Good* for her,' Ma said. 'Good to know that some people can still fly out of their cages.'

'You're right,' Chacha laughed, in a way that did not mock the seriousness of her statement, yet preserved the lightness of the moment. 'Maybe you should send this Hero off too,' he said, winking at Adi. 'I'm sure he'll get a scholarship, he's a sharp one.'

Ma laughed and nodded, but gave Chacha a meaningful look that Adi could not decipher. He couldn't understand why they were talking about sending him off to boarding school – it was something only his father ever said, usually as a threat – and he worked his brain to come up with a way to change the topic.

'Bhaiya?' Chacha called out, and they all stopped.

His father was rushing down the stairs with his car keys, still in the white kurta-pajama he wore for his visits to the temple. He looked over them, examining their shopping bags, but did not say a word.

'Is everything okay?' said Ma.

'Where were you?' His father's voice was calm, almost resigned, but it still carried the sting of accusation.

'We just went to the market to buy a few things,' said Ma.

'I was going to drop these off and go to the hospital,' Chacha added.

'They called,' said his father, looking at Adi. 'They have been calling all day.'

In the silence between them – in his father's eyes downcast and tired, no longer glowering with rage and in the gasp that Ma tried to swallow – he knew something terrible had happened. He knew, somehow, before he even realised it, that Amma was gone.

'Wait, Bhaiya. I'll come with you.'

Ma took the box from Chacha as his father turned and walked to his car. Adi thought of offering to come along. He would have insisted on it, if only his father had not given him that look. It seemed to hover over him now, making his hands, with their bags full of fancy gifts, shiver in the sudden chill. He wondered if it was all his fault; if he had been too selfish, too stupid. He had tried to escape from reality, to construct a fiction, if only for an afternoon, where Ma was happy and he had all the comic books he wanted and his father was nowhere in sight. Did he really think he could get away with it? He had spent a day laughing, daring to dream. Now, perhaps, he would have to pay for it.

*

Chacha and his father left for the hospital, and Adi came home with Ma and waited for the phone to ring. After quickly making him some Maggi, Ma grabbed her maroon handbag and told Adi she was going to the hospital too. He wanted nothing more than to go with her, but he simply nodded.

He sat with the plate of noodles gone cold and flicked through the channels playing the same old shows and movies. His attention was focused on the phone, however, and he could not hear anything but the throbbing silence, the absence of the phone's shrill, needy ring.

Turning the TV off, he pulled the curtains aside and stepped out onto the balcony. The cold evening air brought some relief, cutting through his thin sweater and jolting him into life.

'You there?'

'Greetings, Mr Sharma. How are you today?'

He found the vulture perched on a different roof this time, closer than the one it usually preferred.

'I did it. I made Ma happy.'

'Oh, very good. Why your face is hanging then?'

'Huh?'

'You made Ma happy, you say. Then why you are looking like your buffalo has gone in the water?'

'I made her happy for a little while. But now I think she's going to be sad again.'

'Of course, Mr Sharma, you cannot expect to keep her happy through seven lives. Even your great gods cannot do such a thing. Making someone happy even for one moment is a great achievement.'

'It's also,' Adi hesitated, unsure how to articulate his current, debilitating fear. 'I think Amma may be in trouble. Because we went to the market and there was no one to answer the phone so when the hospital called there was—'

'Hold, please, Mr Sharma. You are confusing me. You think your Amma is having problems because you went to a market?'

'No. I mean, if we had been at home when the hospital called—'

'Yes? What, then? What were you going to do? Go and become doctors, is it? She is in the hospital already, they will take care of it.'

'I guess. It just, it felt like I did something wrong.'

'Mr Sharma.' The vulture sighed and took on a kinder, softer tone. 'You are feeling guilty because you think that you are not allowed to feel happy, that you do not deserve any joy. You fear that by being happy, you will anger your gods, that they will send you a special magic curse in return for every smile.'

Adi frowned, confused by the vulture's words that seemed absurd, yet somehow made all the sense in the world.

'Believe me,' the vulture nodded slowly, 'we vultures have seen the world, we have watched all of history, we are the keepers of mankind's memories, and let me tell you, our entire Historical Archive is nothing but sorrow and pain. When you get a chance to be happy, even for one second, you must grab it with both hands.' The bird lifted one leg, its long fingers ending in thick, black claws curved like sickles, glinting in the grey night like crescent swords. 'You are understanding?'

'Yeah,' Adi shrugged, trying his best not to sound impressed, even though the vulture had lifted his mood more than he had expected.

'Good,' said the vulture. 'You were afraid that your Ma will never be happy again, but you gave her one whole day of happiness. When one is stuck in a hopeless situation, it is an act of great courage just to smile. And it is an even greater achievement to make someone else smile. I am thinking, Mr Sharma, it is time to see your next file.'

He was tired, hungry, desperate to sleep, but he knew he was going to spend all his time lying in bed and waiting for them to return, while dreading it at the same time. It was better to keep his mind occupied, just so he could stop it from replaying all the imagined accusations in his father's eyes.

'Okay.'

Adi leant against the balcony door and took a deep breath and closed his eyes.

DHA/HA/TS/1977(4)

The first thing that strikes him, as he looks around in the darkness, is that piercing, persistent chatter of crickets he remembers from his childhood. From the inky black fields rises a two-storey bungalow, its balconies and porches lit by lanterns. Hallowed by a yellow glow in the thick, humid air, it reminds him of bhoot bungalows – the haunted houses in B-grade films with hunchbacked caretakers and creaking doors – and it makes his arms tickle with goosebumps.

Most of the windows are shut except one, which is covered by a fine mosquito net. As he leans forward, his gaze zooms right in, bringing him to the windowsill. On the far side of the room lies a long sofa running the length of the wall, and on it are two men sitting far apart from each other, like patients waiting at a doctor's office. One of them is Adi's father. The other is Dada, his father's father.

He looks around the room he vaguely remembers. It is a large hall with high ceilings and ornately carved furniture, lit by a giant chandelier that casts soft shadows around the walls. On the other side, opposite the sofa, there is a large black-and-white TV sitting in a wooden cabinet, the face of a news-reader with thick, black-framed spectacles flickering on its curved screen. A sprawling red carpet separates the TV and the sofa, like a bloody sea flecked by little white flowers, and Adi finds its patterns mesmerising. Staring at it, he realises that the carpet is falling apart, its threads fraying all around the edges, many of its flowers rubbed out from years of trampling by careless feet. The entire room is in a state of disrepair, he can make out now, the furniture and the dim lights unable to hide the cracked plaster on the walls. The whole house has the air of a once proud palace eaten hollow by the years, its vaulted ceilings waiting to fall.

With a deep breath, he turns back to his father. It really is him. It is not just the difference in the physical appearance – the slim, muscular frame and the head full of wavy hair – that makes him unrecognisable. Those things Adi has seen in old photographs from his parents' wedding and their honeymoon in Kashmir. What he has never seen is the look in his father's eyes, afraid yet hopeful, like someone impatient for his future – like a child. His father looks at the time on a tall, wooden tower, with a long pendulum swinging gently under a glass-domed clock. It is the same clock they have at home, Adi realises, minus the pendulum – his inheritance, ticking away the tense moments.

He turns to Dada, who looks nothing like his father, not even at his father's present-day age. He is tall and broad-shouldered and his face has a stern, angular look with lips pursed in a thin line, like a military general who only opens his mouth to give orders. He sits bolt upright on the sofa, his feet flat on the floor and his head held high. Leaning next to him is a cane topped with a silver handle that glitters in the pale light. It is the only thing in the room that has not lost its shine.

Ma's voice jolts Adi out of his trance and he looks around desperately. It is her voice, he has no doubt about it. She seems to be moaning in pain but he can't see her anywhere. He leans out to look at the house again, and nearly opens his eyes when the vulture whispers in his ear: 'Patience, Mr Sharma.'

There is nothing to see outside. The house stands still in the quiet night, all its doors and windows shut. He peers into the room again. Dada says something and his father gets up and walks across the room, and turns the volume up on the TV.

'—*Prime Minister Indira Gandhi submitted her resignation to the President today. The new government is expected to be sworn in*—'

Dada shakes his head slowly, his jaw set tight, and finally, Adi sees the resemblance to his father.

'One strong leader we had in this country, but all these illiterates . . .' Dada trails off as his father sits still, biting his lip. Somewhere in the house, Ma's voice is getting louder, more pained.

'—*with the revocation of the Emergency, fundamental rights of citizens have been restored, including the right to freedom of speech and expression, the right to assemble peaceably without arms, the right to move freely through the territory of India*—'

Ma's voice rings out again, drowning out the TV. It is a scream now, drawn out and tired, and Adi remembers where he has heard it before. From Nani, when she was giving birth to Ma.

'Is Ma having a baby?'

'Yes, Mr Sharma. Please pay attention.'

'So . . . this is my birth?'

'As you can see from the very exciting news on the TV, this is before your time.'

'Before my time? But . . . how can Ma be . . .'

A double door at the end of the room flies open and a woman walks in, holding a baby in her arms. It is crying in the way that babies cry, like the world is about to end.

The woman is Amma, Adi realises with a shock. She is wearing a bright yellow sari and is bedecked with gold jewellery, her ears and nose and neck and wrists all glinting as she strides across the room. His father gets up but she holds out a hand to stop him and turns towards the window. Adi lets out a little gasp as she looks right at him, her eyes glowering with a fury that he just cannot equate with his frail little Amma. Can age really do this to people, he wonders – suck the life out of someone's eyes, leaving pale, clouded marbles in place of blinding suns?

Amma is looking at someone squatting just below the window, he realises. A short, dark man with cropped grey hair rises to his feet, wearing a pale blue shirt over a faded white dhoti. It is probably a servant, Adi reckons, seeing the way he stands before Amma, his chest shrunken and his back hunched, like he has spent a lifetime bowing before her. Amma says something that Adi can't catch and hands the baby over to the man. The servant, chewing something behind blackened lips, looks at the wailing child with bloodshot eyes but says nothing.

'Wait!' his father interrupts, looking at Dada, but Amma warns him with a forbidding finger. 'How?' his father yells, more confused than angry. 'We did the test, the ultrasound—'

'She lied!' Amma hisses, her eyes burning red. 'Lies, all lies. The whole village knows we are expecting a grandson. But your woman has made a fool of us, had our nose cut off in the community. The honour of the whole house she has scattered in the dirt. We cannot live with this shame!' She sneers at the baby, who is crying even louder now, as if to compete with her, and Adi realises that Amma is using 'we' for 'I', just like she still does.

'No!' Amma turns back to his father, her head shaking slowly, her locked jaw grinding out her words. 'Either you let us take care of this right now, or we swear upon Shiva Mahadeva, we will eat poison and end our life right now.'

His father stands speechless, stunned and shrunken. Dada's eyes are still on the TV, as if nothing else is happening before him, but his fingers are wrapped tightly around the silver handle on his cane, extinguishing the only spark in the room.

'Move, Kusésar!' Amma pushes the servant towards the door and follows him out, leaving the cavernous room echoing with the baby's shrill, urgent cry.

*

Ma's screams have stopped now and Adi strains to listen. Doors slam somewhere in the house and he can make out women's voices, whispering words he can't pick apart. He leans out again and looks around the bungalow. All the windows are still shut, the hairline gaps between their wooden slats glinting with secrets, and he leans in to check each one, hoping to find a crack wide enough to peer through.

The sound of footsteps draws his attention away to the side of the house. A metal door clangs open and the servant walks out. The baby is still in his arms, Adi can tell, though it has stopped crying. Swaddled in layers of cloth, it is no longer even moving.

Walking slowly across the dark, featureless land, the servant goes up to a small shed and lights a lantern. As the flame flickers and grows, it reveals a pile of tools and farming equipment inside the shed. The servant picks up a large earthen mutka, the kind used to keep water cool in the summer. Gently, he drops his black bundle into the pot, and ties a cloth around the gaping mouth of the vessel. He then takes the pot and walks around the shed, the lantern spilling pale yellow puddles across the flat fields. He finds what he is looking for, sets the lantern down and lowers the pot. It disappears into the ground. Picking up a shovel, he begins to toss black earth over it, covering up the hole that has already been dug.

In the house, Ma screams out with such bone-chilling ferocity that Adi can't help but yelp himself. The servant stops and turns towards the house. Beyond the closed windows of the bhoot bungalow, Ma goes on howling, her animal cry silencing the crickets and toads and curdling the darkness around the house into a thick, black soup that seems impossible to escape. The servant spits out a stream of paan juice, and it glimmers deep red in the glow of the lantern. There is nothing to see, so he turns and carries on shovelling.

15.

A mound of grey ashes,
a cloud of stinking smoke

'The Nigambodh Ghat is the oldest funeral ground in Delhi,' said the pundit. 'Thousands of years ago, Lord Brahma was caught in a conundrum. He was cursed by the Holy Yamuna, *yes*, and lost all of his wisdom and his memory. As we know, Brahma is the creator of the *Vedas* and lord of all knowledge, so the curse meant that the *Vedas* were also lost. Finally, when Yamuna-ji forgave Brahma, he came and took a dip in the waters right here, *yes*,' he pointed towards the steps leading down to the river, 'and so the wisdom of the *Vedas* was restored to this world.'

As the pundit smiled, all the people gathered around him nodded solemnly, perhaps wondering if they were meant to clap. Adi couldn't help but shake his head. It was not just that it made no sense to tell fantastical tales at such an occasion, but the story itself was nonsensical. Why was Brahma cursed by a *river*? Why was he forgiven? Why had he not written down the *Vedas* if he was so smart?

'We will now begin the last rites of,' the pundit glanced at a piece of paper, 'Shrimati Shakuntala Sharma. Her sons Mohan and Mahesh Sharma are with us today, to send their mother's soul to the Supreme Soul. We pray that she is liberated from the endless cycle of birth and death, *yes*, and finds Moksha by becoming one with the Creator. The men can follow me to the pyre, the ladies can stay here.'

'Pundit-ji?' Chacha raised his hand. 'We would like the women of our family to be present for the last rites.'

'Oh.' The pundit nodded – or shook his head, it was hard to tell. 'As you wish. I only said because most people still follow the old traditions. But,' he smiled a tired smile, 'the times are changing, we must adjust to modern ways, *yes*?'

Chacha did not say anything, and his father simply walked off. They had had a fight earlier in the morning about the type of cremation for Amma.

'What do you think about the electric crematorium, Bhaiya?' That was all that Chacha had said. His father had taken two sips of his chai and exploded.

'Can we not even give our mother a proper Hindu cremation? For thousands of years we have followed our traditions and now they are too dirty? You know what those Muslims do on Eid, butchering goats on the streets? Nobody ever blames them for the filth. Why is that only Hindus should always feel ashamed of our rituals?'

'I was just saying,' Chacha mumbled into his teacup. 'Just that it creates a little less pollution, but never mind—'

'O-ho-ho!' his father laughed his chilling laugh. 'For thousands of years we have cremated people and the air has been tip-top. Suddenly it is all our fault?'

'No one is saying—'

'Do you know how much pollution your flight from America created? If you were so worried about the air, you should have stayed there.'

Chacha decided not to say anything as his father left the table with a smirk, shaking his head. They had not said a word to each other since then.

*

The pyre was set up on a concrete platform overlooking the lifeless waters of the Yamuna. It was marked number 21 in a long series of similar platforms, many of them in different stages of the cremation process with men arranging wooden logs or poking heaps of smouldering ashes with long sticks. Down by the riverbank, there were a few more pyres burning, looking like crude copies of the ones up above, some of them surrounded by crowds of people in crumpled white clothes. Every once in a while, the breeze blew the smoke up towards the concrete pyres, making the people above cover their mouths and noses with their starched handkerchiefs. It didn't really matter, thought Adi. The sharp, sour stench of the black river overpowered everything, cursing the ones above and below just the same.

Amma was laid out upon a pyramid of wooden logs, dressed in a gold-bordered white sari and garlanded with yellow flowers. He had not seen her since the night in the hospital – his father and Chacha had made the arrangements for the funeral, and she had been brought over in a van directly from the hospital early in the morning. Ma, along with some distant aunties, had given Amma a bath and dressed her in a new sari. Now, she looked better than she ever had at home, even though she wasn't even wearing her teeth. For the first time since she had come to stay with them, she did not look like she was in pain. Her face was shiny, almost radiant, and her lips, though pursed taut, seemed to curve in a gentle smile.

He could not bear to look at that smile.

The pundit invited Chacha and his father to step up to the platform and finish building the pyre, laying lighter logs over Amma until she was completely covered. His father, being the elder son, was handed the flaming torch to set the pyre alight. He stepped up to where Amma's head was, and paused. He turned and nodded to Chacha, who rushed up and stood next to him, bowing slightly. There were tears in both their eyes, Adi could see. His father turned to Adi and nodded, inviting him up, but he pretended not to see him. When Ma nudged him, he finally stepped forward and joined his father and Chacha, adding his hand to the torch. If anyone was going to set fire to Amma, it should have been Ma, he thought, but that was perhaps a little too far even for the modernising pundit.

The three of them leant as one and touched the torch to the spots the pundit pointed out as he chanted his Sanskrit mantras. Slowly they circled the pyre, bending, touching, retreating, watching the wood sputter and catch, its crackling bursts echoing in the solemn silence like Divali firecrackers. In the end, at the same spot where they had begun, they bent and blessed Amma's head with fire.

They stepped back from the pyre, joining the circle of relatives and friends, and watched in silence as the orange flames leapt from log to log, burning so hot that Adi could feel his skin tingling. When the smoke grew thick and floating bits of ash began to rain down on their heads, the pundit asked everyone to retreat to the prayer hall and leave Amma in peace. It was going to take the whole night for the fire to die down and the ashes to cool, which were then to be immersed into the holy waters of the Ganga. The prayer meeting was to take place after that, on the thirteenth day. For now, there was nothing more to be done.

The guests started dispersing quietly, nodding their condolences to his father and Ma and Chacha with folded hands and forced smiles. When the last of the relatives had left and the pundit had been paid, the four of them started walking towards the parking lot – his father leading the way, Ma and Chacha walking side-by-side behind him, and Adi trying to keep up. As they turned towards the exit, he stopped for one last look at Amma.

He did not want to go home. He wanted to stand right there and watch the fire grow higher and hotter. Knowing what he now did about Amma, he wanted to make sure that all that was left of her was a mound of grey ashes, a cloud of stinking smoke. He would never, ever understand how Ma had agreed to have Amma in her home, to take care of that woman when her own sons would not, to bathe and dress her even after she was *dead*. How could one even begin to forgive a person like that? No, some people did not deserve to be forgiven, he decided; they deserved to burn slowly, polluting the air just as they had poisoned lives.

And yet, he could not stop the tears. Had he really developed a fondness for Amma that was hard to let go of, even now? Had he grown so used to having her in the house – of reheating her lunch and telling her the time every half hour and secretly treating her to rasgullas – that he could not bear to have her taken away? Or was it just that he was growing up and realising what it really meant for someone to be dead: that everyone would one day be dead, everyone you loved and hated, the ones you prayed for and the ones you cursed, until all that would remain was you.

Ma came up and put an arm around his shoulder, and he realised what it was. He found it so hard to leave because he knew that Amma's death was going to change things. At first, he had blamed her for disrupting their lives and awakening the old demons. Now, he knew better. In a way, Amma had been the only thing keeping their family together, deflecting his parents from each other, taking up all the time that could otherwise be turned against themselves. Now that she was gone, the old emptiness awaited them again, and he was afraid of what might be coming to fill it.

16.

Peace?

'Mohan?' Ma knocked on Chacha's door (Amma's door) and waited.

Adi could hear the shower crackling in the bathroom down the corridor, but he did not say anything. His father had bathed already and changed into his saffron kurta to do his puja, but he was sitting in front of the TV instead, watching the news.

'—*Former finance minister Manmohan Singh could be a possible PM candidate . . . known for his honesty, simplicity and non-controversial nature*—'

'Hah,' said his father. 'Sardaar-ji will never be PM as long as the Gandhis are in control. They think it is their birthright to rule this country.'

'Mohan?' Ma knocked again. 'Will you have some tea?'

'Arré, ask us also,' his father said. 'We, too, can have some tea.'

Adi turned a page in his book. Captain Haddock was drunk in outer space.

The bathroom door opened and Chacha came out, rubbing his head with a towel. 'Sorry, Bhabhi. I was having a bath.'

Ma turned and laughed. 'Oh, I didn't realise . . . will you have some tea?'

'Yes, please. Thank you.'

Please, thank you, sorry – it was nice to hear those things in the house, Adi thought. Especially when they were said to Ma. She was owed more pleases, thank yous and sorrys than he and his father could ever give her.

'You sit, I will bring it.' Ma led Chacha to the drawing room and went off into the kitchen. Adi looked up to find Chacha standing at the edge of the room, looking at his father whose face had grown tense but was still focused on the TV.

'Chacha,' said Adi. 'Do you use email?'

'Yes, Hero.' Chacha came and sat next to him on the divan, smelling of American soap, of how Adi imagined snow to smell. 'Do you use it too?'

'Yes. We learnt it in school.'

They had not – he only said it so that his father would not get suspicious about him using the PC at home. All they were taught in computers class were useless things like DOS commands. One morning, when the teacher had left them alone to revise for exams, Mikki had shown him how to set up an email account.

'Oh, very good. What's your email address?'

'Um, that . . . I don't remember.'

As a joke, Mikki had given him grandmasterpaadi@ hotmail.com and told him to create a new one later. He had not yet had the chance to do it.

'No problem,' said Chacha, and fished out his wallet. He opened it and took out a business card. Dr Mohan Sharma, it

243

said, followed by some abbreviations, a Chicago, IL address, a phone number, a fax number and an email address.

'You can send me an email there and I will get your address.'

Adi nodded, but he was distracted by Chacha's open wallet. In it, he could see a thin stack of long, green banknotes – US dollars!

Chacha saw him looking and asked if he wanted to see a dollar 'bill'. Before he could nod, he was holding in his fingers a slim, crisp twenty-dollar note. It had '20' in each corner in big, bold circles, and on top, 'The United States of America' and 'In God We Trust'. There was a sketch of the White House that seemed extraordinarily detailed. Adi thought of getting his old magnifying glass to examine it more closely but thought better of it and handed the note back.

'Keep it, Hero.' Chacha thumped Adi's back. 'Buy me a coffee when you come to America.'

Looking back at the note, Adi thought of the places he could hide it, to keep it stiff and spotless until the day he went to America. Of all the gifts Chacha had brought him over the years, this one, he decided, was his all-time number one favourite.

'Give it back, Adi.'

His father was still staring at the TV and, for a moment, Adi wondered if he had really heard the words. It had been his father's voice, he was sure, but he did sometimes hear that voice in his head, usually when he was about to fall asleep. He wondered now if his brain was playing tricks on him again.

'It's okay, Bhaiya,' said Chacha, and Adi knew it was not just him. 'It's only—'

'I said give it *back*! Can't you hear?'

'No,' he wanted to say. '*No!*' he wanted to scream in his father's face. But there was something different, this time, about the fury in his father's eyes.

He handed the note back to Chacha. Was that all it took to turn him back into a child? A blustering bark, a flash of fangs.

Chacha held the note in his hands, turning it around carefully, like it was something dangerous, like its razor edges could slice through skin and bone. Adi knew Chacha was going to say something – he knew it was a bad idea to say anything, anything at all, when his father was like this – but he could do nothing to stop it.

'Tea is ready,' Ma called out as she walked in from the kitchen, carrying a tray with three of the fragile, flowery teacups reserved for guests. 'Adi, clear the table. See, your books are everywhere. That's what happens during every vacation,' she rolled her eyes at Chacha. 'And when school opens, he will run around the house trying to find all of them. Come, béta, make some room.'

Adi got up and collected his books, and Ma set the tray down on the table.

'Suddenly it's so cold, na?' said Ma, stirring sugar into the cups. 'Looks like Chicago's air has followed you all the way here, Mohan.'

No one laughed. It was hopeless.

'If you have a problem with me, Bhaiya,' Chacha looked his father straight in the eyes, 'then say it to my face. Enough of these crooked comments.'

Fuck-shit-tuttee, Adi shook his head. That was it. Chacha had made the ultimate mistake. The only way to deal with his father's fits of rage, as Ma did so well, was to indulge him a little and let him exhaust himself on silly things – rants about the Congress Party and the Muslims, snide remarks about Ma's cooking or Adi's unkempt hair or general grumpiness about all that was wrong in the world. Never had Adi seen him challenged like that, like a bully being poked in the belly.

'O-ho, leave it,' said Ma. 'We have all had a long day. I'll make dinner early and we can get some rest.'

'No, Bhabhi.' Chacha's voice was stern yet respectful. 'I want to hear it.'

'You don't want to hear anything.' His father gave the TV a sneering half-smile. 'You just want to hear that you are a successful doctor, a very big man from America who comes here once in five years and hands out dollars to poor people.'

'Arré, it's only a little gift, Bhaiya. Can I not give—?'

'You want to hear,' his father continued, louder, 'that you are richer, more educated, more cultured than us backward people. That you can come and tell us how to live our lives and we should join our hands and thank you for it. And you want to hear,' he finally looked at Chacha, 'that you would be a better father to my son, a better husband to my wife. And you know why? I can tell you why, psychiatrist sahib. It is because, to this day, you haven't accepted your defeat.'

Defeat? Adi looked up at Chacha, at Ma. They were both shaking their heads.

'Listen,' Ma whispered. 'Not now, Adi is—'

246

'No-no, why not? Let your son hear it, he is old enough. Yes, *Hero*.' He smiled at Adi – a smile that seemed to have the power to shrink him back into a scared little child. 'Do you know your Chacha wanted to marry your Ma?'

'That is not true,' Chacha said, but he was ignored.

'Yes, we were all together in the same college,' his father continued. 'These two were pukka friends, always together, always chatting chapar-chapar in the library while I was busy studying. But when the offer for marriage came, guess whom it was for?' He leant back on the sofa, beaming with pride.

Adi looked at Ma. She was looking at his father in a way that scared him – not because she looked angry, or even sad, but because she looked like she had had enough of it, like she was wondering why she sat there every day and listened to this drivel. Why she didn't just walk away, once and for all.

'It's true.' Chacha turned to Adi. 'Your Ma chose your father, and I was happy for both of them. She and I were just friends, we never wanted to get married. I always wanted to go abroad and study, and she wanted to——'

'Buss. Enough,' Ma hissed, barely loud enough to be heard, but it made the two of them shut up.

She sat quietly for a while, staring at the teacups sitting untouched on the table and Adi could hear the ticking of the ancient clock in the hallway.

'Both of you think you know what I wanted, just like my father,' she said, her eyes closed. 'But who has ever asked me? Papa was going to arrange my marriage with some village boy from Punjab. All he asked was if there was anyone I had in

247

mind. You two were the only boys I knew then, and you,' she gestured at Chacha, 'you had your eyes on America. So I was left with you.'

She turned to his father. 'If I had to get married, I figured it would be better to go for someone I knew. What do they say, the known devil is better than the unknown angel?' She shook her head and snorted. 'I suppose I should be grateful that I at least got that choice. Not many do.'

Adi glanced at his father and found him, for the first time, looking truly heartbroken.

'But, Bhabhi . . .' Chacha hesitated. 'If you didn't want to get married—?'

Ma chuckled at this, her eyes scrunched up like she was genuinely amused. 'My father was a saint in many ways. He always encouraged me to study, to go to college, but he knew he was not going to last long. All those cigarettes he smoked, he knew he would have to pay their debt one day. He didn't think I could survive without him, a helpless woman all on her own.'

'I remember Uncle-ji,' said Chacha, smiling. 'He was a very progressive man.'

'Even progressive men have their limits, when it comes to their own daughters.'

'But,' Chacha persisted, 'he may have understood, if you had told him. I didn't know him very well, but I remember him as the kindest man I ever met.'

Adi saw what Chacha was doing, trying to brighten up Ma's mood by talking about Nana, and he was impressed that

Chacha had figured out the trick that only he knew. It didn't seem to be working, however. There was a smile playing on Ma's lips, but, once again, it was the wrong kind of smile.

'The world works differently for you and I, Mohan,' she said, her voice low and tired. 'For you it is easy. You know what you want, you go and get it. Now, you are in America, the land of the free. Your world is so big, so full of choices. Here, the world is different. It was always smaller for me than it was for you, and it has only grown smaller with time. From a lecture hall to a bedroom to a kitchen, to cleaning bedpans in a toilet – that is how the world shrinks for a woman.

'What does it matter what I wanted? If I had wanted to go abroad, become a doctor, have my own house and fly around the world like it was no more than a bus ride, so what? I wanted a mother too, did I get that? Wanting things is a luxury I learnt long ago to live without.'

There was a long silence and Adi stopped himself from turning a page in his book. His father continued to gaze at the TV still playing the news. It was talking about Pakistan expelling an Indian diplomat for spying, but he did not react at all to it. Chacha had put the twenty dollar note away and was now fiddling with his ring, turning it slowly around his finger. Ma went on staring at the tea, and Adi wondered if she was most sad about that. She had sweated in the kitchen to make the tea and now it had gone cold, covered in wrinkled brown skin that spread across its surface like moss on a placid lake.

'You never told me,' said his father, his voice down to a whisper.

Ma dabbed the corner of her eye with the end of her sari and took a deep breath. 'I never told you because it did not matter. When I married you, I devoted myself to you. All I wanted after that was a daughter of my own, so I could give her the choices that were never given to me. But you could not even let me have that.'

It was a reference to what he had seen in the last memory, Adi realised. He looked at his father but there was not the slightest trace of remorse on his face.

'That was Amma's doing, you know that. You know how she used to be. You think I don't regret what happened? I never forgave her.'

'And what good did that do? You did nothing when I needed you and when she was old and bedridden, you became a babbar shér, a brave lion roaring in his den. Who was left to take care of her, then?'

'Arré, I told you we could send her to that old people's ashram! You insisted on bringing her home.'

'No,' Ma shook her head. 'You can never abandon your family. Never.'

'Why do you blame me, then? If *you* couldn't let her go, even after what she did—'

'I don't care about what *she* did, Mahesh!' And Adi nearly fainted; he had never heard Ma say his father's name out loud, not once. 'I married *you*, not her. I walked seven times around the holy fire with *you*. I needed *you* to be on my side.'

His father was quiet for a moment, but Adi saw the drops

of shame slowly hardening back into anger. 'What does the fire matter to you?' he sneered. 'You're not even a Hindu.'

Peering between the pages of his book, Adi held his breath as his father's words circled the room.

'Yes, and you are the avatar of Lord Ram yourself,' replied Ma, laughing. *Laughing!* 'After all, that's what the *Ramayana* has taught you, isn't it? Being suspicious of your own wife, treating your own children worse than orphans.'

He did not dare to look up at his father, certain that he was going to start screaming and throwing things at any moment.

'Let me ask you just one thing, Bhabhi.' Chacha's voice was like a splash of rain on a burning afternoon. 'What do you think will give you some peace, now?'

'Peace?' she laughed. 'I have looked for peace everywhere. I have gone to temples, gurudwaras, mosques, churches. Every day for the last few months, I have been going to the ashrams of gurus and babas, listening to their sermons and singing their songs. And still, every night I see them in my dreams – my dead mother, my lost sister, my murdered daughter. You tell me, Mohan, you are the expert. What will give me peace?'

It was the first time he had ever heard Ma talk to Chacha like that, almost challenging him to a fight. Chacha, however, looked unfazed. He pushed his glasses up and nodded quietly, as if he was just a doctor noting down a patient's complaint.

'And you, Bhaiya?' Chacha turned to his father. 'What about you? What will give you some peace?'

'Me?' his father said, as though he were being accused of a crime. 'I am completely at peace.'

Ma scoffed and rolled her eyes, and Adi felt a sudden, irrepressible urge to giggle. He bit his tongue, hard, and winced, waiting to taste blood.

'All I wanted,' said his father, raising his voice to mask the embarrassment of being laughed at. '*All* I wanted was the truth. But all I have got, from day one, are *lies*. Lies about who she is, where she has come from, who her parents are. Can you blame Amma, really? She thought she was marrying her son to a Brahmin girl from a good family and then we find out, on the *wedding day*, that leave aside Brahmin, she may not even be a Hindu! Is she a Sikh? Is she a Mussalman? She herself does not know.'

'You found out because I told you,' said Ma. 'And I told you as soon as I found out. How was I supposed to know, my mother died before I—'

'Despite all that,' his father continued, ignoring Ma and addressing Chacha. '*Despite* all that, I *still* accepted her, you know this. I fought with Amma for her, but maybe that old woman was right, after all.'

'Look at that,' Ma smiled at Chacha. 'Even now he takes his mother's side. He lives in the house my father gave in dowry and says he "accepted" me. Wah! What a great favour—'

'I *wanted* to marry her,' his father roared. 'I stopped talking to my own mother for her. All I asked was that my own family respect me, tell me the truth from then on, but what do they do? They keep lying to me! They go running around like rats, hiding their secrets, talking to God knows who, thinking I am too stupid to notice.'

Adi felt his fingers go stiff. Did his father know about the vulture?

'The *truth*?' Ma yelled. 'What is the truth? You tell me the truth if you know it. That's what I have been trying to find out all these years, but that is also a problem for you. My mother and father lied to me too, you know. Now they are dead and there is no one left to ask. And your answer to everything is to forget it, never talk about it, bury it all like you buried my daughter. No, I'm not going to take it anymore, I—'

'I know,' said Adi, and the room fell silent.

He bit his lip and tried to breathe, and ages went by. Like Ma, he had had enough too. He could no longer sit around and stare at the TV and do nothing as Ma kept getting closer to leaving for good. He could not end up like his father.

'I know, Ma.' He looked up at her. 'I know what happened to Nana and Nani. And your sister, my Maasi . . . Kammo.'

Ma's hand flew over her mouth and his father frowned at him like he was talking gibberish.

'How?' was all Ma could manage to say.

How? He hadn't thought it through, he realised. Telling them that he had travelled back in time with a blabbering vulture would have definitely broken up their fight, but it would probably have taken him straight to the notorious mental asylum in Agra.

'He has been listening to our conversations, how else?' said his father.

'But I have never talked about Kammo, never in front of him!' Ma was still looking at Adi, her eyes wide with worry but also bright with awe.

'Children listen and observe things more closely than adults,' Chacha said to Ma. 'Maybe he remembers something you have forgotten? Something you or someone else, maybe your father, may have said long ago?' He turned to Adi and nodded, encouraging him to continue.

'I just . . . I know Kammo Maasi was in Punjab. In India.'

'No, Adi. Your Nana told me she was lost in Pakistan, before Partition, and they came here by themselves. Anyway, I have searched all over Punjab already. I went to Jalandhar and Amritsar long ago, when you were a child. I checked all the ashrams where the lost women were kept, just in case. There were no records of her. Then back in the summer, I found some distant relatives of your Nani, but they didn't know anything either.'

'Yes, but you checked in Pakistan too, didn't you? She wasn't there either.'

'That's true,' she said, looking down and lowering her voice, 'I went there because your Nani's relatives told me where to find her old in-laws, in Lahore. I found them, but they acted very rudely.'

Toshi's in-laws – they were the people from the first memory, he realised. The woman who doused her kids with kerosene. The old lady who chased Nani with a cane. The drunken Sardaar-ji with the sword. Some of them must have survived that night, or perhaps their children. Is that who he had spoken to on the phone? Just the thought of it was enough to make the hair on his neck tremble in terror.

'They don't know anything, Ma! They wanted to burn Nani and Kammo Maasi. And you, too! I'm telling you, Maasi was with Nana-Nani, with you, when you all came to India. She was kidnapped by the Sikhs and the Hindus, they had an army and they killed all the Muslim people and they made the little girls dance naked—'

'This is too much!' His father turned to Chacha. 'She has spent years chasing secrets and lies, now she has spoilt her son's brain also. I don't have time for this buckvaas.' He got up, tossing the remote on the sofa. 'I'm going to sleep.'

'Will you not eat?' said Ma. 'I was just going to—'

'I'm not hungry,' came the reply, followed by the banging of the door.

Chacha sighed and shook his head, and Ma did the same. The room immediately lightened with his father's departure and Adi knew that the conversation was over. What else could he have added anyway? It was not like he knew where exactly Kammo Maasi was, or if she was even alive.

'Don't worry, Bhabhi,' Chacha smiled at Ma. 'Sometimes, it can help to get these things out, it can make things better between the two of you.'

Adi glanced at him and wondered if he even believed it himself. Ma did not seem to be paying attention anyway. Her face was grey and heavy, her forehead etched with deep lines, and she was staring at him in a way that made him squirm.

'He is old enough now, you know?' Chacha said, as if reading her mind. 'He understands more than you think, you can tell him things.'

'*Yes! Yes! I'm old enough!*' Adi wanted to scream but stopped himself. After all, that would not have helped his case.

'I've tried, all these years,' Ma said, turning to Chacha. 'I've tried to protect him from my past, from my pain. Why should he have to suffer for our sins?'

'It's his past, too, Bhabhi. He will need to know, sooner or later.'

Ma looked at Adi again and nodded for what seemed like forever. Finally, she smiled: 'You must be hungry, béta. Shall I make you a sandwich?'

That was it, then. She was never going to treat him like a grown-up. He did not need her protection, could she not see? He was old enough to know more than she did. He was old enough to protect *her*.

'No,' he said, even though he was starving.

*

'Hero, are you awake?'

Adi opened his eyes to find Chacha standing before him in the drawing room, dressed in his long coat with his four-wheeled suitcase next to him.

'Listen.' Chacha sat down on the divan. All Adi wanted to do was turn over and go back to sleep. Why did everyone have to keep *leaving*?

'I know you are worried about your Ma and Papa. I have known them for a long time and I can tell you that they really care about each other. They are just going through a difficult time . . . you know this, don't you?'

He knew more than Chacha would ever know, but he kept his mouth shut. There was a tenderness in Chacha's voice that was hard to fight against.

'It became more difficult for them when Amma came. And now . . . death affects everyone in different ways, even if it is the death of someone distant. This was someone very close,' Chacha nodded, his eyebrows raised in high arches over his slim spectacles. 'They will need time to grieve, and things will be hard during that time.'

Adi had to bite his lip to keep himself from saying something. He was the one who took care of Amma all day, the only one who bothered to listen to her dazed ramblings and sneaked her rasgullas when she was sad. He was sure that in their house, he was the only one who actually missed having Amma around.

'I just want to tell you that . . .' Chacha paused and looked around, like he was looking for words floating in the cold, still morning air. 'They care about you very much, and they feel bad that you are affected by all this. But just remember that this will pass. Things will change, maybe sooner than you think. Right now, it may seem like everything is falling apart, but trust me, it's going to be okay. In the end, everything is going to be alright. And,' he smiled, 'if it ever gets too difficult, or you feel like talking to someone, you have my card, yes? Whatever you need, you just have to ask.'

Adi nodded, then smiled. He did appreciate what Chacha was doing – it was more than his own parents ever did – so he did not have the heart to tell him that the hope he was offering, the very change that he was promising, was what he now feared the most. On some level, he had always believed that Ma and his father would work things out, find a way to coexist. He had grown up hearing them fight, and frightening as it was, they had survived through all those years. What scared him was the sense that they were both too tired to keep fighting. By bringing their hushed whispers out of their room, spilling their secrets for all to see, they were no longer trapped in silence. In a way, they had freed themselves, and in a way, it was all Chacha's fault. When he had asked them what would give them peace, Adi had known straightaway that a new door had been edged open. Peace was the one thing they were never going to find in that house, with each other. If peace was what they wanted, the only way was out.

*

The day Chacha left, Ma and his father spent the entire afternoon in their bedroom – not fighting, not screaming, not accusing each other of lying; just talking like a pair of grownups. Their calm voices were hard to hear through the bedroom door and Adi decided he didn't want to hear them anyway. Their even, resigned tones were far more disturbing than their muffled screams had ever been.

He turned on the TV and spent the afternoon watching the highlights from last year's Friendship Cup series between

India and Pakistan (played in Canada, for some reason). It had been cold and rainy, and the batsmen, laden with heavy sweaters, had struggled to score. The high point of the series, however, had been the incident with Inzy. The big Pakistani had been heckled by an Indian fan carrying a loudspeaker, calling him 'Aloo'. It was a common nickname for Inzy but this time, it had sent sent him into a fit of rage. He had charged the spectator stands with a bat and almost knocked the guy's head off. Adi could see why, now that he thought about it. Calling someone a potato was hardly an expression of fondness. It was just like Mikki's nickname. It may have sounded cool – cooler than Paadi, at least – but it was still an insult, poorly disguised. It was a constant reminder of his surname and what it represented, and it only worked because Mikki pretended that he didn't care. Maybe deep inside, Mikki felt just like Inzy, boiling with fury, wishing he too had a bat.

The bedroom door opened and he held his breath. His father came out into the drawing room and took his spot, but in place of his usual scowl, there was an easy smile.

'Fantastic series,' he said to Adi. He did not reach for the remote. 'It's good to send this Tendulkar out to proper bowling pitches abroad. Here, on our flat pitches, he acts like a lion but look at him now, standing with his tail between his legs.'

His father laughed and the laughter was not coated with sarcasm. It flowed lightly, warm as the winter sunshine, and Adi wondered whether he needed to slap himself to check if he was awake.

'Who's hungry?' Ma walked into the drawing room with her sari tucked into her waist.

'Samosas would be heavenly, no, Adi? Especially if your mother is making them.'

'Ask your father, Adi,' Ma said without missing a beat, 'didn't we just decide that it's time to stop dreaming?'

Adi bit his lip and stared at the TV, waiting for the house to explode at any moment. Instead, his father laughed again.

'Arré, tell your mother I'm only joking. I will go and get them. I will get the sweet chutney she likes too.'

Ma shook her head, but on her face, in place of the usual hardened, weathered lines, there was something approaching a smile. As she went into the kitchen, Adi felt his body relax, like it was letting go of a weight it had been dragging around for years. Maybe Chacha had been right, he thought. Maybe things were really going to change for the better, now that everyone had left and a new year had dawned. And even if all that changed was that Ma rediscovered this smile of hers and his father laughed in this jolly way – that, he told himself, would have been enough.

17.

The present is a made-up thing

'Oye, Omi.'

Adi threw his bag under the desk and held his hand up for a high five. His bench partner looked up at his hand, then at him and, after a momentary frown, chuckled and shook his head. A high five was too much to expect, Adi knew, but he was glad to see that his new nickname had been accepted. He had been right: Mikki was not a kind name for his friend. It was not a reference to the mouse. It was a mark of his caste, a constant reminder of his untouchability, meant to never let him forget his place. He only wished that he could have figured this out earlier.

'Hi,' said Noor, walking up to her desk in front of theirs. They both stared at her, dumbstruck, as she took out her notebooks and arranged them in her drawer, pretending like there was nothing different about her.

'Your hair!' said Adi.

'Oh, yeah.' She touched the back of her head. 'How does it look?'

'It's . . . like a boy.'

'It's not!'

'No, I mean, it's . . .'

She turned and sat down, but Adi could not stop staring at her head. Noor's hair was almost as short as his own. Gone were the shining curls that swung wildly each time she turned her head. He could see the shape of her neck clearly now and her ears with their dangling disco balls, and the top of her freckled back under her loose collar. It was as if she had taken off a piece of clothing and he found himself feeling excited and embarrassed, like he was the one who was exposed.

The morning assembly was held over the PA system; January was too cold even for the teachers' cruelty. Through it, he struggled to keep his eyes off Noor. There was something scary about the way he felt, lightheaded and restless, his back tingling with tiny pinpricks. His stomach churned like he was hungry, but it was a hunger like no other, aching somewhere deep in his belly.

After they had all mumbled along to the national anthem, most of them mispronouncing the words, they sank into their seats for the first class of the day: the dreaded Ghost Time. Ma'am Mishra began scrawling her usual bhoot kaal verbs on the blackboard, each stroke of the chalk screeching through the cold morning, making him clench his jaw.

'Oye,' he whispered, and Omi looked up, shocked. Unflappable as he was during most classes, brazenly reading his magazine whenever the teacher was sitting down, sometimes even slipping in his earphones, something about Ma'am Mishra made Omi grow tense and watchful, and Adi could never understand why she alone had that effect on him. She was the only teacher who could make the big guy act like a scared little child, haunted by something no one else could see.

'I need to set up a new email address,' said Adi.

'You have one.' Omi's voice had already broken and he often seemed unable to control it. Even when he tried to whisper, it came out as a croak loud enough to make Noor turn and shush them.

'I know. But you gave me a funny name. I need a proper one.'

'Just do it in computers class. It takes five minutes, I showed you—'

A piece of chalk came zipping through the air and slammed Omi's forehead. The short, sharp knock, like marbles crashing, rang through the room like a crack of thunder. Omi sat stunned, looking like he had forgotten where he was, who he was.

'Omprakash Valmiki,' said Ma'am Mishra, looking down at him over the top of her gold-rimmed glasses. 'I am sure you would like me to kick you out of the class so you can roam the halls like a goonda, but I will not let you off so easily. Get up and sit over there.' She pointed the stub of the chalk still in her fingers at Noor's desk.

Omi looked at Adi, who realised his mouth was hanging open and quickly shut it. Noor was already moving her bag down to make room on the bench.

'Don't look at Adi,' Ma'am Mishra thundered. 'You are spoiling him too. Thanks to you his marks are going down. You better stay away from him in my class, at least. And for *your* own good,' she turned to Adi, 'in other classes too.'

Adi looked down at his feet and saw the white bullet she had shot at Omi. He bent down to pick it up and closed his fingers around it. All he wanted was to get up and fling it, with all the strength in his tightly wound body, back at her smug, jowly face.

'Good,' she said, as Omi got up and carried his notebook to the front desk and slid in next to Noor. She picked up another piece of chalk and began scribbling on the blackboard, and Adi turned to his notebook. He did not look up again.

*

Fasaana-é-shab-é-gham unko ik kahaani thi
Kuchh aitbaar kiya kuchh na aitbaar kiya

Noor stepped aside and froze in position, like a statue of an angel serenading the gods, and Adi stepped forward:

The tale of my dark nights was a story to them
Some of it they believed, some they did not

'Bravo!' Noor clapped as he rose from his courtly bow, terrified that she might give him a hug. She did not.

They had spent a week practising the same poem, a long Urdu ghazal by Daagh Dehlvi that Noor and Adi took turns to recite in their different languages, twirling around the room as Omi sat still in the centre, doodling on a notebook. It had taken so long because Adi had struggled to get the timing and the rhythm right. Noor insisted that they recite the poems together, one couplet at a time, so he had to match her musical verses that made his own words sound like the drone of a bored teacher.

It was not fair, he had pleaded – he could not be expected to mirror Urdu's poetic grace with a language such as English – but Noor would have none of it. It was about the *feeling*, she kept saying, not the language. English could be just as musical as Urdu; it only required a little effort to bend and shape it. She had spent hours practising with him, telling him to study the movement of her lips, picture the curl of her tongue and try to add the same stresses to his words. Such suggestions had not made it any easier to focus, so he was glad that he had finally got it right.

'Is it time for Ghost Time?' Noor asked, checking her flower-strap watch.

'No,' said Adi. There were still eleven minutes left.

'Yes, let's head back.' Omi shut his notebook and rose from his chair.

'Great job, guys,' said Noor, running her hands through her hair, damp with sweat despite the cold. 'What acting, Omi,' she said with a mock-impressed nod. 'You almost look like a poet. If only you had a beard.'

'You would have looked like a dancer too,' said Omi. 'If only you had any hair.'

Noor pounced on him and slapped him hard across the arm. Omi tried to hit back but she was too fast. Before he could move his hand, she was dancing circles around the desk, laughing hysterically. Omi shook his head and slowly walked away from the table, stretching his arms like his back was stiff. Just as Noor lowered her guard and went to pick up her books, he lunged at her. She tried to step back and stumbled over a big cardboard box. It ripped under her weight and she fell on a heap of rainbow-coloured confetti, trapped before the towering Omi.

'Buss, Omi,' said Adi. 'That's enough.'

Ignoring Adi completely, he leant over Noor with a mock evil laugh, and for a moment she looked scared. He reached over and flicked her earring, and she stopped struggling to get up and looked him in the eyes. 'That's it. You're dead.'

Adi came running and slammed against Omi, surprising even himself with the force of the impact. It sent Omi stumbling halfway across the room before he steadied himself and looked back at Adi, confused and bemused in equal measure.

'What's the matter with you, Adi?' Noor shouted, rising to her feet and brushing off confetti from the folds of her skirt. 'Have you gone mad? We're just fooling around.'

'Yeah? So was I.'

'You hit him really hard,' she said, looking at Omi with concern. 'You could have hurt him. You've never done anything like this. What's wrong with you?'

'What's wrong with *you*?' He turned to Omi to include him too. 'Aren't we too old to be running around and hitting each other?'

'It's fine, yaar, leave it,' Omi said to Noor, picking up his book again. 'Let's go, we'll be late for Sanskrit.'

'Oh, yes, your new favourite class,' sneered Adi.

'What?' Omi turned, and Adi saw a flash of anger in his eyes. Rather than scaring him, it made Adi feel bolder.

'Yes, what's that about? You hated Sanskrit, didn't you? You used to skip it every time, before the holidays. We still have the note, we can still skip it, no? So how come you're suddenly so desperate to be there? Is it because your new bench partner makes "Ghost Time" more exciting?'

Omi looked at Noor, who was still picking out bits of paper stuck to her shirt. They had no answer, Adi could see. Suddenly, he felt sick at the sight of them, like he couldn't bear meeting their eyes one more time.

'I'm done,' he said. 'Since the two of you are having so much fun, you can do the play yourselves. All the best.'

He stormed out of the drama room and ran towards the staircase. In his rage, he did not even stop to realise that his legs were finally long enough to accomplish what he had yearned to do for so long – racing up the stairs two steps at a time.

*

When he had recovered his breath, he leant back on his chair and looked around. The library was empty, and the librarian was snoozing at her desk as usual, so he put his feet up on a chair and looked out of the window.

The winter sun was hanging low in the sky, bathing the tall, white-barked eucalyptuses with its mild, golden glow. The thick green leaves that shaded the road in front of the school now looked pale, shivering in the cold breeze, waiting for the spring to bring back their colour.

He found the vulture perched upon a high branch at the end of the street. 'Where have *you* been?' he mumbled.

'Ah, Mr Sharma. I wanted to ask you the very same!'

'I've been busy. Amma died.'

'Oh, yes, please accept my deepest condolences. She was a nice lady.'

'She was not,' he scoffed. 'You *know* that.'

'Yes, but one must not speak ill of the dead. And all of us have some good in us, even your Amma. That is why you are missing her, is it not?'

'I'm not missing her. She's dead, it's all in the past.'

'A wise man once said: "The past is never dead, it is not even past."'

'*Not even* . . . what does that mean?'

'It means, Mr Sharma, that the present is a made-up thing. What we call present, by the time we catch it, is already past. The past is where we live our lives, and there is no difference between things that happened yesterday and last year and a lifetime ago. They are all mixed up, tangled up in each other like the roots of great big trees. And the future is caught in the middle, writhing like a trapped worm. Have you never wondered why your word for tomorrow is yesterday?'

It was true, he realised; he had never really thought about it. Kal was the word for both – the coming kal and the bygone kal were the same. It was a wonder they were all not constantly confused, lost in this maze of time. Or, were they?

'That is why our work is so important, you see? We need the Historical Archives to make sense of our lives, to untangle the threads of time and arrange them in the right order, so we can free ourselves from the knots of the past that tie down our future.'

'Uh . . . okay.'

'Hrr-hrr, worry not, you will understand. Now, we still have one more file left for you. Do you have a fear you can address in return?'

'I was thinking—'

'Oh, *good*,' said the vulture, bobbing its little head, but he ignored the quip.

'I'm worried that my parents . . . they might get a divorce.'

'Because they are fighting?'

'No, that's the thing, they've been acting *happy*? That's why it's so weird.'

'Oh, Mr Sharma,' the vulture sighed. 'This is because you are not trusting happiness.'

'No, it's not that. I'm telling you, I have a sense about these things.'

'Oh, I see! We are in the realm of the supernatural now, is it? You have suddenly developed a sixth sense? Next you will say you have a third eye, like your Shiva.'

'Why don't you offer a suggestion, then? Don't *you* have any ideas?'

'Ideas? I certainly do not waste my time on such things. I am a simple functionary sent here to carry out my duties as per the rules and—'

'Abé, *yaar*!' He nearly yelled out a 'behenchod' but stopped himself just in time. 'Okay,' he took a deep breath. 'If I did something to bring Ma and my father closer, will you count that?'

'It depends.'

'On what?'

'On what you actually *do*, Mr Sharma.'

'How about I do what I did with Ma and Chacha? I can take them to Lajpat Nagar market. They never go out anymore, maybe they'll have a good time too?'

'Hmm,' the vulture nodded.

'What? You have a problem with that?'

'Problem? No problem. You are welcome to try.'

'Oh, you think I can't do it? You want to bet?'

'Gambling? I am a respected senior official, not some roadside astrologer's parrot. How dare you suggest such an activity to me, the DDG of DHA, in charge of—'

The school bell tore through the dusty, deserted library and cut the vulture off. Gathering his books, Adi shook his head and rubbed his eyes. How long, he wondered, would he have to endure this behenchod bird's buckvaas?

18.

A man of action

The doorbell rang with a series of short, sharp bursts, and Adi knew his father was home. It was only 17:57 – he was at least an hour early – and Ma was still in the bedroom talking on the phone to Chacha. Adi was not sure if Ma knew the precise pattern of his father's bell. She must have assumed it was Rina Auntie, who had not yet shown up for her evening shift, so she did not stop talking. Standing in the middle of the drawing room, he wondered if he should go and tell Ma when the doorbell rang again, more insistent this time.

'Papa!' he greeted loudly as he opened the door. 'You're home early!'

'Yes,' his father grunted, out of breath from climbing the stairs.

'Are you going to the office on Saturday? Can we go to Lajpat Nagar market? I have to buy a costume for my school play.'

'Where is your mother?' his father asked, then glanced towards their bedroom when he heard her laughing. Adi saw a shadow of rage passing over his face, and he knew there was going to be no more laughter tonight. Pushing his dull brown leather shoes to the side of the door, his father headed straight for the bedroom.

'Oh, you're here?' came Ma's voice, surprised but not in a guilty way. 'I'm talking to Mohan. Do you want to speak with him?'

Without a word, his father came back into the drawing room and took his place, reaching for the remote. In a moment, Ma came rushing out, tying her hair in a bun.

'Mohan called to give some good news.' Her voice was quivering with excitement – or was it dread? 'The date is fixed. He is getting married on 5 August!'

'Hmm,' said his father, switching to the news. Elections were coming up and the news was all he watched now, even when the cricket was on. His mood, however, had been far better than before. The BJP were being predicted as the winners – the party that supported his two favourite things: temples and atom bombs.

'I am so happy for him. After so many years—'

'Don't be so happy; he is not marrying you.'

Adi started sneaking out of the drawing room, circling around Ma and pretending to look for something on the dining table, careful not to make the slightest sound. The silence in the house was so thick he wondered if they could hear his heart hammering against his chest, just like his father sometimes pounded the door when his second bell wasn't answered.

'Why do you have to spoil every happy moment?' Adi could practically hear Ma's teeth grinding.

'Arré, don't blame me, it's the law. But maybe you can find a way around it. After all, among your people, it's okay to marry four times, no?' His father laughed and Adi felt his fingers go numb.

'Again you are starting with this nonsense?' Ma hissed. 'If you have such a problem with me—'

'*I* have a problem?' His father turned away from the TV and looked at Ma. 'You are the one bent on ruining my life.'

'What?'

'Don't do your drama now, you know what I am talking about. First, you said you wanted to go to Pakistan to look for this Kammo, this ghost of a sister dreamt up by your father, and I didn't say anything—'

'You didn't *say* anything!' Ma laughed. 'You broke my brain, so much hulla you made.'

'But I got you tickets myself, didn't I?'

'Only so you could keep track of me,' Ma mumbled.

'And *then*,' his father's voice grew louder, 'we start getting letters from over there! At my address! I still didn't say anything. But now *this* ...' He reached into his pocket, unfolded a piece of paper, and flung it at her. '*This* has crossed the line.'

'The telephone bill?' said Ma, frowning at the paper.

'Yes. With a call to Pakistan on it. It was just by chance that I spotted it before I filed my claims. You know what this could do to me if the Department found out? Do you not understand who I work for, what I do? This one piece of paper could ruin me. It could put me in *jail*! Is that what you want?'

273

'I . . .' Ma stared at the bill, and Adi could not bring himself to move. It had to be the call that he had made. Ma must have realised it too, since she had not done it, but she did not turn to Adi. 'I will be more careful,' she said, folding up the bill.

Sensing surrender, his father became more aggressive, raising his voice higher.

'Let me explain to you again, since simple things don't get into your head. I am working on a top-secret national security project now. I'm not even allowed to tell *you* what it is and thank God for that! Who knows whom you will call up and blabber to? There are spies everywhere – ISI, CIA, KGB – but here I have a traitor in my own house.'

'Enough!' Ma shouted back. 'There is no need for babbling so much. I told you I will be careful. Matter closed.'

'No! You will stand right here and listen to me. I have had enough of your lies.'

Ma simply turned and walked away and slammed their bedroom door shut. His father was left fuming on the sofa, his belly heaving like it was about to explode, and Adi finally willed himself to move out of range. He tiptoed across the dining hall, past the kitchen, and into his room and edged the door shut.

He was back in his room now, for good. He had resisted it for a week after Chacha had left and the room had become vacant again, until Ma had moved his things in herself, laughing at his laziness. The room had been cleaned out thoroughly, even before Chacha had arrived and, by now, it was just like it used to be. His old desk had been cleared of medicine bottles and the drawers were full of his notebooks again. Even the mattress had been aired and flipped, and the bedsheet smelled of lavender-scented Surf Excel. There was no sign of Amma ever having been in there.

He drew the curtains open but the bright streetlamp that he had grown used to in the drawing room, that shone through the thin curtains and chased out the darkness with its yellow glow, was not visible from his bedroom window. Even with the lights on, he had struggled to fall asleep here, and he had wondered if he could move back out. He knew he would have to explain it to Ma but did not know how to. He imagined how nice it would be if he could move to the balcony – if he could build a little room for himself out there with roll-up bamboo curtains for walls and a half-mattress covering the narrow floor – but the impossibility of it made him chuckle.

Outside, he heard his father stomp across the dining hall. He held his breath until he heard his parents' bedroom door creak open and slam shut again.

No matter how hard he tried to tell himself that he was being stupid, he knew his old room would never be the same again, never be his own. But there was nothing to be done. He could hear his father yelling now, his voice radiating from the walls and echoing in the empty house. This house too – the place he had grown up in, the only home he had ever known – had begun to seem more alien with each night, but there was no place else to go.

He opened his cupboard, got down on his knees and reached into the back of the bottom shelf to retrieve the blue plastic bag. Opening it slowly, careful not to make it crackle, he took out his most prized possession and got back under the blanket. He ran his fingers over the smooth plastic again, marvelling at its metallic sheen, tracing the raised silver letters that spelt 'Sony Walkman'.

He had discovered it in his school bag, on the last night of the holidays, and it had terrified him. It felt silly now, but he had thought that it had appeared by magic, or that the vulture had put it in there. It was from Chacha, he had realised – the same one they had bought together – only when he had seen the little note Chacha had left in the cassette compartment. He took it out and read it again:

For my one and only Hero
Love, Chacha

He slipped the headphones on, drew the blanket over his head, and shut his eyes.

*

A loud crash rang through the walls like thunder before a winter storm. He sat up in bed, pulled the headphones off, and listened. After a moment's silence, there was another crash, followed by a shriek that pierced right through his chest. He jumped out and ran across the house and pushed his parents' door open. His father was on the far side of the bed,

276

274

his face warped with anger, his yellow teeth bared in a madman's grin. Near the door, Ma stood with her arm raised, holding a small idol of Ganesha in her hand. Behind his father, Adi could see bits of painted plaster on the floor – the shattered remains of fallen gods.

'Adi!' his father roared. 'Get back into your room.'

He looked at his father and held his gaze, and a long-forgotten memory flashed before his eyes: he must have been no older than five or six, because his father had loomed as large as an idol of Lord Ram. He had stood right where he was standing now, but Ma had been on the bed, holding her face and sobbing. Adi had run up to her and hugged her, and when he had kicked his father on the shin, he had received a slap too. Ma had screamed, and so had he, and his father had stormed out of the house.

This was why he had stopped going into that room, he now remembered. It was incredible how he could have forgotten something like this, but perhaps that was the nature of memory. Perhaps some things were so painful to remember that our minds decided, for our own good, to file them away in some secret drawer never to be opened again. Until it became necessary to do so, when the drawer became too stuffed to take any more.

His father's bloodshot eyes blinked first. Even though he had grown heavier with age, he looked diminished too; a pale shadow cast through the years, fading before Adi's own fiery eyes.

Adi stepped forward and held Ma's hand. 'Béta?' she said, trying to slow down her breathing. 'Don't worry, everything is okay, we are just—'

He pulled at her hand, quietly, but with more force than she had expected. He was not a toddler tugging at his Ma's finger. He was a son standing beside his mother, no longer afraid of hollow plaster gods.

Slowly, Ma got up and followed him out. Without another look at his father, he shut the door and led Ma into his bedroom.

'You will stay here now,' he said, leading her to the bed.

'Listen, béta,' she began, but he held up his hand.

'That's it, Ma. Enough.'

He shut the door and walked out to the drawing room. Taking his place on the divan, he switched on the TV. *Die Hard* was on. He turned the volume up to 50.

*

After the final credits had faded, he turned the TV off and spent a while trying to sleep, but he couldn't bring himself to stay still. He got up, pulled the curtains apart and looked around.

'Have you finally left?' he said, no longer worried that Ma or his father would hear him talking.

'Not yet, Mr Sharma,' came the reply, and he looked up to find the vulture on the lamppost across the street. In the glow of the yellow lamp, all he could make out was a black silhouette.

'I lost our bet, you'll be happy to hear.'

'Oh, no.' The vulture pulled its head back. 'I am afraid you are mistaken. I have never indulged in gambling, not once.'

'It looks like everything I do goes wrong. Maybe I should just give up fighting and run away from home.'

'Hmm. Maybe you should. When it comes to fight or flight, one must be a fool not to take flight. But I am biased for obvious reasons. I am a dignified vulture, after all, not some rowdy crow.'

'I was just trying to bring them closer. But I managed to do the opposite.'

'But what happened?'

'I . . .' Adi was surprised to find his voice shaking, choking like he was about to cry. He coughed to hide it and took a breath. 'They started fighting again, really badly. I was scared that my father was going to . . . hit her. Like he used to. So, I went and stopped it. I gave my room to Ma, so I'm sleeping here again.'

'Help me understand, please. You are telling me that you went into the situation that scares you the most, like the Rani of Jhansi riding into battle, and you *stopped* the fighting?'

'Um, yeah, I guess.'

'Oh, Mr Sharma, you should be proud of yourself! You are exceeding my expectations once again.'

'Really?'

'Of course! This is the first time you have acted like a grown-up, instead of hiding behind comic books and watching everyone like a mouse. You are finally becoming a man of *action*, Mr Sharma. Actually, I am counting this as a completed task. You have confronted a great fear and defeated it. Congratulations, you have earned access to your Ma's fifth and final file. Are you ready to see it?'

Feeling a little better about himself, he thought of checking his Casio, worried that it might be too late, but then shook his head. Sleep had been chased away for tonight, he was sure; he might as well get this business over with.

'Okay,' he said, closing his eyes and taking a long, slow breath. 'I'm ready.'

DHA/HA/TS/1987(5)

He recognises the place as soon as the fog clears – it's Lajpat Nagar market. The streets are nowhere as crowded as they are now and there is almost no traffic. There are only a few small shops, mostly restaurants and household stores and the odd chemist, and even the park in the middle – now a barren dump with gates chained shut – is full of children chasing each other. Instead of the usual cacophony of car horns, he can hear birdsong.

'The house next to the park,' says the vulture. 'The one with pink walls.'

He spots the house instantly, hidden behind a gulmohar tree just beginning to grow its green, bullet-shaped buds. He has never been to it, he is sure, but it still looks familiar, like a long-lost home. Peering through the iron-grilled window, he finds a small drawing room filled to the brim with things. There are tall shelves lining the walls, packed with hardbound maroon books, and they make the room look dark and dingy despite the sunlight flooding in through the wide windows. There are things scattered all around: stained mugs and crusty plates and towels and rags and slippers and empty water bottles, and medicines – more pills and bottles than Amma ever had. The room is quite large, he realises; it's the clutter that makes it seem claustrophobic.

A long, low groan attracts his attention and he turns to find an old man lying on a narrow bed in the corner of the room, facing the wall. The man turns, struggling to push away the pale blue sheet that covers him, and tries to lift his head but fails. His hair is a brilliant white that shimmers in the sunshine, but it is so thin that it barely covers his pale, pockmarked scalp. His face is long and rugged, his leathery cheeks glinting with a silver stubble, a monumental nose rising in defiance of his age. He opens his eyes and smiles. Adi knows those eyes well by now. Despite their drooping lids and the specks clouding their once-bright cores, he can recognise those eyes anywhere. They belong to Nana.

'Papa, you are awake?' a woman calls out, and Adi gasps. She walks in with the end of her sari wrapped and tucked around her waist, carrying a dusting cloth and wiping her forehead with the back of her hand. She looks just like her old photographs, only stronger, taller, way more beautiful.

'Come, get up,' says Ma. 'Sit up for a while, I will put some tea on.'

She walks up to Nana and runs her fingers along his cheeks. 'First, I will clean up your face. Have you seen the mirror? You look like some goonda with that beard.'

'Paani,' says Nana.

'Raju!' Ma yells in the direction of an open door. 'Get some water for Papa.'

After some clanging in the kitchen, a short, reedy man walks out, carrying a steel glass in one hand and a newspaper in the other. He walks slowly, with a slight stoop, although he doesn't seem old. He holds the glass out towards Ma but she frowns at him, amused more than annoyed. 'What? You will make me drink it? It's for Papa, give it to him.'

The man smiles sheepishly and sits next to Nana. He gently lifts Nana's head and holds the glass to his twitching lips. Nana's Adam's apple bobs up and down as he swallows the water in hungry gulps.

'Will you put some tea on?' asks Ma, once the man is done.

'Ji, madam,' he gives her a circular nod. 'Two cups?'

'Make it three. Sahib will be arriving soon.'

'Ji, madam,' he nods again and shuffles back into the kitchen.

'Raju?' Ma calls after him. 'Make it four. One for yourself.'

'Ji, madam,' comes the response.

'He seems like a good boy, Papa,' she says to Nana, who looks more awake now. 'Give him a few days, he will learn.'

'He wants to slit my throat,' Nana says, his voice ragged and faltering.

'The things you say, Papa! He doesn't want to slit your throat,' Ma laughs. 'It was an honest mistake. You don't make it easy, either, moving your head all the time like a little spar-row. Don't worry now. I have got you disposable razors, the new Gillette ones. They won't give you any cuts.'

'The best,' Nana sputters then starts again, speaking in English. ' "The best a man can get." '

'Yes,' Ma laughs. 'You are watching too much TV these days, no?'

Nana begins to say something but the bell rings and Ma gets up to open the door. His father walks in, dragging behind him a little boy. 'Too hot out there. Why isn't the fan on?'

'Papa feels cold.'

The boy snatches his hand away from his father and runs to the sofa, and Ma bends over him to check his forehead. It is *him*, Adi realises, no more than two or three years old.

'Was everything okay?' she asks his father, who shrugs.

'The shot took one second but your son did so much drama, as if his leg was being broken.'

'Poor child.' Ma runs her fingers through little Adi's hair as he sits slumped on the sofa, fiddling with something in his hands, his cheeks streaked by dried-out tears. Adi looks at his child self, examining his spindly legs and side-parted hair and ears that stick out like a little monkey, and he can't believe what a loser he used to look like.

His father pulls out a chair from the dining table on the far side of the room and switches on the fan. 'How is he?'

'Not getting better,' Ma whispers. 'He kept calling me Toshi in the morning. I brought him out here for a change but he lay down and fell asleep again.'

His father shakes his head and Ma turns back to Nana.

'Papa? You're still lying down? You have to get up or your back will start hurting. Come, I will help you.'

'Kammo?' says Nana. 'You're back?'

His voice is faint. Ma doesn't catch it, but Adi does. He looks around the room, half-expecting to find Ma's lost sister, but there is nobody else.

'Come, Papa, make some effort.' Ma tries to pull him upright. 'You are still too strong and heavy for me.'

'Kammo, puttar, saara kasoor méra si,' says Nana, switching to the same poetic Punjabi he spoke in the older memories. 'Kammo, my child, it was all my fault.'

'Kismat si, Papa, tuhada kasoor nai siga,' Ma replies. 'It was fate, it was not your fault. Ma was sick. You did everything you could, but she had lost the will to recover.'

'I never—' Nana coughs, recovers. 'I never forgot about you, child. Your Ammi said I abandoned you to save Munno, but she is wrong. You are my daughter too, Kammo. You remember when I used to take you to Mall Road, to Anaarkali Bazaar? We used to get ice lollies, orange for you, lemon for me. Your tongue would go red and you would stick it out at the Angrez officers, you remember?'

'It's okay, Papa,' says Ma, leaving him to lie down. 'Get some more rest, you are tired. It's probably all of these medicines you are taking. I will call Doctor Batra and ask him—'

'I just wanted, I just wanted to protect your Ammi, my Toshi,' says Nana, his eyes welling up. 'I went back to look for you, Kammo. I went back many times. I asked everyone in the village but I could not find you.'

'You . . . you went back?' Ma's eyes are wide as a child who's just seen a ghost. 'So, Kammo was alive? But, you told me—'

'Toshi,' he chokes a little. 'My Toshi never forgave me for leaving you. She never forgave herself either. Seven years, seven years she mourned for you, until she could not go on anymore. She could never love Munno like she loved you.'

'Do you know what he's talking about?' Ma turns to his father, who is flipping through an *India Today*, pretending not to listen. 'I thought Kammo died of pneumonia, as a child. Now he says she was alive?'

'What do I know?' says his father. 'You and your family, even God does not know your secrets. Or should I say Allah?—'

'Where did you go to look for Kammo, Papa? Is she still alive?' Ma says to Nana, ignoring his father.

Nana's eyes are glazed over, however, peering past Ma's shoulder into the fog of time, into moments long gone but never out of sight.

'She never recovered from losing you, Kammo,' he continues. 'Nobody,' he sniffles, 'nobody can take the place of your first child.'

'That you are right about, Papa.'

'Oh, here we go,' says his father, flipping another page. 'Don't start again now.'

'I am just agreeing with Papa.' Ma glares at him.

'I know what you are doing,' says his father. 'You are trying to distract me from your own lies. You act as if your own family are angels and only mine are demons.'

'I came to see you, Kammo.' Nana's voice is growing fainter. 'I never told Toshi but I found you.'

'—Are you going to take your mother's side again?' Ma rises to her feet. 'Papa got you a government job, gave us a roof to live in Delhi. You can be a little more sympathetic to him.'

'I'm not taking her side.' His father shrinks a little. 'I don't even talk to Amma anymore, do I?'

'I came to Jalandhar, I saw you there, at that Gandhi Ashram.' Nana's voice is down to a whisper now. 'But I . . . I was afraid.'

Ma is still looking at his father and Adi is struck by her eyes. They remind him of the blue flames on the stove, frightening yet mesmerising, burning so hot that they send a chill through his bones.

'It's not some great favour you are doing to me,' she says. 'It's for your own good.'

'Acchha, okay,' says his father, trying to placate her, but Ma turns back to Nana.

'—You knew me as Tariq, you never knew Tarun. I was afraid you would tell them I was Muslim. They would take everything, everything from me again. But who can know Allah's will?' Nana wails, and lets out a pained, unbearably sad laugh. 'He took everything away anyway. He took my Toshi.'

The chair screeches across the stone floor as his father gets up, tosses the magazine on the table and heads for the door. 'I am going home.' He picks up his keys. Little Adi sits up on the sofa and begins to whimper, but his father shuts him up with a withering glare. 'You and your family can stay here.'

'Forgive me, Kammo, it was all, it was all my fault.'

'It's okay, Papa, it's okay,' Ma whispers, caressing Nana's wrinkled hands. Those once radiant eyes fall shut again, and the world goes dark.

19.

A *cunning plan*

'Omprakash Valmiki,' said Ma'am Mishra, as soon as she had set her handbag down on the teacher's desk. Even the way she said Omi's name made Adi wince. It was just the way his father said 'Mussalman', like the word was a sour, stinking thing that needed to be spat out.

Omi rose and began to slowly gather his things.

After their fight in the drama room, Noor and Omi had been practising their play without Adi, but they always made it back before Ghost Time, and each time, Omi came and sat in his old spot, next to Adi. He waited for Ma'am Mishra to call him out before slowly stepping up and moving to Noor's bench. Ma'am Mishra, too, began every class by repeating the ritual, waiting for Omi to move up and settle down in his new place before continuing. If Omi was hoping that she would eventually get tired of it, she showed no signs of it. In fact, each minute she spent waiting for Omi only served to make her angrier; each time she was forced to speak his name was another drop of fuel for her burning eyes. Now, she decided she had had enough.

'Stop.' She raised her hand. 'Enough of your disrespect. Don't you have any shame? Do you think I am your servant, that I should remind you every day of your place? You go and stand there now.' She pointed to the far corner of the class-room, away from the doors.

Omi stopped and stared at her, and for the first time, Adi saw anger blooming on his friend's face, flaring his nostrils and pursing his lips into a thin, trembling line. He dropped his notebook on his desk and shuffled across the classroom.

'Hurry up,' said Ma'am Mishra. 'Some people are here to study.'

Omi reached the corner and turned around and stood with his hands in his pockets, like he was daring Ma'am Mishra. She took the dare.

'What is this? Are you taking a stroll in the Mughal Gardens?' The class tittered. 'Raise your hands over your head.'

Omi glared at her but she did not blink. Adi was sure that his friend would say something, that he would not let that witch treat him like a fifth-standard child, but he was shocked when Omi slowly raised his arms, straight as rods and stood staring at the floor like he had a gun pointed at him.

'Good,' said Ma'am Mishra, and turned back to the black-board with a smug smile.

As she went on scratching tense tables on the board, Adi rose to his feet. Pens stopped moving and whispers died down and the class held its breath as he walked across the room, behind Ma'am Mishra's back. Taking his place next to Omi, he turned and raised his arms.

As the class sat still and Ma'am Mishra's chalk went on screeching, Adi and Omi stood and watched Noor tiptoe across the room to come and stand next to them, her arms joining theirs in parallel, looking less like a punishment and more like a revolutionary salute. She grinned like they were doing something adventurous and exciting, as opposed to an act of mutiny that was sure to land them in Father Rebello's dreaded room. Nonetheless, Adi and Omi couldn't help but smile.

Ma'am Mishra turned and saw them and stopped mid-sentence. Adi could almost hear her brain creaking, trying to get around the problem. Most of her time was spent devising ways to torment unwitting students; there were no rules for dealing with self-imposed punishments. It was driving her mad, he could see, especially the half-bitten smiles on their faces, but there was nothing she could say.

There were two loud knocks on the open door and they nearly jumped. Ma'am George was standing at the edge of the classroom, frowning at the three of them.

'What's going on here?' she asked, turning to Ma'am Mishra.

'They are being taught a lesson,' Ma'am Mishra replied. She did not switch from her traditional, pundit-style Hindi, knowing that it was a language Ma'am George did not speak too well.

'What did they do?' Ma'am George was sticking to English herself, even though she could clearly understand Ma'am Mishra's words.

'They don't study, they disturb the whole class, so I am dealing with them.'

'That's surprising.' Ma'am George turned to the three of them. 'They are very good students in my class.'

'Look at that,' Ma'am Mishra laughed, and going by the mocking edge in her voice, Adi could have bet that she was related to his father. 'So you can study English but you have no interest in your own language?'

Adi rolled his eyes. The only time anyone heard Sanskrit being spoken was at weddings and funerals and even then, no one knew what the pundits mumbled. Of all the useless things they were taught at school, this tongue of ghosts took the top prize.

'Sanskrit is not my language,' said Omi. 'It is the language of Brahmins. And as you know very well . . .' He looked up at her. 'I am not a Brahmin. My language is Marathi.'

Ma'am Mishra's face grew pink – with embarrassment or anger, Adi couldn't tell. He glanced at Omi, who was staring at his nemesis with unblinking eyes; a rush of pride made him stand tall next to his friend.

'And mine are Urdu and Punjabi,' said Noor, her eyes glinting with mischief.

'Yes,' Ma'am George smiled. 'And mine is Malayalam. They are all our languages, and so is English.' She gave Ma'am Mishra a look carefully balanced between a joke and a warning.

'Good,' said Ma'am Mishra, shaking her head. 'The language of the gods is wasted on people like you anyway. What does a monkey know about the taste of ginger, no?' Her smirk was aimed straight at Omi.

Ginger? The three of them looked at each other, doing their very best not to burst into giggles.

'What do you mean by that?' Ma'am George was suddenly enraged. 'What are "people like us"? Say what you mean clearly, so everyone can understand.'

The room fell silent as the teachers stared off, and Adi felt like he was beginning to understand what was happening. There were some things that grown-ups were not allowed to say openly, like why Ma'am Mishra was repulsed by Omi or why his father was forever frothing about 'reservations', even though these things were as much a part of them as the blood pulsing in their popped veins. Thanks to this unspoken rule, Ma'am Mishra had now been checkmated. She could not admit to her irrational hatred for Omi, and she could not drag them to the principal's office either, because scary as he was, Father Rebello was famous for being scrupulously fair. He would have asked Ma'am Mishra to explain it all, forcing her to say what she was not allowed to say in a school with the motto, 'Love thy neighbour as thyself'. There were no exceptions for neighbours belonging to lower castes.

'Put your hands down, for God's sake,' Ma'am George said, and they quickly brought down the arms they had completely forgotten about. 'Come. I need to talk to you in the staff room.'

Ma'am Mishra turned her back to the class and began writing on the blackboard, pretending that nothing was happening. The whole class saw through it, however. The three of them had done the impossible – stood up to that down-talking, chalk-shooting bandit of bhoot kaal, that demon of tenses past. Now, as they walked proudly across the classroom, like the cricket team taking a victory lap after winning the Silver Jubilee Independence Cup, they felt their audience's astonishment turn into admiration, and Adi almost felt like punching the air and cheering.

*

'So, Adi Shankar Sharma,' Noor said, after Ma'am George had left them in the staff room and they had finally stopped laughing. 'Are you still going to act like a baby?'

'What?'

'What do you mean *what*?'

He did not want to say what again, and he did not know what else to say, so he turned to Omi and found him barely containing his laughter.

'Are you not even going to say *sorry*?' Noor said.

'Sorry?' Adi frowned, genuinely baffled. Noor took it as an offer of apology, however, and seemed to calm down a little.

'It's fine if you don't want to do the play, you know. But it would be nice if you at least discussed it with us and didn't just go, "Umm oim not dooing it." It's rude.'

Omi broke into a full-blown laugh, his crackly voice sputtering like a two-stroke engine. Noor's impression of him was funny, Adi had to admit, but he wondered whether she was exaggerating or if he really sounded like that, like a sulking little boy.

'I did explain it to you,' he said, making his voice deeper.

'And it made no sense. We've been practising for so long. You're good at it, you liked doing it. What happened that you're suddenly so scared?'

'I'm not *scared*.' Noor flinched, and Adi realised that he had yelled. 'I'm just . . .' He paused and gathered himself. 'I don't feel like it. It's a lot of things.'

'Is there a problem at home?'

He looked up at Noor. There was not a hint of awkwardness in her eyes, like it was the most natural thing to ask someone if there was a 'problem at home'. If she was not embarrassed, he was not going to be either, he decided.

'Yes. Many problems.'

Noor nodded, like they were grown-ups discussing grave issues. 'Your dad?'

'Um, no,' he said, but his voice was so feeble he wouldn't have believed it himself.

'It's okay, you can tell me. My parents are crazy too. My Dad left my Mom two years ago and married some other woman, but he used to hit her, so I'm glad he's gone. My Mom is so much happier now.'

'No, that's not . . .' He didn't even know how to respond, so shocked was he at Noor's admission, and the ease with which it was made. 'I mean, yeah, my father's always a problem, but I'm more worried about Ma.'

'What is it?' Omi said. 'Does she beat you?'

'No!'

'Oh, okay,' Omi shrugged, like it was no big deal even if she did.

Adi sighed. There was not enough time in PE class to tell them about everything. He had to begin at the end.

'My Ma,' he said, then swallowed. 'She has a sister who got lost, long ago when they were kids. She's trying to find her now, and I think I know where she might be.'

'Where?' asked Noor.

'How do you know?' said Omi at the same time.

'In Jalandhar,' said Adi, ignoring Omi. 'In Punjab. I don't know if she's really there but I . . . I have a feeling. Ma doesn't believe me, though. I guess it sounds stupid. It's not like I have an address or anything.'

'Maybe I can help you find out,' Noor said, tapping her chin with her finger. 'I think I have some relatives in Jalandhar.'

'You're Punjabi?'

'Aho, puttar,' Noor said. 'Yes, son. Actually, we are from the other side of Punjab. You know, from the *enemy* side,' she whispered dramatically, then laughed. For the first time in days, Adi felt joy rushing through his head, clearing the cobwebs of confusion and despair. Perhaps he was not so alone, after all.

'This aunt – your Maasi – do you know her name?' Noor asked.

'No. But her nickname was Kammo.'

'Kammo,' she nodded. 'Sounds like a Sardaar name, like Kamaldeep. Was your Maasi a Sikh?'

'Um . . . yeah, I think so.'

'So that means your Ma is a Sikh too?' Omi frowned. 'But you're a Hindu. Sharmas are Brahmins, no?'

'Yes,' he said, not wanting to dwell on this topic that he had tried to untangle on many sleepless nights. His Nani was Sikh and his Nana Muslim, which made Ma zero per cent Hindu. But Nana had become Hindu later, so did that change Ma's lineage? Or was religion assigned at birth, injected into every newborn's blood, never to be shed or mixed or replaced? And in any case, what did that mean for him? How much of him was Hindu and Muslim and Sikh? The question made his head spin if he thought about it too much. He had never been good at maths, and this seemed like the hardest equation to solve.

'Anyway,' Noor said, frowning at Omi for his irrelevant questions. 'Do you know your Ma's parents' names? Your Nana and Nani?'

'Yes,' Adi nodded. 'Santosh Sharma and Tariq—' Noor's eyebrow popped up and he quickly corrected himself, 'Tarun. Tarun Sharma.'

'Oh-kay.' She narrowed her eyes. 'So your mother and father had the same surnames even before marriage?'

'Yeah.'

'Wow, that's lucky.' She nodded slowly, her eyes twinkling like she understood. 'So, Santosh Sharma and Tarun Sharma. I'll ask my Mom to find out.'

Before Adi could find a way to thank her, Omi cleared his throat.

'Er, there is a faster way to check, you know?'

'What?' Noor said, mildly irritated.

'On the internet?' said Omi, like he was talking to a slow child.

'Internet?' Noor's frown deepened. 'How can you find people on that?'

Omi rolled his eyes, like he had no time to explain such basics. 'Come on,' he said, rising from his chair and heading for the door, 'I'll show you.'

*

In the hush of the computer lab, they closed the door softly behind them and looked around at the row of monitors, all sheathed in plastic covers like precious new cars not to be touched, or a battalion of tanks not to be toyed with.

The lab was free for the next hour, the timetable on the door showed, so they took a computer at the far corner of the room. Omi took a while to figure out what he needed to do. As much as he knew about computers, his knowledge was mostly academic, gleaned from the *Chip* magazines he read down to shreds. He did not have much practice on actual computers, and even controlling the cursor was a challenge, making him slam the mouse on the desk in annoyance. Adi knew that Noor was the most adept among the three of them – she had a computer in her own bedroom – but she let Omi take his time and did not make fun of him when he typed slowly with one finger, like he was poking a ball of dough.

'Yes!' Omi was staring at a page called *AltaVista* crammed full of blue, underlined text.

'What's that?' asked Adi.

'All the search results from Jalandhar with your Nana and Nani's names.'

They began clicking on each of them – there were over 10,000 results – but each turned out to be a false flag, lacking any useful leads at all. At this rate, they'd have spent the rest of the year in that lab.

'Try Toshi,' Adi told him. 'It was my Nani's nickname.'

T-O-S-H-I, Omi poked the keyboard, and hit Enter. After a few seconds, a new list appeared, shorter than the last one but still running into the thousands.

'What's that?' Noor pointed to a link at the end of the page.

It was a news article about traditional fashion boutiques in Punjab. Omi scrolled the clicker wheel on the mouse, and they scanned the article. He stopped at boutique number 7, titled 'Toshi Designs'. It was a small shop based in Jalandhar, known for 'modern adaptations of traditional Punjabi designs', the article said. It was run by a woman named Kaamna Kaur. Kaamna, it took Adi a moment to realise, meant hope, desire, a fervent wish. It was a synonym for Tamanna, Ma's name.

There was no photograph of the owner, but there was one of their bestselling design – a long green kurta printed with bright pink flowers that seemed to glow even on the flickering computer screen. Adi leant back in his chair and closed his eyes. He couldn't breathe. It was the same kurta Ma had; the same one he had seen Nani wearing in the very first memory. He knew he had found Kammo.

'Are you okay?' Noor asked and he nodded.

'This is the one.'

'Are you sure?'

'Yes. One hundred per cent.'

'There is an address here,' said Omi. Noor had already found a piece of paper and was writing on it in her neat, beautiful script.

Adi looked at his friends hunched over in front of the screen, and he chuckled. It was all he could do to keep himself from crying.

*

He waited until 23:42 and he could wait no more. Tiptoeing out of his room, he peeked across the corridor – there was no light under his parents' door. He could hear his father's snores, loud as the fighter jets that roared every morning in preparation for the Republic Day parade. Ma had decided to go back to her room, and once again he wondered how she ever managed to sleep next to *that*. He straightened out his mattress, picked up his slippers and opened the front door, praying for it not to creak. It did not.

It was delightfully cold on the terrace, the breeze cutting right through his sweatshirt and making him shiver. The fog had returned, burning orange halos around the streetlights. It obscured everything beyond the nearby apartment blocks and made the streets dissolve into the haze, making it seem like their little piece of land had been lifted off the Earth and suspended in the clouds.

Taking his place on the ledge above the terrace door, he allowed himself a little smile. The Delhi winter lasted for less than two months, but during those months, he could almost pretend that he was somewhere else, some faraway country cold and grey where he did not have to dread the return of the merciless summer sun.

'Where are you?' His whispered words stirred the hushed night.

'Good evening, Mr Sharma.'

He followed the voice and found the vulture sitting atop a water tank on the same building, just two terraces away from him. It was the closest it had ever come, and he was startled to see just how big the bird was. With the fog blurring its outlines it seemed even larger, like a genie ballooning before his eyes, growing bigger with every breath.

'Yes, Mr Sharma? What is the matter? The cat has taken your tongue? Hrr-hrr.'

As much as Adi dreaded this, it was the only option he had left. He had tried telling Ma about Maasi, the day he had found out about the boutique, but Ma had lost her temper before he could finish the sentence. She had warned him not to mention Maasi's name ever again.

'Listen,' he cleared his throat. 'I really, really need your help. There's a lot of trouble at home, they are fighting again and I think Ma might leave this time. I know where Maasi is and I even found the address but Ma won't believe—'

'Slow down, Mr Sharma, calm down. I am here to help you only. Your wish is my command.'

'I need to see that last memory again, the one with Nana's death. He said something to Ma, I can't remember—'

'Out of the *question*, Mr Sharma.' The vulture cocked its head in a show of determination. 'The rules are clear, as I believe I informed you in the very beginning. You can access each file for one time only, no more.'

'Just for a minute, a few seconds, please! I just need to know what Nana said about Maasi. If I can find a clue there, I might be able to make Ma believe me and she might be able to find Kammo Maasi.'

'You are not listening to me.' The vulture slowly lifted its head to the sky, its eyes shut. 'What you want is irrelevant. The rules cannot be bypassed for anyone, otherwise we will have *anarchy*.'

'Okay, fine.' Adi leant back and took a deep breath. He had given the vulture a chance to help him. Now, he had no choice. In one smooth motion, he leapt up to his feet, pulled the catapult out of his back pocket, loaded its leather square with a marble the size of an eyeball and drew the rubber band all the way back, as far as his arms could stretch. There he stood, like Arjuna taking aim at the mighty Indra himself, ready to do his duty.

Finally, the vulture turned and opened its eyes. After a moment's silence, made heavier by the weight of his taut, trembling bow, Adi said: 'Last warning. Help me, or you die.'

The vulture shut its eyes and began to shiver, and it took him a moment to realise that it was not quivering in fear. It was laughing.

'What, Mr Sharma? I thought you had grown out of such childish toys—'

'I'm going to count to three.'

'—Ah, please, please stop—' the vulture was struggling to catch its breath.

'One—'

'I am telling you again, hrr-hrr, it is not in my hands.'

'Two—'

'The rules, they cannot be broken under any—'

The band snapped and the marble went whistling, streaking like a meteor through a starless night, and it filled Adi with terror. He had not meant to shoot, only to scare, but his fingers had slipped. Now, as the marble headed right for the vulture's heart, he turned away with his eyes shut tight: *Shit-fuck-tuttee, what had he done?*

Slowly, he opened his eyes and looked up, holding his breath.

There was nothing – no burst of black blood, no cloud of feathers, no cry of surrender. The vulture was staring back at him, shaking its head. The shining bullet had been swallowed by the inky blur of its body, leaving nothing but a deep, disappointed silence.

'I must say, Mr Sharma, that was *not* very nice of you.'

Adi sank back to the ledge, feeling relieved but also despondent. Was there really no way out?

'—I understand you are upset, but this is no way to treat a senior officer and an elder. Now, since I have shared all the necessary files about your mother's case, my work here is done. I wish I could say that it has been a pleasure—'

'Um, actually . . .' He sat up, seized by a realisation. The vulture may very well be some mythical being – ancient, immortal, impervious to fear – but it was also a civil servant. And those were beings he understood. It was not fear that drove them; they considered themselves invincible, infallible. It was the desire for things they felt entitled to, petty privileges they knew they so richly deserved.

'Yes, what now?' The vulture's long neck bent forward, its bright, black eyes peering through the darkness, trying to read his face.

'Just that . . .' He mulled his theory over for cracks. There were none. 'You're saying that you've shared all the five memories, so your job is done?'

'Correct. I have fulfilled my duties as per the Department's protocol.'

'So, tell me one thing . . . why are you still here?'

The babbling bird went quiet, for once, and he smiled. 'I'll tell you why. Because you may have cleared your "files", but you have not done your job.'

'Oh? And how do you know this, may I enquire?'

'Even with your super sight you can't see the obvious. You said your job was to clean up the mess of history, yeah? To solve our "family matters", isn't that what you said? Take a look at my house. Do you think you have sorted out our problems? If anything, you've made things worse!'

'I am only following my instructions, Mr Sharma. I cannot be held responsible for anything beyond that. If the matter is not resolved, the case will simply be passed on to another department, or labelled 'B.S.' and filed away with all the others.'

'B.S.?'

'Beyond Salvaging.'

'Okay, but . . .' Adi paused for a deep breath, yet again tempted to add a 'behenchod'. 'Would it not be so much better, for *you*, if you could salvage this mess? You could go back to your office and tell all your vulture bosses that you solved the case, and who knows, they might even give you a promotion.'

'Hmm,' the vulture grunted, and Adi knew that this time, he had struck its little heart.

'You know, maybe you can even save the Department, set an example for all the other vultures. Then you could become a DG instead of a DDG.'

'I have been waiting for a promotion for many years now, it is true. A comfortable cabin, a peon to make chai. This field work is not easy at my age, you know, talking on and on with . . .' The vulture stopped, then added, 'Delightful young-sters such as yourself.'

'Yes, you will get moksha,' Adi nodded. 'Freedom from this cycle of misery.'

'Hrr-hrr, very good, Mr Sharma.'

'Okay, so you will let me see the last memory again? I mean, if you don't have the authority because you're only a *deputy*, then I understand—'

'Oh, I have the authority, don't you worry about *that*. You are forgetting that I am also Additional Joint Secretary of the Department. I am authorised to approve a one-time exemp-tion under Section-7, Sub-section 13 of H-A-H-A.'

'Oh, wow! So you *can* do it, that's very impressive! Thank you so much!'

'Okay-okay, Mr Sharma. But, I must say one thing – this is for one time only.'

'One time only,' he nodded, putting on his best maths class face.

'And I must remind you, you need to behave yourself at all times. No monkey business, you promise?'

'No monkey business, pukka promise.'

He held up ten fingers to show that none were crossed. In the darkness, he hoped that the vulture could not see his feet dangling under the ledge, his big toes crossed over to cancel his vow.

DHA/HA/TS/1987 (5)

The quiet, empty streets of Lajpat Nagar market emerge again from the crackling haze, shining brightly in the afternoon sun. This time, Adi finds the pink house behind the budding gulmohar tree and zooms straight up to the barred window.

There's Nana, lying in the same position on his half-bed, his face turned to the wall. Looking around the room again, Adi notices several things he had missed the last time – photographs of Ma as a little girl; an old-fashioned music player with a big, golden speaker blooming like a flower; ancient newspapers preserved in a glass showcase; and a large photograph of Nehru, dressed in a closed-neck kurta with a red rose sticking out from the third buttonhole.

There is a small temple mounted on the wall next to the door, like the ones he has seen in many houses, usually carrying little idols of Ganesha. This one, however, is like no other. It is a temple dedicated to Nani. There is a large, framed black-and-white photograph of her in a black gown, holding a book in one hand and a rolled-up paper in the other, wearing a square black hat. The photo is garlanded with strings of dried-up flowers and surrounded by smaller pictures of Nani at different ages, some in faded colour and others a lifeless yellow. The big photo is the only one in which she is smiling.

Nana groans and turns, tears away the blue sheet, and tries to lift his head. Adi can hear Ma's voice in the kitchen inside, instructing the helper, Raju, on how to properly boil an egg. Adi has never eaten an egg – he always thought Ma was a vegetarian, just like his father.

'Papa, you are awake?' Ma walks into the room, wiping the sweat from her brow with the back of her hand. Once again, Adi is stunned by how different she looks; how much more striking than he has ever seen her in real life.

'Come, get up,' she says. 'Sit up for a while, let's have some tea.'

She sits down next to Nana on the bed and caresses his cheek. The memory plays exactly like before, and even though that's what Adi was expecting, he's still surprised. He watches as Ma jokes with Nana and waits for the housekeeper, Raju, to enter with a glass of water, spilling some of it along the way.

As Nana drinks from Raju's hands, Adi notices the plastic bag hanging from his side, half-filled with pale yellow water. It's a bag of pee, he realises, repulsed and fascinated, and wonders how it would be to have such a bag and pee any time you wanted. It would be useful in Sanskrit class, he thinks, especially for Omi, who is still terrified of asking Ma'am Mishra for permission to go to the toilet.

'—Don't worry now, I have got you disposable razors, those new Gillette ones. They won't give you any cuts.'

'The best . . . The best a man can get.'

'Yes,' Ma laughs. 'You are watching too much TV these days, no?'

The doorbell rings and he prepares himself. His father walks in, complaining about the heat, but Adi can't take his eyes off his younger self trailing behind, wearing a Mickey Mouse T-shirt. He watches himself run to the sofa, his face puffed up with all the crying.

'Poor child.' Ma ruffles his hair and the little grump turns away, like he is angry at her. Looking closer, Adi realises what the boy has in his hands – a green gulmohar bud – and he suddenly remembers what he is doing here, what he loved to do as a child. He is ripping the bud open to take out the frail stamens and pit them against each other, locking their little heads and pulling until one breaks; the other wins.

'Kammo?' Nana says. 'You're back?'

Adi leans in and sits still. This is it, the one chance he gets – he can't miss it this time or it will all be over.

'Kammo, my child, it was all my fault,' Nana says, and this time, Adi can't help but feel proud that he doesn't even need to pause to translate the Punjabi.

'I never . . . I never forgot about you, child,' Nana continues. 'You are my daughter too, Kammo.'

As Nana goes on, he tries to read Ma's face, searching for signs about how much she knows, how she feels about all this, but she has always been good at hiding these things.

'I went back to look for you, Kammo. I went back many times. I asked everyone in the village but I could not find you.'

313

'Y-you went back?' Ma says, her eyes widening. 'So, Kammo was alive? But, you told me—'

Adi can see he was right to return to this memory. This is where Ma's search began. Now, he needs to make sure his father doesn't ruin it, as always.

'—Seven years, seven years she mourned for you, until she could not go on anymore. She could never love Munno like she loved you,'

'Do you know what he's talking about?' Ma turns to his father. 'I thought Kammo died of pneumonia, as a child. Now he says she was alive?'

'What do I know?' says his father. 'You and your family. Even God does not know your secrets. Or should I say Allah?'

Adi lingers on his father for a moment, marvelling at how different he looks. Looking closer, however, he catches a glimpse of the father he knows – the sneering smile, the malice in his eyes, the anger rippling from his soft jaws to his large forehead. This may have been a turning point for Ma, but his father, he can see, is already beyond redemption.

'—I know what you are doing,' says his father, and he snaps back to the moment. 'You are trying to distract me from your own lies. You act as if your own family are angels and only mine are demons.'

'I came to see you, Kammo.' Nana's voice is growing fainter, and Adi swallows. This is it, his cue should be coming up any second now. He shuts his eyes tighter to make sure he does not miss a single word.

'—I never told Toshi but I found you.'

'Are you going to take your mother's side again?'

Ma rises, and Adi takes a deep breath and screams at the top of his voice, louder than he has ever screamed before, as urgent as a newborn's cry: '*MA!*'

'Mr Sharma!' the vulture shrieks in a shrill, childish voice. 'What are you—'

'Shh,' Adi whispers. 'Pay attention.'

Ma turns to little Adi, frowning, but finds him sulking in the same spot, tearing open another bud. She shakes her head at his father and sits down again. His father goes on muttering but her attention is once again focused on Nana.

'—I came to Jalandhar, I saw you there, at that Gandhi Ashram,' Nana whispers, and Ma leans in to catch his words. 'But I . . . I was afraid.'

Ma pats his bony hand again, smiling, though she looks like she's about to cry. Adi finally allows himself to breathe – his work here is done.

'—You knew me as Tariq, you never knew Tarun. I was afraid you would tell them I was Muslim. They would take everything, everything from me again. But who can know Allah's will?' Nana wails. 'He took everything away anyway. He took my Toshi.'

The chair screeches, his father rises, but Ma does not turn.

'—Forgive me, Kammo, it was all, it was all my fault,' Nana weeps.

'It's okay, Papa, it's okay,' Ma whispers, soothing his restless hands with a gentle caress, until he sighs and closes his teary eyes, and Adi opens his own.

20.

She had Ma's eyes

'You want something more?' asked Ma, and he shook his head.

He had gobbled up his sandwich in four bites, as usual, and had been sitting at the table staring at his empty plate, mopping up the ketchup with a finger and wondering if the time was right.

For over a week he had waited for the right moment to approach Ma again. He did not know how long it would take for the edited memory to seep into Ma's awareness, to remind her of what Nana had said. It could be weeks, months for all he knew, and he wondered if he could do anything to move it along, place some more hints for Ma to rediscover what she had forgotten. He could print out the article about that boutique named after Nani, owned by someone with a name synonymous with Ma's, and leave it on the dining table. He could bring up Nana again, in the hope of refreshing her memory.

'Oh, listen,' said Ma, acting all nonchalant as she wiped the table and rearranged the condiment bottles. 'That day, when we were, uh, talking . . . You were saying something about your Maasi? You found something on the internet? In Jalandhar?'

'Mm-hmm,' he nodded, and examined his jagged nails, trying not to smile.

'Was it the Gandhi Vanita Ashram?' Ma asked. 'Because I called them and checked again, they don't have any records—'

'No, no, it was a shop, a boutique.'

'What?'

He sprang out of his chair and ran into his room, emptying his bag on the bed, flinging the books and notebooks around before remembering that he had saved the note in a place he rarely touched: the Sanskrit notebook.

'What are you doing, béta?' Ma asked from the doorway, her eyebrows joined with worry.

He unfolded the note with the address written on it in Noor's neat, even hand. 'I think Maasi is here.'

Ma stared at the note, taking way longer than needed to read the two lines of address. 'Are you sure?'

'Yes.' He wasn't sure, but in a strange way, he was too. He was starting to suspect that all the odd happenings of the past few months – Ma's disappearances, the vulture's memories, his friendship with Noor and Omi, their confrontation with the Sanskrit teacher and their discovery of the boutique named after Nani, selling dresses like the one he had seen in his visions, just like the one Ma had found in her storeroom – none of them had been coincidence.

'Come with me, I'll show you.' He got up and walked into his parents' room, flung the cover off the computer and turned it on.

Ma stood behind him as they waited, first for the computer to start up, then for the modem to beep and croak and shriek, until they were finally online.

'How do you know all this?' Ma said. 'Do they teach you at school?'

He just laughed and went on scrolling, searching for the link Omi had found. How *did* they know? How did kids know what to do with a ball, or how to climb over fences, or the art of picking nicknames that pierced right through your deepest insecurities? They just did.

'Here.' He let Ma have the chair.

He watched as she read the article, her eyes scanning rapidly until they were caught by the image of the flower-studded kurta. He read Ma's face – the sideways movement of her jaw, the slight dip of her chin, her forehead lifting and her eyes widening – and he knew what she was thinking.

'I'm coming with you,' he said.

'Where?'

'There.' He nodded at the note still clutched in Ma's hand.

'Adi,' she said, looking at the screen, then back at him. 'How will you . . . you have exams coming up. You don't have to worry about these things. I will just go and check, it will only take a few days—'

'I'm not asking, Ma. I'm telling you. You're not going alone this time.'

Ma turned to the screen again and was quiet for a long time.

'Ma?'

She looked up, her eyes brimming with tears, and nodded. Adi could see she wanted to say thank you, and understood why it was so difficult for her to say. It was for the same reason that he could not reach out and give her a hug, even though every muscle in his body ached for it.

*

Across all the sixteen platforms at the New Delhi Railway Station, the Shatabdi Express to Amritsar was the best-looking train. It was painted a deep, rich red and, unlike the small, barred windows of all the other trains, it had massive, tinted panels that gave it an air of importance. Sitting upright in the plush blue seat by the window, Adi couldn't help but feel it too, like he was an intrepid traveller going on an important journey, visiting distant lands in search for signs of life – a kind of 'Explorer on the Moon'.

'Ma?'

'Yes, béta?' She was busy looking through her maroon handbag, making sure she hadn't forgotten something important. He knew the look she had on her face, the twitches that betrayed her rising panic. She was probably anxious, afraid of not finding Kammo yet again – or terrified of finally meeting her. He had to distract her, he thought, just to calm her down.

'Why is the train called the *Shatabdi Express?*'

'Shatabdi means a century.'

'I know, but a century of what?'

'These trains started in '86,' she said, glancing up at their small suitcase sitting on the overhead rails, checking to see if it was still there. 'Or maybe '88. It was Pundit Nehru's hundredth birthday, so they were named after that.'

Adi nodded, then remembered the vulture's third memory. It seemed like such a long time ago, but he could still see it all vividly – the blood-covered baby, the sweat-darkened back of Nani's kurta, the joy in Nana's sunken eyes, the dust on Nehru's shiny shoes.

'Ma? Did Nana know Pundit Nehru?'

As always, the mere mention of Nana made Ma smile.

'Oh, yes,' she said. 'He used to say he met Pundit Nehru once and it changed his life. He never told me where he met him, or what Nehru did, but your Nana always remembered him as a great man. He always said that it was the British who accidentally gave birth to India, but it was Nehru who nurtured the country like his own child. Without Nehru, India may never have survived.'

He thought of asking why, then, his father so hated Nehru, but thought better of it. Ma may have read it on his face anyway, because she shrugged and said: 'Now, some people don't like Nehru very much. He had some faults too. He made mistakes, like we all do. Those are the things people remember now. But that's what happens when a country changes and grows up. It's just like a child that way,' she smiled. 'When children are young, they see their parents as perfect. But when they grow older, all they can see are the faults.'

He looked at Ma, trying to make out if she was trying to say something about him, but she just laughed and mussed his hair.

After a brief pause, he decided it was a good time to ask the question that had been on his mind for days, ever since he had overheard Ma talking to his father about their trip.

'Ma? Are we going to get Maasi back with us?'

'I don't know, béta.' She chewed her lip. 'Let's see if she is even there.'

Ma had told his father, making it clear in her calm, determined voice, that if she did find her lost sister, she was going to bring her home. To Adi's surprise, his father had not argued against it. He had listened quietly, his eyes hooked to the TV, and grunted. But then, he could not really oppose Ma now, after she had spent months taking care of his mother. Himself, Adi could not have been more pleased at the thought of a fourth person moving into their house again. Not only would it distract Ma and his father from each other, it meant that he could move back into the drawing room.

'Listen,' she said, 'I should have . . . I didn't tell you about these things . . . When I left, um, I should have . . . I thought it was best if you didn't know.'

'I know, Ma. You were protecting me from bad things in the past.'

'Yes, but . . .' She paused to look out of the window, and he stared at his hands. 'I – I was ashamed of my family, of myself. And your father and Amma, they . . . I always felt like it was my fault, like I was . . . You know, your Nana and Nani, they were not married. Actually, she was married to someone else, but she ran away with your Nana.'

'Yes, I know. They ran away to save their lives. And your life.'

Ma looked at him again, the way she had looked at him when he had set up the computer and the modem. 'I don't know how you know these things. You must have a great memory if you remember your Nana talking about it.'

He had a little help from a friend, but he wasn't going to tell her that, certainly not now. He could sense her foot tapping furiously underneath her sari.

'It's okay, Ma,' he said, reaching out to touch her hand. He wanted to say a lot more, to tell her that there was no shame in being the daughter of Tariq and Toshi. They had lived through hell and they had tried their best to hold on to love, to each other and to their two daughters and they had suffered enough for it. He was proud to have them as his grandparents, and he was proud to have a mother who never gave up. He could not bring himself to say any of it, but it didn't seem to matter. He could feel the tension leaving Ma's fingers, and he could see her face transforming, slowly, with that warm, radiant smile that he had almost forgotten.

*

It began with the slightest of movements, a barely perceptible jerk and it took Adi a moment to realise what it meant – the train was moving!

He leant back and watched the platform begin to slide past the window. As soon as the train had cleared the station, it sped up, tracing its path through a narrow channel cutting across the city. The tracks were sandwiched between unending rows of houses with bare brick walls, sitting so close to the train that he could peek into open windows and catch glimpses of women bent over stoves in dingy kitchens. It would be cool, he thought, to live in such a place, close enough to feel the thrilling roar of the train in your chest, but realised that it could be rather inconvenient, especially when you had to study, or sleep, and the Shatabdi Express went thundering across your window, rattling your bones like the rails of a rickety bridge.

*

He woke up with a start and found the train standing at a station. Looking around for one of the signs that had the stations' names painted in a circle, he spotted one in the distance. It was Jalandhar.

'Ma? We're here!'

'Not yet, béta.' Ma didn't even open her eyes. 'This is Jalandhar Cantt. We'll get off at Jalandhar City.'

Adi sat up and rubbed his eyes, cursing himself for falling asleep. He had vowed to stay up through the entire eight-hour journey, through all of the towns and cities he had never seen. He had been thrilled to be speeding away from Delhi, away from everything and everyone he had ever known. Flying across the endless shades of green that seemed to stretch out all the way to the horizon, he had felt freer than ever before. But sometime in the afternoon, as he had stared mesmerised at the sunshine reflecting off the railway tracks – a little flash racing alongside the train and jumping over the gaps and forks in the tracks like a video game character – he had drifted off to sleep. He had to admit, though, it had been the deepest, most peaceful sleep he had had in a long time.

When they finally stepped out at Jalandhar City and made their way out of the station, he was surprised to find how different it was from the place he had imagined. It felt like a small town but somehow seemed more crowded than Delhi. Beyond the chaos of the taxis, tempos, buses and cars outside the station, he spotted a group of cycle rickshaws. The address they were looking for was not far from the station, Ma had said. Lugging the small suitcase with one hand past red-shirted coolies squatting idly, he went up to a rickshaw-vala and decided to practise his Punjabi. The tall, skinny Sardaar-ji was not wearing a turban – his hair was tied up in a bun on top of his head and wrapped in a small piece of cloth, like they did for Sikh children. He said something Adi didn't understand and laughed, but it was a warm, friendly sort of laugh and oddly infectious too.

Ma came and repeated what Adi had said, but this time the Sardaar-ji understood. He turned to Adi and said in slow, beautifully enunciated Hindi, 'Come, sahib, have a seat.'

Once again, Adi was annoyed at the unfairness of it. Everyone in the world, it seemed, could speak more than just Hindi. Everyone had a local language, a mother tongue they could call their own, that came to them as naturally as blinking, plus they could speak at least one or two more languages with ease. All he had was English, a language that belonged to none of them, that they were forced to adopt, twisting its words with their unaccustomed tongues.

As the rickshaw crawled out of the station and into the city, his annoyance gave way to wonder and he began pointing things out to Ma, who seemed just as excited. She was distracted by the constant chatter of the rickshaw-vala, however, and he stopped trying to listen and quietly observed the city.

They passed a cinema hall larger than any he had seen in Delhi, with a giant hoarding for the movie *Border*, still playing here months after its release. The hoarding was hand-painted, he realised and, seeing the rage in Sunny Deol's bloodshot eyes, he could hardly believe it wasn't a photograph. They looped around another roundabout – the city was full of them, each street meeting the next in a circle that seemed to work smoothly without any traffic lights – and a large market emerged, overflowing with candy shops and toy shops and shops selling all kinds of costumes, from generic gods and Santa Claus to forgotten freedom fighters. It was like a wonderland for kids, this city, and he wished he had come here a few years earlier: how exciting he would have found it then.

As the rickshaw swung around yet another roundabout, they passed a shop called Lovely Sweets and the rickshaw-vala got even more excited, stopping and turning around to tell Ma she should buy the famous laddoos of Jalandhar.

Ma laughed and shook her head, telling him they were in a hurry, and his face fell as if his mother had made the laddoos with her own hands.

'On the way back,' Ma said to console him.

Adi realised that even though his ears could disentangle the language and prise the words apart, his tongue could not put them back together in the same way. There was a rhythm to it, a gentle cadence that his lips, stiffened by the toneless drawl of English, would never be able to sing. Perhaps the choice had already been made for him – he would just have to love the language that had chosen him.

But wasn't he falling into the same trap as his father, thinking of English as a foreign language, a symbol of slavery? It was their twenty-third official language, Ma'am George had said; the language of the laws and the Constitution that had created independent India. Had he not grown up reading, writing, speaking it? Had he not learnt A-B-C before ka-kha-ga, Ba-Ba-Black-Sheep before *Chanda-Mama*? Above all, he had spent all those nights flipping through *Roget's Pocket Thesaurus*, marvelling at the magic of its words. No, he was not going to feel ashamed of it anymore. English was his own tongue, as much as Hindi and Urdu and Punjabi and Bhojpuri, and he was going to love them all just the same.

'Lo-ji, here we are,' said the rickshaw-vala, turning into a residential street and stopping.

As Ma fumbled through her bag for the money, Adi jumped out and stood before the house. He had been expecting a shop, a boutique, but this was a two-storey bungalow, smaller than the ones around it but many times larger than their own flat in Delhi. It had a small, well-kept lawn in the front, ringed by a row of flowerpots, and even though the walls were faded and crumbling in places, the house exuded a feeling of strength and solidity, like it was too comfortable to bother about such trivial things as cracked plaster.

He turned to find Ma still looking through her purse and fished out a ten-rupee note from his jeans' pocket. The rick-shaw-vala took it with a smile and waved goodbye as he pedalled away.

'Come, Ma,' he said, but she didn't answer; she didn't move. She had grown quieter as they had drawn closer to their destination, and hadn't said a word since they had passed Lovely Sweets. Now, she seemed afraid of even looking up.

He walked ahead to open the wide metal gates. With his first step in, the gruff barking of a dog rose from within the house and he jumped back.

'Who's there?' a voice called out, and a woman appeared behind the screen doors. Even in the fading light of the evening, even with the blue mesh of the door veiling her face, Adi knew they had made it. She had Ma's eyes.

'Kammo?' Ma called out, the name formed slowly, carefully on her hesitant lips.

The door was flung open and the woman stepped forward, then stopped. She looked younger than Adi had expected, leaner and taller than Ma, and her face had a hardened stern-ness to it. For an instant, he wondered if they had made a mistake.

'Who are you?' the woman asked. 'Who told you that name? Only my mother knew that name.'

'Yes,' Ma answered. 'Our mother. I am Tamanna, Toshi's daughter.'

The air stood still and the birds stopped chirping, and they stood frozen in their spot as Kammo stared at Ma, her frown deepening. Suddenly, her face crumpled and she reached out to hold the wall, and nearly stumbled down the two steps outside the door. Before Ma could say anything, Adi ran up to Kammo and held her arm, until she had steadied herself again. She looked up to him and squeezed his shoulder, then slowly turned back to Ma, her eyes brimming over.

'Sister. You have found me?'

Ma came running up the path and leapt up the two steps, and she grabbed her sister – the sister she had spent half a lifetime searching for; the only one in the world who shared her unforgotten past, who carried their unspoken memories in her bones.

'Sister,' she said, 'I never lost you.'

*

Dinner was a slow, confusing affair for Adi. At first, he was thrilled to have a seat at the dining table, finally being treated as a grown-up. Maasi told them all about her boutique – she had a workshop on the first floor where she designed and tailored clothes. She talked about her friends who came over every Friday to cook lunch together and she insisted that they stay for a week to meet all of them. Hearing Maasi talk about herself, he felt a jab of resentment. He had come expecting a helpless old lady. Instead, he found a woman with a robust voice and a free, easy laugh, living a life full of friends and Friday feasts. He should be happy for her, he told himself, knowing what he did about her. Why, then, did it feel like a betrayal?

As dinner was served, however, the conversation wandered around all the useless things that he had no interest in. They talked about the weather, the traffic in Delhi, the rising prices of onions. More than anything else, they talked about the food. Ma seemed fascinated by the Punjabi dishes on the table – leftovers from a party the night before, Maasi told them – and they discussed the recipes in detail, from which kind of chillies to fry in which kind of oil, to how long to pressure cook different mixes of daals.

Through it all, Adi sat quietly, trying to swallow small mouthfuls of all the things he hated – weird, weedy spinach saag; watery daal with bits of onion and tomato and thick rotis slathered with stinky ghee. He could not understand how they could waste their time over such trivial things. How could the sisters united after a lifetime's wait behave like new neighbours, like strangers studying each other for clues?

When dinner was finally over, Maasi showed them the guest bedroom. Used to sleeping on the divan in the living room now, he would have preferred his own room, but at least there were two single beds. Ma told him to change and get into bed while she went for a shower. Tired from the long day, he lay down and was surprised at how hard the mattress was. Even then, he struggled to keep his eyes open as his mind ran over all the things they had done since waking up before dawn, the distance they had covered in a day.

It took him a while to realise that Ma had been gone for way longer than her usual showers. He turned to lie on his back, silenced his mind and focused his ears, and he was pleased to discover that he hadn't lost his superpower.

'—Don't blame our mother, Munno,' Maasi was saying. 'She had loved Tariq since she was a little girl.'

Now, they had started talking about the real things, as soon as he was in bed? Fine. He was going to lie awake the whole night and listen in. He was used to it.

'But it was '40, or '41,' Maasi continued, 'and there was already talk of a separate Pakistan. It had become impossible for a Sikh girl to marry a Muslim boy, if it was ever possible. Her family were afraid of the scandal it would have caused, so they quickly married her off to some Sardaar from the villages, a military man injured in the big war. But she could not let Tariq go. She was crazy. It was never going to work. How long can you hide a thing like that? But love makes people lose their minds, no?'

'So are we both . . .' Ma lost her words halfway through the question.

'Tariq's daughters?' Maasi completed it for her. 'Only Wahé Guru can know for certain, but I think so. Or at least I hope so. Seeing you now, I think it might be true. We do both have the same broad forehead, don't we? And these big noses of ours, we certainly don't get them from Toshi!'

'Oh, it doesn't matter,' Ma said. 'But I can tell you this: he loved you like his daughter, right until his last breath.'

'Yes,' Maasi said, quietly. 'He was always good to me. And to our mother. Her husband was not. I was glad when Tariq took us out of that prison. In the end our kismat was broken, but I am glad they tried.'

'So, tell me,' Ma said, 'what happened to you after . . . when they took you . . .'

Maasi must have already told her about how she was kidnapped. He, too, was desperate to know what had happened to her after that, but there was a long silence.

'What happened,' Maasi finally said, 'is what always happens to women, to girls when they fall in the hands of men.'

He heard Ma gasp, and felt the silence thicken. Although he wasn't sure what exactly Maasi meant, his body seemed to know, tensing up by itself, hurting at the pain in her voice.

'It feels strange to talk about it now,' Maasi continued. 'It's like someone else's story, something I may have read in a book. How old was I – four, five? The truth is that I hardly remember a minute of it. It is like Wahé Guru took mercy on me and wiped my memory clean.'

'Yes, perhaps that's for the best.'

'I do remember a kind old woman who hid me in her house and fed me halva. There was barely any sugar in it, let alone ghee. Just a lump of boiled semolina with a hint of jaggery. God knows where she even found that during those times, but it was the best halva I have ever tasted.'

'This woman saved you?'

'I suppose you can say that. I remember hating her for a long time, though. I hated her for leaving me at the ashram. What is a child to do? You grab whatever you can find and you try not to let go. I loved Toshi too much to hate her for leaving me behind, so I took all that anger and poured it over that poor old woman.'

'But,' Ma interrupted, 'I looked for you at the ashram here! I called twice, I even came and checked, they said—'

'I was not in their records. Yes, I know. That woman gave me a new name. I remember her asking me my name, but I think I may have gone mute for a while. So, she gave me the name she said she had saved for the daughter she never had. I only changed it back when I turned eighteen.'

'Is that also why you are, um . . .' Ma hesitated for a moment, but Maasi guessed what she was going to ask.

'Why I am a Sardaarni, after what the Sikhs did to me?' Maasi stopped and sighed. 'My religion is not the religion of those thugs and murderers. It is not the religion of the ten Gurus or the scriptures either. My religion is only the memory of my mother. I am a Sikhni because that is what Toshi taught me to be, to believe in self-respect and the service of others, to treat every person with compassion. Once she was gone, what else did I have left?'

The two women were quiet for a while and Adi fought to keep his eyes open, digging his nails into his palms to stay awake.

'Anyway,' said Maasi, her tone betraying a smile. 'If you can't run from religion, it's better to have one that treats women as human beings. At least on paper,' she added with a mischievous, high-pitched chortle.

'That's true,' Ma said. 'Maybe that's what Papa thought too, that if it was not possible to escape religion, even in the new India, then it was best to go for a high-caste Hindu name. Do you think he would have got two houses and such a high position in the government with a low-caste name, let alone a name like Tariq Ali? And God forbid if we had been Sikhs, what would have happened in the '84 riots? Even Giani Zail Singh, the President himself, almost got his throat slit by the Hindus.'

'By the Congress mob,' said Maasi. 'It was about power, as it was in '47, as it is today. Once you awaken the animal inside humans,' – she paused, and Adi could almost hear her shaking her head – 'it ignites a junoon, a madness much older than all our gods. That's how our people, our neighbours and friends, turned into rabid dogs and ripped this country apart. Hindu, Muslim, Sikh, whose sword cut whose throat? And what difference did it make?'

'Maybe,' said Ma. 'But the name worked for Papa, no? Picking the right religion worked for him. He rebuilt his life from nothing.'

'It didn't work for you,' said Maasi, and to Adi's surprise, Ma laughed. Had she told Maasi about the trouble with his father, with Amma? How they never really accepted her because she wasn't a high-caste Hindu? He must have fallen asleep for a while and missed it.

'It could have worked. Who knows?' Ma replied. 'If he hadn't gone senile in his old age, babbling on about Tariq and Toshi and, most of all you, his Kammo. All those years he kept it all in, but in the end, the memories turned into termites and ate him away from within.'

It was Maasi's turn to laugh, though it was a muted sort of laugh, weighed down by a sorrow that had grown so old, so comfortable in her, that it had lost its painful edge. Listening to Ma and Maasi, Adi was reminded of a poem, a ghazal by Mirza Ghalib:

Ishrat-é-qatra hai dariya mein fanaa ho jaana
Dard ka hudd se guzarna hai davaa ho jaana

He remembered the verse in Noor's voice, swerving as she danced around the stage in the play that had earned them a standing ovation from Father Rebello, and a big hug from Ma'am George. He tried to remember the English translation that he had recited. It had only been a couple of weeks, but somehow that dizzying afternoon seemed like a distant memory, vague and slippery, a blur of fact and fantasy.

To be consumed by the torrent is the drop's ecstasy
Pain, beyond endurance, becomes its own remedy

Adi had practised the couplet countless times, recited it in front of the whole school, but the meaning had evaded him. Now, he felt like he was beginning to grasp its edges, even as the weight of sleep finally grew too heavy to hold back.

*

He woke up to sunlight streaming in through the windows, bathing the room in its mellow warmth, and he sprang out of bed and checked his Casio. 11:42. No one had woken him up? Had they all left? He rubbed his eyes and tried to reason with himself. Where would they go? Why would they leave him here? Where did that fear even come from? Would it always be such a part of his being, the trembling marrow in his very bones?

He wandered into the kitchen, looking for something to calm his grumbling stomach, and was struck by just how large it was, larger than the entire drawing room in his house. Almost a quarter of it was taken up by tall shelves, stocked with sacks of rice and flour and countless unmarked tins and jars. It seemed like there was enough food in there to feed all of Jalandhar, and he couldn't fathom why Maasi needed so much when it was just her and the dog living in this house. He found an open, rubber-banded pack of Marie biscuits on the kitchen counter and walked out into the drawing room.

Sinking into the sofa, he admired the soft touch of the worn-out blue fabric embroidered with pink and green flowers. Everything in the house, from the heavy curtains to the cushions on the chairs, was finely embroidered with every kind of flower imaginable – a riot of clashing colours shining bright despite the erosion of the years. Even the coasters on the table looked like the marble panels of the Taj Mahal, each with its unique, intricate pattern of petals. In spite of its general air of an antique shop, with its chipped furniture and faded rugs and strange light switches that looked like ancient white domes, the house had a warmth that seemed to glow even on that grey winter morning.

As he sat and looked around the sprawling drawing room, with its long dining table on one side and a cluster of sofas and armchairs on the other, he realised what was missing: a TV. All the chairs were arranged in a circle around the large coffee table, facing each other instead of being pointed towards a screen. An entire wall behind them was lined with bookshelves stretching from floor to ceiling, packed with more books than he had ever seen outside a library. Craning his neck, he wondered how Maasi ever managed to reach the high shelves stacked with heavy, hardbound books.

Most of the books were in Punjabi or Urdu, and he picked one from a lower shelf. It was a thick volume with frayed, yellowed pages held together with sellotape across the spine. *Tedhi Lakeer*, it was called. A crooked line. The author's name was Ismat Chughtai – a name he found breathtakingly beautiful, like Noor Farooqi. If only he had a Muslim name too. If only Nana had not changed his name, Ma might have grown up as a Muslim and he would have got a sleek, elegant name like Mir, Firaq, or Faiz, as opposed to his mealy mouthful of a name, full of podgy 'sh' sounds. If only Nana and Nani had not cycled across an invisible line on that fire-lit night, he might have grown up in Pakistan and studied Urdu instead of Sanskrit, recited poetry instead of chanting tense tables. All because of one small turn of fate half a century ago, he was now unable to read the pages fluttering before his eyes.

He heard the click-clack of its footsteps before he saw the dog, and he was seized by panic. How had the beast freed itself from its chains? Could he make a run for the door? Could he climb up the bookshelf? Three years had passed but he still remembered it vividly – the incident with the dog in the park. He had discovered a puppy, tiny as a toy, hiding in the bushes and mewling. As soon as he had picked it up, the mother dog had appeared, racing towards him with bared fangs.

'Dogs can smell fear,' his father had told him. 'Never show your back to them,' he had said. 'Never, ever run.' So Adi had stood his ground. Seven injections he had had to get, thanks to that advice. Seven in the butt.

The dog walked over slowly towards the sofa, panting and wagging its tail, then sat before him like an obedient child, looking up with eager eyes. It wanted the biscuits, he realised. Gingerly, he took one out and dropped it on the floor. The dog ate it in one go, lifting its head up and gulping it like it was a pill. It made a distressed face, a childlike grimace that made Adi chuckle. The dog shook itself, as if trying to get rid of the taste, the very memory of the dry, powdery biscuit; it turned full circle before laying down right next to his feet.

In a way, his father had been right, Adi realised. He should not run from his fears, but that did not mean he had to stand frozen in place.

*

It was late February, but, unlike the thick, dusty air of Delhi that already seemed to be heating up for the long summer, the Punjabi afternoon was crisp and cold. Ma was sitting on a cane chair, sipping her tea and waiting for Maasi, as Adi lay on the grass reading his book.

'I have something for you,' Maasi said, walking up to Ma. From a blue velvet pouch, she carefully took out a piece of jewellery, something small. He couldn't quite see it, but, going by the look in Ma's eyes, it was something precious.

'Our mother gave this to me.' Maasi was staring at her palm like it held a painful memory. 'It was the only thing she took with her, when we ran away from that side. The only thing small enough to hide, sewn into the band of my salvaar. But it was also the most precious thing she had, this pair of earrings. They belonged to her own mother, our Nani, who died long ago, during the Bombay Fever. This is the only part of her dowry that Toshi managed to save from that drunkard husband of hers. She gave them to me, to keep safe. I did.' She looked up at Ma with a smile. 'But I couldn't give them back to her. Now, I'll give them to you.' She held her hand out to Ma.

'No-no, behen-ji, I can't take these,' Ma said, looking like she was terrified of the glinting gemstones. 'They're all you have left of our mother, how can I take them from you?'

'Hayé, puglee,' Maasi laughed. 'Oh, silly girl, I have *you* now.'

Ma finally took the earrings. Slowly, she turned her head one way, then the other, slipping them into her ears. She pushed her hair back and showed them to Maasi, who clapped like a little child. Adi could see them too, now. They were made of silver, he thought, shaped like a peacock's feather, studded with little gems of different colours that fanned out around a large white orb, a pearl that shimmered in the winter sun.

'What happened, behen-ji?' Ma asked, suddenly worried. Adi looked up at Maasi and saw her face drawn. She tried to smile, but she looked like she was in pain.

'Oh, these memories.' Maasi shook her head. 'They never leave you, do they?'

'I think I should—' Ma said, pulling the earrings off.

'No, no,' Maasi stopped her, 'it's just . . . I suddenly remembered something I thought I had forgotten. These earrings, they once caused such a fight between Toshi and her in-laws. Those hyenas always had their eyes on them, but Toshi protected them with her life. She saw them as a symbol, I think, her last embers of hope. They could take everything from her, treat her worse than the skinny mule in their stable, but Wahé Guru knows, she never let them break her spirit. Maybe that's why, through the fires of hell, I held on to these little trinkets.'

'Oh.' Ma sat up and bit her lip. 'Actually, I met them, Toshi's in-laws, when I went to Lahore.'

'Acchha?' Maasi raised an eyebrow. 'What did they say?'

'They . . . they were not nice. This old woman I met, she was just horrible.'

Maasi roared with laughter, but there was no joy in her voice. 'I know who you must've met. Did she have light brown eyes?'

'Yes! You know her?'

'She was Toshi's sister-in-law. She lived with us.'

The woman who poured kerosene on her children, thought Adi. And probably the same one he spoke to on the phone. He looked at Ma, who seemed to be confused.

'But, you said last night, they . . . they wanted to burn themselves?'

'Oh, I knew she wouldn't. She just wanted to get rid of Toshi and me. She was always mean to us. She controlled the kitchen, the food cupboard and kept everything for her children. She would make all kinds of sweets, laddoos, kheer, halva, but she would never let me have any. I remember the whole house smelling of sugar and ghee, while I drank plain, watered-down milk.'

Was this why, Adi wondered, Maasi's kitchen was so big and well stocked now? Was this why she had eaten so little at dinner, even though the table was covered in food?

'So strange, no? The oddest things that you remember from childhood, like they happened yesterday?' Maasi laughed, but Ma did not respond. She was turning the earrings over in her hands, caressing them gently like they were fragile little things, baby birds in need of a warm touch.

'I'll just – I'll go and keep these away,' she finally said, and walked off into the house.

Adi turned back to the book lying open in the grass before him, but it did not hold his attention. Maasi had told him he could take any books he liked, and he had made a list of the interesting ones – short stories by Saadat Hasan Manto (he loved the name Manto), a brick of a book by a Russian named Leo (he had always wanted to be a Leo, he hated being a Cancer instead), and the Ismat Chughtai book that he could not read.

He glanced at Maasi and was again surprised by just how different she looked from what he had imagined. It was the same little girl, he had to remind himself, whom he had seen in the vulture's visions. He was beginning to discover that the glimpses he had caught barely scratched the surface of her suffering through the years. And yet, she was an idol of calmness, a smiling Buddha, looking like she had no complaints against life. She was at least five years older than Ma, he knew, but she looked younger, healthier, her face not as lined with worry, her eyes always sparkling with a barely contained smile. That smile filled him with hope. If she could put it all behind her and build a life full of colour, so could Ma. Now that they were together, perhaps Ma's life was going to change too.

'I have something for you,' Ma said, as she walked out into the garden holding a small bowl. 'We cannot change our memories, but we can create new ones. All those people, those times, they're gone. Now, when you think of halva, you think of me.'

Maasi took the bowl and stared down at it in silence. Slowly, she scooped a small spoonful and put it into her mouth and held it in there for a long moment before swallowing. When she looked up, she was crying.

'No, behen-ji, no more tears,' Ma said, but her own voice was breaking, and Adi had to look away. He had been waiting, he realised, for Ma to break down. He hadn't expected it from Maasi, who had looked so composed. Maybe he had missed what Ma saw – the pain of a past that still flowed deep within her body, waiting, like lava, for years, decades, aeons, until a crack in the calm surface let it all out.

'Munno, now you promise me you won't leave,' Maasi said, trying hard not to sob, but failing. 'Promise . . . promise me you'll stay.'

Ma bent down to hug her tightly, cradling her head in her arms. 'You have me now. You'll never be alone again.'

Looking at them as they held each other, enveloped by the afternoon glow, the realisation hit Adi like a piece of chalk on his forehead. He had got it all wrong. All along, he had hoped that uniting the sisters would give Ma the peace she was looking for and he would no longer have to worry about her leaving. But Ma needed more than just peace, he could now see. After half a century of suffering, living a false life that had been rigged from the start, what she deserved was liberation. And he was not the one to give it to her, to rescue her like he had so often dreamt in his childish fantasies. No, he was the one holding Ma back, her five-foot baby forever tugging at her dupatta.

He closed his eyes and sighed. It was time to let go. It was still the fiftieth year of Independence, after all; it could be their year of freedom too. And if he truly wanted Ma to have it, he knew he would have to first set himself free.

It was time to confront his final fear.

21.

This son-of-an-owl

The evening sky was clear, almost transparent, the moon glowing bright before the sun had fully set, and he could even see a few stars shining through. Climbing onto the concrete platform that carried the water tank, he surveyed the neighbourhood. Large, solid-looking houses were spread out all around, many of them just as gracefully old as Maasi's, with muted pastel walls, carved window arches, and sprawling lawns. In between, there were a few new houses that seemed entirely out of place. They were taller, starker, with air-conditioning units instead of large windows, and sparkling cars in long driveways in place of grassy lawns. He wondered if Jalandhar too would one day turn into a cramped, cluttered city like Delhi, its old bungalows replaced by grey apartment blocks and all its little roundabouts jammed with traffic day and night. For now, at least, it was quiet.

'Are you there?' he whispered. He hadn't spotted the vulture yet and he wondered if Punjab was too far for it to bother flying all the way.

'Ahem,' came the voice, and he turned to find it on the house next door, perched on a water tank right in front of the setting sun.

343

'You made it all the way here? How far will I have to go to get rid of you?'

He said it as a joke but he knew the vulture would not take it as one. He was not wrong.

'You are disappointing me, Mr Sharma. Even after all of your progress your manners have not improved. May I remind you that you have come looking for me. If you are wanting to get rid of me—'

'Relax, baba. I was only joking.'

'Ah, yes, your sense of humour. Very refreshing.'

Adi rolled his eyes. 'Okay, I'm ready for the last challenge now.'

'Oh? And what is your last challenge? Once again you are going to trick me?'

'What, are you still angry that I messed with your memory?'

'It is not "my memory", Mr Sharma. They belong to all of us, and the rules are there to protect them.'

'Oh, calm down, they're only memories, no?'

'*Only* memories? What is the past but memories?'

'Yeah, but they're like recordings of things that happened, didn't you say? Does changing them actually change the past?'

'Hmm.' The vulture looked up at the fading sky. 'No, I suppose it does not. But it is still risky, it can change what people remember. It can change the future.'

'Exactly.' Adi couldn't help but break into a grin.

'Anyway, what is done is done.' The vulture nodded, looking secretly impressed, as though it was biting down a smile. 'Let us move on. You said you are ready for something?'

'Yeah, so . . .' Adi took a deep breath. 'My biggest fear, the one I didn't tell you earlier, because I—'

'I know, Mr Sharma. You are feeling ashamed to admit it.'

'You *know*?'

'Of course! I am knowing since day one. Anyone can see it just by looking at you one time.'

'So, why did you not say something?'

'I was waiting for you. You have to admit it yourself, that is the rule. Which, may I remind you, you are still not doing.'

'What? Oh. Okay, so my number one all-time greatest fear is . . . Ma leaving. And never coming back.'

'Very good,' the vulture mumbled. 'And how are you going to address it now?'

'Oh, I thought you would—'

'What? Tell you? But I cannot, Mr Sharma. You have to find the answer yourself, those are the—'

'Rules, yes. God forbid we break those.'

'I have never told you what to do. If you recall, you told me your fears and you addressed them one by one. I merely recorded your updates in my report.'

'I guess that's true.'

'It was easier because they were simple, like the fear of your father's high temperature. But a fear like this is complicated, no? Fear of your Ma leaving? When she is here, you are afraid she will leave. When she leaves, you are afraid she will not come back. What to do? What to do?'

'What if *I* left?'

'Hmm.' The vulture bent its long neck, bowing its head as if it was examining the ground, and nodded. 'Very interesting, Mr Sharma. But where can you go?'

Where *could* he go? To Sunny-Bunny's house, where he had spent so many a peaceful summer afternoon? He did not even know where they lived now. To Chicago, IL? Chacha had his own life; he was getting married. He may have loved Adi and all that, but it did not mean he would want to adopt him.

'Oh!' He sat up with a jerk and his head hit the concrete casing of the water tank. He did not even notice the pain. 'What if . . . what if I went to England?'

'England? What is there in England? They are not even good at cricket anymore, and it is always raining.'

'And I love the rain!' The more he thought about it, the more it made sense. England, of cloud-filled skies and red double-deckers and Famous Five adventures. That was the answer.

Or was it? He was not sure.

He tried to expand the idea in his head, to turn a flash of inspiration into a detailed plan of action, but his head began to spin. All he knew for certain was that it was the most excited he had ever felt, even more than when he had sat in the train and watched the world he knew speed past him.

'I . . . I just know, I remember Chacha saying . . . okay, I have to go,' he said, leaping off the platform and ran towards the staircase. 'I'll tell you later, you'll see,' he yelled.

'Indeed I will,' came the mumbled reply, but Adi was gone.

*

On the first floor, he took a deep breath and nudged the door. It was open. He stepped into Maasi's workshop and looked around the long, narrow room. The windows stretching across the length of the room had no curtains and there was still enough light outside to make the room sparkle. There were rows upon rows of hangers standing at attention all through the room – a fancy-dress army of kurtas, saris and skirts. Some of them were unstitched and they flapped loosely in the light breeze from the open door. Some looked as finely finished as shop-window pieces, covered in embroidery and gemstones and glittery threads. All of them were beautiful and unmistakably Maasi's creations.

There was a computer at the far end of the room, wrapped in plastic casing. He turned it on, dragged a chair from the sewing table and waited. After staring at the blinking lights on the internet modem for a while, he realised he had to disconnect the telephone and plug the wire in. Finally, it croaked and coughed and shrieked, and the little Earth icon appeared at the bottom of the screen. Opening hotmail, he briefly considered creating a new email address but decided there was no time for all that. He clicked on 'New Email', entered Chacha's address, which he had memorised, and stared at the blank screen.

Where was he to begin?

*

He woke up slowly, stirring from a sleep deeper than he was used to and his legs stretched out under the plush duvet, flexing muscles that seemed to have grown overnight. He prised open his eyes and looked around the guest room. It was small but comfortable, with dark wooden cupboards and an earthy smell and, in just two nights, he had begun to feel at home in its warm embrace. The time had come to leave, however, and he pulled himself out of bed.

Out in the drawing room, he was not surprised to find Ma fully dressed and ready to go, sitting next to Maasi on the sofa with a steaming cup of chai. Their train was to leave at eleven – there were still four hours left – but Ma preferred to wait at the station rather than at home.

The sudden snort of the dog in the corridor, right behind him, made him yelp and jump into the drawing room. Ma and Maasi turned to him and started to laugh.

'I was just going to wake you up,' said Ma. 'Come here, I need to talk to you.'

Adi tried to prod his brain into action, running over all the possible things he could have done wrong. He had taken four books from Maasi's bookshelf – was that too many? Maybe Maasi had found out that he had been in her workshop and was unhappy about the intrusion? Was it the bloody dog? Had it fallen sick after eating all those biscuits that he had shared with it last night?

'I spoke to your father this morning,' said Ma. 'He said Chacha had called, looking for you. So I called him back.'

'Shit-fuck-tuttee,' he muttered, incensed at the betrayal. He had specifically asked Chacha to keep his email Top Secret. It had taken him two full minutes just to figure out how to underline 'Top Secret' and make it red.

'I'm not angry, béta. I just want to talk.' There was a hint of a smile in Ma's eyes, so he breathed in and went up to her.

'You want to go to boarding school? In England?' Her voice sounded incredulous, but her expression was neutral – closer to amused than angry, if anything – and he couldn't decide how to respond.

'Chacha had said . . . when he was here, when we went to Lajpat Nagar . . . he talked about someone who went to school in England, a girl who got married there.'

'Oh!' She laughed, surprised that he remembered the story. 'Yes, but—'

'And he had said that I should go too. He said I could get a scholarship.'

'Did he?'

'Yes! And you had agreed.'

'I don't remember this, Adi. Maybe I wasn't listening. But I don't want you to go. If that's why you are saying this, then you don't have to—'

'Ma, I want to go.'

'Oh.' She looked at Maasi, who, for the first time in three days, was not looking at Adi like he was a little child. 'Arré, but,' Ma turned back to him, 'what's so bad about your school? We sent you to a convent school in South Delhi to get the best education. Do you know how hard it was to get admission there?'

'But they don't teach us anything! Half our teachers are always absent. When they are there, they just write things on the blackboard and ask us to copy them. The only thing they like is punishing kids for stupid things, like forgetting our notebooks or not combing our hair properly or not talking in English. If I have to talk in English all the time, I might as well go to England, no?'

'There are many good schools in Delhi. You should have told me if you didn't like it, we could ask Papa to—'

'I don't *want* to ask Papa, Ma. It's not the school, I don't want to live in that house. I don't want to live with *him*.'

'Adi—' she started with a stern voice, but he cut her off.

'Does he even want to live with us? All he is interested in is doing his puja and getting his promotion.'

'Your Papa works very hard so he can support the family. He is not a bad man, béta. He is just under a lot of pressure at work. He feels unappreciated sometimes, like we all do. He used to be very different, you know? He was not always so angry. You were too young, you won't remember, but he—'

'Used to slap you? That I remember.'

Ma looked away, wincing as though she had just been struck, and he bit his tongue. He hated doing this, reminding her of things she tried to forget. But he had to.

She sighed, then turned back to him. 'Listen to me, béta. Every family has some problems. These things happen sometimes, people get angry and they say things, do things, that they regret later. It doesn't make them bad people.'

'What makes someone a bad person, then?'

Ma's jaw tightened, and he could almost hear her teeth grinding. It would have scared him on any other day, but today, his rage burnt hotter and brighter than any of his fears.

'Behave yourself, Adi,' Ma hissed, but he saw through her attempt at evading the question. He wasn't going to let it go.

'No, tell me, Ma. You keep saying he's not a bad person. He hits you, he talks badly to you, he doesn't appreciate anything you do for him. And I know what he did to your . . . to my . . .'

Di was the name he had given to his sister; he could not share that with Ma, however. He did not know how, but he had known about her, even as a child – he had felt her absence strongly enough to create an imagined version of her, a ghost to comfort him through the long nights. But no longer could he have his sister stay buried like some shameful secret, like a cursed family jewel locked away in a grey Godrej safe.

'. . . to my sister!' he blurted out. 'I know, Ma.'

He looked at Maasi, wondering if Ma had told her about Di yet, but she was frowning in confusion.

'What is he talking about, Munno?' Maasi asked Ma, who was looking down now, her entire face trembling like a pot of tea about to boil. The dog came trotting up to Maasi, panting for attention, but sensed the tension and quietly fell to the floor.

'I had a girl,' Ma said, her voice down to a whisper. 'Before Adi. I never saw her. They took her away when she was born, and—'

'Oh. So that's why . . . I was wondering why you had him so late.' She slowly shook her head, her eyes telling Ma that she understood, that no more was needed to be said.

'Ma?' Adi's tone softened at the sight of his mother's shining eyes. 'Papa may not be a terrible person, fine, but he is never going to be happy with us. He has a problem with who you are. And me too. He has a problem with our blood, just like Amma did. How can we change that? So if he wants to be angry all the time, let him be. Why should we keep suffering it? What is the point in living like this, where we dread coming home every day?'

'We can't break up our family, Adi. We have to adjust and support each other, and sometimes we have to compromise—'

'The family is already broken, Ma!' he yelled, losing his patience. 'There *is* no family, can't you see?'

'Buss!' she screamed back, rising to her feet. 'You will not speak to me like that!'

'Acchha, now listen to me.' Maasi reached out and grabbed Ma's hand. 'Just listen, Munno.' She smiled with such kindness that Ma's anger deflated a little and she sat back down.

Maasi turned to Adi with a theatrical scowl. 'This is no way to talk to your mother, boy. Say sorry to her now. Come on.'

Adi was fuming, but, seeing the twinkle in Maasi's eyes, he sensed that she had something more in mind. 'Sorry,' he mumbled, avoiding Ma's eyes.

'Shabaash,' Maasi said. 'Very good. Now, you listen to me, sister. In my life, I have seen all kinds of men, good and bad. I have also seen some that you cannot imagine. And you know what's common among all of them? They are all phuddoos.'

A little snort of laughter escaped from Adi's nose. He had heard the insult before, the Punjabi word for a fool. It used to be a favourite of Sunny-Bunny because even though it sounded vaguely obscene, it was technically not a gaali and therefore easier to get away with.

'Stupid cowards they are, all of them, like mules,' Maasi went on. 'They can change, sometimes, but not without a kick or two in the behind.'

'Behen-ji,' Ma said, her voice hushed, her eyes growing wide. 'What are you saying?'

'Your boy here has a sharp tongue.' Maasi frowned at Adi again, but there was a smile playing on her lips. 'But he is right. If you keep being a pativrata, such a good husband-worshipping wife, why will your pati-parmeshvar, your exalted husband-god, bother to change? He has got every-thing – someone to cook his food, wash his chaddis, warm his bed. If you want him to change, make him do all that himself. Men in our country are treated like gods' gifts by their mothers, they are brought up like avatars of Lord Vishnu. Left to themselves, they struggle to wipe their own asses.'

A crack of a smile spread across Ma's face, and Adi felt bold enough to chuckle.

'So, do one thing,' Maasi said. 'Send this one to England, Amreeka, Kaneda, wherever he wants to go. Give him a chance to make his own choices too. If nothing else, he will learn to feed himself without crying for his mumma. It will be more than most men know around here. Anyway, what's left in this country for young people? All we care about is temples and cows. And then,' she smiled, 'you come and live here with me. Just try it for a few months, see if it brings any change. If it does, then good, you can go back. If it does not, I am here for you, no?'

Ma was too touched to speak, but he could tell from her eyes that her defences were crumbling. Maasi held both her hands and waited until Ma met her eyes.

'The innocent spend their lives in prisons until they turn into their own guards, while the criminals roam free. No, Munno, enough of that. You are not breaking up your family. For fifty years you have lived a partitioned life. You are giving yourself a chance to become whole.'

Ma nodded, but said in her choked-up voice, 'How can I send my child away?'

'I am not a child,' Adi shot back.

'You will always be a child to me, béta.'

'No, Ma. I can't always be a child, not even to you. You have to see me as a grown-up, only then can I be one, no?'

Ma looked at Maasi, who was once again smiling her bright, naughty smile. 'Wah, Munno. This son-of-an-owl is wiser than our own crooked-nosed father.'

Ma chuckled, and Adi felt a wave of relief crashing upon him. 'Fine. But you have to score well in your exams, then you have to see if you get a scholarship.'

'I will.'

'And then we have to tell your Papa.'

'Don't worry,' Maasi said. 'Let him take care of his studies, we will take care of your man.' She used the Punjabi 'marad' for man, somehow adding a sarcastic tinge to the word that robbed it of the very manhood it was meant to represent.

'How, behen-ji? You don't know him, you don't know how—'

'I know, Munno. I know.'

There was something about the way Maasi said it, the way she dismissed his father with a shake of her head, that told Adi she knew what she was talking about. Behind those bright eyes and ever-smiling lips, there was a quiet confidence that came with knowing how to solve problems like these – how to escape from prisons that other people built around you.

'Puttar,' said Maasi, patting Adi on the back. 'You have a train to catch. Go to the toilet and do your work quickly,' she grinned at him. 'Don't leave it for the train. You city boys can't squat on those desi-style toilets like us old hags.'

Finally, the tension broke in the room and Adi couldn't help but giggle. He got up and was walking towards his room when Ma called out his name. Just as he turned, she crashed into him, wrapping her arms around him in a tight, trembling hug. He looked up at Maasi, smiling sheepishly, but she had turned away. As she walked out towards the kitchen, he caught her wiping her eyes with the back of her hand. He wanted to do the same, but his hands refused to unlock themselves from their grip around Ma.

22.

Now, finally, we have grown up

It was not yet seven in the morning but the sun was already burning up the empty sky, throwing shadows sharp enough to cut the pavement blocks into black and white. Summer was here and he hated it.

As he stepped inside the school gates, his feet were lighter, but his hands felt jittery. He was not supposed to be here. He had no classroom to go to, no desk to claim. He made his way up the stairs, going straight up to the fourth floor to make sure no one would see him, and rushed towards the library. Midway through the open corridor that connected the school buildings, he stopped. The hot, dry air suddenly seemed hard to breathe and his feet refused to move.

He had to take a deep breath and remind himself that it was only a matter of days. Soon, he would be going to a cold, grey place, away from the glare of the sun and he would never have to hide again. In a week, he would be in England. People actually looked forward to summer there, Chacha had told him. They celebrated when the sun came out. It sounded utterly absurd. He was sure he would never miss this blinding, suffocating heat.

Over the past few weeks, after their return from Punjab, things had happened so quickly that Adi was often left in a daze. Ever since the new government was elected in March, his father had been spending long hours at work, coming home late at night and leaving again early the next morning. It had been a few blissful weeks of calm evenings and dinner conversations with Ma, discussing Adi's boarding school options.

At school, during the quiet weeks leading up to the exams, he had spent hours in the computer lab with Noor and Omi, researching all the different schools and trying to convince them to apply with him. 'Maybe next year,' they had said, but had helped him find the one for him. It was a school called Rugby, in a place called Warwickshire (the second 'w' was silent). It was the school where Lewis Carroll had studied, Noor told him, and that was all he had needed to make up his mind. Ma had secretly enlisted Chacha to help him apply, and he had even earned a scholarship that covered most of his fee. Ma had planned to take out a loan to cover the rest, until Kammo Maasi had found out. She had offered to bridge the gap with her savings, saying, 'What is it for? How many more books does an old woman need?' When Adi and Ma had protested, she had threatened to come to Delhi and spank their chuttars with her chappal. Adi, for one, had believed her.

Now, the exams were over and the new school year had begun, and he had come back one last time, just to say goodbye to his friends. He crossed over to the other side of the corridor and looked down. It didn't take him long to find his old class, now in a new classroom. And there they were, right at the front desk by the window, standing side-by-side for the

357

morning assembly. Seeing them together – just a boy and a girl sharing a desk – made him smile. It nearly made him start crying.

No, he couldn't do it. How was he supposed to say goodbye to the only two friends he had? They had made so many promises to each other – they would keep in touch on MSN, they would call every weekend, they would meet next year and travel to Scotland. They would all go to Cambridge and live in a single dorm room. But saying goodbye now seemed wrong, like a bad omen. He was not going to do it, he decided. He was going to hold them to the promises they'd made.

He waited in the library until the recess bell rang, then made his way to the now empty classroom. At Noor and Omi's desk, he saw a brand-new *Chip* magazine in one drawer and a dog-eared copy of *The Complete Poems of Emily Dickinson* in the other, and he couldn't help but laugh. He couldn't think of two people more different from each other, and he felt a little proud of having played a small role in bringing them together. He opened his bag and took out the only two books he was carrying – Manto's short stories for Noor and Tolstoy's long story for Omi. Ismat Chughtai he had kept for himself, for the day he would learn to read its flowing Urdu letters.

Rushing out through the deserted corridors and down the empty stairs, he realised he had forgotten one person: Ma'am George. He kicked himself for not bringing a book for her. She would have loved one of Maasi's old, hardbound editions of Dickens, he knew. It was too late, now. Perhaps he could write a book of his own one day, he thought, and dedicate it to her. That's what she had taught him, after all, that there was no shame in being whoever you wanted to be – reading poems, talking to ghosts, chasing little daydreams of your own.

*

'Arré, did you hear what Chairman Sir said?' His father picked up another oily, orange laddoo from the box that was already half empty.

'No, sir, what did he say? Tell me, no?' Laddoo Uncle played his part, beaming like a dog eager for a treat.

'He said it best,' said his father, before popping the laddoo in his mouth, clearly savouring the moment.

Laddoo Uncle was just a junior scientist – Class C or D; Adi could never keep track of the civil servants' own little caste system – so he had not been involved in the 'Operation'. His father, too, had only worked on the sidelines, but it didn't matter to him. In his own eyes, he was one of the handful of heroes who had made the country proud. The 'Op Shakti' that Adi had tried to unlock on the computer all those months ago had finally been executed. India had exploded five atomic bombs deep in the deserts of Rajasthan.

For the past week, the papers had been full of 'nuclear news', with pictures of pot-bellied politicians and the slow-talking, dhoti-wearing Prime Minister, all peering into a smouldering pit, grinning like the neighbourhood boys who went around blowing up letterboxes on Divali. The TV, too, had been blaring non-stop, with retired colonels making grand claims about India's military might while insisting, somewhat confusingly, that the bombs were necessary to ensure peace.

Adi had read all about the different types of bombs, including the thermonuclear H-bomb codenamed Shakti-I. It was a combination of fission and fusion stages – the heat generated by the breaking apart of one kind of nucleus made possible the coming together of another kind.

'When the first bomb went off,' said his father, swallowing, 'the Earth rose up, like the ground had turned into water, and Chairman Sir said, "Now I can believe the stories of Lord Krishna lifting a mountain." Isn't that fantastic?'

'Wah-wah!' cried Laddoo Uncle, appropriately impressed. 'It is true. People today think these are all just stories but our ancestors had all these technologies. Aeroplanes, satellites, atom bombs – all these are mentioned in our *Ramayana* and *Mahabharata*, they all come from our *Vedas* only. The tragedy is that we have forgotten all this knowledge. Today, Angrez people are studying Sanskrit while we are busy learning English. The Angrez have left but we still behave like their slaves.'

His father nodded in agreement. After all, Laddoo Uncle's words were so familiar, steeped in such self-assured ignorance, that they could just as well have been his father's own.

Adi had assumed that his father would not be thrilled about him going to the land of the 'Angrez', but Ma had told him to leave it to her. When they had put everything in place, she had walked up to his father one Sunday, as he was eating, and told him what was going to happen. Listening to Ma's voice, slow and gentle yet hard as steel, his father had grunted and shaken his head. He had asked only one question: was Chacha paying for any of it? He wasn't, though he was doing much more – travelling to England to meet Adi and help him settle in. His father did not need to know about that, they'd decided. It could be their secret mission, their own buried bomb meant to keep the peace.

'Now you see?' said his father, wagging a finger at the TV. 'These Americans are creating trouble, threatening their sanctions. Whoever gave them the licence to meddle in everyone's affairs, like they are the whole world's uncle? They are only upset because they were fooled. We did it in broad daylight right under their noses! All the CIA satellites in the sky could not even get a hint of what was happening.'

'It is truly a miracle, sir,' Laddoo Uncle nodded.

'But I can give you one thing in writing,' said his father. 'All this is drama only. Now they will treat India with respect, you just wait and see. That is the custom of this world, only strength is admired. This is what that Gandhi never understood. Going around begging and turning the other cheek never earns you any respect. Now, finally, we have grown up.'

'Adi?' Ma called out from the bedroom.

'Coming, Ma.'

He dumped his remaining comic books into the cardboard box, to be sold off to the kabaadi-vala. The only ones he was taking with him were the Tintin books that Chacha had bought for him.

In his room, he stopped at the door and looked at Ma as she struggled to zip up a swollen suitcase. Rina Auntie had offered to stay late and help Ma pack, and she was now kneeling on the suitcase to push down its lid, giggling uncontrollably. He had never seen her like this, like a little girl going on an adventure, and he tried to snap a picture in his mind. This was how he wanted to remember her, always.

'Béta, are you sure you haven't forgotten anything?'

'Yes, Ma,' he said, kneeling down to help her. She was leaving in two days, and even though her suitcases were already packed, she kept finding some useless little thing she had forgotten to keep. He was leaving late that night, and even though he was going so much farther away, he had less than half of Ma's luggage. All that he needed – all that mattered – was burnt in his memory, never to be left behind.

'There,' he said, pulling the zipper shut, and stood up.

'I just need to finish this.' Ma waved at the two other suitcases lying open on the bed. 'Then I will have a bath and we can eat. We leave for the airport at ten, okay?'

Adi looked around his room again. Stripped of its posters and emptied of all its books, the room looked so much larger than it had on all the noisy nights he had spent in there. But then, it seemed so much smaller too, like a pair of shorts he had grown out of, that he could no longer imagine ever fitting into. Was he going to miss it? It seemed impossible, but then, he knew better now than to use that word lightly.

'Mémsahib,' said Rina Auntie, throwing Adi a shy glance. 'I have made Chhoté Bhaiya's favourite dishes tonight, matar paneer and bhindi.'

'Arré wah! See, Adi?' Ma laughed. 'Rina Auntie knows you even better than I do now. She is going to miss you too.'

'Ma,' he said, glancing at Rina Auntie. 'Can Auntie have dinner with us tonight?'

'Oh,' Ma frowned. 'But we have—'

'I don't want my last meal to be with them,' he nodded towards the drawing room, where the two men sat. 'I will serve their food now and they can eat in front of the TV. We'll eat later at the dining table.'

'What do you say, Rina?' Ma smiled. 'Will you eat with Chhoté Bhaiya?'

Rina Auntie looked down and nodded with a slight, circular motion that Adi found hard to make out as a yes or a no. But he could tell that this woman, who had worked at their house since he was old enough to walk, whose hair had gone grey frying their potatoes and mopping their floors, now had tears in her eyes.

*

As he put the dinner tray down on the coffee table, Adi looked at his father, and for some strange reason, felt the urge to laugh.

'The salt and green chillies are here,' he pointed. 'And there are extra bowls for the curd. Do you need anything else?'

His father shook his head ever so slightly but did not look up.

'Very good, béta.' Laddoo Uncle seemed impressed. 'I heard you got a scholarship to go abroad? Well done.'

'Arré, all their Oxford–Cambridge were built with our

money only,' his father said. 'They are not doing us any favours, handing out a little scholarship.'

Laddoo Uncle smiled at Adi, and he smiled back. That's all his father had to say too – *well done*. Two little words would have been enough. Instead, he had to settle for a stranger's smile.

'But, sir,' Laddoo Uncle continued. 'Very good thing you are doing, this, sending your boy abroad. Schools here are useless. And there is so much competition for the good colleges.'

'Yes-yes,' his father nodded, like the whole thing was his idea. 'It's not like it was in our time. With all these caste reservations, even the brightest students don't get admission these days. Nowadays, I tell you, it's better to be a Scheduled Caste person than a Brahmin.'

Laddoo Uncle laughed dutifully, before clearing his throat and changing the topic. 'But, sir,' he added with concerned eyes. 'How will you manage with Bhabhi-ji going to Punjab? Is she . . . is she going for long?'

'No-no, she will keep coming and going. Her sister is older, and she lives alone so she needs some help. We will manage. After all, family comes first. If someone needs help, it is our duty. We can always adjust, no problem.'

'That is very noble of you, sir. First you and Bhabhi-ji took care of your Amma-ji, now her sister. In this day and age, not many people are so big-hearted.'

Adi cringed, biting his lip and wondering if his father truly believed all the things that flowed so effortlessly, so shamelessly, out of his mouth.

'Oh, it's nothing!' His father dismissed Laddoo Uncle with

a wave, showing just how modest he was. 'Anyway, I will be moving out of here myself.'

'Oh, really?' Laddoo Uncle's eyes lit up. 'Your type-seven bungalow, it's approved?'

His father nodded with a half-smile, pretending like it was not a big deal.

'Wah, sir, congratulations! Then what's the problem? You will have your own chauffeur, gardener, chef, everything. What more does one need? Chalo,' Laddoo Uncle sighed, 'at least this government is recognising the people who do the work, unlike the Congress thieves who only promoted Muslims for their vote bank politics.'

'Yes,' his father nodded. 'All that is going to change now.'

Finally, Adi tore himself away from the farcical show to go and set the dining table. He set three places, using the nice guest plates that had not been packed yet and took care to use all the same cutlery for Rina Auntie's place. He knew his father was not going to believe it – the maid at the dining table, sitting on the chair reserved for him, putting into her 'small-caste' mouth the very spoon that he used. But his father could go to hell, he shook his head. And join Amma there.

Ma was still in the bedroom when Adi was done, talking to Rina Auntie. She was supposed to go for a bath before eating, so he had some time. He walked to the door and slipped his chappals on.

In the drawing room, Laddoo Uncle had finally turned to the reason that kept bringing him over, his own super weapon in the quest to earn his superior's favour. He had pulled out his briefcase arrayed with rings of different shapes, studded with stones large enough to knock planets off their orbits, and he was busy telling his boss which one he needed to keep his good kismat safe. His father was holding his fingers up to the chandelier, the glint of the gemstones reflecting off his wide eyes. Neither of them noticed as Adi walked out and shut the door behind him.

*

On the roof, the dry heat was like a blast from a tandoor, and it made him gasp for breath. Climbing the wall dividing the terraces, he heaved himself up to the ledge above the door. The fall to the floor below no longer looked as frightening as it had on that distant rainy night when he had first dared to climb this high. He looked around, breathing a little easier in the slight breeze, and realised that everything – the grey apartment blocks around him, the tall lampposts, the great gulmohar tree finally in full bloom – looked smaller, somewhat diminished.

'Are you still here?' he said out loud, scanning the rooftops.

It had been nearly three months since he had last spoken to the vulture, and he was not sure if it would still be around.

'Good evening, Mr Sharma.'

He turned to find it two terraces down, sitting on a water tank with its shoulders caught in that permanent shrug around its little bald head, like an old man watching the sun set behind the heat-blurred horizon.

'And to you, sir.' He gave the vulture a little bow.

'Ah, you have finally found your manners, I see. Very good, very decent.'

Adi rolled his eyes but couldn't stop himself from smiling. He had avoided the vulture because he had not wanted to jinx things, not until he was certain that nothing was going to go wrong. Now, at last, he felt safe looking the bird in its gleaming eye.

'Listen,' he cleared his throat. 'I . . . I know I broke your rules, shouting in the middle of that last memory. I had to do it, you know? It was the only way to get Ma to believe me. But anyway – I'm sorry.'

'O-ho, no need to apologise, Mr Sharma. I am understanding completely.'

'Wait a minute,' he said, sensing that now familiar tongue lodged in a cheek. 'You – did you *know* I was going to do that?'

It was possible. The vulture could have stopped the memory if it had wanted to. And it had harped on about 'behaving yourself' a little too much, now that he thought about it, almost as though it was trying to give him ideas. Could it all have been part of the vulture's plan all along?

'Sadly, Mr Sharma, I cannot know the future. Until it is in the past, of course.'

'But . . . but you knew that I was going to—'

'I, Mr Sharma, am merely a humble servant following the rules and regulations—'

'Yes, yes, I know, the rules and regulations of Section 42 of H-A-H-A.'

'Correct. That is all. Now, by chance I am also having some good news to share with you. I have submitted your report to the Department Head Office and I can inform you that it has been accepted. Meaning, your case is finally closed.'

'So, your job is done, then?'

'Yes, Mr Sharma. But yours is only beginning.'

'What do you mean?' He sat up. 'I wanted to grow up, to stop being scared, and I've done that. I faced my all-time number one fear of Ma leaving and I defeated it. Now, *I'm* leaving, going all the way around the world, and I'm not even scared!'

'*Very* good, Mr Sharma. I applaud your bravery, no doubt. But—'

'But what?' he said, and barely moving his lips, muttered, 'Buttface.'

The vulture laughed its cackling, cawing laugh that made Adi wince, but he could not resist being infected by it and bit his lip to keep himself from giggling.

'*But*, Mr Sharma, overcoming childish fears is merely the first step. Growing up is not like making your two-minute Maggi noodles. It is a journey of a thousand steps.'

'Great. So, you're going to follow me until I complete a *thousand* more of your stupid tasks?'

'Oh, no, no! I, Mr Sharma, am only entrusted with simple procedures appropriate to my limited skills. For subsequent tasks, you will be needing the intellectual insights of teachers wiser than this humble servant.'

'Right, right,' he chuckled. God knew he had had enough

of the vulture's rambling, unending buckvaas. Still, he had to admit, it had sometimes made him smile, often when he had needed it the most. Now, he wondered if he would ever get to roll his eyes at this nonsense again. 'How will I ever find such a great guru,' he said, trying to keep a straight face, 'wiser than your humble self?'

'I cannot help you there, unfortunately. I am but a lowly functionary, I try to maintain my distance from such people. The more evolved you humans are, the more dangerous you become.'

'Wait a minute,' he said, realising what he may have missed. 'Does this mean you are getting your promotion now?'

'Oh, look at that!' The vulture's head bobbed up, its black eye glinting with childlike mischief. 'I *completely* forgot about that. Yes, it is true. Yours truly is going to be the Director General of the Department.'

'Ah, I see.' Adi shook his head, smiling. 'So that's what all this "humble servant" business is about.'

'Certainly not! A Director General in the Department is a highly respected position, I am not denying. But in the end, you see, we are all humble servants, in service of someone or the other.'

'As long as you're not serving me,' said Adi. He was trying to sound cool and sarcastic but he could not hide the sudden pang of sadness that had seized his voice.

He remembered the day he had seen the vulture for the first time, the day Ma had left – how terrified he had been by its serpent-like neck, its shining, unblinking eye. He could never have imagined that he would one day come to miss this odd, inexplicable creature, this blathering beast who had made the cold, dark nights so much more bearable, the burning afternoons a little less sad.

'No, Mr Sharma, I am sure that you do not need my services anymore, at least for now. In fact, I must compliment you on your performance throughout all our tasks. I confess that I did not expect much from you in the beginning. When I first saw you in your half-pants, legs like a Siberian crane, sneaking around in the night like a little mouse—'

'Um, is this your way of complimenting me?'

'Yes-yes, of course . . . oh, never mind,' the vulture sighed. 'You will not be needing me as long as you remember the one thing that I have tried to teach you—'

'Oh, really? And what's that? Talking in riddles?'

'—As long as you remember to take care of your memories, keep careful records of them, preserve them like they are precious jewels. Because our department is not going to be around forever, I am afraid. *I* am not going to be around for much longer. You will need to remember the past by yourself. It is not an easy job, but it is one that needs to be done.'

'Why?' said Adi, even though he knew why. He knew now how important it was to face the past, especially when no one else was willing to do it, even when they continued to suffer from it. He knew, but he wanted to provoke the vulture into another ranting monologue. Now that this fantastical adventure seemed to be nearing its end, even though he was tired of it all – even though he was eager for all the new beginnings that awaited – the little boy in him was still terrified of all the things that could go wrong, wishing that this day didn't have to end. Was that boy *ever* going to grow up?

'Because,' said the vulture, and paused as it bent its head and crouched low, as if preparing to leap. 'Memories make us who we are. Because the past is all that there is. All the answers you need are waiting in its pages. So, whenever you look around and find yourself lost, or scared, like you are stuck in a bad dream—'

The vulture began to unfold its wings, raising them high over its head.

'—whenever it seems like there is no hope, that there is nothing you can do to change what is written on your palm, that things can only go from worst to very worst, just remember—'

The wings came sweeping down to lift the great bird into the air, and the still summer evening echoed with a booming cry, '—close your eyes, Mr Sharma, and *see*.'

Adi ducked as the vulture swooped towards him, gliding gracefully with measured flaps of its vast, black wings. In a blink, it had passed over him, heading towards the burning horizon, chasing after the sinking sun. He watched as the vulture flew in loops, spiralling higher and higher, until it was no more than a flickering dash punctuating the blank, boundless sky.

Acknowledgements

It began with a boyhood memory, no more than a passing feeling that made me miss my stop one morning. A sentence, a word, a stare at a time, it gathered the shape of a story. Across years and continents, through upheavals and lockdowns, it stayed with me; it kept me going. Now, as I prepare to let it go, there are things that keep coming back to me: places that I miss, people for whom I am grateful, moments that will always be a part of this story. It seems only fair to give them a place in these pages.

The long evenings at the hawker centre on Keong Saik Road, Singapore, where I scribbled countless pages only to scratch them out.

That rainy afternoon at Dasa Book Cafe, Bangkok, where I discovered *Black Swan Green* by David Mitchell, the book that somehow unlocked this one.

The British Library and the Birkbeck Library in London, where I learnt so much about a past that is rarely remembered yet never forgotten, from writers who have kept its stories alive.

The 'Alumni' shelf at the University of East Anglia book-store, where I first let myself imagine, if only for a moment.

Jean McNeil's workshop room, where the lights would go out if you sat still for too long.

Giles Foden's office, where I found the courage to kill ten thousand darlings.

The Student Union Bar, where we sighed and vented and laughed; where we lifted each other up.

Bina and Arun Balakrishnan's house in Bangalore, where I was made to feel at home; where I gathered the strength to pick this novel up one more time.

That monsoon-drenched corner of Chapel Road, Mumbai, where I stood as Caroline Ambrose told me that this jumble of words, this piece of me, had won the Bath Novel Award.

The long phone calls with Julia Silk, my agent, who saw more in these pages than I did; who seemed to be able to read my mind.

The thousand kindnesses of Jo Dingley and Nico Parfitt, my editors, whose efforts brought this novel to life; whose faith in my writing, while sometimes befuddling, was always inspiring.

My father's car, where I conquered my own fears; where he did eventually apologise.

The magazine-vala in Lajpat Nagar market, Delhi, where my mother bought me all the *Jughead's Double Digests* she couldn't afford.

And, most of all, our little house on Norman Street, London, where we held each other as the world was burning;

where you created a space for me to come back to, filled with laughter and light and the aroma of Brooke Bond Red Label tea. And cake – all the cake.

Here's to more of these memories blooming, over time, into stories of their own.